THE PARIS PREDICAMENT

SASHA LAUREN

Black Rose Writing | Texas

©2020 by Sasha Lauren
All rights reserved. No part of this book may be reproduced, stored in a retrieval system or transmitted in any form or by any means without the prior written permission of the publishers, except by a reviewer who may quote brief passages in a review to be printed in a newspaper, magazine or journal.

The author grants the final approval for this literary material.

First printing

This is a work of fiction. Names, characters, businesses, places, events, and incidents are either the products of the author's imagination or used in a fictitious manner. Any resemblance to actual persons, living or dead, or actual events is purely coincidental.

ISBN: 978-1-68433-552-7
PUBLISHED BY BLACK ROSE WRITING
www.blackrosewriting.com

Printed in the United States of America
Suggested Retail Price (SRP) $21.95

The Paris Predicament is printed in Plantagenet Cherokee

*As a planet-friendly publisher, Black Rose Writing does its best to eliminate unnecessary waste to reduce paper usage and energy costs, while never compromising the reading experience. As a result, the final word count vs. page count may not meet common expectations.

Cover Image: Black Cat on Paris Rooftop, by Jiel
https://www.jiel-artiste-peintre.fr

I dedicate *The Paris Predicament* to Khristina Atkinson,
who was my biggest fan, "Er ma gawd,
Matt and Lucy are enchanting;
you totally made my day."

ACKNOWLEDGEMENTS

Thanks to my mother for full bookshelves and library trips as a kid; John Gai for his love, wisdom, and friendship; Susan Soranno for her enthusiastic, astute feedback all along the way; Zahra Akbar for picture prompts; Khristina Atkinson for her bubbly support; Todd Hunter Campbell for his inspiration from Beirut and London; and special thanks to Alex.

Half way through the book, I asked Facebook friends from around the world to suggest words for me to incorporate in the chapters, i.e., "Give me a word that begins with the first letter of a pet or child." They challenged and inspired me with their choices.

THE PARIS PREDICAMENT

"It is strange, in Paris I never draw fauns, centaurs or mythical heroes like these, and they always seem to live in these parts."
~ Pablo Picasso

THE PREDICAMENT

I wasn't used to short hair: short-short, like newly grown grass a week after seedlings were planted. I'd habitually run my fingers through my streaming chestnut waves since I was a kid out of nervousness and preening both. Now I ran my hands through nothing.

A flip of my stomach signaled something was wrong, like the time someone stole my car from its spot outside Sunday Market; that ticky-tacky turn of the intestines, then a drop down into a roughshod rabbit hole, hurtling me, no heed for motion sickness, towards the center of a molten hot core, without care, stripping my soul bare.

My three and a quarter inch heels clunked down the Montmartre steps like a quarter horse: clomp-clomp, clomp-clomp, clomp-clomp. They know my name, but I keep moving just the same. My car, registered to me, an American ex-pat who'd found my overseas haven, will give me away.

Buenos Aires. Please god, please. I'll do anything. I'll walk, stow away, tele-transport myself out of France so I can have a new chance. Live alone, no need for romance. Like Shawshank Redemption, only there will be no redemption.

He looked to be about five-years-old. A mass of brown curls, olive skin, dimples, brown hoodie, chocolate scarf, tan pants. I didn't hit him directly; my automobile knocked over the pole that toppled the awning on him like a Gulliver foot squashing an ant.

I considered myself kind, ethical; I volunteered for a homeless shelter, tithed my income to a global micro-lending organization, held doors for the elderly - for anyone - gave up my seat on the Metro before the masses reading their periodicals or hash-tagging their way through their catatonic commute even looked up.

Why did I drive today? Why today when that bundle of boy went out to play and got in the way while I was on my cell having my say? It's Brigitte's birthday. I'd called to wish her a happy day.

I'd considered myself a good soul - never questioned it - right until the moment I hopped out of my car and ran; I ran for my life, a life no longer worthy of living.

I killed a boy in Paris today.

Adrenaline is a strange animal. Only two hours from the accident I'd bought hair cutting shears, ducked into an alley behind a convenience store, lopped my locks as closely to my overwrought skull as possible, bought a baggy brown outfit in a friperie, ditched my colorful former set in the dumpster behind, and ran, all without forethought or consideration.

Heart pounding, panicked, any moisture I'd had in my mouth transferred to my palms, which dripped sticky, fear-filled liquid that slid onto my fingertips. Meanwhile, my mouth, desert dry, could not summons a drop of saliva no matter how hard I tried.

I'd killed a boy. How could that be? This one moment, an accidental act (my fault for looking down at my phone while behind the wheel) leveled my life; when I killed the child, I died too, existentially, if not in form.

I thought of killing myself, but first I needed a drink. A hibiscus tea would be nice, but I settled for water-no-ice in a cafe off the beaten way. The garçon dropped a tray, and I jumped as though shot, so scared that police would catch me, darting eyes barely dared to look at those looking askew at me. All I wanted was to be free again.

Twenty-seven years old, everything to live for, I'd moved to France three years before. I drew chalk portraits on the sidewalk in front of the Louvre to pay my way through graduate school. One makes a surprisingly sturdy income kneeling on cement and pressing pastel impressions onto the pavement that wash away the next day. Tourists took pictures and left magnifique tips in my upturned hat. I'd crawl around a drawing like a cat, and just like that, my wallet got euro fat.

Normally on a vegan, non-gluten, pristine diet that would put even my health nuttiest friends to shame, I ordered a flakey, buttery, steak and cheese croissant. Apparently, killers require carbs. I followed that with a lemon fig curd tart, and of all things, a glass of Australian wine, then another, then another, then another, until I could finally think.

Lifting my hands to run through my non-existent hair in my now non-relevant life, I hatched my plan.

I headed straight for the one person who would have my back no matter what: Bertrand, the busker from Brussels with a penchant for The Beatles, Buffalo Springfield, and the Blues.

Bertrand and I teamed up at work nearly two years ago. As I began a portrait, Bert would ask a few key questions of an individual, couple, or family and sing them a personalized *Song on the Spot* while I wove the information into chalk or charcoal portraits. People loved the blending of services so much, word spread like prismatic sunrays on the Seine at six a.m. on a summer's day. We gained slight fame for this, garnered regular write ups in local papers and high, exclusive 'recommends' from the Louvre walking tour guides. Daily we'd hear, "Pardonnez-moi, êtes-vous Bertrand et Camille?" Yes, we *are* Bertrand and Camille, the busiest street artists this side of Belgium.

Because of our famed partnership, I was hesitant about contacting Bertrand. I'd shut my phone down in fear several hours before, imaging the calls I'd be getting would not be good. I am not the savviest person with computers, so I wasn't even sure if the phone had a tracking device, which might alert officials as to my whereabouts, thus, I considered tossing it. Habit and suspected need, however, edged out impulse, and led me to hold on to it for the time being.

"I am a wanted woman," I marveled, 90% still in shock, 5% abject terror, 5% dramatic intrigue, and zero clarity. I touched the one-quarter inch hairs on my head, "Wanted." Then, un-deux-trois, my knees buckled and my bottom took refuge on a dirty curb where I sat and cried for the tot in the tan pants and his family. The cry wasn't soundless, wasn't loud, wasn't shy, wasn't proud, closed out the sun, shrouded me in a remorseful, inconsolable cloud of contrition under a darkening Parisian sky.

"Merde," I cursed into the air before I lifted this altered-universe self up off my arse and re-positioned my body in the intended direction of my mission. My legs walked themselves; I observed from the treetops. Each pair of left-right, left-right, left-right, left-right steps ridiculed me, "Want-ed, want-ed, want-ed, want-ed."

For the reason mentioned above - our connected fame - I snuck up to the back door of Bertrand's flat, gave my trademark rat-ta-ta-tat, ta-ta-tat-tit rap on the violet door and waited.

Rather than seeing my friend's familiar face, I heard a rumbling voice I was unaccustomed to ask, "Qu'est-ce?" from the other side of the wooden panel. I froze. I surmised this baritone was Leonard, Bertrand's new lover, a man more delicate in dimension and demeanor than his weighty voice would infer. Leonard, an Uber driver-art student, gave off covetous envy towards my business and the symbiotic relationship with the man he called, "Our" Bertrand.

Before I had time to decide whether to run, Leonard peeped suspiciously through a crack in the door — when he saw it was me, he opened it and stood speechless for several slow moments, finally uttering one word as a query.

"Belle?" he whispered.

The soft sound of the Belle, Bertrand's pet name for me, sounded comforting and threatening. The confrontation sent my heart through a percussive pattern, playful under more auspicious circumstances, but racing under current conditions. My ears, exposed without lush hair to tuck behind them, pinked up hot and shameful like hazard blinkers on my head.

"Oui," I barely breathed out.

Leonard grabbed my waist and whisked me inside. My French is good, but he insisted on speaking something that resembled English if one spoke English with a rag stuffed in one's mouth from inside a burlap sack, yet with a saveur poétique that made his voice sound like a verbal baritone ballet. I focused on the smooth deep rumble, captivated by the undulating movement of his scarlet lips, characteristic of gentle waves upon a lee shore.

His intensity at once gave away that my name was on the news. Then, to drive home the point, he spoke in suddenly discernible English, "They are looking for you, Belle. Tell me all what has happened?"

I looked around. Bertrand's salon didn't seem at all familiar without his presence.

"Your eyes look bigghair withh your short hair."

"Où est Bertrand?"

"Chhhe is, Berrrchtraund in zee home of his mother. Shheeee is dying."

"Bertrand, he's in Brussels?"

"Oui."

"Now?"

"Oui."

"He's not here?"

"Non."

Leonard could see that I was in shock. I wasn't myself - part of me still hovered above the fray; the rest of me remained with the tan legged, dimpled boy I'd named Pierre in my head. I pictured his mother, father, sister, and brother wailing to excess, wailing just enough, wailing and rightfully cursing my name, Camille.

I was angry with Bertrand for being with his dying mother and not there for me. Rather than single-focused concern for my good friend and his family, I thought of myself, which caused me to doubt my patronage as a person. Who am I to have such self-centered thoughts? Floundering like a kite in a kinetic storm, my knees gave way again, and the world went black.

I came to on the couch with an icepack on my forehead, Leonard, like an angel, leaned in to me, his long, artistic fingers petting my warm head. Any jealousy he had vanished, replaced by a full concern for me, Camille, the killer of innocent Pierre.

"LOL."

"Excusez-moi?"

"That was the last thing I texted Brigitte before the pole jumped in the way of my car."

Leonard sat still.

"Poteau stupide."

"Excusez-moi?"

"Poteau stupide! Stupid pole!"

"Tell me all what has happened," he was persistent.

I talked, slowly at first. Given the language barrier, I'm unsure how much Leonard understood, but I told him everything and he kept his attention trained on my now bigghair eyes the whole time.

I began my story in the middle and circled round like a helicopter buzzing overhead searching for bandits biding their time in the bushes.

Brigitte, my bestie from Université, would surely be beside herself with worry. The last she heard from me was "LOL." This was in response to a selfie of her feigning the look of astonishment she planned to affix to her face at her party, which would be anything but a surprise. Jacqueline had spilled the beans by mistake, as only Jacqueline can do, coyishly, cluelessly, cute as a Koala, no way to hold a grudge against her.

"Brigitte, she will remember this forever on her birthday! Poor Brigitte!"

I grew faint again and lay back down on the settee where I continued my story like a surreal psychoanalysis session. Leonard played Freud with the conviction of Montgomery Clift in *The Secret Passion*. He fixated on me, my bigghair eyes, pixie hair, pale cheeks, and delicate delivery, a former contender, suddenly a pretender; he nodded his head, stroked his chin, and encouraged me along.

"Oui, continue."

I love the French, France, Paris, being the best chalk artist with the best busker, le meilleur partenaire, Bertrand, and now his new boyfriend, justifiably jealous of me, with the baritone intone of 'bigghair' and 'continue.' The beauty of life was still tangible to me in the day's tragedy. For the time being, anyway.

I majored in Art History against advice from college advisors and concerned friends. "Your only career choice with this major will to be a professor," rallied their tough-love, bullshit, battle cry.

"And why wouldn't I want to be a Professor?" I said as I secretly planned to be an extraordinary chalk artist until Kingdom Come, or my retirement, which would be slow to arrive as I neared the Century mark, so enriched was I by the enthrallment of my patrons. I tapped into my knowledge of art through the ages to embellish the tenor of my temporary creations. Temporary on the pavement, but captured on film, video, and in the memories of children, lovers, friends, and families who left generous tips, providing more than an ample living for an innovative artist.

"The child! Leonard, I killed Pierre!"

"Camille, we stop now."

I half expected him to tap his watch, "Your hour is up. See you again next week," but he steered me pragmatically, "Would you like a bath while I order food and then we will continue?"

"Yes." I wanted to wash away this day, to soak out of my pores the petulance I had caused. "Yes. Yes."

"Camille, come. Stop saying yes. Ere es your servette."

He handed me a monster-sized, eggshell blue towel and closed the door. Once alone, I sized up the stranger in the mirror. The haircut suited me. I looked like a beguiling Twiggy with massively mascaraed eyes a la the swinging sixties on Carnaby Street. Within moments I cried; my image replaced by that of Pierre — I saw him being born, brought to his mother's breast and lovingly blanketed, as she breathlessly smelled his downy baby head.

I saw the boy I called Pierre take his first unsure steps on the ginger grass to rounds of applause, bowing beneficently like Sir Richard Burton, another baritone, in an award-winning play directed by Benthall.

I saw him fly wooden planes, play with Choo-Choo trains, wrestle with his brother and sister, both of whom I was sure he had. Later, clad in feetie pajamas, he lied down to rest with snuggly toy and patted it until the patter of his young heart slowed for slumber. I quietly undressed as I intermittently pressed my hand over my eyes to shut out the scene that was played and replayed on my inner screen.

The tub nearly overflowed by the time I touched back to the present circumstance. I tiptoed into the hot water, wondered if this might be my last bath for a while, surmising what my limited choices and the repercussions might look like.

The warmth of the water lulled me into a fairly deep flutter-eyed sleep where my own first steps and feeties floated through my field. I awoke to waterlogged hands, held them in front of me and marveled at the whirly marbled fingertip patterns, patterns that surely would compliment the borders of my sidewalk art if I hadn't hit the pole that knocked the awning that killed Pierre.

"Camille! Are you there! The story is on the news!"

I popped up from the tub, a jack-in-the-box whose coil had sprung, pulled the puffy powder blue servette from where I'd draped it on the bidet, animated as a film sped up on triple time. I patted dry, wrapped in the bath sheet, knotted it under my right armpit, twisted the crystal door handle open and launched myself, adrenaline addled, into the Bertrand-less salon.

"I will turn myself in!"

"He's alive!"

"What?"

"Who?"

The earth had been pulled from below my feet. Now the stars were plucked from the heavens too. I floated somewhere in the middle where the fish and birds meet in ocean-sky, unable to swim, unable to fly.

"Will you feed Natalie Mouskers?"

"Who?"

"Miss Mouskers!"

Don't ask. We three, Leonard, Bertrand and I, had named her one night while testing out a bottle of fine French wine, the kind that Boise Idaho girls like myself fly ten hours and thirty-seven minutes to sample.

"She's not your cat, she's a feral bitch who roams the neighborhood."

"Natalie Mouskers is my cat! She has BECOME my cat! She's the only one who will miss me while I'm locked up for killing Pierre."

"Luis." Leonard announced.

"What?"

"Es name es Luis Fernando. Es family is visiting from Columbia. Ee's still alive in intensifs in hospital."

"Critical condition! Oh, no. Why couldn't he just have died instead of hanging on and suffering? He'll probably live a long life with a crippled body and brain injuries; his family will have to mortgage their house to pay for special caretakers for Pierre... Luis."

"Maybe he will live and be a happy boy."

No, the awning crushed him, there's no way, I thought, and then, lip trembling and teary, I retreated for a selfish moment back into a pocket of self-pity that made me feel like such a shitty person.

"No one will miss me."

"BERTRAND will miss you! I think ee loves you more than me!!"

There, he finally said what we'd been dancing around for months. The truth, stinging and pungent like a raw onion, provided the perfect seasoning needed for this emotional stew.

"And, if zee need be, we will feed your damn cat. We will adopt her and bring ere here if we have to, but you're not turning yourself in. If zeese boy dies, you will get time in jail, and Camille, as strong as you are, you're too fragile for zeese fate."

Fragile? Moi? *Non.* I'm the one who cared for my parents as they both were dying of cancers - skin and pancreatic - as my friends planned their sweet sixteen parties. I'm the one who lived alone for the two years following in that haunted hilltop house, chopped the wood, kept the drive clear of snow, stayed in school and graduated with a four point oh, sticking with geometry even when the letters and numbers hid under my bed and leapt out to tease and torture me at night as they danced the tarantella with my grief. I would stand ON the bed, stand ON my head and kick my legs as I recited formulas out loud while imploring my departed dad to impart his math whiz wit to me. This worked, lit me from within, and kept the mumbling math bullies at bay inside my head, all my family dead, I forged ahead and graduated as Valedictorian. Fragile? *Non.* I don't think so.

"I don't want you to go, Camille," Leonard enveloped me in a wholehearted hug that never would have happened had Our Bertrand been here. I was à la carte vulnerable. I swallowed a largish lump in my throat and tugged to keep the towel in place. "Va t'habiller - go get dressed, we'll eat, and discuss zeeese in a clear head."

There was nothing to discuss. I toddled off like a bébé embarking on a new bissel of balance, unsteady feet on an undulating ground capable to tossing an anchor from even the steadfast Andes.

A knock came on the door. This time I didn't jump. Our food had arrived.

"Je suis affame."

The acid in my stomach washed up over my gums, transforming the alluring smell of quesadillas into a nauseating nuisance. I was famished, but forcing food when one is in shock-grief-mourning is a cumbersome challenge. Perhaps a serving of soft, plain yogurt might have been a wiser choice considering that my nervous system was wreaking havoc with me on this day, turned night?

Parisians, especially those transplanted from the West Coast of the U.S. and their young French counterparts in University, fueled the demand for more quality Latin American foods in France. There was a peppy place, Sabroso Plato, my group frequented, where patrons rolled out their own tortillas; I didn't partake of this activity though since I abstained from wheat. Leonard had recalled this health habit of mine: the quesadillas were for him, a black bean and brown rice corn taco and salad for me.

My need to draw superseded my body's need for nourishment.

"I left a jue de craie here. Do you recall where they are?"

"Non."

"May I look for them?"

"Our house is yours. Do as you wish."

I tentatively, then vigorously, opened and slammed drawers like a junkie jonesing for a fix a dry-day and dollar too late. I looked in both bedroom bureaus and found them in the second one's bottom drawer.

"Do you have any drawing paper, Leonard?"

"Je ne sais pas… Ah, there, use that," he pointed behind me to a fax machine stocked full with pristine white sheets that beckoned me from across the room. Like a marble tumbling down a steep incline, unable to stop my momentous roll, I buzzed over to the pad, plucked a half-inch pile, fell to my knees and began my draw, occasionally, dutifully, munching a bite of the too hot taco to energize my efforts.

Art is my prayer.

I drew in layers. Beginning with brown ringlets that just glazed his collarbone, like a Kerry blue terrier, only darker, tighter, and so beguiling on a little boy.

"Leonard, do you have a thin black marker?"

He did. Caught mid-chew, Leo obediently got up and fetched me the tool while his mandible continued to mulch the Mexican meal.

Chubby hands next, small, thick fingers that hadn't yet slimmed with age. Fingers with quintessential wrinkles like a Pug's mug. Shaking, weeping, I tore through my tour of Pierre's form, arms, shoulders, torso, legs, knees, feet, in a rabbinical fervor, davening the divine, a dervish whirling for peace.

The dark sky shone indigo through the pane giving me momentary pause. I thought of Brigitte at her party. I wondered if the events of the day dampened the festivities fully, or maybe my fate provided fodder to galvanize the glitzy, gossipy girls? I half hoped that the mood, spiked with such worry for my well being and concern for young Pierr... erm, Luis Fernando... might disable their fun enough for a postponement, or at least blot the celebratory tone down to a dull roar.

Then, back to my tremendous task. The Tinkerbelle Effect totally took me over. Clap your hands if you believe. Clap loudly enough and Tink will come back to life. This is the ferocious, magical thinking I drew Pierre with. Each stroke of the pen and flush and blend of the pastels came from a guttural place; if wishes were horses, I could fly and Pierre Luis Fernando, the sweetest child that ever was, or ever would be, would not die.

Please God, why, why, why.

She encircled herself in a protective cocoon; her feet, which were bare for dancing, sat flat on the studio floor. Friends and party guests were at a loss, streamers strung with gaiety earlier in the day hung like limp spaghetti from the ceiling, blue, orange, yellow, red, mocking the sad scene. The cake, with a melted candle that proclaimed HAPPY 25th remained uneaten, nibbled on the sly by a hungry few.

Brigitte was inconsolable, rambling on, repeating the same story like a Merry-Go-Round. Twin cousins of shock and remorse like a runaway train took her on a circuitous course.

"It's my fault. I kept her on the phone. She said she was driving and it was not safe to text. 'One more picture' I said. 'Look,' I said, and sent her a silly face and she laughed in her delicious way. It was I. I hurt the boy and now dear Camille's life is a ruin. Sweet, supportive, Camille who always shares a meal with the homeless outside the Louvre, considérez-vous Camille who wouldn't hurt a fly and who puts spiders on a piece of paper and deposits them outside instead of killing them. The phone went dead. I feared the worst. I felt it. I knew."

Kendra from Quebec, usually the leader of the bunch, had no words. She shifted from foot to foot like a three-year-old waiting to use the bathroom. Dominique, usually meek, sat close on the floor and soulfully laid her head on Brigitte's shoulder. Jacqueline was the first to speak. "Twas an accident, Brigitte. An accident. The boy, for now, he lives."

If she meant this to comfort, it had quite the opposite effect. Poor coquettish Jacqueline never seemed to say the right thing. Brig burst out crying, wailing, and howling. Some guests grabbed their coats and slipped out the garish, green door. Only a loyal few remained to sit with the birthday girl in her pain.

"Where is she? Why won't she answer my calls? She hates me, my sweet friend, she hates me," head bowed back down momentarily in her lap until, as if on cue, her phone rang.

"Salut?"
"Brigitte. It's me, Bertrand."

The cacophony in my head was so loud, rapid, and ridiculing, I purposefully placed a song in there instead. Stress, to the extent I was experiencing it, induced artistic amnesia in me. I frantically searched through my inner file as though rifling through a blotted out blog, hoping, praying for the disappeared ink to rewrite itself, but no such luck; my macro-musical catalogue was bereft.

Momentarily, the chorus from *Alouette* made a jaunty appearance, but I avoided this tune, the first French song I'd ever learned. My mother used to sing it while bathing me when I was baby. Since I desired to keep as clear from added emotional memory as possible, I swiftly moved on.

The next song my mind DJ-ed up, interestingly, was also a song from childhood, *Kookaburra*.

"*Kookaburra sits in the old gum tree*
Merry, merry king of the bush is he
Laugh, Kookaburra! Laugh, Kookaburra!
Gay your life must be."

This first verse calmed me as I walked, as nonchalantly as possible, several long, perfect blocks to my loft, past protesting eco pirates and young sellers of street side tapioca who graced my darlingly dappled, liberal quartier. Leonard had kindly offered to drive me to my flat on his way to pick up an Uber patron from the Charles De Gaulle airport.

"Belle, I will drop you three blocks away so as not to arouse suspicion. I worry for you going back zhere unless you are sure you are emotional-ee read-ee to be in custod-ee."

I was in new territory and deposited into a reality I neither cared for nor knew how to navigate. I wanted to turn myself in - had an overpowering compunction to do so before they tracked me down. After soul searching, the sort one might not imagine until placed in such a predicament, I was clear I wished to spare Pierre's family the pain of a chase, a fight, denial, or any inch more anguish than I had already caused them. For me, Camille Lisette Portraro, this was the only way. It wouldn't make anything okay, but it wouldn't make the situation worse for them, and sometimes, less harm is the best option available.

When my father was sick, the doctors who committed preventable malpractice, lied, denied, and fought me on every front, legally, financially, and emotionally. It was the worst of humankind I had ever seen or ever hoped to see. I firmly believe that if one inadvertently causes hurt, then the ethical action is to accept accountability, express remorse, and set on a course to make amends now and until the river of time runs dry.

I set my soul on taking this course, but being petrified, I chose to tidy up a few things in my life first. Also, I needed to feed Natalie Mouskers.

With my new look, short hair, bland brown ensemble, flat shoes, and cool demeanor, I readied the key and slipped in the complex's rear, suspicious only of one car on a street side, but confident and determined to take care of what I'd come for.

As Leonard drove away, I noticed him texting, probably to Bertrand, with barely an eye to the road. Merde. People never learn. Luis Fernando lay in critical care, yet my compatriot's fingers flew on the phone with one hand on the wheel at three o'clock, regardless that this same act decimated the lives of a boy and his family that morning.

Why is it people always think it will happen to the other guy yet they are immune? He waved to me, protective, and gave a wink to say I'd be okay. I was furious and wanted to rip that phone from his claw and forbid anyone to get so easily sidetracked while driving.

This forlorn moon gifted me, finally, just the right song to settle in my cerebellum. Simon and Garfunkel's *The Boxer*. My cells sang it with all the bells and whistles, crashing in a crescendo on the chorus. The lie-la-lies too gleeful for the situation I found myself in, fallaciously so. The song kept me going when fight, flight, or fear had every justifiable reason to freeze me. If you ever find yourself in a life predicament with no way out, I highly recommend belting out *The Boxer*. Lie-la-lie.

A mouth full of Belgium crispy-rice chocolate didn't stop Bertrand from his stream-of-consciousness conversation. So intent was he on speaking, he didn't realize for several minutes there was no response from Brigitte, neither an "oui" or an "umm-hmm" or a sigh. She was quiet as a buzzy fly on a summer windowsill, hoping to avoid a swat.

In an uninspiring waiting room in a small white building on a quiet street in Brussels, far from the dramatics of friends and fiancé in France, Bertrand paced past plastic plants.

"Moeder is een l'hôpital. She might die any time now. I've been awake, by her bedside, without a good meal, for twenty-four hours now. One would think a hospital would have better food! I received a cryptic text from Leonard early today. Belle, he said, has been in an accident de voiture. I asked if it had hurt her, but he didn't answer. He only said she wasn't dead, he didn't give any information, there a knock on the door, he had to go. I'm waiting here, I've got to know."

He swallowed, took a swig of water sin gas, sat on a stiff orange chair, ran his hands through his hair, took a gulp of air, and continued; still no sound from the other side.

"Leonard said we should not be in contact in case they monitor our calls. Belle is in trouble. He wants to house her for now if need be. Please tell me Brigitte all information you have... Hello? Salut? Are you there?"

Muffled movements like a chair scraping across the floor came from the other end, then -

"Hello? Bertrand?"

"Oui."

"It's Jacqueline."

"Ah, Jacqueline. Hello! Where is Brigitte?"

"Brigitte refuses to eat today. She doesn't drink. She cries, rubs her eyes, she is morose, like Ophelia. She's like Ophelia, Bertrand! She blames herself for the boy, for our Belle. It's Brigitte's birthday and she wants to die. Bertrand, please come. Come quickly!"

The phone went dead.

Bertrand again sat and rubbed his head. He was lost, untethered, uninformed, and adrift.

His phone vibrated. Ah, Brigitte, he thought, but no. Finally a text from Leonard! Before he had time to read it, this call came from the hallway -

"Monsieur, come quickly, your Moeder!"

Vanilla pumpkin spice puffed from the new tubby cream-colored candle I lit in the dark, hoping to remain undercover. I'd planned to give that one, still wrapped, as a gift to Brigitte. The lavender was too sensuous for the moment, the violet one, too pretty, and peppermint, too peppy. Pumpkin spice fit the mood for a young woman in hiding from pursuing police, possibly to take me away, deservedly so, and booked for involuntary manslaughter or whatever they call it in France, IF young Luis Fernando died.

It was comforting to be home, yet my things had taken on a decaying and Daliesque tone; the meaning my life had the day before was outdated.

One of the first things I noticed was my physiology textbook and class notes. There was a test on metabolic processes scheduled for Friday. "A thin person may be obese and conversely a person who looks fat may be very fit, or possibly starving — appearances may be deceiving." Curly, artistic cursive festooned with detailed dolphin doodles framed the page. That lecture seemed to have droned on and on and on. I'd squiggled in my seat, eager to get back out to my chalk corner and draw the children visiting the museum with their families.

I drew cartoons, modernistic, realistic, cubist, impressionistic, expressionistic, fauvist. Any of the *'istics'* I could do! I walked my talk and my talk was chalk. I was chock full of chalk chatter. Now it no longer seemed to matter.

There, tossed casually on my desk was an unopened envelope Brigitte gave me the night before; a light lapis note with a hand-drawn rainbow in the corner. The rainbow at once innocent and sophisticated wrapped itself like a too tight scarf around my neck. So long ago, last night! When we left the skating rink, she tucked it in my pocket and said in her signature sultry and silky way, "Eer, Belle, a love note for you. Read it later and I'll see you tomorrow at my party." She lifted on tiptoes, kissed me sweetly on both cheeks and disappeared in a whirl. That was the last time I saw my closest girlfriend in the world.

A shiver snaked through my spine like Kundalini only it wasn't raising, it was quaking, and the sourdough feeling in my stomach returned. I worried in waves all over again about Brig. I should check to see if she called; she must be going out of her mind.

Hesitantly, then defiantly, I turned on my phone. Not sure what to expect.

Forty-nine voice messages.

I scrolled through, counting.

Sixteen from Bertrand — ah, poor Bertrand! He, my main man, partner, and baritone busker, has his hands full in Brussels with his mother and has to think about the unintended mischief I have caused!

Twelve messages from Brig, hmm. I expected more. Twelve, well, that's about one per hour since this morning - or perhaps they came in clusters of four?

The others were from various and sundry other concerned friends who wondered why I didn't show up to help with the fête. My dry cleaner called. An aunt from Hailey I wasn't close to, three private numbers, and five unregistered. Noticeably absent was Jacqueline. This sank my heart like a massive iron anvil; the rackety weight rattled me like out-of-control Moroccan marimbas.

I shut the phone down. Didn't even count the texts. I needed air before I even looked there. I looked around for colors to ground me. Red on the Webster's dictionary. Orange, the tangerines in a yellow daisy flowered bowl. A vintage jacket, forest green, embossed fabric, with a torn label that boosted SILK. Blue, the clear sky in the photo of Brigitte and me on my chalk corner. Purple, a vase with flowers, drooping over now, hanging their heads sadly in shame and sadness for the serious situation in Paris. The predicament. The pernicious, noxious, baneful, deleterious Paris Predicament.

With business to attend to and potentially a limited amount of time, what I did next made little sense, but it was the only way I could collect my thoughts.

I began by scrubbing the oven, a job I'd avoided for five months. I ate mostly raw and didn't like to use the teeny-tiny steel shoebox for fear of fire – it had smoked up the place with a smell of burning rubber mixed with turpentine when I baked Monkfish last January. I'd since resigned myself to a garlic, fennel infused Bouillabaisse as my fish dish of choice, a saffralicious recipe bought from Favaurant, a commedia dell 'arte juggler who performed near my chalking place.

Next, the rest of the kitchen, pantry, bed area, (including the trundle drawers beneath), foyer, closet, and bathroom got a going over. I still had art supplies, personal papers and desk area to go through, but mental exhaustion caused me to quit for the time being. I turned on the old movie channel, avoiding news stations like a gazelle avoiding a team of rabid tigers, hungry and ready for the kill. On came *The Philadelphia Story*. Katharine Hepburn's east coast affected accent echoed in my head.

"The time to make up your mind about people is never."

I flipped to another channel searching for something darker, grittier tuned to the tenor of the time. Hitchcock - *Strangers on a Train* - perfect, my favorite movie.

"I may be old fashioned, but I thought murder was against the law."

I clicked off the set.

Momentarily I fixated on Bertrand and wished to the point of cosmic appeal that he could tell me what to do. I trust his grounded, intuitive way in the world implicitly. Integrity flew out his fingers onto the frets of his golden guitar, rectitude rose from his diaphragm, vibrating up and out his throat, past his expressive lips. His voice reverberated into the well of each crowd who assembled and moved through our portion of the universe in search of art, inspiration, wonder, and colorful refuge from a beige, sometimes terrible, banal branch of humanity that trickled like a fjord through everyday life.

That desperate desire of wanting someone else to make my decisions passed with nary the forcible fanfare it had arrived. Much advice I'd gotten in my life was wrong. Well-meaning folks sometimes misled me because of their own blind spots and biases.

Bertrand saw everything in a bluesy way which often juxtaposed my perky Pollyanna rose. I continued to speculate what he might say in this moment.

"Belle, you never should listen to anyone, not even me. You knew better than to stay on the phone with Brigitte. She's a sweet girl, but you need always to listen to your gut!"

"Belle, do the right thing. Turn yourself in. You can't run from your own reflection."

"Belle, find out how the boy is. This is all that matters now. The rest of your life is about rectitude for him and his family."

"Belle, RUN!"

Perhaps that last one was my own inner voice. Fuck fear. I didn't want it near.

I spotted the unopened letter from Brigitte. It was the first she gave me. I toyed with it; outline it with my gaze. Lapis. Rainbows. Not yet. I was not ready to open it.

CLUNK. CLUNK. CLUNK.

The icemaker, accidentally turned on when cleaning, was alive and kicking. I thought they shot me! Grabbed my side, feeling for a hole. Picked up the phone to call Bertrand. Reconsidered. Turned on *Black Magic Woman*. Danced in defiance of darkness, danger and death, not my own, but Luis Fernando's. I knew I would turn on the news soon.

Oye Cómo Va followed, and the music moved my body, releasing pent up apprehension, swinging out some tension; if anyone saw me now, they might miscalculate and assume I was mad or unremorseful. I was neither... though perhaps I was *going* mad.

I turned on my computer, avoiding news, social media and email - chugging straight to YouTube where I danced to one more song: Elvis Presley. *Jailhouse Rock*. Love how he moves. No wonder they call him the King.

He leaned his head in the passenger window, "Uber?" His accent was undeniably Spanish; South American flavor. All these runs to the airport had attuned Leonard to the unique musicality of each country's dialect.

"Oui. Je suis Leonard. I speak English. Do you need help with bags?"

"No, thank you. I just have this," he gestured to a small forest green hand held case whose better days had long since passed, the nicked kisses from lurching down luggage carousels shone light on a busy man, well traveled. No luggage for the trunk? It was odd for a pickup at Terminal international at de Gaulle.

He got in the back, white teeth, brown skin, and sincere smile with a smattering of sorrow. The handsome man, early sixties, leaned forward and firmly shook Leo's hand, then handed him an address of a hospital. "Juan Alberto. I'm here to see my grandson. There's been an accident," he sat back and sighed.

Leonard sighed too, only silently so. He adjusted the rearview mirror and tried, unobtrusively, to take in all that he could about Juan Alberto's countenance. If he was going to the hospital, that meant Luis Fernando was still alive, fighting for his young life. The subtext of the trip to town became about the boy and sussing out how he was doing, without letting on.

The Aéroport Terminal ramp was jam-packed with traffic. Leonard held his hands tight to the steering wheel at ten and two o'clock, kept right at the fork, and followed signs for A1/Paris-Lille /A3/A16/A104/Marne-la-Vallée.

The fifty-five minute drive was at first silent. Cordial conversation about Paris and the weather led Leonard to share about his art studies and passion for landscape portraiture. Juan Alberto spoke eloquently about his position at the International Center for Equatorial Agronomy and his mission to combat global warming and food insecurity.

By withholding information about the accident, Leonard felt like a fraud. The more Juan Alberto talked, the greater Leo's reverence for this kind soul grew as the reality of the tragedy crashed in upon him. As Leonard turned onto hospital grounds, Juan Alberto focused on what he might encounter. The mood was grim, yet he maintained his dignity.

"Do you have another call now, or is it possible for you to wait while I see what the situation is? I may need to get something to eat or freshen up at my hotel. It's been a long day. I will compensate you well." With that he held out euros the equivalent of EE-Gads! Leonard didn't want any money, but how could he explain?

"I will wait. Please, no tip necessary."

"Ah, but what is necessary for the heart is a different matter." With that, he left currency in the car, picked up his lovingly battered old case, and headed up to see Luis. Leonard piloted his car to a waiting zone, and parked, his shoulders heaving with the heaviness of heart, the depth and breadth of which he could not have conceived of just yesterday.

The stench of rubbing alcohol made Bertrand woozy. That, lack of nourishment, the Paris predicament, and the emotional swell of seeing his hearty mother, so small now, swallowed up by the hospital bed, billows of pillows, dwarfed by a beeping silver screen overhead that monitored a heart frequency like a series of earthquake aftershocks, all combined to give him a spinning sensation.

"Son," she held his hand, fine fingers calloused from passionate play on string instruments — her own still strong, so recently capable, soft, wrinkled knuckles emanating with love.

"Oui?" He leaned in close to better hear his mother's dying words.

"Son."

"Oui?"

"SON!"

"Oui, what is it, mother?" He held more tightly onto her hand like a life raft adrift on an open, unpredictable sea.

"Son, answer your damn phone! That's the tenth time it has rung in the same amount of minutes."

"Ah! Oui. Salut?"

Leonard spoke through a crackly reception.

"Bertrand... there you c-c-c-rackle... Bertrand... ooo-c-c-c-crackle, I have to go!"

Juan Alberto stood outside the driver's door with a stone-faced man and woman by his side – they retreated into a robotic-like reality; their bodies on this plane, but their beings far, far away.

Leonard tucked away his phone like a naughty poodle caught ripping apart a pair of expensive, new, leopard print slippers. Juan Alberto leaned down with a forced casual, "Would you, erm... mind... erm... taking us to the estación de policía? A suspect... umm... a suspect has turned herself in." He suddenly looked like a lost four-year-old in a crowded mall. Leo breathed in, but not out. Perhaps he indicated that, yes, he would drive, because the three of them fell into the back seat like dominos.

The women crossed her leg with the unselfconscious grace of a young gazelle in the forest unaware of gawking spectators. "This is my daughter, María Rose." She nodded from a faraway universe. Leonard was aware of her innate geniality beneath the twilight veil that had descended on her this day.

The young man extended his hand, "I am Luis Fernando."

"I thought this is the name of the…" Leonard stopped himself.

"Luis Fernando is my grandson, my son and my father's name. I stand alone as Juan Alberto." He laughed, more from habit than anything, the chuckle out of place in the deaf tin in this trench.

"How is he, your grandson?"

Three heads shook sadly. Three pairs of faraway eyes settled expectantly on Leonard, waiting. He thought of Belle. He thought of getting out of his car and abandoning it there, he thought of calling Bertrand again and asking what he ought to do. He thought of moving to Buenos Aires, but he turned the ignition and drove.

A lone leaf fell on the hood of the car. Leonard fixated on it during the drive to the station like a yogi staring at a flame waiting for enlightenment. Maroon, crisp and curled at the edges, the leaf rode the lonely way with him. "I'm here, still here," it seemed to say, so he winced at its loss when it flopped with finality onto the ground before he parked.

Members of the Jiménez family exchanged only a few half mumbles during the journey. Leonard picked up that the child was still alive, unconscious, and on life support, with his mother still by his side. Maria Rose repeated, "I never should have moved to Paris" like the rosary, as though her journey abroad were to blame for the day's tragedy.

Luis Fernando sniffed a lot - a sharp double-sniff, towing the line of anger-tinged grief. Juan Alberto was calm. Not heroic or stoic, but solid and brave. He was the spine of his family and any community lucky enough to attract his peaceful, paternal presence.

Fascinated by the electrifying, doubt-defying urban transformation of Colombia in recent years due to the bold bettering of even the worst barrios, the South American Republic was on Leo's bucket list. HAD been on his list until listlessness flooded him as he watched his little leaf fall. Under ordinary circumstances, he would have engaged Juan Alberto in conversation about his country, but this wasn't any normal.

Upon arrival at the police station, Leonard stepped up to open the doors. He helped Maria out, took her hand, and supported her under her arm almost as if she were old and infirm, her body quivering almost as if she were dying. He opened the heavy door to the station, and stood tall as if to impart, in unspoken terms, his sorrow at their suffering.

Once inside, the solemn mood shifted like tectonic plates scraping against each other, tilting the earth to its core. There, crumpled like a pile of twisted dirty laundry she laid, forehead to the floor, lamenting, "I did it! I did it! It was me who hurt the boy! Put me away, lock me up, throw away the key, it was me!"

Four officials and Jacqueline stood by saucer-eyed. The largest officer, two meters tall, didn't have the courage to speak. This Shakespearian display made even the strong weak.

Maria Rose gasped and ran outside for some fresh air so she wouldn't faint. Luis Fernando II punched his fist into a wall with such an ancient caterwaul it sent shivers up and down any spine within earshot and stopped Bridgette's wailing from the floor.

Juan Alberto's reaction was the most regal thing anyone there had ever seen. He got down on the stone cold floor, wrapped his arms around the young woman, and stuck there like a grape leaf encircling rice. He laid his head prayerfully on her shaking shoulder.

Time, a wily, worthy opponent, was in a race against me. A rooster that crows on the hour adorns the Art Deco clock on the buttercup-colored kitchen wall. She crowed loud and proud, reminding me to redouble my pace, no dawdling - "Cock-a-doodle-doo!"

Time shadowed me in multiple ways on this evening. I'd heard it said that in moments of crisis one's life passes before one's eyes. As I spent my efforts to organize and manage my belongings, my twenty-seven years paraded like a techno color film in Sensurround. I saw and tasted events large and small that transpired in my days on earth. The triumvirate of joy, delight, and triumph commingled with the death, devastation, and despair that is familiar - that I was so acquainted with - in my moments.

When dad was dying, and I fought with the evil doctors, supposed life givers, oath takers who acted with Hippocratic hypocrisy, negligent in his diagnosis and care, I was overcome with the IS-ness that life wasn't fair. I, just sixteen, newly bereft from the loss of mom, shouldered the system alone while caring for dad in our modest Boise home.

People cared: Neighbors and friends brought by an occasional home cooked meal. Once, my ceramics teacher, Kurt Karling and his wife Carlene came by to help with laundry. Their kindness made me cry, yet for big-ticket issues, it was just dad and me. My father, in his daily misery, was supportive to the end. I pondered why bad things happen to good people. Why is the world as it is, one born into wealth, another to squalor?

After dad took a steep downturn, a new neighbor moved in. Andrika was a night nurse who blocked our driveway with her truck, stole our clean trashcans, held parties until ungodly hours when in our house we just needed a little peace to sleep. I dealt with Andrika with kid gloves, considered that she'd suffered abuse, made excuses for her rudeness, said please and thank you, and told her I'd like to foster a good neighborly relationship, but there was no getting through to her. A witness saw her smash the pale blue crystal vase in our driveway. My tires crunched over the pieces, going flat when I had dad buckled in on the way to the ER.

Why? I wondered. Why did this soused louse move next door to our house, especially at such a precarious time? Life wasn't fair. Or was it? Had I inadvertently deserved it? Had I thought wrong? There are those who say, "You create your reality by what you think." Did I THINK my parent's dead? Might I have thought an easier life instead?

Life wasn't fair now for Luis Fernando and his family and I was the louse. That precious boy played no part in thinking an awning knocked over by a pole hit by a car by someone - me - distracted on a cell phone would fall on him.

Keep moving, Camille, keep moving before the rooster crows again.

"Natalie Mouskers! No, no, no!" I scooped her under her soft belly, gave her a light kiss between her perky ears, and plopped her on the worn, woven Guatemala rug under my desk. She'd been clawing on the four Manila hemp envelopes I so carefully prepared.

The top envelope said, "Luis Fernando and family." In there, neatly stacked, in ascending order were €5,000 with a note on white paper written in block letters with black ink because this was too serious a situation for cursive or color.

"I'm sorry. I have no words. Camille."

The next envelope in similar no nonsense lettering was for my landlady who had been nothing but decent, proper, and welcoming of me. When I was new to town and moved into the flat, she had a gift basket of food waiting for me brimming with bread, cheese, grapes, tomatoes and olives along with a typed card that listed grocery stores, post office, and other important points of local reference.

She always fixed my plumbing and appliances toot suite when necessary. In return, I was a clean, quiet - except for occasional fits of dancing - tenant, fairly drama free, even though I'd been through two boyfriends in the three years of my residence.

I walked her nippy dachshund, Beau, when she was on holiday to Versailles. Most importantly I paid my rent early each month in cash from tips I earned while living my chalk artist dream in front of the Louvre, in Paris, the City of Lights, where I cherished life, the days to the nights. She counted on my timely contribution to her pale pension.

"Madame Trouli. You have been an angel. If I don't come back, here is the €1,400 rent for January and another 300 for the trouble of dealing with my things. Choose whatever charity you like for the nicer items and trash my personal things. I caused an accident. I'm sure you'll hear about it soon. The anguish is unimaginable. I apologize for not giving you more notice or hugging you goodbye. All my best, Camille."

I kept my tip money - wads of bills - hidden amid kidney beans and black-eyed peas in bell jars at the top of the pantry. No robber would think to trifle with the legumes. My home safe deposit box pleased me, more so now that I needed immediate access to cash.

The last two envelopes, for Brigitte and Bertrand, remained unfinished. Stuffing both packets to bulging with pictures and trinkets was as far as I'd gotten. I had not even had a moment, or the nerve, to open the long lapis one so patiently waiting for me.

The rooster crowed again. Natalie Mouskers and I looked at each other panicked. She knew. She rubbed round my leg like it was a midsummer Whitsun maypole. We would miss each other. That thought broke me. When I bent to pet her, I instead squatted on my haunches, then leaned over in the child's pose and sobbed into my hands like when my mother - and then my father - had died.

"Cammy, you're a stronger person than me. I couldn't handle it," Winona used to say on our way to school when my father was in the thick of his decline.

"It's not like I have a choice, Winny."

"Yes, you do. You're there for everyone. You stay steadfast. I couldn't do it. You're a much stronger person than me. We each only get what we can handle."

I hated when she said such things, as if tragedies befell me because I could handle them. This repeated squabble nearly cost us our friendship. I wondered how Winny and the others back home would react to the news. It would sadden everyone except that nasty nurse neighbor. I was the local hard luck girl done well and Idahoans often came to stay with me at my Parisian pad.

What is taking the police so long? The anticipation of the knock on the door was killing me. Do they even knock? Fatigued, I had to lie down. Natalie Mouskers and I collapsed, curled onto the couch and slept soundly into the night.

"Your old Moeder will live," she patted his hand like she was pounding out dough for Speculoos, Bertrand's favorite shortbread biscuit since he was a little boy. Helga, famous throughout Belgium for her spectacular Speculoos, secreted away her special recipe. Family, friends, and her community commonly speculated her simple spiced pleasure contained these ingredients: pepper, cinnamon, ginger, cloves, cardamom and nutmeg.

Bertrand didn't believe for one moment she would rebound, so notched down she seemed since he'd last seen her a fortnight ago. Frightening how quickly that happened out of range of his watchful eye while he'd been having fun singing with Belle, his muse, and asking for the hand in marriage of Leonard, his eager young partner of six months.

Something vexed him, anyone could see it: the verpleegsters, their aides, orderlies, and patients gossiped with ferociousness behind his back, some out of concern, others out of judgment, as people do.

Helga, straightforward as redirected turbine wind, kicked courtesy to the wind and asked, "Son, what's bothering you? We have always been honest with each other; it's no time to deceive now." She adjusted the plastic tube that threaded from her nose down her throat.

"I gather you're worried about your friend - what's her name?"

"Belle."

"Yes, well, I think you need, (deep nose inhale, more adjusting of tubes), to go straighten that out. Go eat, find some cell reception, find out what you need to, then come back to your dear mother's side." She coughed, a filthy, phlegmy cough, her hand pat was soft like patting talc on a new baby's bottom.

Now it was his turn to sniff. He removed his hands gently to swipe through his hair, feeling five years older than when he'd arrived.

"What is it? I can tell there's something else."

"Oui."

"Wat?"

He hung his head, "I would like to get... I would like... Please, your recipe for Speculoos."

"No. It's not the time."

She said it with such force he believed her, or told himself he did. His last heel exited the room as another sharper inhale of breath came from beneath the beige hospital blanket.

Maria Rose returned into the station, a trace of color fleshed in her face from the fresh air. This scarlet faded to pale pink then drained to white again as she saw her father in a fetal position enshrouding the woman on the floor. She stepped forward then back as if approaching a fire and rapidly retreating from the molten heat. Her father was who he was, regardless of the situation in life, embodying integrity in his own inimitable way.

Brigitte, knocked a tether from her keening, finally lifted her head. She put her hand ever so tepidly on the elder's cheek, "Je suis désolé, lo siento. I am sorry." The pair exchanged a private moment in a public sphere, searching each other's souls in sorrow.

Jacqueline helped her up. Juan Alberto followed, twice flattening out the creases on his slacks, quiet as a crow in between caws.

"She did nothing. You did nothing," Jacqueline kissed the top of Brigitte's head like she was a babe being put down to nap. "It 'twas an accident. Camille was in the car. Camille was driving. Camille... Camille... Camille..." her eyes fixed on a splotch of uneven paint on the wall opposite. "Camille," she uttered once again, trailing off.

"Leonard?" Brigitte asked this.

All eyes turned: the four officials, now five, Juan Alberto, Maria Rose, Luis Fernando II, Jacqueline, Brigitte, and two strangers in the station to report other crimes and trespasses. Twenty eyes trained on him. Make that twenty-two - the lady in the red coat cradled a Yorkie in her arms, a matching red bow clipped in her hair. As if on cue, the Yorkie curled her lip and barked, "Rrrrr..... uuffff!"

Leonard stood still like a Beefeater at Buckingham, a teen in a mannequin challenge, a deer spotted by the King of the Jungle, a corpse three days post mortem, an Uber driver-art student in an awkward, salacious situation, wishing he could vaporize like Sabrina or Samantha at the snap of his fingers.

No one moved. No one dared even breathed. Even the Yorkie stayed silent until a weak, "Oui. Salud, Brigitte," he lifted his right hand in a wee wave.

The Yorkie was having none of it. "Rrrr..... uuffff, rrrr... uuffff, rrrr... uuffff, rrrr... uuffff!"

Three a.m.
I awoke more refreshed than I had a right to be. Natalie Mouskers seemed appropriately worried and then decided she still had time to sleep and claimed my warm spot on the bed for another catnap. She lay

curled in a blissful ball while I, bare feet on the cold floor, circled through my home reviewing my life.

The amethyst heart given me by my father on my twelfth birthday hung around my neck, tucked in the cleavage under my tee. I filed precious photos of mom, dad, and Winny like hotcakes in a flat file set into a blue rucksack along with two bottles of travel shampoo.

I stared for fifteen minutes at the corrugated corkboard that displayed over fifty photos of my favorite chalk drawings. I would get rid of anything current or with my name on it.

I worked my entire life at being a good person. I had an "A" for my attitude and actions until yesterday. I mean, I made the requisite mistakes: wore plaids and stripes together (an intentional artist thing), grew impatient in the post office when I was too tired, and picked the wrong boyfriends.

All of my friends text and drive; I didn't even go that fast... flow of traffic and all. I still blame the pole. It came up out of nowhere, like I was on a slippy-slide.

All day and night the visual of Pierre, erm, Luis Fernando, falling face down played through my head as he repeatedly fell like a rag doll being tossed onto the pavement by a petulant child. This image pushed past any other thought I had. I fled the scene out of shock and a survival instinct I didn't even realize I had. I could forgive myself that, but I would not forgive myself if I continued to flee.

If... I... continued... to... flee...

Confounded, choices fluctuated in my mind. I prepared to spend my life in servitude trying to make up for the harm I caused, but could not prepare for prison; it was impossible for me to wrap my mind around being searched in delicate, private areas of my body, being at risk of violation by prisoners who hurt those who hurt children, and eating non-nutritious slop. So at the same time I promised myself I would be noble, I simultaneously packed my sack as though in a dream.

I worked up a sincere speech that expressed my deepest remorse to Luis Fernando's family. I churned through what I would say to Bertrand, Bridgette, Aunt Molly, Winona, my school advisor, the police...

Where WERE they? How is it no officer had found me yet? What is going on? How were my friends holding up? Was Luis recovering? Had he died? Was he suffering? The not knowing gnawed at me like a mouse chewing through plaster to get into a warm house during a monsoon.

I turned on the télévision. Flipped to the news. Sat through the weather forecast, (chance of snow), a preview of a fashion show, a wrenching report about refugees, and some silly banter between the anchors I tuned out. Then, there it was. My picture flashed onto the screen; it was a candid shot Brigitte had snapped at the Patinoire De Boulogne Billancourt, our roller rink.

I looked happy.

"The driver of a hit-and-run is wanted for an accident that has left a young boy fighting for his life tonight. A distraught friend turned herself in to the police. The police refuse to hold her because she is not guilty of the crime. The suspect, Camille Lisette Portraro, is still at large. If you have seen Camille or are aware of her whereabouts, please call our anonymous tip line at...."

I turned the set off. Natalie Mouskers was purring peacefully. I picked up Brigitte's letter with hesitation and forced myself to read. Oh! Poor Brigitte! Such a secret she harbored!

Lucy Perelle. Isn't that swell? Here I am in post accident hell. I chose 'Lucy,' the name of Coach Franameyer's lucky, plucky Minx cat that clawed through our volleyballs until they deflated. I'd witnessed at least five episodes in which she ought to have lost her life, but landed regally on her white paws. Each time she casually strolled away from near death by truck, car, Doberman, Dalmatian, or skunk spray splay.

Lucy. Lucy it was.

I have no idea where 'Perelle' came from. It just announced itself as the surname for my fake ID so Winny, Cathy, and I could get into real nightclubs to dance, get drunk, and meet twenty-year-old carousing college boys when we were sixteen. I kept the license stuffed away in a scrapbook I'd sorted by year. I never once thought I would use it again.

Still pitch dark, no cops, and a million things to do. I was so lost in remorse, regret, and anguish over Luis, Brigitte and Bertrand that I could barely see the reality in front of me.

Bertrand depended on me for his living. It is unusual for a busker to rake in the cash Bertrand did without such a famous partnership as we enjoyed. He was Sonny to my Cher, Fred to my Ginger, Jack to my Gracie, and John to my Yoko. We supported, inspired, amused, relied on, loved, and admired each other as we filled each other's bean jars in bulging rolls of bills.

Meanwhile, my bestie Brigitte had rawly revealed herself in a rainbow-sticker adorned letter. I never saw it coming; I would have been sidelined by her confessional inquiry even IF life had continued on as expected in that alternate universe, the one I was so comfortable and challenged in eighteen hours before.

The slightest thought of Luis and family trumped all. I'd erected a wall around my heart so I could even sift through scrapbook art for the Perelle identity, which from this day forward would be mine, in sickness and in health, till death do us part.

I'd worked through my things quickly - shredded journals and letters, and pulverized private, precious moments from my personal life. Then I packed my sack, laid down with my kitty, and told her I was not coming back. She scrunched up her nose and her eyes slit contentedly closed as she purred in containment of the NOW, grateful for our cosmic connection that saved her from the streets.

The rooster clock crowed again as if to proclaim the cavalry. I sprang up like an coil cut loose from a Chevy Truck, catapulting high through the air like the daring young man on the flying trapeze. Natalie Mouskers even deigned to open her eyes to see why I had stopped scratching her chin.

A soft spritely snow fell flush. The same flakes he used to catch on his tongue and gobble hungrily as a child stuck to his eyelids as Bertrand escaped the icky stench of the infirmary and turned the corner of this otherwise equable straat.

His lungs naturally expanded in the fresh night air; oxygen molecules readily traveled like water rushing down a ravine, gurgling, gushing along, speeding to heed his body's neglected needs. How is it one forgets to breathe when one's mother is in hospital?

Leonard's name, on speed dial, was easy to punch in. The buttons responded musically, conveying to Bertrand they were doing their part: Er, um, er, um, er, um, eeer. Then: ring, ring. Ring, ring. Ring, ring.

"Bonjour. C'est Leonard." Leonard's voice like an empty echo informed Bertrand, "I cannot answer. Please leave a message."

"Bonjour, Leonard! C'est Bertrand. S 'il-te-plaît réponds. Comment va Belle? Comment allez-vous?" Bertrand begged him to answer and inquired how everyone was.

Click. Next up, Brigitte.

"Bonjour, hello. C'est Brigitte. I must be at the beach. (Giggle) Please leave me a message."

"Bonjour, Brigitte! C'est Bertrand. S 'il-te-plaît réponds. Comment va Belle? Comment allez-vous?"

Then he tried Camille — five times.

The brightness of the snow dimmed. Three blocks down, Bertrand stumbled upon a Pool and Snooker hall, Le Fellini. There he had three martinis, two games of pool, (won one, lost one), four games of darts, and a heavy flirtation that would cost him Leonard's trust if he didn't rustle himself together. It's a shame the worry and stress for his mother, concern for Camille and their business, along with his frustration at being cut off mixed unwieldy with the high blood levels of alcohol. His cells cried out for food, his spirit craved comfort.

"Another martini, please. Extra olives."

THE PASSPORT

He was home.

I'd never seen the man look more perplexed. Was I unrecognizable with cropped hair, a wan face, and fearful eyes? Had he forgotten me? Was he wondering why, after telling him two years ago he was a lying scumbag and to never, ever, ever, ever contact me again, I was suddenly standing at his door at 4:35 a.m. hugging a gray rucksack like it was a suckling baby? Was this too late - or too early - to call? Was it something else?

"Who's that?" His gaze was at my feet.

Oh! That cat! She had followed me. She'd never done that before. She knew. She knew. "Natalie Mouskers!" I stooped to pick her up. Miss Mouskers vibrated in the crooks of my arms as Nikos scratched the white spot between her eyes with such tenderness he seemed almost human.

God, I love this guy.

I'd fallen in love more times in my young life than a person should be allowed in fifteen lifetimes. Bertrand said it wasn't love, but it was for me, and with Nikos, I'd fallen especially hard and fast and plummeted into a pleasure garden he'd pruned purposely for me. He had ferociously flirted with and courted me. In retrospect he stalked me when I was new to Paris, a freshman to the street artist scene. This was before my museum corner graced me with Bertrand, and pre-Brigitte, Jacqueline, or any of my now former life friends. I was a giggly girl, wide open to the world, and wide open for a man like Nikos to use a crowbar to pry his way into my sanctuary.

In the beginning, before God made the earth, there was Nikos Ramanos, a package of power, magnificence, and simmering artistic talent so brilliant it burnt my corneas. Inaugurating me with intellectual intrigue, his mind worked like a maze and opened doors to perceptions not previously conceived. He mesmerized and magnetized me into his aura. I was a malleable magnet and he was symphonic steel.

"You look good, Cammy. What do you need?"

"A camouflage passport."

His beautiful eyes, burning to bargain or barge his way back into my life, flashed respect.

"Cammy, have you been a bad girl?"

God, I hate this guy.

Nikos was a sociopath. Lied to me about everything. He was a poker cheat. Ran a million euro undercover scam online until they shut him down one day. No penalties, no accountability, just blocked access to the site. Two, three, or nine timed me while professing his undying love in such a poetically pleasing, literate way, He could lob out Shakespeare's Sonnets with more soul than Mark Rylance strutting and fretting upon the New Globe stage, then his backhand would score him points for his ready references to Tennyson, Thoreau, Whitman, Frost, Dylan Thomas, and the trifecta of Morrison's: Jim, Van, and Toni. This drove me wild.

"Can you help me or not?"

"I can, but it will cost you."

I was prepared for this, but Natalie Mouskers who raised her fur, screeched and hightailed from my arms to crouch aquiver behind the red rawhide couch, wasn't. I reached in my pack and plucked out the gold lame bikini. He ran his hand over my newly shorn head. "No braids anymore. Where's the fun in that?"

My life was on the line. I stood steady, waiting for this gorgeous, mercenary Greek to decide what he would do. "You want to get out of France? Dance, sister, dance." He kicked the door shut with a BAM!!

"Rrrr..... uuffff, rrrr... uuffff, rrrr... uuffff, rrrr... uuffff," the Yorkie, flummoxed by the falciform friction that sliced the air like a bagging hook, barked her red bow right off. Plop! It fell at the feet of Officer Girard - the tall one - who yelled over the yapping Yorkshire to his counterpart a quarter meter shorter, two decades older, and with a handful of hair less on his back crown.

"Moreau! Move 'em out of here!"

"Madame, this way," Moreau took the lady in the red coat by her arm.

"Don't touch me! Assault! ASSAULT! This man is assaulting me! Help! Assault!"

"Rrrr..... uuffff, rrrr... uuffff, rrrr... uuffff, rrrr... uuffff! .... RUFF!"

Leonard was secretly and selfishly satisfied with the scuffle for it gave him a momentary reprieve from all of the prying eyes that shone like sarcastic stars in a blackened sky.

"Joubert!" Girard nodded at the sorrowful looking squared jowled sire to his left. Joubert flanked Red on the other side as he and Moreau smoothly scooted her and her little dog too out of sight, out into the night. The ruff-ruff-ruff's faded to gray, at which time Girard had something to say.

"Well," he trained his full authoritative gaze onto Brigitte, "If you're ready to talk, we're ready to hear."

Rachelle Rousseau, the only female officer in sight, fastidiously grabbed an electric notepad at the ready to record every word.

Juan Alberto approached Leonard, his calm, dignified demeanor cracking, top lip curled into quaking question. "You know HIM?" Even the sharpest English speaking Colombian mixes up their pronouns in Paris under stupefying stress.

"Oui." Leonard stepped defiantly next to Brigitte to signify his loyalty to her with rueful regret at dislodging his comradeship with this respected elder. Brigitte hugged him, buried her head in his shoulder and sobbed again.

"Leonard, I love her. I asked her, did she read my letter? She told me YES. I asked does she love me? She told me YES, I love you too, Brigitte, and then BOOM. I heard BOOM, and then nothing. Nothing more from my Camille, my Belle until I found out we hurt this boy, this innocent boy. It was me; I did it, Leonard."

Now it was Maria Rose's turn to collapse on the floor. The BOOM had toppled her. And who runs in, but the Yorkie escaped from her leash! She slip-slides on the slippery floor over to Maria and licks her face. Maria Rose couldn't resist this bundle of dog. She picked her up, clipped back on her bow, smiled, and gave her a kiss right on her forehead just like Brigitte had done to Belle at the roller rink.

Moreau sat down, head in his hands, defeated. Rosseau, next in command, geared up to take control of this cylindrical situation, when Luis Fernando II grabbed his own hair, "Get that phone already! It's been ringing non-stop for fifteen minutes!"

Leonard took his phone from his shirt pocket.

"Salud?"

"Leonard! There you are! Please, tell me, what is going on?" Bertrand, drunk as a skunk, put up his hand to wave away the bartender whose hand sat sensuously on his thigh.

For the next ten minutes Nikos didn't seem interested in talking.

"Use the condom. Utilisar le préservatif. The last thing I need now is to get pregnant," or contract any diseases, I wanted to add, but restrained myself for fear of insulting the man whose help I sought.

"Oui bien sûr," he lied. Then, a breathless, "I've missed you, Cammy."

I reached out and pet Natalie Mouskers, my pussycat, as each moment exploded in effortful eternity. She interspersed pleasure purrs with pleas of protest. Her hyper vigilant furs stood up static straight. Something in Nikos' vaniteux attitude upset her. Her claws flared, as she became the closed kitty I'd met on the street before I'd tamed her.

When it was over, I got up to go to the toilette. Miss Mouskers followed me.

"You can go to Saint Kitts and Nevis," came the call from the bedroom.

"What? Where?" I fumbled through a messy cupboard to find a new paper roll.

"Caribbean. You can live under the radar there. They are loose on asylum."

"No, too sunny, too remote. I need someplace to make chalk drawings."

I pulled on my clothes and sat on the far end of the bed, "Or jump off a 30,000 foot cliff."

"What did you do, Cam? What are you running from, my angel?" he reached for me out of lust, habit, and perhaps genuine concern.

I sat silent.

"Can't help you if I don't know."

So, this is what hell feels like. I figured I did a bad thing and was being punished. How else to explain that I looked to nefarious Nikos to untie this knot that was strangling me?

I wondered about Luis Fernando, scanned the room for a television set. Closed my eyes and tried to contact the spirits of my father and mother for comfort, guidance, and encouragement, but sad to say, they had jumped ship, left me floundering amidst a flotilla of futility. In that formerly familiar inner space, rather than sanctuary, I found a tunnel pitching into the dark. Nikos clasped my hand and turned my chin towards him.

"I was driving down..."

"Driving? In Paris?"

"Yes."

"Whose car?"

"Mine."

"You have a car in Paris? You - a student, an artist?"

"Yes."

He laughed, not a kind laugh.

"Oh, you spoiled American girl. This is what you spend your money on?"

"I didn't buy it. Someone left it for me."

He could read it in my eyes.

"Who? Someone died?"

"Yes."

"A lover? A rich lover?"

My eyes roamed again looking for the set, searching for escape, a piece of rope or knives sharp enough for my wrists. I thought of Pascal and sighed. Nikos let go of my chin. Perhaps I was paranoid, but it seemed more like a push.

Once again, all eyes were on Leonard, Twenty-six this time: the officials, Moreau, Girard, Joubert, and Rousseau, Juan Alberto, María Rose, Luis Fernando II, Jacqueline, Brigitte, two strangers there to report other crimes and trespasses, including the lady in the red coat back in the station, (her Yorkie still in Maria Rose's arm stopped licking her to look at Leonard), and now, two smartly dressed reporters carrying microphones.

They heard a desperate male voice rise through the phone, "Je t'aime, tu me manques, Léonard, dis-moi ce qui se passe, comment va Belle, ce qui est arrivé à Brigitte, je ne sais rien." Juan Alberto translated this roughly to English in his head, still trying to piece this peculiar puzzle together, "I love you, I miss you. Please, Leonard, tell me what is going on? How is Belle? What happened to Brigitte? I haven't been told anything."

Leonard swallowed; the contraction of his throat was so tight it made a loud click. Eight of the eyes turned to the Yorkie, in anticipation of another round of barking, but no. She remained quiet, as eager to hear what came next as much as everyone else.

"I love you too, Bertrand. I am sorry. I cannot talk more now. I am.... indisposed." Again, his dry swallow, one of guilt, fear, apprehension and fright, pulled on his neck muscles, popping out the jugular vein, now a sick greenish blue.

Click.

Bertrand looked at his phone as though it might speak and explain this quick conversation, this night, this life, to him.

"Indisposed? My lover, my new fiancé, he is having an affair!"

The bartender, not yet twenty-five, but with a belief he was more worldly than he was, put his hand back on Bertrand, this time on his shoulder; a gentle, steadying hand, just the kind Bert needed now.

"When... when do you get off?"

Rémy sized up the paltry patrons in the bar. A couple kissing in the back, two drunken derelicts betting on their seventh game of billiards and an Orthopedist, just off his shift at the hospital, nursing a Whiskey Sour like the last drops of canteen water in a desert.

"Come on, everyone out. We're closed!"

His take-charge attitude excited Bertrand.

"But I haven't finished my drink."

"Take it with you, Doc. The glass is on me."

At the station, five people spoke at once.

JUAN ALBERTO - "I don't understand. You have met these people?" (To Leonard)

REPORTER WITH A LOOSELY DOUBLE WRAPPED SILVER SCARF - "Are you the suspect?" (To Leonard)

OFFICIAL RACHELLE ROUSSEAU - "Tell me everything you know." (To Brigitte)

JACQUELINE - "Where is the toilette. I don't feel well." (To no one in particular)

BRIGITTE - "Camille is a safe driver. She doesn't normally talk or text and drive. I pushed her to do so. I asked her over and over if she loved me. She wanted to hang up, but she held on for me. I sent her this picture, see?" (To Rachelle)

Brigitte took out her phone and clicked open a photo. Rachelle came close to inspect it.

JACQUELINE - "The toilette?" (Loudly to the lady in the red coat)

The Yorkie listened to everyone, turning her face from one to the next, cocking her head inquisitively, her bow tilting attractively with every move. Humans are a curious bunch.

"How soon after we split up did you date this rich, older, man?"

"He wasn't much older. WE didn't split up. I left YOU because I didn't want to be part of your harem or associated with your illicit... activities."

Stop. Stop Camille, from being so confrontational with this man, the only one who might help, came the call from inside my head as I again pictured life in prison as a child killer. Images like a flipbook unfolded an unfunny cartoon, which traumatically flashed in my mind without warning, flapping closed with a finality that didn't portend banality.

"You're telling me a young man died and left you a car?"

"Yes. Are you going to help me or not, Nikos?"

"The whole thing, she makes little sense."

"It makes sense, it happened!" I rarely shouted, and when I did it was like the last few minutes of popping corn, a full out kinetic splay of kernels in all directions, incapable of stopping, heated to combustion as they were.

"You haven't even asked me what I have done. You're fixated on the car. The stupid car I wish I never had! I met Pascal a few weeks after I stopped seeing you. We fell in love. He was everything I wanted in a man, in a partner. Everything." I lashed this whip at him with an accusation, because he had not been.

"We soon found out he was sick. He didn't come from old money, if that's what you're thinking. He was a self-made man, only thirty years old, he worked as an avocat, a lawyer, and he died in the prime of his life.

We used to drive to the country together. He left his daughter and ex-wife everything except the car which he willed to me."

"An avocat, yet you detest the bullshit authoritative system? I can't see you, a rebel, loving a lawyer."

"Pascal was different; he worked for humanitarian causes."

"Ah, of course he did."

He sat down. This monster, as I had thought of him for the past two years, looked every bit a lonely man who failed to find his dreams in life and was incapable of loving those who cared about him wisely. His father, a tourist florist in Mykonos, exhibited a gentile spirit to me when we met on our last excursion there, yet could never show Nikos the unconditional acceptance his son craved since boyhood.

The quest to please one's parents may haunt us all our lives. Before I met him, Nikos gave up on seeking the approval of his patérasa; like a worn boxer, he'd squandered his resistance, thrown the towel in the ring in the third minute of the twelfth round. I had always made excuses for him until the day I left him. History here repeated itself as I told myself, yet again, that this was a good man who never got a break in life.

"I will help you regardless of what you have done."

"Why?"

"I love you, Camille; you're a good person," he lifted my chin again. "Now, tell me everything, we'll make a plan, and I will help in whatever way I can."

He was a sociopathic pathological liar, but I believed him. I had no better options.

I'd forgotten the Lucy Perelle ID! Gah! That's what that niggling feeling was about!

When we were dating, Nikos and I spent all our time at my place, draped in delicious natural lighting that beamed in through the front pane. Fecund flowering plants spilled wildly like the waterfalls at Niagara I'd seen the summer of my sixteenth year, the last normal year before my father died. Sweet and sassy frankincense, lavender, and rose saturated the smell molecules and the riotous rooster clock always elicited a chuckle; this terrific totality made mine the place of choice over Nikos' bachelor pad, a bit cluttered, musty, dusty, and dull.

He'd rushed off to nab the Lucy license in the same breath as I mentioned I'd left it on the kitchen counter. He knew where the key lay hid, and before I could overthink it, he left me alone, (with a sleeping Natalie Mouskers), in his flat feeling flat.

"The porn is under the bed, the money is... well... everywhere, and I'm sure you'll find other things of interest. Do nothing I wouldn't do," were his parting words to me. Since we'd broken up years before, what more could he be hiding?

I began my snooping the moment the door shut. I checked the bean jars first. Yep. Wads of cash stuffed in disarray amid his lentils, corn meal and pasta. That was one of the best things I learned from him. I needed cash; it was oh-so-tempting, but I kept my decency even in dire circumstances. That was his money, however illicitly gained. The harm I'd caused was a stupid mistake I would take back in the micro fission division of a nanoparticle, but I couldn't. There was no need to add sins to my already leaded load.

From the pantry, I moved to his desk. The usual office supplies filled the top drawers, then... the motherlode. Three wide bottom drawers held photo albums and videos of his sexual conquests. It shocked me. Shocked I hadn't caught a disease when we were together. Shocked I was so clueless for the year I thought we were "in love." Shocked to see several files of Nikos with men, in threesomes, and in an artistic shot with a Boa Constrictor wrapped around him. Yes, really.

I missed Idaho. I missed my parents. I just wanted to be a girl again in the carefree days of sledding, skiing, and swimming, when my sketchbooks were filled with portraits of those I knew and loved, not strangers from Stockholm or Shanghai.

A helicopter flew low overhead. I imagined they were looking for me. I pictured squads of officers lined up in camouflage gear stalking me, ready to pounce.

I finally found the television and turned it on to see if I could catch the news.

Lively Spanish guitar played. Leonard turned to Luis Fernando II who clucked his lips with the hesitancy that said, 'If I don't answer, it won't be true.' Rousseau, annoyed at all the interruptions, halted her interrogation and feigned a look of concern.

"Bueno."

A woman's intermittent wail echoed out.

"Sí. Sí. Sí."

He hung up, hugged his sister who gave him three slap-pats on the back like she was burping a colicky baby, motioned to his father, "We go now."

No one asked. No one needed to. Juan Alberto matter-of-factly nodded at Leonard, "Come."

Jacqueline, refreshed upon her return from the bathroom, watched the crew file out like a small child watches ants march for the first time under a magnifying glass.

"Leonard?" her tone betrayed dismay at being left in sole charge of a shattered Brigitte. Brigitte had no expressions left and angled back to Rosseau ready to continue her testimony like an old gramophone someone had lifted the needle from but now set back down in the groove of GO.

Dawn was breaking, the sad, silent, solemn sort of dawn that will stick with a family forever. Leonard, ever the gentleman, opened the door for Maria Rose and again held her arm as she slid in the backseat, her elegant legs crossed with the affliction of an Auntie who would never again blow bubbles, make balloon animals, or tuck in nephew with *Goodnight Moon.*

Once everyone was back in the cab, the car moved mindlessly through a maze of rear view mirrored minions maneuvering through French morning haze, Juan Alberto leaned forward, elbows on the seat ahead. His half whisper, half cry, "So..." echoed in the air.

Rémy handed the dapper, brooding doctor the bottle of Whiskey and shoo-shooed everyone out of the bar. He winked sideways at Bertrand as he fluidly closed up shop with the grace and agility of an Olympic swimmer. He quickly counted and pocketed some cash, locked the money drawer, tidied up the pool cues, picked up darts, and finally pulled down an iron screen over the door.

"Smoke?" He offered a Disque Bleu cigarette, which, much to his own surprise, Bertrand, a non-smoker, took. Everything about this night was different and acting from reason seemed a most unreasonable way to proceed.

"Merci."

This is where the conversation ended. The two men, in alternate orbits, had accidentally come together for a noir movie moment on a drizzly dawn. They walked in regretful, smoke-filled silence, both trying to find an exit on this awkward turnpike. The chilled, red-orange tinged air slapped Bertrand out of his half drunken daze; he coughed a passive aggressive, "Ka-hah," stomped out the cigarette and stopped, feet planted a foot apart.

"Rémy... I apologize if I have... umm... misled you... my moeder, she's ill in hospital. I must… umm… I must... I must now get back."

"Yes, I see. Well, best wishes, Bernard."

"Bertrand."

"Yes, best wishes." He pumped his hand like a car salesman closing the top deal of the day, happy to have a get-a-way.

Bertrand ambled like molasses down the sanitary corridors of the icy institution, not in a rush to see the pale puddle of his moeder. Imagine his surprise when he found her flush out of bed, in high spirits, animatedly telling stories to the nursing staff, her hands waving like magic wands in a fairy forest.

"You look awful, son, go get some rest, otherwise you'll give yourself a coronary and then who shall I, your poor mother, cook my prize bread for?"

The nurses, eating out her hand, tittered like schoolgirls.

On his way to his mother's home to sleep off this deleterious day, he picked up his phone and dialed with all the lost hope of a pirate heading gainfully down the plank. It rang and rang and then a doleful, "Hello?"

"Belle!"

Dawn unfolded more quickly than a rose on its prime day of bloom. I felt safer in the dark, unseen, like a child covering his plump face during a playful game of peek-a-boo.

I checked my messages one last time before destroying my phone. After practicing anchor knots, I realized I'd never be able to kill myself although despair ate up sacred portions of my soul I'd so carefully coaxed back into being via chalk, travel, study, and friendships.

My mind splashed in multiple directions mainly because of Brigitte and her lovely, lengthy letter; how could I have been so blind as to not see that my bestie was in love with me! All of those crushingly close flirty arabesques at the roller rinks, the late night confessional phone calls, the almost reverent rendering of my life through her eyes. As I was clearing the clutter of voice messages and text trail, the phone rang. It was Bertrand!

"Hello." The casualness of my tone surprised me.

"Belle?"

"Oui."

"What is going on? Please fill me in."

Ah, my friend, my confidant, my partner, my dear, dearest Bertrand. I wish he never had to learn what became of me. He would go through his own mourning, his business would take a hit, but I had to believe he would revive it, as I formerly had, my soul.

"He's dead, B. He's dead!"

"Who is dead? Leonard!"

"No! Luis Fernando. He didn't make it. He's gone!"

Just then, the front door blew open with the quick click of a key. An itty-bitty woman with a wash of black hair looked surprised to see me.

"I have to go B. I love you." I hung up.

"Who are you?"

"Um... I'm Camille. A friend of Nikos'."

She was the most beautiful creature I'd ever seen. Her lips like a sensuous sea dipping and bobbing a boat out to sea. Her eyes shone like a metallic meteor shower. Her hips like a fertility goddess were curved just so like the crescent moon, inciting curiosity. My knees were weak, my spirit meek. My mind scanned the pictures I'd seen in the bottom drawer, trying to place her face, her body. Nothing. I stumbled, stuttering...

"Who are you? Are you... are you... you and Nikos...

"What?"

"Ya know..." I gave a shimmering shrug that indicated sex, passion, and love - all the above.

"Oh. No! Nikos is my cousin! We're double first cousins."

"Double first cousins?"

"Yes. My mother's brother married his father's sister. We are cousins twice. We are like this." She crossed her first finger over middleman, middleman, middleman like a swan's neck gracefully folding down to peck food into her cygnet's mouth.

I flashed on my girlhood, skiing at the bright, sun-drenched, boldly beautiful Bogus Basin, Mormons and mountains surrounding me, never imagining I'd be in Paris in such a predicament.

"I'm Tanu." She gently took my hand in hers. I wanted to kiss her, to gobble her up, to imbibe her sanguine life force.

Nikos arrived like a cannon shot into his own home, fevered, as if he was fleeing evil itself. "Cammy. Go! We have to get you out of Paris soon! Oh, yeia sou, Tanu..."

"Did you get the Lucy Perelle driver's license?"

"Yes," Nikos slapped it on the coffee table, "Tanu, find me the scissors. You can't use this Camille. While I was there, the police came. I fled just in time. They may have followed me. You need to leave NOW."

This somehow validated that *finally* the officers were taking this seriously.

"Here, cousin," Tanu up offered a pair of titanium shears, no questions asked.

He cut the card in two. "To be safe. We need to make you a new ID. Leave town now. Get your bag, buy a new cellphone, and keep in close contact. It will take me perhaps a week to get your new papers, identity, and life. You can trust me. I love you." He clasped me so tightly my breath released with a huhhhh, like a squished helium balloon.

"I should turn myself in. I want to do the right thing. I don't know where to go."

Nikos grabbed out a handful of cash as big as my face from the polenta jar. "Get your pack!" I did. He stuffed the cash inside. "Here. You'll need your healthy food." He took apples, cheese, and nuts and packed them in amidst my toiletries and scarves.

"I read the letter in your bag. Brigitte loves you very much. Beware, however, Cammy, lovers may deceive. Be careful whom you confide in. I'll get you the documents, I promise you that. I owe you that much and more."

"Where shall I go?"

"I can't tell you. Wherever you decide, don't tell me so they can't get it out of me."

"What about Natalie Mouskers?"

"I'll take care of her. She likes me, look," he picked her up. She yowled, wriggled free, and hid in her place behind the settee.

"She's hungry. Please feed her and love her."

"We have no more time. GO!"

I ran into his room.

"Where are you going? Do you want to go to jail?"

"No. I have to pee!" A stream of liquid let loose like my kidneys had been retained water behind a dam. I heard the double cousins speak in a soft stream of Greek in the other room. When I emerged, the door was open. Daylight's amber hand jostled me awake.

"Tanu is going with you."

"I'm coming with you," she said.

Nikos pushed us out the door. I didn't even get to say goodbye to Natalie Mouskers.

The mid morning Monday rush was on. We ambled down the avenue. I pinched myself, unsure if I was in a bad dream.

The sun glared harshly in judgment, perturbing the delicate corneas of my eyes. I never knew Paris could be so cold. Who was this Tanu, so beautiful and bold, to accompany me nary a question asked? I missed my knitted hat with the hanging bunny earflaps; the frost turned my nose strawberry red, lips Burberry blue, and ears stinging scarlet.

Moist mid morning mist hissed out my mouth, "Why are you doing this? Uprooting your life to come with me?"

"I'm unemployed, unengaged, and unimpressed with my life in Paris at the moment," came the droll reply.

Unimpressed with her life at the moment? Would any place impress her, if not Paris? Then it hit.

"Are you getting paid for this?"

"Ναι, Nikos pays very well."

Nikos, who betrayed me so badly, loves me. His double first cousin, Tanu, whose countenance I am so topsy-turvy taken with, is my paid escort. The great golden life-giving orb won't get the fuck out of my eyes. A meter away from the curb, I stop to scrounge for my sunglasses. An occupied Taxi with an orange light on its head toot toots at me. The driver yells unkind cuss words from the passing wash of his window.

Reality rushes in, reminds me of the boy who is dead, his relatives in mourning. Brigitte, who poured out her heart and soul to me in a letter I read too hastily, too late to placate her, would at this moment be suffering on account of me. Bertrand, lost in his hobnob hurt, cities and centuries away, was cut off from communication at this dire hour for his family. His sensitive soul would soar in sorrow.

I'd lost my past, present, and hope for a better tomorrow, unable to comfort those I loved, guilty for the harm I'd caused. Eyeing the uncourteous cross traffic, cars, like hunting arrows shooting at terse targets unseen, I bolted into the melee, hoping to be smashed to smithereens.

Tanu earned her top salary that day. She tackled me, pulled me out of the way of the frenetic fray of French horns and lay atop me on an icy sidewalk in the cultured country I'd dreamed to live in since I was seven-years-old and selling Girl Scout cookies in front of the WinCo Supermarket. I cupped my ears to warm them. My hat… my hat…

Tanu never said a word about the fact that I'd just thrown myself into oncoming traffic. Never reprimanded me, comforted me, encouraged me. She got up, clasped my arm to help me up and walked me stat to her flat.

To say that she lived in a shamble would be a compliment. This stunning creature kept a dizzyingly, disheveled house. Portraits of her in half naked come-hither poses lined the hall, dirty dishes filled the sink. There were few spots on the floor to step without tripping on expensive, slinky fabric. She had a fetish for pink flowers and peekaboo designs.

"Hungry."

"Yes."

"You eat eggs?"

"Yes."

"Onions okay?"

"Yes."

"Cheese?"

"Yeah, sure."

She clattered around her filthy kitchen, chopping, mincing, whisking, and served me up the best vegetable cheese omelets this side of the Atlantic. We ate in silence. I eyed the mildewy wallpaper as I chewed a bite of garlicky broccoli and pulverized olives that exploded with flavour in my mouth.

"I will put makeup on you and then we're going to Lille."

"I don't wear makeup."

"Today you do. You look like death. You have pierced ears?"

"Yes."

She cocked her head. "Three inch hoops."

"I can't."

"Up to you, trying to help."

"Okay. Whatever. You're the boss."

She softened, "Yes. I am."

Coincidence is a remarkable concurrence of events or circumstances, which have no apparent causal connection with each other. I'd experienced these phenomena at several prime moments in my life in the form of serendipity, a fortunate happenstance.

I first heard Bertrand sing at Le Blue Chateau at Brides-les-bains ski resort in the South Eastern French Alps. This, on the first weekend away from the city proper that Pascal and I spent together. His music responded to my homesickness for the slopes of Bogus Basin. My vision was of partnering with this marvelous songster - his melodies, my pictures - yet it seemed an image culled from thin air without proper reasoning or rhyme behind it.

Ah, it seemed so, until the following Saturday when we bumped into each other on the Avenue des Champs-Élysées outside of Station Charles de Gaulle. I heard his rhythmic, reaching version of *Rocky Raccoon* ring out through the buzz of the bustling crowd.

"Bertrand?"

"Oui."

"Je suis Camille. We met last weekend."

"Of course, with Pascal! Belle, (he nicknamed me immediately), what song would you like to hear? Anything, I sing whatever you like in French, Spanish, Italian, English, Dutch."

"*Fly Me To The Moon*, en français, s'il vous plaît."

And that was it. We had been inseparable ever since, co-conspirators, Troubadour and his Muse, best comrades, twin souls.

Now, another coincidence occurred but with a sourdipitous flavour.

On our trek to the nearest route national by the service station just a mere three kilometers from Tanu's place, who should drive by but Leonard on an Uber run? My pupils expanded like inky food dye dilating in water, survival chemicals pumped poisonously out from my adrenals. I froze like a deer just feet from the stroll of the King of the Jungle, weight on his paw pads, muffling his movements, stalking past. I literally stopped in my tracks, unable to ambulate. No frosty exhales because all breathing had ceased. The moment hung like tea-stained 1950s wallpaper in a suburban den.

Leonard didn't notice me, but a man in the back seat did. His jawline, (pleasingly strong with a brush of five o'clock shadow), set hard as he lowered his glasses, locking his eyes upon mine; his face had a vague familiarity as he stared, nearly glared, fixedly at me.

I was self conscious in my heavily made up mode. The bright berry lipstick was layered on lips cracked dry from anguish. Silver blue powder lined my lids like a lily gilded with grapes, and blush swashed smoothly, expertly across the natural flush of my cheeks made me feel like a red rose awkwardly gawking from a florist's display of daisies. I grabbed off the hoop earrings that hung heavy on my lobes.

"I can't wear these." I told Tanu.

"Suit yourself," she shrugged, nodding vixen-like at the man with the silver-grey temples in the rear cab of Leonard's car. He looked like he wanted to reach out for us, as if he had something to say, a story to tell. That moment haunts me to this day.

THEO

"Où allez-vous?" He inquired where we were going.

"Lille."

"Get in, ladies, I'm going that way."

I'd hoped Tanu might be more discerning about whom we entrusted our lives to, but no. The helter-skelter of her apartment, the rashness of her decision to accompany me, her "Suit yourself," retorts, racy photos displayed in her lair, and the company she kept with her cousin, all informed me she was not the careful sort. This was a woman who seized the bull by the balls and was on a rollicking ride, now taking me along too. I blamed myself for the actions that led me here, so had little room for my own objections. Used to being kinder to myself, I found this new uncompassionate self utterly exhausting.

Fabien, (about forty-five but looked sixty), had a molten pallor as if he'd hid from the sun and partied hardy since the first moon landing. The pungent pine freshener barely soaked up the stench of two-day-old onion smothered fajitas and post-fajita belching.

I used to hitchhike back in Idaho where half the locals knew me and the other half knew of me, but here in France, sticking out our thumbs to grab whatever the universe offered was alarming. Why then was I so thrilled? Perhaps I secretly wanted to get killed?

"What's your name?" Fabien looked through the rearview at me. By the sour look on Tanu's face, I surmised he'd asked several times already.

My name! Shoot! What was my name? I was no longer Camille, Cammy, Cam, or Belle. I couldn't even rift behind Lucy Perelle. I didn't want to let go of the name Lucy though. I fancied her as my new self.

"Lucy," it came out as a question. Tanu shot daggers. I smiled back in defiance, my heavily coated lids batting up and down.

"You're beautiful, Lucy. Are you a model?"

"Moi? No. No. Merci."

"Here," he flipped out a calling card boosting a black-and-white photo of a young vixen in a cape and not much else. "I pay well. Call me sometime." Now Tanu beamed as if she were a proud parent responsible for my physical form. "You too," he flipped her a card like a magician pulling quarters out of children's noses, "We'll do a double shoot."

"We'd love to," Tanu, flattered, replied with a finality that fixed a fresh new fantasy into Fabien's mind and provided me with an additional subject for that night's nightmare.

Thankfully, the rest of the two-hour trip passed pleasantly enough: my traveling compatriots chatted in singsong French about the history of Lille and the differences between French agriculture as compared to that of Greece. The warm air fogged up the panes as I pressed my forehead to the glass and watched buildings and landscapes fly past to the sound of the Spanish guitar piping soft rhythms from the speakers.

Our destination was a skinny, brown brick blockhouse where childhood friends of Nikos and Tanu from Mykonos lived. We said our goodbyes, grateful for the door-to-door service. As I stepped from the car, I thirsted for art like a parched capuchin monkey in Majorca thirsted for a soft water spring. A couple, Jon and Theo and their young, runny-nosed brood of three greeted us warmly. I held myself in check during the small talk. All that was on my mind was, "Where are the crayons and is there any chalk here?"

The inside of the house was quaint, bright, and busy. Messy finger paintings hung askew and unframed, taped in random corners of the room. They had scattered alphabet magnets on the lower third of the fridge, and oversized abstract art splashed colors on the walls in loud circles and exhilarating triangles. Every angle seemed to cry out LOOK AT ME!

"This looks like a Kandinsky."

"It is."

They introduced me to each of the squiggling, giggling children. Harquint and Gilberto, the twins, held up fingers to show me how many they were. One, two, three, four, five, six we counted. This pleased them no end and to celebrate they leapt around the living room like airplanes flying amok in a shooting contest with Manfred von Richthofen, aka The Bloody Red Baron from Germany. Sugar, I imagined, fueled these wild kids.

The little girl, three-years-old, dark and beautiful in the same etheric way as Tanu, was shy and reticent. Theo lifted her up to meet me. "This is Bob. Bob, say hello to Lucy." She looked at me quizzically like she was calling my bluff. "What's your real name and what did you do to Luis Fernando?" she asked telepathically.

"Bob?" I inquired in a half tone so hushed it was like the wind through the whippoorwills.

"She is Bubindina. Bub for short." I nodded as if to signal that I understood.

Tanu emerged like a Western wind from the toilette. "Mamá, mamá, mamá!" The children flocked to her knees, wriggle-waggling their fingers as a message to pick them up. She took turns lifting and smothering them in kiss-kisses.

"Why do they call her mamá?"

Theo, who stood in Tree Pose, twinkled. "Because she is their mother," Jon crossed his arms at the elbows, hooked his hands, and lifted up to stretch his trapezius added. "Our egg donor and the gestational ecosystem for our babies."

The unexpectedness of the situation, yoga poses during conversation, and mention of babies and new life gut punched me with a fast jab-jab-jab.

"Do you have any chalk?" The words spilled out.

"Chalk, like... to draw with?"

"Yes." I felt naked with my clothes on. Raw. Vulnerable. Exposed.

"Sure, yeah." Theo returned in twelve seconds with a child's set of flaky, peg-shaped, nearly colorless chalk: the pink, more milky white than blush, the blue, paler than a Robin's egg, the green, a weak, watery tea, the yellow, like sunshine on a cloudy day. Only the purple had pizzazz.

Tree Pose, Jon and I stood gawkwardly in a semi-circle as mama and children reunited slurpily and chirpily stage right.

"I'll come with you, I like to draw too." Theo led me outside as though asking for chalk was the most natural thing to do in this situation. I will always love him for this. I dropped to my knees as one does when visiting the sidewalk art alter, took hold of the cheap, chunky chalk and drew a rainbow rose. Theo drew a sun, clouds and birds. Together we created a universe to step into and momentarily glide away on.

Lille was just over half an hour from Brussels by Eurostar. Bertrand was so close that his presence - like a grief-stricken ghost - dogged us from half a block behind. Each time I turned to gaze upon him, his gilded image would shimmer and disappear among the red and brown brick of our beautiful host city.

"Why do you keep looking behind you? You think we're being followed?"

"No."

"No one knows we're here, Lucy. Not even Nikos. Relax for a minute. Calm down. You're a good person; a bad thing happened, but whatever happened, you must remember who you are."

Calm down. Calm down. These two words had the greatest ability to rile me up. So invalidating those two words, a judgmental command to stuff one's reasonable response, to force one to act rationally in a disordered reality. I let pass my impulse to fight and took in Tanu; this was the first I'd heard her opinion of what I'd done and me.

The weather, though cold, was warmer than Paris. "Here is the market I told you about. We don't have much time. It closes at 2:00." Tanu steered me by my forearm into Marché Sébastopol, a food market in the City Centre, just past Le Théâtre Sébastopol. The place, a piquant produce and people haven, was a world I dreamt I could partake of, but any life for me now would be far, far away from France.

"We will make a feast for my family!" She was excited, elated by her brood, and I could see why. "Captain Fun," Theo's nickname, was a blast. He spoke in rhyme, held yoga poses amid serious conversations, drew pink clouds, and kept the mood elevated and electric. Jon, an urban planner, seemed lovely though much more reserved than his househusband. Perhaps if we were well acquainted, I might find him irritatingly uptight, but he welcomed me in his home without question, so I had no quibble with him.

Harquint and Gilberto, though hyperactive, shone brightly like the twin stars they are, shadowing and mimicking each other, a delightful doppplegang ing double vision, like the first moments when drunk on lime daiquiri punch. And Bub, the most riveting light body in the family galaxy, had an extrasensory perception - three-years-old and nobody's fool.

"Pick out some new potatoes, leeks, and mushrooms. I'll get the cheese. We will make a casserole. You recognize me, no? I watched you for a year drawing portraits. I saw your work evolve when you met your music partner. I watched your transformation, Lucy. I'm well aware of your talent and kindness. Fifteen minutes, I will meet you back here."

She said so seamlessly. Dropped the bomb just like that in the middle of leeks and potatoes. I recognized her now! She looked different, more mature, with hair grown out and her new stylish fashions. As she disappeared to the dairy section, I was swimming in a stew of questions, none that would have rational answers, I was sure.

A child of five, dark curly hair and tan pants just like Pierre, tugged at my skirt.

"Où est ma mère?" He asked.

"Calm down. Calm down," I told myself as my mind spun out of control and I gasped for a breath.

"Laurant!" An exasperated young mother swooped the boy up in her arms, causing him to dissolve in tears of anger and relief. He laid his beet-red face on his mama's shoulder, stuck a thumb in his mouth, held onto his nose with his fingers, and eyed me woefully as the clipping of her heels carried him away. Who needed prison? I would live every day in emotional agony, constantly reliving the trauma I'd caused little Luis Fernando. This was a caged in situation that no prayer, penance, platitudes, or persuasion could pry me out.

Tanu rejoined me with a breezy air as though she hadn't just let on that she'd stalked me in Paris. As we exited the marketplace, she gleefully led me into inquiry by her silence. I don't take kindly to manipulation, but I asked. "Why were you watching me? For how long did you watch? What did you see?" If she told me to calm down now, there might be a Tanu-sized woman picking up cheese and vegetables strewn all over the street.

"Nikos."

"He had you spy on me?"

"Yes. At first it was him, and then it was me."

"When? Why? He paid you for this?"

"Yes, Camille... Lucy. Years ago, when you were dating... after you broke up."

"I never cheated on him! He cheated on me!"

"He was jealous. He asked me to do this. First, I needed the money, then I found you fascinating and couldn't stop even after he stopped paying." She sounded bored or ashamed. I couldn't read her. My people-meters were haywire.

"Oh, my god." I had so many questions, but the gears in my mind ground to a halt. The rest of the way to the house we spoke of the weather, my thoughts a million miles away.

We cooked, served, and ate dinner in seamless harmony like a colony of penguins marching in rows, an interconnected weaving of natural design. The casserole was delicious even with my stomach sour from stress.

I fixated on Theo, Captain Fun, who became my safe spot in this storm. The twins adored me, threw paper airplanes at my head, and clung to me until it was time for bed. Bub remained suspicious. She was so pure she could sense my fear and tensed up whenever I got near. They set the twins in sleeping sacks on floor pillows in Bub's room. Tanu and I set up in the twin's trundle beds. It was a steamy silence once I turned out the lights.

"Tanu?" I ventured in the dark. She either was asleep or pretending to be. I peeled away layers of blankets as quietly as I could and tiptoed out of the room. Theo flipped on the living room light as I was reaching for the chalk.

"This is where I was going too. Put a scarf and hat on, it's cold out. I'll wait outside."

We drew together in the sanctity of silence for seven minutes. Theo rendered a baby elephant, rearing high on hind legs, trunk upturned in triumph. I relished his creative zeal. I choose abstract since I couldn't focus on a subject and wished for my chalk statement to be unassuming, non confrontational.

"What is it, Lucy?"

"Just an abstract."

"What's wrong? Do you have anyone to speak with honestly, candidly, fully?"

"No."

"I consider us friends. Kismet from the moment we met."

I nodded, evading his questions, and curious all the same. "How did you meet Tanu?"

"Nikos, her older cousin, and I were best pals in Greece. I dated Tanu for two years before I came out as gay seven years ago."

"That must have been a shock to her. Did you know at that time?"

He set down the yellow chalk with which he was drawing sunflowers spouting from the baby's hose nose. "Yes, it was. Yes, I knew. You cannot imagine the guilt I carry."

"How did it come about that she mothered your children?"

"Penance. Atonement. I needed to give her something to love fiercely, to add back to her world in a positive way since I'd subtracted from it." He stood up, brushed colored dust from his knees. "So, we're friends. I keep secrets. I'm here to listen if you need."

Captain Fun looked solemn as stone. It hit me how jumping to conclusions about anyone was jumping too high. Venus burned brightly as if to say. "Hear-hear, you can trust this man." I ran my hands gratefully over the pavement; gravity was all I had to ground me.

"Friends." I believed him.

We stayed at Jon and Theo's for five weeks as we waited for Nikos to come through with the Lucy passport; weeks filled with sleet, snot, and strain. The entire household came down with some cutthroat cruddy flu that was going around. Poor hoarse Harquint got it twice. The silver lining is they weaned him from sweets during his convalescence and his hyperactivity quieted, concentration increased, and he was a calmer, happier child.

The adults, while wiping our own noses, all pitched in running after the twins and Bubindina with cotton rags. Once we caught a child, we placed the kerchief over their face and gave the command, "Mouche ton nez." We six were swimming in a sea of peach-tinged yellow mucous. Oddly, this brought us all quite close.

Bub warmed to me by then and propped herself upon my lap, little legs dangling, while we, (both sick as sogs), read *Babar The Elephant* together in French and English. She is such a smart child. She picked up my language and dialect like a hooker in the heyday of the Haight gathering diseases like bouquets of daisies - fast and indiscriminately. When we made paper cut outs one day, she patted her head and announced with a perfect Idahoan accent, "I want a crown like Babar for my head." And she got one.

The Babar series was strange, engaging, slow moving and, for me, relatable. Babar is an elephant who ran away after hunters murdered his mother. Thanks to a benefactor, he lives in a large home, dresses elegantly, but is homesick. What drew Bub and me to the books were the bold, bright pictures. I had a longing now to chalk out some elephants. I promised myself that as soon as I got over this crud, I would, but I couldn't seem to shake the nausea. I threw up at the same time early every morning.

"You're pregnant," Tanu tossed that worry ring onto my heap from her trundle as I got up for the third time on a Thursday to upchuck.

"No. I'm not."

Theo pulled me aside later that day. "Are you pregnant? You have a glow." I remembered his offer to listen. With a downcast of my eyes he announced, "Lucy and I are going out for a while. Keep this spinning smoothly while we're gone."

Jon protested that we were too sick to go out, Tanu sulked, hurt and left out of our special friendship, and Bub ran over to me clutching *Le Voyage de Babar*. I got out one of the snot rags, held it over her nose and commanded, "Mouche ton nez." Harquint whispered, "Have a good time," and we were gone.

Our favorite cafe near the Marché Sébastopol had a winding queue like the mythical serpent Titanoboa, so we ventured further on to a quieter, less lustrous place. Theo and I sat cross-legged on our chairs, leaning in, warming our hands on our respective tea mugs: cool mint with lemon for me, chamomile with honey for him.

When there is trust between two people, words can be scant. A nod, fractional flick of the eyes or a sigh may communicate volumes. Theo did ninety-nine percent of the talking. I did one hundred percent of the squirming. Our one-way conversation sounded like this:

"Are you in trouble, Lucy?"

"What's your real name, it's not Lucy, is it?"

"Your life is a mystery to me. It seems odd you're waiting so long for papers. Tanu hasn't spent this much time at our house since the twins were born. You said you draw portraits, you've mentioned school, but I hear little about your past except you're from Idaho."

My look gave away that the Idaho info was unintended — a mistake I let slip out.

"When you read Babar with Bub, you congratulate her on sounding like an Idahoan. Living a life of secrets is a hellish existence, Lucy. I've been there. I lived that way for years. You're a good person. I feel it in my gut, my gut is never wrong. If you share your troubles with me, perhaps I can help?"

I studied the inside of my mug like a famous psychic reading the spearmint leaves. In it, I saw what used to be my life. I missed the cobblestone streets of Paris, mom and dad, our house, Boise air sipped like fresh elderberry wine, childhood friends who knew me better than I knew myself. Missed the often fascinating, sometimes tedious, art history lectures, long, lovely days spent with Bertrand creatively lighting up "our corner" with music and a backbeat of sweeping sidewalk lines formed fastidiously into friendly and freckled faces. Missed nights skating sensuous circles with Brigitte. I even missed math class, missed my hair, my quirky clothes, my past, my present, my future.

Theo touched my arm bringing me back to the hum of this Lille eatery on a day so cloudy the precipitation moistened us to our bootlaces.

I missed my period.

"Do you trust me, Lucy?"

I blink-nodded. Yes.

"Talk to someone. It doesn't have to be me, although I wish it was." He looked despondent for me.

"Whatever it is, there's always a way out. I mean, it's not as if you killed anyone."

I coughed out the tea and excused myself to the bathroom.

Five antsy, annoyed patrons looking at their watches shot me the stink eye when I finally opened the door from the toilette. They had already re-peopled the table we sat at. New customers animatedly gave their orders. I looked about wildly for Theo. There he stood, half out the door with my coat, hat, and scarf draped neatly over his arm like a rack drying out soaked bath sheets.

I thought he was sour with me, but as we clipped along in the dewy downpour, Captain Fun was all business.

"Look, Lucy, tell me or not, secrets have a way of coming out. You have in me a friend to the end. Now, we will stop in at the store and pick up some items you need. When we get home, I want you to make a note of my private post box address. Keep in touch with me. You'll need someone who cares. Jon is blissfully unaware of my box. I have investments overseas I keep to myself and I stay in touch with old lovers he wouldn't approve of and need not think about. I'm honest and faithful to him, but he's a jealous partner, and that makes me crazy because I am not."

He turned into a store. I followed like his lost, hungry puppy. He sailed through the aisles: pregnancy test, soda crackers, and fizzy ginger soda.

"I don't eat wheat."

"Now you do, dear. The crackers will help quell the morning sickness. Tanu had it something terrible with the twins. We will have to get you to a doctor."

"Not until I'm out of France."

"Suit yourself." There it was - Tanu's phrase. I set my jaw forward. Theo gave me a quick hug. "We have to make haste. How long do we have to prepare you to leave? It would help me help you if I knew what you're dealing with."

I was frozen.

"Think about it."

Once home, Theo set me up at his computer. "Clear your searches when you're done," he instructed. I was like Holmes, without cap or pipe, plugging in names, jumping page-to-page searching for information about Luis Fernando and his family. I was curious about where they lived, what they looked like, their history, occupations, how they fared. I took copious notes. The worldwide web is a worldwide wonder, I could practically find out their shoe sizes.

A pair of hands clasped my neck tightly from behind. It was Tanu. She kneaded my tight shoulders. "I have some news for you. Next Thursday, Nikos is coming with your papers. Tuesday we have a photo shoot with Fabien - one thousand euros each. The money will come in handy when you travel to... wherever you're going."

Before I had time to object, a search I'd done flashed a news article about me onto the screen. Tanu and I, heads bobbed together, raced to read it. Woozy, I put my hand to my forehead and slumped forward.

"Ladies, dinner is ready!" An aproned Theo, waving a spatula like a conductor's baton, appeared in the doorway. He moved from doorway to desk at Eurostar speed and gulped in the article, *"Je suis désolé, Luis Fernando and Family,' Message Left by Hit And Run Driver Before Her Disappearance From Paris Earlier This Month."* The story included that photo of me from the roller rink and a clear shot of my bathroom mirror with my apology scrawled across it in lipstick. I'd forgotten about that gesture done in my shock and grief.

"Please give us a few minutes, Tanu," Theo seemed remarkably composed until the door closed behind her. His tomato sauce splattered apron came off with a whip. He sat hunched, rocking and crying for a respectable amount of time, then got up and beat up a blue, gold and green cushion adorned with wrens. I circled the room like a caged deer in fear of an encroaching cougar.

"You were beautiful with long hair."

I fell into a squat, exhausted.

"I mean, you're beautiful now too."

I stood, shaky, scared, and ready to run.

"Would you like to tell me now what happened?"

I nodded.

"Fine. Let me get the family set up for dinner. I made a beautiful meal: roasted vegetables, spaghetti, fruit, cheese."

I don't know why but I replied, "I don't eat wheat."

Theo's eyes filled with tears. He clasped me in a thirty-second hug, which seemed to last forever. "I made the spaghetti out of zucchini for you." He gently patted me on the cheek like the Godfather and stepped from the room. I cleared the computer history as I wondered how I might get to the hardware store to purchase rope. Where might I hang myself without traumatizing Bub, Gilberto and the now healthier, happier Harquint?

When the door opened again, it was Tanu. The pieces never fit in the puzzle that is Tanu. She could be at once superstitious and superfluous or sweet as Mulberry pie. Her moods swung like a reckless monkey from a chandelier: pensive to contrite, volatile to delight. This Tanu came bearing a plate piled with salad, oven roasted greens, and zucchini squash spaghetti and a stash of soda crackers.

"Theo said he needs time to compose himself. We thought you might be hungry." She slipped back out without another word. I ate every bite of this meal cooked with love then fluffed up the pummeled chirpy wren cushion, closed my eyes, and waited.

I had a dream that Natalie Mouskers jumped on my chest and pawed at me, digging her claws in deep. Then she licked my ear to communicate that though she was pissed, I was also missed. I awoke to find the three kids jumping on me, tickling me under the chin to get me to open my eyes.

"Bonne nuit, Tante Lucy, Bonne nuit!"

"Bonne nuit, Bubindina! Bonne nuit, Gilberto! Bonne nuit, Harquint!"

Harquint, with a cough, kissed me smack on the lips. Great. That's all I needed is to get the crud again on top of everything, but I didn't want to make him feel bad, so I clasped him in a hug with a head ruffle for good measure. His jealous brother Gilberto pulled him aside with such force, a pajama button popped off and flew across the room. He gave me a MWAAAAAHH kiss too. Bub attached herself like an aviator scarf around my neck so tightly Jon had to pry her off.

"Bonne nuit, bonne nuit!" She stuck her thumb in her mouth, which I hadn't seen her do before. Perhaps she was regressing because of the strangulation of stress I gifted their harmonious home with? Way to go, Tante Lucy.

Jon smiled at me with what seemed to be pottery glaze in his eyes. Obviously he could see this strange woman brought drama into his home, stayed well beyond the three days that Ben Franklin recommended for fish OR visitors, and now was hogging one of his bathrooms each morning with a virus and / or morning sickness.

I wondered if there might be huge fights about my stay when I left. "Who is this woman and why do you insist on taking in strays, Theo?" I imagined him yelling, his left eye twitching.

As the kid crew piled out, Tanu and Theo filed in. Tanu sat herself nearer to me than she ever had done before. Theo paced the entire time: six strides this way and six strides that.

"I'm your friend, Lucy, I always will be. As a parent, I am mourning this young boy. We have no time to lose in talking about your choices. I have a lawyer friend in Paris, Helene, if you turn yourself in. There might be a range of outcomes - perhaps community service or a short time in jail? It isn't good that you ran. People are angry."

I drew a piercing inhale. I had stopped considering the option of going back to Paris.

"In prison, inmates hate people who have hurt children. When I think of returning for the sake of giving the family closure, I enter a darkness I can't describe. I think of bridges and ropes and bloody wrists. I tumble down a rabbit hole of horror, although I realize Luis Fernando's family is suffering beyond comprehension too."

Tanu rubbed my knee. She looked like one of those puppy puzzles I used to do with Winona, the ones with the great big eyes. "I couldn't go back if I were you."

Theo continued, clomp, clomp, clomp, clomp, clomp, clomp, and turn. "If you continue on your way, I will still love you and be here for you. The only line I have is that I will not put my family in jeopardy. I don't know what I'd do in your situation. Although I'd like to think I would go back, when I was hiding my secret, I kept running and could not do what others thought I ought. It's possible you may be ready some day. I sympathize with you and with the child's family. This is a very sad day."

He finally sat.

"Your life may be hell on the run. Secrets have a way of catching you. You have a loving, compassionate heart, so I can only imagine how this tears at you. We also now have a possible pregnancy here, another life to consider. There is much to discuss, and the clock is ticking. Tanu, would you mind giving Lucy and I some time alone?"

"No." She looked relieved to leave. "Goodnight, Lucy." She kissed me softly on each cheek. "Bonne nuit, Theo." She gave him the same.

And then there were two. Overwhelmed by how I'd let Theo down, I thought of my father. Although I was unsure if I believed in life after death, if he was aware of this, his heart would crack apart like a dried coconut in the scalding sun.

Theo reached over to the dresser top. He took down a family portrait of himself, Jon, Tanu, and the three kids, all dressed in coordinated shades of blues and greens. They looked like the ocean - Tanu's efforts, no doubt. His back remained towards me for ten minutes, shoulders shaking. I wondered what it might feel like to drown in a tub.

"Hurry, we're late." Tanu loomed over me, hopping from foot to foot as I finished my business, head bowed unblissfully over the bowl after which I stood unsteadily. I brushed my teeth three times, then forced down two loosely scrambled eggs, "I don't eat wheat," dry dark rye toast, and a few sips of fizzy ginger water. Grabbing a handful of soda crackers, we headed out into the soft, pink light of the new day.

Fabien's studio was as spacious as a gymnasium, airy as a coniferous forest, and bewitching and curious as closely cut, cuneiform crop circles. Two crystal pitchers of water sin gas awaited us, one with lemon wedges, the other laced with mint leaves. We poured the drink into Jingdezhen porcelain Chinese dragon teacups. A matching yellow infuser holding some sweetly stinky mystery herbal concoction sat patiently nearby.

An assistant laded the dressing room with racks of clothes (half clothes, really), in our sizes: filmy scarves, and bowler hats, and bells and whistles - literally, belly dancing bells and whistle on chains. Plush chairs the size of my former living room sat waiting for our behinds. This was not the hole-in-the-wall I'd expected. Fabien gregariously greeted us.

"A girl could get used to this," the look in Tanu's large puppy puzzle eyes filled with childlike delight.

This slightly scandalous shoot would not make my parents proud, but this day, at least this day, would be a good one. And oh how I needed a good day! I spent the last two taking a pregnancy test (positive), convincing Theo to pretty please NOT yet make appointments with either an obstetrician or his lady lawyer friend in Paris, even though he assured me the avocat would keep my story in strict confidence. Yeah, right, and storks deliver babies, the tooth fairy piles bills under a child's pillow, and Santa shimmies his hefty form down the narrowest of chimneys, Norway first, Jersey last.

The constant discussions with Theo brought us both closer together and moved us further apart. We spent our evening outdoors making chalk drawings. When the hour and weather permitted, the children joined us, and once, Tanu, who drew a fantasy scene with flying sheep and a very acrobatic Little Bo Peep, pepped up our party. I would miss their company. My departure loomed just two days away with Nikos' arrival on Thursday.

Fabien had us dress in matching silver tasseled, deep, dark, emerald green crop tops, wraparound pants, tennis shoes with two inch cleats, and, oh yes, the whistles. It was more fun than it ought to have been. My nausea hid away for the afternoon. We two posed together like pros.

"A girl could get used to this," I winked at Tanu as I took a sip of herbalness that made me feel feisty. Overcome with apprehension that this potent potion might harm the baby, I switched back to the plain Jane mint water as unobtrusively as I could.

As if Theo and I didn't have enough secrets to keep, I added one more to the wobbly stack. Although she suspected, I didn't want to tell Tanu I was with child because I didn't want Nikos to be alerted; that wrench could make a wreck of my already reckless plan. The signs, however, were as shrill as the whistles around our necks, as obvious as the perfect nose on Tanu's goddess face, and as wide as my waistline would soon be.

"Twist to the side a little more, Lucy. Tanu, drape your arm further around her waist, look at her like you mean business, more, more, more, that's good, and.... CLICK CLICK CLICK CLICK CLICK... got it! Take a break. These shots are spectaculaire!"

"What month are we going to be?" The sticky, sweet herbal tea, resplendent daylight steaming in through the sky lit studio, our bell and whistle improvisations and surprising sensuous and comedic chemistry had all three of us in a light-as-a-feather mood.

"My fetching Fabian Fresh calendars go by sign, not months. You are Gemini."

"Fantastique! I always wanted to be a twin," Tanu giggled. "Me too," I confessed. "Here's my address. Send our calendars to me, and merci beaucoup for this." Tanu counted out 2,000 euros and peeled off half for me. A girl could get used to posing in plushness, being catered to with treats and specialty foods, and playing dress up for cash.

"Take a souvenir, each of you. One item of clothing."

Without hesitation, Tanu clutched the green crop top to her chest and nuzzled the silky fabric against her face. I was thinking more practically these days, planning for my foray into the wide, wild world alone.

"May I take this?" I gave a quick toot on the silver whistle.

"Suit yourself," Fabian waved his hand with a flourish. There it was again! That phrase! I never wanted to hear it again.

Everything seemed to move at double time after that. The walk home was brisk.

"Tanu, I'm worried that someone might see me on the calendar. This was a bad idea."

"Lucy, you have a fat wad of cash in your pocket. Once you leave town, you'll be on your own. I will not be there to take care of you. There will be no roof over your head but what you pay for. No food on your plate but what you buy. I did this for you. Your pseudonym will help. I like the new name you choose. I should change my name too, no?"

She twinkled mischievously, mocking me about my name changes. Tanu had a bite to her delivery she tried to disguise as playful teasing, but it often smarted.

"Why did you follow me all that time after Nikos stopped paying you? The truth."

She stopped, looked at me sideways like she was studying a Van Gogh and stroked my cheek with the side of her nails. "I think you're a brilliant, fascinating person. I am forever obsessed with you, Belle." Then she kissed me on the lips. Right there on a busy street in Lille as parents scurried home to cook their evening meals, a woman pushing a stroller jogged past, and a bird cried overhead. Hers were the most velvety lips I'd ever met. Such soft lips on such a hard guarded person.

I suddenly knew I had to get out of this town as soon as I could. I needed perspective on everything and everyone. My heart raced like a marble clipping down a marble staircase, tat tat tat, picking up speed, tat tat - tat tat tat - tat TAT TAT tat tat.

"What are you going to do about the baby, Lucy?"

"I'm not pregnant!"

"Silly girl," she cackled.

I wiped her kiss from my lips and we walked on, estranged. Three blocks down, she stopped again. "Here, I have enough clothes." She laid the shirt smoothly in my bag. "I'm his cousin. If you have this baby, I want to be part of his life."

"I'm NOT pregnant!"

Why did she think it was a boy? Oh, god! What if I was carrying the soul of Luis Fernando! If I spent my life loving this child and gave him the life HE should have had, would this be the way I could find redemption?

Quickly rounding the corner to Jon and Theo's flat, we spooked Affrodile, the neighborhood Calico cat. She jumped off the roof with a shriek - one less life to go. Directly below where Bub's tricycle was parked Nikos sat on the top stoop looking suave and handsome, like he was all that. Tanu was giddy when she saw him; she stamped and whinnied like a new foul caught in a whirlwind. Nikos stood. The cousins ran towards each other like lovers in a shampoo commercial. He lifted her, twirled her around, joy turned to ecstasy. "Jeez, get a room," blew through my mind as I wondered which one I might be jealous of... or perhaps envious of their positive family connection?

"Hi, Nikos, you're early."

"That's it? That's my whole greeting? I've spent weeks to help you and all I get is 'Hi Nikos, you're early?'"

He was right. I didn't seem grateful, but I was. I opened my arms to give him a hug and WHOOOOOP — he lifted me in the air and spun me around too. It was fun like being on the Tilt-a-Whirl when I was a girl, trees spinning past, and clouds milling circles like clotted cream being stirred into chocolate espresso.

He set me down and pulled out a folder covered in camouflage print, "Here is your camouflage passport, Glika mou. Look." He was proud of his work.

I loved the artistic touch. He knew I would. The chemistry between us was always electric; he hooked my heart early on and it was hard to unlock. A man walking past noticed the magnetic mystery that ricocheted back and forth between us and turned, intrigued. Tanu bubbled green. I opened the folder like a child at 6:00 Christmas morning, ripping the first silver paper from a pretty pile of presents.

Luciana Petrokov.

What I saw disappointed me. It showed.

"It was the closest we could get to Lucy. Lucy is... can be a nickname."

I couldn't connect to the name, tried to hide my upset, but out spilled this, "Am I Italian, or Polish?"

"You're family history is whatever you wish to make it. You're American by birth." He uncovered the next paper in the stack: a college diploma from the University of San Francisco. There was my name, Luciana Petrokov, Bachelor of Arts, Design.

"There's a birth certificate and other papers you may need. You'll see." He closed the folder.

I was at once relieved, touched, grateful, guilty, scared, and disgusted by the imposter I was becoming. The spirit of Luis Fernando sat on the stoop mocking, deriding, and taunting me to go back to Paris, to turn myself in in his name.

I touched my stomach. Our baby would be beautiful. I wasn't ready to tell Nikos he was the child's father or even that I was ripe with this young life. Tanu pressed her lips together. Her thick, perfectly arched brows held high. She would not tell either. I hugged Nikos, this time, for a long time.

When we released, he hugged Tanu too. "Well, I better get going."

"What? You're not staying?" I hadn't expected this.

"No. My job is done. Goodbye, Camille." He held my hand; fingers lingered then slid away, his words threw a shovel of dirt on the grave of Camille Lisette Portraro. As we watched the back of his head disappear down the street, I wanted to shout, "Wait, you bastard! You got me pregnant, now what am I supposed to do?" Instead I yelled, "Thank you, Nikos!" I blew kisses and waved like the Queen of England.

"Luciana Petrokov, Luciana Petrokov, Luciana Petrokov." The first fifty times I tried on the name I winced like someone had taken a winding blow to my windpipe. Then I gradually got the hang of it. The pronunciation of Luciana in two Italian syllables, (Lu ciana), rather than the American four (Lu chi ah nah), made the name sing for me. Petrokov begged for the emphasis to be on the P, then a soft tumble into rokov. PET ro kov. Luiciana Petrokov. Well done, Nikos, well done for a girl on the run.

Lille grew weary of me, or me of Lille, in the time it took a flash flood to overflow a basement in the plains. You know that feeling the last day of school after they hand report cards out and goodbyes said, but you still have to wait for the 3:00 bell? Well, I was not having it. Watching Nikos walk off down the road was my bell. I hung the whistle on a string around my neck, changed into the green shirt from Fabian's joyous Gemini photo-shoot, and surreptitiously packed out of sight of my comrades in arms.

Tanu was in the kitchen when I went to gather my food. This inhibited me from packing my wares, as I didn't wish to call out my plan. Secrecy had become my middle name, Luciana Secrecy Petrokov. I planned to slip out without the hullabaloo of goodbyes. Three crying children, I didn't need - it would tear their hearts and mine. Better that Tanta Lucy just waft away like wisps of a dandelion globe on a summer day.

Theo and I had said our adieus for days. He'd gifted me a book, left wordlessly on my trundle, *Famous Architects For The Archophile*. Inside he wrote his post box number, 8675309. Easy to remember since it was the name of a catchy pop song, "867-5309/Jenny," that Noni, Cathy and I used to dance along to like a box of firecrackers.

I, meanwhile, drew and framed a portrait of the family. I riffed off the ocean blues and greens of the sitting room piece and attired the crew in rainbow hues. Bub, yellow, Harquint, orange, Gilberto, red, Jon, green, Theo, blue, Tanu, purple, and Affrodile, the Calico who often cozied up with us, a white-violet. Affrodile was a symbolic stand in for me. Theo choked up when he opened it. He ran his fingers over the image of the cat and cried. He knew. He got me. Why put us through any more?

"I thought you might head back to Paris with Nikos when he left, Tanu."

She stirred her tea with a rough clink against the sides of the cup. "No. I still have business here."

I didn't ask. I knew her well enough by now not to pry.

"Fabian asked me back for another shoot."

"Oh!" I was rejected. Not that I would have wanted to go or anything.

"He asked for both of us, but I told him you're leaving town. Of course, you would be most welcome to come. The shoot is booked for Friday. 1500 euros each, Lucy. Our price went up."

She clinked again.

"Yes, I'd like to go." I knew I needed more money on the road and my morning sickness could use more time to settle a bit. Plus, there was the chance Tanu might kiss me again.

I did an about face and headed to unpack my toothbrush.

AU REVOIR

Deuxième partie, part two, of the photo shoot was a bust; it was that second date let down after the first date elation. My head was far, far away - in Colombia to be exact. The pitchers of flavored water were flat, Fabian was a lecherous rat, and Tanu was crabby, yet oddly the photos again turned out spectacular. Go figure.

Tanu and I separated at day's end. I'd worn running shoes so I could go for a jog. I'd been running up to two hours a day. It put me into a state of mind that allowed me to plod on through the haywire mire my actions had sired. In the park I saw several loving couples with babies, playing, laughing, changing diapers, and picnicking. I'd killed this future for myself when I texted Brigitte on her birthday. The world now seemed like a movie screen in which I was an audience, not a player. I needed to leave town NOW.

Went home, showered, packed, (again, on the sly), ate with the family, read Babar to Bub, helped put the kids to bed, slept until 4:00, crept out of bed, threw up, and then whistle in place around my neck, money and passport strapped in elastic carriers around waist and ankles, I snuck out the door.

I almost got down the block before a hand grabbed me from behind. It was Jon.

"Tu es en train de partir?"

"Oui."

"Sans dire au revoir."

How could I look him in the eye and tell him I left without saying goodbye? I couldn't. I fiddled with the whistle and cast my eyes down. "Oui."

"Here, you forgot these." He handed me the soda crackers and fizzy ginger water.

"Merci. Jon?"

"Oui?"

"What's your opinion about me?"

"You are a beautiful artist and a loving Auntie for my children. Bon voyage, Belle." He disappeared as quickly as he came.

Why did he call me Belle? How much was he privy to? What the hell am I doing? The sanity of the four o'clock hour saved me as I continued to the station.

The station was eerily quiet when I arrived. The next high-speed Train à Grande Vitesse was to leave in an hour. I paid my €19, went to the toilette, and found a solitary bench nearby to wait. My battered blue notebook kept me company. On the back page, I made a graph, twenty-seven across, ten down. I labeled my years from birth to present, listed the following items and began to fill up squares with information, reviewing my life to check where I fit on the "good person" scale.

1) Family
2) Friends
3) Health
4) Homes
5) Good Deeds
6) Regrets
7) Favorite Memories
8) Main Challenges
9) School, Work, Career
10) Travel

I got but a few minutes into my project when the train doors opened revealing a packed coach. Our small crowd of Lillian's jumped like jack-in-the-boxes, each eager to get a clean seat. I slid into a prime spot next to the window, settled in, and looked up to see a tall, crooked man of about eighty standing sadly by the door, all seats taken.

I got up. "Monsieur, s'il vous plaît, prenez place."

"Non, merci, vous asseyez." He seemed embarrassed, determined to be strong and independent until he could no longer stand upright.

"J'insiste." I explained I'd been sitting too long and preferred to stretch my legs. I wasn't going far anyway, I said. He looked relaxed and content once he sat, nodded gratefully at me, and turned to watch the scenery as it rolled by. I contemplated my blue book graph; glad to have a check on Luciana's good deed for the day.

Goodbye Charles de Gaulle! Goodbye Opera House! Goodbye Théâtre Sebastopol! Goodbye, dear, sweet Theo.

Thirty-six minutes later, we rolled into Brussels-Midi/Zuid Station, a destination I'd set my mind on for the past five weeks. With dark shades and Tanu's three inch earrings in place, I checked my bag at the station and hurried off to the home of Bertrand's moeder, unsure who might greet me or of the consequences of my appearance here.

I tentatively gave my trademark knock, rat-ta-ta-tat, ta-ta-tat-tit rap. A familiar rumbling, baritone voice asked, "Qu'est ce?"

Leonard!

I ran to hide in the bushes as he opened the door, galloped down the steps and demanded, "Qui est là?" He looked older and more worn than I recalled. These past weeks had aged him. A dark Labradoodle pup bounded out and sniffed round my corner. I stayed still.

The adorable Labradoodle tore at my ankle; this was the ankle that was strapped tightly in the tan neoprene padded elastic holster that held wads of tip cash from my bean jar, including the generous gift from Nikos, *and* the earnest earnings from Fabian's fantastic photo shoot. "Shhh. Pssst. Sssssssss," I whispered to this tail-wagging cur with its empennage bobbed so short, it brought to mind the vestigial rump of a rabid, capybara out in a savage savannah far away from this posh, proper part of Brussels.

"Ssssssss!"

"Pippin," came the call from the porch, "Venez ici, nous devons partir pour le cimetière bientôt."

They have to leave for the cemetery? Ah, so Helga *had* died. She was a good sort, most welcoming of me into Bertrand's small, selective family of friends. Once again, poor, dear, soulful Bertrand! He would be distraught, inconsolable, and morose. For all of their mother-sons tiffs, they were as sweet and smooth together as blueberries and cream.

Pippin ran off to pull on the leg of the lady clipping up the front walk to deliver a rainbow wreathed funeral spray. It was just Bertrand's style to go all out like this for Helga. The florists interwove kumquat colored roses in an artistically random fashion with the first purple Iris reticulate of the season.

Straining forward in the bushes, I caught burbles of the turgid conversation between the florist and Leonard. There would be a small ceremony at Woluwé-Saint-Lambert Cemetery, near to Tomberg. I knew this place! Bertrand and I had passed by on one of the late night supreme tours he gave me of his hometown. That night was sumptuous, enjoyed under the stillness of sultry skies that illuminated the pellucid, no frills simplicity Bertrand and I preferred in our outings. There were no famous tombs there, no remarkable monuments, just a solely birdsong, and public benches around flowerbeds. A quiet little Public Park. Perfect for the under-the-radar funeral service that had become custom in Brussels recent decades.

In many urban European areas, traditional practices, including wakes and funeral processions behind the hearse, have almost completely disappeared. Death, previously a more public event, is now more often in the private domain.

I began plotting how I, a roving waif in a city I knew but superficially, might metro my way to the service to pay my respects to my friend's moeder and suss out if perhaps a dialogue was feasible with my partner. First though, I would have to reunite with my bag and don black clothes so I might better go undetected in the event's background. As I was contemplated execution of my tasks at hand, Helga's crisp voice rang out from the porch, her cuneiform face showed signs of new grief: red eyes and sallow skin. Her body language was languid.

What could this mean? If she was alive, then who died? *Where is Bertrand?* Why hadn't I yet seen him, the master of this domain? *Why was Leonard here?* Oh, no! My heart splattered as if I'd been tossed alive from a tier during the 1419 defenestrate in Prague.

Pippin once again rankled with my ankle and so I made my exit stage left, just like Snagglepuss.

The detour for my dark clothes detained me longer than expected. On the way I stopped for a bowl of Moroccan tomato chickpea soup that warmed me inside out, as good soup does. Sussing out wholesome sustenance on the road routinely swallows up one's time and cash - even as a savvy, intrepid traveler I have yet to find a way around this.

When I arrived at the cemetery, the service was already in progress. It was akin to slipping in the back of a movie theatre late, the audience, popcorn half eaten, slumped in their seats, biting the back of their thumbs in tense anticipation of Who-Done-It. I was chagrined by my tardiness. The rainbow wreath stood proudly in front. Helga had wrapped herself in a bright silk shawl with spunky Flamingo dancers tap-tapping all over it. Leonard, leaning on her like a toppling Pisa, sported a royal blue shirt with a Nero collar, also silk. They mourned vividly in Belgium.

There was a small, tight-knit bunch, all festively adorned but for one butterscotch-brown-haired young woman wearing not fifty, but four shades of grey. She was Margaret, Bertrand's favorite cousin who had visited us three times in quick succession on our corner in Paris before her sojourns abruptly stopped. Bert broke the news to me she was unwittingly pregnant. Sure enough, she carried a full belly before her, yet I spotted no partner nearby. This put me in immediate emotional solidarity with her. I had to reign in my desire to throw arms round her and lay my head heavily on her shoulder.

In black dungarees, a mop neck, and dark glasses on an overcast day, I appeared odd and out of place. I positioned myself behind a chestnut tree and looked feverishly for Bertrand. *Surely he is alive, here to lay a relative to rest?* Not over three weeks ago, we were having the time of our lives as "Camille et Bertrand," the most highly sought after sidewalk artists in the history of the Louvre. Our last day together, he played *Louise*, by the Yardbirds, fervidly freewheeling as a ruddy rival for

Clapton; his harmonica blissfully braced round his neck, he blew that harp with the passion of a flock of Canadian geese crying for their mates through a blistering, blinding Calgary blizzard.

We had people packed in for blocks, stomping and clapping, the city on creative fire. I stopped my drawing, bounced to my feet and twirled like a dervish, not a care in the world. That day we met Marius and Anna from Norway, who had lost their only son, Matthias, to leukemia the year before. Their first trip since their loss, the art helped ease them back to enjoy life again. After I finished their portrait, they took the usual set of selfies and group photos with Bertrand and me, then we four went out to lunch.

Bertrand, glowing like a Super moon rising over the Grand Palace in Bangkok, chewed on a well-earned sandwich. He grabbed my hand and squeezed so hard, my eyeballs popped. "Belle," he said, "I'm so fucking happy."

I gave one more rabid look around. Bertrand was nowhere as far as I could see. Leonard stepped to the podium to speak.

You haven't lived until you've heard Bertrand play *La Vie en Rose* on acoustic guitar to a jigsaw assemblage of locals and tourists on our art corner. He knew better than to sing the words alone; he encouraged the crowds to join in. People would move into a tight circle, sway together, openly weep, and hug total strangers as he made the spine of his Yamaha guitar quiver with delight, and strummed soulfully, like he was petting a Maine Coon cat.

Bert, a master musician, was also a master of manipulating and elevating moods. When he spotted a lovey-dovey honeymooning duo, he'd tear jerk them with *Time In a Bottle* played with almost a sadistic, sappy slowness, then to follow, segue into a peppy version of *Standing On The Corner* and group tears would transform to laughter. It was so cute and corny, no one complained in the name of feminism or ever questioned if our dishy singer preferred a different dream team.

Perhaps my favorite memory was when Bertrand surprised me with one from his vast repertoire: David Byrne's *This Must Be the Place (Naive Melody,)*, which he sang with the same sweet, simple sound of Shawn Colvin's soaring version. When I was ten, my father and I took a trip to San Francisco during spring break, just the two of us, while mom flew solo to her twenty-year high school reunion. On the Saturday we spent in Berkeley, just after our hike up the Strawberry Canyon fire trail and before a shopping spree at Amsterdam Art, a young girl from the Midwest on Telegraph Ave. sang this song. We were transfixed. I mentioned this once to Bert and so on my birthday, this was his gift to me. That is the quality of man he is. Was.

Tradition was that at sunset on Fridays as it grew too dark for me to continue the portraitures, Brigitte, Jacqueline, Leonard and various other chums would gather at our corner just in time to hear Bert kick off the evening portion of the concert with *Waterloo Sunset*. We'd go on a collective Kinks kick until his fingers wearied, when we'd rumble off to dinner and late night roller rink regalia. It was wholesome fun; a beer or glass of wine too much once in a while was the most reckless we got.

We had our regular bits. When I saw tie-dye in the crowd, I'd wink at Bertrand and nod, GO, which alerted him it was time for a set of *Uncle John's Band into Box of Rain into Scarlet Begonias / Fire On The Mountain*. What we loved about Dead Heads is they never failed to get everyone dancing.

His love for the Beatles - everything from *I Want To Hold Your Hand* to *Rocky Raccoon* to *Revolution* - fired up our wedge of the world. I, the Blues girl, encouraged more-more-more Muddy Waters to flow. Requests were good-naturedly fielded too. A repeated shout of "BETH ORTON, *I WISH I NEVER SAW THE SUNSHINE*," met with a one-two-three punch of Orton leading into Rufus Wainwright's *California* blending into Dire Straits *Walk of Life*. It worked. Trust me, it worked like stepping on stones into the sky.

After the terrorist attack of our city, crowds gathered for a week to hear Bertrand lead them in Imagine, gracefully followed by the CSNY anthem *Carry On*, guiding us collectively to evening's end of those difficult nights.

Our best work came when Bert and I worked together. He would ask key questions of our customers and fashion a *Song On The Spot* for them, as I blended their essence into bright sidewalk scenes. It was hard to tell who was happier, Bert and me, the throngs, or the gods grinning agog in twelve dimensions. Life was great, tips and smiles, generous.

Leonard tripped and righted himself at the podium. He took out a paper that looked like an origami experiment of a mountain lion. His breath crackled in the microphone IN OUT. Centering on the written words, he read.

The heavens chose that moment to cry. A mid afternoon sprinkle caused us all to cover our heads as we sopped up the sentiment. Our Bertrand silenced too soon.

I wish I never saw the sunshine then maybe I wouldn't mind the rain.

I spied Speculoos, Helga's infamous shortbread biscuits, Bertrand's favorite, on a crooked-leg foldout table in back, next to a stack of peach programs. Spooky cemetery shadows, my invisibility, and the implausibility of the situation rendered me like a ghost at a service in which I ought to have been host. As Leonard read in a voice that crackled like a fourteen-year-old boy on a quick collision with puberty, I kept my eye on a large piece of Speculoos, readying myself like a gull to swoop in for this treat and then lift off in retreat before anyone could train their focus upon me.

"Our Bertrand," he read, wrestling the paper like a small California quake. "Ahem. Ahe-he-hem — Our Bertrand, sorr-orry." (Sniff), he looked up with the innocence of a four-year-old, hand caught in the cookie jar. "I cannot believe his life ended so unnecessarily... and like this. This man, this awful, vicious man, this bartender, this thief! The... thi.... thief... he stole Our Bertrand." This broke Leonard.

What? Someone killed Bertrand! Every instinct in me wanted to rush up, wrap Leonard in my arms, and mourn together, but this role now was Margaret's. She waddled her way upfront and held him as he shattered on her shoulder, patting him like she was burping the babe she was soon to birth.

He regained his words and read a private poem penned by me about Bertrand. Oh, he had gone through Bert's things, all my notes to him now exposed; the dream of walking down the street naked was real.

The sonnet rolled out in grim measured meter like William Butler Yeats reading *The Second Coming*. I wasn't sure I'd make it without squealing like a seal caught in a net, so I made my move. Speculoos in one pocket, program in another. I turned to leave and ran smack into Margaret. We squared off, each unable to speak. Unsure if she recognized me, I hugged her in solidarity, in grief, in thanks for her support of Leo and Bert's mother. "I'm so sorry for your loss, good luck with your baby, you'll be a wonderful mother," double kissed her on the cheeks and ran like Mo Farah all the way back to the station.

I collected my pack and caught the train I needed within minutes. The moment I heard the whir of wheels, I pulled out the program and inhaled its contents without the ability to assimilate it. Rémy Jacquard, a twenty-five-year-old bartender, was at large for Bertrand's murder. Stabbed him twenty-four times, chest to shins, all for some shitty cash. There was a witness. The family pleaded for the capture of the criminal, "It would assist with their emotional closure."

How could such evil exist as to kill a beautiful soul like Bertrand with such vitriol? And how different was I? Some in my circle called me a 'life affirming angel,' as did my customers and even strangers on the street, yet I was guilty of negligence. Brigitte's cloying kept me on the phone that day, longer than I wanted, but it was my decision to look down at a device when I ought to have been watching the road. Though I didn't kill Luis Fernando on purpose, he was forever dead and a family needed closure. Would it serve them for me to turn my pregnant self in? Would the fact that I was with child protect me from the anger and perhaps violence of others? What was best for this new life that was growing in me? I wish I'd taken my tablet with me instead of destroying it at my flat. I'd not yet researched what the punishment is for a hit and run murder in Paris.

Speculoos spices played at my nose. I unwrapped the tan cookie, salivating for it. No. I would not eat it. This represented the body of

Bertrand. I would carry this / him with me until it crumbled. Swaddling it back in layers of linen napkins, I tucked it to sleep in the middle of a ball of woolen socks, cotton tee shirts above, and rayon skirts below.

Shh. Shh. Shh.

French supermarkets have wonderful tinned food in irresistible packaging with contents that live up to the design. My itinerary for the next few days was jam-packed, but the first item of business was clear. I stood corner side holding open a tin of the highest quality sardines, at the ready. Perhaps I ought to have taken greater precautions to protect my identity, however, I headed onward towards my goal - I had to see my love. Make sure she was well. I'd wait as long as necessary.

A grey tabby found me first and attempted to confiscate the goods. His boldness met with my coldness so he tried to purr-suede me with his Chantilly charisma and cocoa-puff charm. I was having none of it and had to walk three times around the block to throw him off my scent. On my final go round, who should strut in my path but Natalie Mouskers, looking elegant indeed? She hesitated for a moment, then our blissful reunion was just as I'd imagined. She rubbed round my calves like a favorite forty-five record spun repeatedly. In her delicate way she sampled the fish, taking time to tell me she'd missed me in happy mews before going hog wild, whiskers wet from the dive into the depths of the tinny-tin-tin.

I was so focused on petting my beloved Ms. Mouskers, I didn't see Nikos walk up. On his arm like a Cartier watch he wore a babe of about twenty-one, twenty-two tops. She made me, a youthful twenty-seven, feel like a dinosaur. Her hair dark like a moonless night, a surge of jealously choked me, "Perhaps she is another beautiful Greek cousin?"

"Parlene, I'll meet you inside," Nikos commandeered her, sticking a key into tiny hands, manicured pale blue with ivory and pink-rosed tips. She looked me up and down, tongue pressed to the left side of her mouth. "I'll just be a few minutes," he kissed her forehead and gave a slight push in the right direction to get her going.

I held Natalie Mouskers to my chest as a buffer between us.

"Cam, what are you doing here!" He spoke wildly in Greek, but the gist came through. Then French. "Are you crazy? You should be on the other side of the world by now!" Then English, "Is something wrong with the papers? Are you in trouble?"

This man loved me with every cell in his solar system.

I was hot and ashamed. He worked so hard to help me; I hadn't considered this reaction from him, though I ought to have. I'd become a wayward oaf. I looked down to avoid his eyes. His scuffed wingtips had mismatched laces. Something about those shoes made me sad for him, for me, for everyone affected by this mess, anyone with lost potential.

He tucked up my chin, the way he does, "What's wrong, my love?" He carefully removed Natalie Mouskers from my arms and set her on the ground, hugging me close. We stood there unmoved, our cat licking his scuffs. I planned to tell him about our baby-to-be, but the presence of Parlene derailed that plan.

"Nikos, tell me something."

"Yes?"

"Am I at risk for any venereal disease? I won't have time to go to a clinic to get checked for a long time."

"No! Of course not!"

"It's just that..." my gaze shifted toward his flat, "... you have many other partners."

We stood distant now, "I use protection. I'm careful, I always get checked."

"You weren't careful with me." I meant this on so many levels.

"Your appearance was unexpected, Camille. You took me by surprise. You must forgive me for this. Forgive me for everything. Please, you are the love of my life. I made mistakes I regret. We all do. It's a tragedy what happened on the street here in Paris. You are a great soul - a living angel. I hope you move forward with life, do good deeds, and spread love, but whatever you do, get out of this town — they dislike you here."

He picked up Natalie Mouskers and covered her in kisses. She licked his face. "Ah, Ms. Mouskers, you have had a treat! Your breath, it stinks!"

I relaxed seeing my cat was safe and cared for. They would take care of each other. In other circumstances, in another world, Nikos would have made a first-rate father.

Parlene reappeared and tugged at his sleeve, "Come on, Koko, we will be late."

"Goodbye Lucy," he said as the three of them strolled away.

THE HÔTEL

The awning, properly replaced, was a regal royal now instead of morose maroon. Spring was in bloom and the street festooned with peonies, irises, lilies, and nasturtiums. I cradled a dozen pale pink rose caninas, symbolizing to me his sweet innocence. Under wrap of a paper-thin grey hoodie, I scoped out my opportunity to pay tardy, incommensurate respects. A family of four turned into a nearby book Shoppe, a tourist couple dipped for a kiss on the corner, and the workaday hubbub hummed hard. I took advantage of my yellow-lit yard of un-people pavement and solidly set down the pink beauties in memory of Luis "Pierre" Fernando, then stepped back in reverent silence.

Wittingly un-witnessed, I scampered around the corner in need of a toilette; morning sickness was visiting late today, or perhaps the grip of sorry remembrance. The car crash played on a litigious loop; my brain perceived this as acute trauma, palms wet, mouth dry, vision blurred, acid burned in my gut as though I'd swallowed kerosene.

Tomorrow would be another full-tilt itinerary, but tonight I would retreat in style. I would blow a wad on a suite in the legendary Hôtel Plaza Athénée - accommodations far above my frugal price range - where I would sleep in style and anonymity after weeks of couches and a tiny child's bed. I was looking forward to TV and complimentary high-speed Internet access in tight trigger range.

I loped into a serene supermarché and stocked up with several tins of sardines, screw my vegan diet, I needed a pow-pow of nutrition to carry me through what was ahead. Also, a few bottles of water - those sardines would render me hecka thirsty, an array of fruits and veggies, a bag of cheddar cheese flavored air popped popcorn, pomegranate chapstick, and a grape toothbrush and orange holder.

I had a little time to whittle away; my plan was to arrive at the hotel exactly at 10:00 p.m. Once in Budapest I'd arrived late and bargained for a five-star room at half price.

"How many vacancies do you have?"

"We are at fifty percent."

"Hmm. So those rooms will stay empty tonight?"

"Yes, Miss."

"What is the rate for a room?"

"Three hundred for the night, Miss."

"How about I give you one-twenty and we call it a win-win?"

"One-fifty Miss."

"Okay. Done."

That night in Budapest, I turned on TV to relax, but found only hard-core porn. Shame. I needed something unaggressive or inane like *The Bachelor*. I shut off that TV, took a two-hour bubble bath, slept still and heavy like waterlogged wood, stocked up on green bananas, waxy apples, and yogurt from the Continental breakfast bar, and caught the early train to Vienna without ever properly seeing the city. Tonight, however, I found a bench near my dream hotel, took out my blue notebook and picked up on the life assessment squares I'd drawn out on the back pages. I was honest and candid with myself, calculating carefully as though I were preparing for my Chemistry final.

At 9:50 p.m., I tucked away the book, gathered my pack and grocery sacks and headed hopefully into the Haute Couture Plaza. Staying here where the smallest guestroom suite could run from €850 a night had been a top item on my bucket list for the three years I lived in Paris. Now was my chance because if not now, then when?

My running shoes squeaked on the ornate lobby floor. Laden with my sacks, my rapidly growing hair tussled like rangy rags on my head, I set my shoulders back with faux confidence, wet my lips, and approached the front desk.

As the impressive music tumbled down the corridor from the lounge into the satin, silk, and chandelier coiffed lobby, I pictured myself in a boat on a river. This was no shopping mall pianist; the Plaza's poised Maestro engulfed guests with a glamorous ambience well deserving of the historic luxury hotel, which has sat proudly at 25 Avenue Montaigne near the Champs-Élysées, boosting striking Eiffel Tower views for over a century.

In earlier years, I might have taken the song *Lucy In The Sky With Diamonds* as a sign everything would be all right, but hard times flap jacked my idealism on its head. I trudged up to the left side of the lengthy front desk, dragging my grocery bags along the polished tile like a functionless extra appendage.

Felicite smiled at me as though I was a long-lost sister she thought had capsized at sea.

"Je suis Felicite. Bonsoir, Mademoiselle..."

"Lucy," my voice cracked.

"Bonsoir, Lucy. How may I help you? Do you have a reservation?"

"No."

"Ah, I'm sorry, we are full up, Ms. Petrokov," she pushed my passport back towards me like we were playing a game of shuffleboard.

The two-by-two picture Tanu had taken and sent to Nikos was a good one considering what my mood had been that day. I looked down at the photo looking back up at me and there, in the luminous light of the fragrantly flowered front foyer of the Hôtel Plaza Athénée, I broke down and cried.

This wasn't a sob, sniffle, whimper, or even blubber; this was a full out howl, doubled over like a four-year-old having a tantrum, only more pitiful. The piano player paused for a few moments from his rendition of *The Entertainer, The Sting Theme*, as if out of respect for my piercing public grieving.

Seven poshly dressed international guests gathered in a semi-circle, each one touched, each one wanting to throw money at the problem and at the very least silence it so they might enjoy another round of rock and ragtime before the coach turned into a pumpkin.

Felicite ran from behind the desk and hugged me, "Shhh, Lucy, Nous allons travailler quelque chose pour vous. Allez vous asseoir et attendez-moi. Je vais chercher le directeur."

Okay, okay, I'll do that. Go sit down and wait for her while she gets the manager. As she ran off, I congratulated myself on making the biggest scene I could. For a wanted criminal who wished to lie low, I scored zero on my test.

"Hello, Lucy. I am Jacque Maynard. I'm the night manager here. I'm sorry to inform you, but we have no rooms available tonight."

A German woman slathered in Gucci and gold stepped forward and held Mr. Maynard's elbow, "Sehen Sie, Mr. Maynard, meine Nichte has-been einen Tag verzögert, würde Ich mag diese junge Dame zu haben sie auf, und was mehr ist. Ich möchte, dafür zahlen."

I recognized the words *Mr. Maynard, night, day,* and *she has.* Jacque turned to me, pumped my hand, and bowed his head; "Welcome to the Plaza Athénée, Frank will show you to your room. I hope you enjoy your stay."

Felicite hugged me again and directed me back to the desk where she gave me a key. *Fly Me to the Moon* trickled in waves from the west.

"I don't understand, what's happening?"

"Mrs. Van der Heffelin's niece will stay with her and you'll get the guestroom she's in."

"Oh, no, I don't mean to put anyone out."

"It's no problem, I'm sure. Her suite is bigger than my entire house, Lucy," she wrinkled her nose adorably at me.

"I haven't yet asked the price. I don't even know if I can afford it."

"Mrs. Van der Heffelin took care of that."

"Oh, no, no, no, I couldn't. That's too much to ask."

"She's happy to do it. She's a rare person, a philanthropist, and an excellent judge of character. She must see something special in you."

"I'd like to do something for her. Please tell her I'm a portrait artist. If she or her niece would like a portrait, I'd be happy to buy supplies tomorrow if they'd like to sit for me."

"Yes. I will tell her. How much for a portrait? I would like one too."

"No charge, Felicite."

"I would like one too," chimed in Frank.

"So would I."

"And I."

"And I."

Everyone who witnessed the spectacle I'd made wanted a picture of themselves or his or her family or friends, and that is how I went into business at the Plaza in Paris.

I didn't wake up until ten a.m., pulled awake only by my need to hang my head over the toilet in the most magnifique bathroom I had ever seen. It was like a stone white basilica in which I kneeled in prayer for five raw minutes during what had become my morning routine. The King, a Rolls Royce of beds, dressed in crisp, soft whiteness had swallowed me up whole like the whale snick-snacking on Jonah.

I didn't remember much from the time I curled into a fetal position in this spectacular French Regency guestroom, found the television hidden in the wall mirror, selected *Easy Rider* to watch in honor of Jack Nicholson going after Diane Keaton in *Something's Gotta Give* filmed at this very hotel. I dozed for an hour, waking to that rat bastard sayin' "Whyncha git a haircut" before blowing Billy away, the most shocking ending to a movie I'd ever seen. Whoops, sorry, spoiler alert if you haven't seen it. All night I dreamt I was riding the open road with Luis Fernando's mother on a bicycle in the next lane waving a bloody handkerchief and sayin', "Whyncha grow your hair back, Camille, you coward," as she spit on the ground beside me.

I opened the curtains onto a view of the Eiffel Tower holding her majestic head high in a cloudless sky; a fairy tale within my nightmare, the juxtaposition of opposite emotions clattered round my heart and flitted down into my hungry belly. Outside the door sat a domed silver food cart, which I wheeled in with a squeal of delight. Next to the ample and artistic food display, I found fifty euros tucked into a napkin along with a note in faultless English. "Meet me in the lobby at 8:00 p.m. for our portraitures. We will sit for them in my suite. I hope this time does not conflict with your plans. Have a lovely day. Sincerely, Mrs. Maria Van der Heffelin."

The eggs beat Tanu's omelets; the toast laid untouched, juices, fruit, and frothy French yogurt eaten gratefully while I alternated my view from the perfect Paris perch to Le Parisian, a daily newspaper of Paris. The town was up to the same old shit: a soccer game here, a terrorist threat there, no mention of Lucy or Camille.

I showered quickly, longing for the nighttime when I could enjoy a bath. The tub was so large I wondered briefly if I might guzzle some wine, turn face down and fall asleep forever in it, but as this was unlikely, I didn't want to risk hurting the baby. Though I'd hoped to scoot out the front door unseen, I had no such luck. The staff all greeted me by name, "Bonjour Madame Petrokov, bonjour." They treated me like royalty; several patrons from the night before inquired as to how I slept, how I was doing, what were my plans for this day?

I made small talk, excusing myself graciously by explaining I was late for an appointment and off I scurried to get my tasks done after a run. Let's face it; it's wiser to meet the cogs of the world after a sound breakfast and jolly jog. I nodded to the Tower; she beamed back at me. I felt fresh, feisty, and frightened as I hoofed foot in France.

My plans for the day were a discombobulated mess, but who was I to complain? I, Luciana Petrokov, (Lucy), formerly Camille Lisette Portraro, was a guest of philanthropist Maria Van der Heffelin in the Hôtel Plaza Athénée where everyone knew my name and the guest list for portraitures grew steadily. It was an enchanting day in Paris, such a spectacularly shining city where the sights and sounds exulted me. Even mundane or merciless tasks here were the makings of miracles. A quote from Picasso rattled round as I ramped up for my rounds. "It is strange, in Paris I never draw fauns, centaurs or mythical heroes like these, and they always seem to live in these parts."

Seven hours, six errands, one convenient well planned metro system; ruefully, I would be too busy for introspection or to tally deeds in the blue notebook. Every day during the three years I lived in Paris I experienced a surge of possibilities; on this day, I felt quixotic, my mood capricious, tempered by the gravity of my predicament.

My first stop was to the storefront in which I rented a private post box. I peeked in and saw Sallee, who knew me well. Merde. I waited outside, paced and re-peeked inside for twenty minutes until her line grew long and the customers became restless. This was my cue to enter. Wrapped in a sea green scarf up past my chin, obscured by dark glasses, key at the ready, I floated fast past Sallee to my box. It seemed stuck - perhaps they changed the lock? Ah, no, it clicked open and out tumbled a month's worth of mail. A few pieces fell to on the floor. I stooped and scooped the pile into my pack and hastened back to the heroic hub of high noon traffic.

Next on my list was my apartment, barely a kilometer away. The closer I got, the greater my ambivalence grew; it was risky to be near old haunts, this I knew, but I yearned to say a proper goodbye. Madame Trouli was out front pruning a robust tree with fleshy petals like a Jackfruit. In the time it took for me to say whoa, the new tenants walked by, said their hellos to her, and left. The couple, in their forties, looked wholly straight laced. Perhaps their rigidity appealed to Madam after the colourful artist who made her place infamous with a bathroom lipstick scrawl? How I longed to enfold her in a hug, catch up on our days, and help her pick weeds a while, but I slipped away unseen.

I popped by a market I had not frequented when I lived there, on high alert for people I recognized. There was Maribel, a nosy neighbor from Norway who lived two doors down. I took an inordinately long time dawdling over limes while she riffled through the snap peas one by one. What was she doing? Looking for the lost land of Lemuria? Upon her phlegmatic retreat I bought vegetables, almonds, an apple and orange for me, and a bit of fresh mackerel for stop number three to see my kitty.

Natalie Mouskers was nowhere in sight and I had a limited amount of time. A stoop on the opposite side of the street served as my lookout. Who should come home as I sat in wait but Parlene with a male friend in tow? I wondered if this was someone Nikos would like to know about? At my heels, finally, a fresh face showed. My girl mewed, jumped on my lap and ate the mackerel in bliss. I leaned over her, smothering her in kisses, one eye trained on the door across the way like a spy.

But this was no lazy day for me and the hours were already getting away like a wind-up top spinning astray. "Make hay while the sun is shining," dad used to say. "We must make haste," was Theo's way of expressing it, so up I stood, once more unto the breech.

"Good bye, Miss Mouskers, I hope to see you again, my love."

Outside of the computer store, a bodacious girl, fifteen-years-old tops, adjusted a teal garter, breasts bolstered precariously high in a ridiculous, colon-crunching, rib crushing waist cincher. I halted, wishing I could lend an ear and impart words of wisdom. Like the proletariat in a coup d'état against the state, she revolted against my watchful eye.

"Qu'est-ce que *tu* veux?" She spat. "What do *you* want," was her snappish accusation as if she knew I too messed up my life.

Inside the store I agonized for half an hour over whether to get an iPad or a mini. The mini would be less expensive, lighter, and easier to travel with, but the iPad, easier to use. I bought the iPad and rushed away to the art store. My money was flowing away too quickly like a kayak caught in a crescendo of cascading waves, yet I knew that evening's art would require the best. Putting off the final errand, I hauled home three packages full of charcoal, paper, pencils, small canvases, and paints.

When I walked into the hotel, staff and patrons who had quickly adopted me like a well-wanted babe from an orphanage greeted me.

"Happy birthday, Lucy," was the rallied cry!

At first this confused me. My birthday, (that is to say Camille's), was in October. I, (she), was a Scorpio. Luciana, an Aires. I was Aires now. It fit. That this made sense scared me. I received my double-cheeked birthday kisses from people I don't recall meeting and hurried to my suite to wash up and prepare for the Van der Heffelin portraits.

I turned twenty-six again. Many people would kill to be a year and a half younger on their birthday. I did, and I don't recommend it.

The phone rang at seven p.m., startling me. Who could it be?

"Hello, Lucy. It's Maria. I thought perhaps we might do the sitting in your suite rather than mine. I imagine you'll be more comfortable there and this will save you from carting your supplies upstairs. To be perfectly honest, there's a bit too much activity here for me to relax." I heard Brazilian guitar playing uproariously in the background. The festivity of it brought Bertrand to mind. Before I voiced an objection, she closed, "See you in an hour, dear," and the phone clicked off, so that was that.

Mrs. Van der Heffelen arrived promptly at 8:00 p.m., not a moment early or a second late. Her punctual work ethic undoubtedly explained her success. I ate sparsely and barely had time to clean up self and room and arrange a sublime makeshift artist's studio in the settee section. I used a foldout table and a soft chair the hotel staff situated me with like a quick scenery change at intermission Brigitte and I saw during Féerie.

When formalities were past, I inquired, "Do you prefer charcoal, pencils or paint."

"CHARcoal, please. My left side is best, don't you agree?" Madam had a pulchritudinous profile and turned both cheeks at an angle apt for Aphrodite. I agreed, albeit I saw no difference before she pointed it out; perhaps I was more suggestible than I realized.

An artist's sitting is silent for some, but mine were often like talk therapy, only better. People trusted me; my clients shared the most private, detailed, and salacious aspects of their lives as though I was their vault and a confidentiality agreement had been signed and notarized. For ninety minutes as I sketched her high forehead, strong nose, thin lips, wisps of grey, Mrs. Van der Heffelen chatted about her life, loves, social contributions, and strengths and weaknesses, beginning with her upbringing in Nazi Germany.

She was seven when the war broke out. Her father, Baron Guntrum Van der Heffelen risked the lives of his own family by taking in Jews, Gypsies, homosexuals and dissidents; they protected them until those in peril safely left the country with an escort. Her tales of growing up while a fanatical, authoritarian National Socialist, Hitler - influenced by extreme right wing fascist beliefs - fast tracked his people into his ferocious, high-faulting fantasy, fascinated me. I was verklempt hearing this well-articulated aperçu of the atrocities and could have listened to her talk forever.

"What are your plans, Lucy dear? Would you like to be my guest here at the hotel for a week, through next Thursday."

Her words, perfect English with sporadic German phrasing thrown in, had me conjugating verbs like I was doing multiplication tables up to ten-thousand as I processed what she was saying mentally and emotionally all at once.

"Oh, no, I couldn't possibly…"

"Lucy," she grabbed my arm like a spelunking cable as if her life depended upon it, "This gives me a chance to spend time with my niece under closer supervision, you see? You would do me a favor, and I will be forever indebted."

What would I do in Paris for a week? I wanted to attend to business and be done with it.

"Why, yes, thank you, Mrs. Van der Heffelen."

"Call me Maria."

"I have enough to go on now, Mrs. Van… umm, Maria. I can finish the portrait later on my own."

"Splendid. I'd prefer to wait to see it until it's complete. I shall send my niece down now. We've been gathering names of staff and guests who also wish to have you do their portraits. If they offer to tip you, take the money, I see you need it. Save your supply receipts, I will reimburse you. I'll send a breakfast every morning, but go easy on room service, as it's very expensive, even for me. Gute Nacht."

She handed me a list of names and numbers and left in a whirl.

Maria's niece flounced in at 9:45 when I was honestly more capable of collapsing on the bed than producing artistic brilliance. In a bombastic blast she bellowed, "I'm Nina LaRue. I've heard so much about you!" Her entrance intrigued and frightened me at once.

"Wooooooo. It's hot in here," Nina fanned herself as if she'd stepped into a five hundred degree oven rather than my perfectly temperate guest suite that her kindly grandmother was paying for so she might have more access to her kin.

"Oh, I'm sorry, I think it's comforta….."

"Do ya mind if I let a little air in from the balcony?"

Without awaiting my answer, she pulled the heavy cords like she was doing The Monkey at a Perry Parker Dance Party in the 60s and opened the double doors onto quite a cool night. A rascally breeze took advantage of the opportunity to rush in and ruffle the sketch paper I'd situated just so for our drawing. Four sheets flapped across the room like the tiger kite Noni and I used to fly in Kathryn Albertson Park. Images of a wild stallion galloping over a New Mexico mesa flooded my vision; I couldn't see the woman for the horse, and wondered how I would draw anything but forelock, fetlock, muzzle and hocks.

"You're an adorable thing, Luc. Do ya mind if I have a smoke real fast before we get started?"

"Yes. I mind. I don't want cigarette smoke in here."

"It's a joint, not tobacco. I'll just step outside for a sec. You wanna hit?"

No! I did not want a hit. I did not want my wonderful room to smell skunk like and attract unwanted attention while I was trying to lie low even though everyone in the damn place knew my name, my birthday, and had signed themselves and their sisters up for sittings.

"Nina. I'd rather you smoke nothing on the balcony, I'm sorry," though I wasn't. "Marie and I had an outstanding session. I'd love the same with you. Will you be able to sit still?"

I don't know where my cajones came from. My meek, "Poor me, I killed a boy and so am not worthy of taking up space on this earth anymore," flew right out the wall length window, which I then closed as I shooed all five foot five inches of Nina LaRue back inside. "Help me get this paper, let's get started before I get too tired to do a good job."

She obediently retrieved three, I got one, and she sat, subdued, like I'd slapped her or something.

"Would you like me to use charcoal, pencils, or paints?"

"You're the artist. You choose."

I softened. "That's a lovely necklace you have on, Nina LaRue. Oh, and call me Lucy, okay?"

"Thank you," as she fingered her two-stranded handcrafted beaded necklace, a bright remembrance twinkled in her eye. It was lovely: peach, white, orange, and olive recycled glass strung 1/4 inch apart with dark brown and ivory strands knotted in between. " I got it in Africa a few months ago."

"It sounds like there's a story there."

"Oh, there is, Luc, there is."

Nina LaRue took her prodigious, wiggly energy and heated my comfortable room with enthralling tales of world romps that captivated me for the next three hours as I pasteled her portrait - one of the best I'd ever done - with nary a hint of a flared horse snout.

We parted fast friends at one a.m., she over-the-moon with her picture, vowing to frame and hang it prominently in her Brooklyn townhouse; I with eyes closing, focused fully on disappearing into the tub just over yonder.

As I closed my leaded lids in a bath full of bubbles, Nina LaRue's ebullient life replayed like a docudrama through my head, starting at her birth. Sigh. When might I have time to process my life? My schedule was back-to-back-to-back for the next few days at least.

Blurp, blurp, blurp - I submerged under sudsy skies, sailing in the stratosphere of a eucalyptus, peppermint, and lemongrass bubble bath. The salt-tinged climatic, chemical concoction turned the water a soapy hue of sage yellow and sapphire blue. I blurped down to the bottom, mint spiraling into my ears, stinging my eyes, refreshing every orifice known to humankind, mind whirring around the labyrinth of Nina LaRue's life. Her name presented to me over and over as she had introduced herself, as one poetic word: NinaLaaaaRue. Saying her name is like riding a roller coaster that is chugging up skyward, then a metaphorical schussing down on angled inclines too fast, stomach left hovering above, arms in hallelujah position, LaRuuuuuuuuueeee!!!! *Whooooooooooo!!!!*

Nina was a product of privilege, a victim of circumstance, her mother died young of cancer; I could relate, we bonded over this in fact. Her father was a trumpet player in a jazz band, loving, but non-apologetically absent, permissive to a fault, dropping young Nina and her brother Jaran into the lavish laps of Mr. and Mrs. Van der Heffelen.

In the magnificent Van der Heffelin mansion in Berlin, the all but orphaned twosome shared a diamond-covered bungalow out back that housed only them. Brown diamonds on cream, a pre-teen's dream, with a thatched roof such as one might find in more primitive villages where building supplies consisted only of straw, reeds, rushes, heather and animal dung; she and Jar painted the door outer space blue when she was twelve, he just ten.

Jar died in an epileptic seizure - his first and only - at lunch break on the schoolyard four years later. An autopsy came back non-conclusive. The then sixteen-year-old Nina absconded to Australia where she hitchhiked around with a band of bohemians, eventually marrying the America, Jeremy Joseph. Jeremy, a civic-minded fellow, became an environmental lawyer. Nina LaRue - refusing to relinquish her maiden name - finished high school, went to college, (History major, Philosophy minor), and prepared to have a brood of little LaRue-Josephs, until years of trial, error, and tests revealed that Jeremy was infertile.

Jeremy, unsatisfied with his life, distraught by right wing denial of global warming coupled with his inability to father children, became emotionally abusive. Nina rebelled by doing the only thing that made sense to her which was to have an affair with their articulate accountant, Jabori, a married jazz pianist, with three children of his own. Jabori was a black man, and Nina, now four months pregnant with had no idea how to explain her miraculous pregnancy, knew the child she carried would be born with skin darker than Jeremy's Middle Eastern olive. She struggled, unsuccessfully, to end her pot habit for the sake of the baby.

I held back from confessing to Nina about my own fertilized state. It was as bumpy as being a picador on the back of a boisterous bucking bull. I held on that strap, stretched to capacity, overtaxed, trapezium tightened, and breathless to burble, thus, the blurping in the bubble bath was such welcome relief. I tried to push her life, her strident strife, out of my pores so I could finally focus on my own botherations. Just as my shoulders released I heard a faint knock at the door like a woodpecker pecking wood but the pecking turned to pounding and wouldn't stop.

Before exploring how I might let the levity of liquid take me to a place where children don't die from falling awnings, a place I'd see my parents again or all consciousness might cease, and Nikos, his cousins, and flitty girlfriends would vanish, I stepped from the warm tub.

"Qu'est-ce?"

"Luc, it's me. Let me in, I left my cell phone here and I'm expecting calls from Jeremy and Jabori."

I begrudgingly opened the door. In gusted Nina LaRue.

"Luc, you have blue bubbles in your hair and have left burgundy puddles on the mauve carpeting."

"I was in the bath."

"I can see that. Go finish up. I'll just sit here and check my messages until you're done."

It took the tenacity of constraining another team of savage beasts not to clock Nina LaRue in the kazoo.

Being beholden to Dame Van der Heffelen positioned me in a very fine, upper crust box with a pianist playing Misty for me. Like a French street mime, my situation confined me. Jacqueline and I once saw an angry, drunk mime get arrested on the Champs-Élysées, close to the hotel. There's nothing more sorrowful than watching a silent clown get dragged away screaming and crying with his full-faced smirk sullen and smudged.

"Don't just stand there dripping, get back in the bathroom!"

"Don't tell me what I should do!"

A vibratory Buzzzzzzzz came from the settee, "Ah, my phone! It's him!"

Yes, but which him, Darren one or Darren two? Nina LaRue, like an Olympian swimmer dove for the gold, hands-over-head, lifted, leapt, and landed on her phone and settled into the couch as if she were in her own home. "Hey, bae, I miss you." She waved me into the bathroom like she was shushing a fly from the melon balls on a Fourth of July picnic.

I hauled my pack into the lap of lavatory luxury, not keen on Ms. LaRue riffling through my stuff. My bath was over. I eavesdropped earnestly on her. Well, she was presenting her mottled melodramas at my door. Her conversation had the same toxic, magnetic magnitude I had with Nikos during our scorching second year together. I bet it was Jabori, the jazz playing player with a penchant for vulnerable, colorful, charismatic women on the line.

Upon exiting my steamy kingdom, I found Nina weeping into her hands, tissues strewn on the floor. The sight of her bent figure tore at my heart. I sat haunch-legged on her left and hugged her; her heart beat like Ali jabbing Frazier. After five minutes of hiccupping sobs, she composed herself.

"That was Jeffrey. He's talking divorce. You're getting my shirt wet. Go dry your hair. Can I stay here for the night?"

Her non-sequiturs flew back and forth like Serena's sets at Wimbledon. Before I answered, she handed me a crinkled paper and smashed the ball past the net, making me sprint for it.

"We booked fifteen people for portraits. You'll work for five days, two days off. We asked them to give you at least one hundred euros each. Ah, ah, don't object, they can afford it; you need it. Three appointments per day: 10:00 a.m., 6:00 and 8:00 p.m. This gives you free time each afternoon. My grandmother will get you some luggage to replace your filthy pack. Oh, and a haircut. You're booked at 12:30 tomorrow. She doesn't take no for an answer. You're a thoroughbred who needs grooming, Luc." She brushed my bangs out of my eyes. I felt like a five-year-old.

"So can I sleep here tonight?"

"NOOOOOOO!" I screamed in my head.

"I don't sleep well with anyone in the room," I stammered.

"Please," she grabbed another tissue, " I don't snore."

"Fine. Just stay on your side of the bed." I had no choice. The box, remember. This wasn't really my room.

"No funny stuff, I promise." Now she sounded five.

"I have a quick call to make, Nina, then I'm turning the light out.... Hello, room service? I don't need rolls, bread, croissants or butter with my breakfasts. Could I have extra scrambled eggs instead?"

"Order me eggs benedict."

"You do it," I thrust her the phone and lay down. I was asleep before she hung up.

Have you ever woken up totally disoriented? The wake up call at 9:00 a.m. stirred me from a dream in which I was sailing upon a turbulent sea. Queasy, unsure of where I was, I surmised I was on a boat, seasick, the fold of the comforter, rolling ocean waves. Then it hit me, I, Camille, was Luciana. Luciana had morning sicknesses something fierce. Nina's side of the bed was empty but her shoes sat and her pants hung nearby. Holding my stomach, I lunged for the bathroom. She had locked the door! Nina was singing in the shower at the top of her lungs. Bits of an off-key version of *The Flower Duet* from the French opera Lakme escaped from beneath the floor slats and shook the window glass.

I needed to find something to throw up in. Fast. First thought: the flowerpot on the balcony. NOT! Second thought: the sink in the kitchenette. Oh, no no no no no. Third thought: one of the plastic bags from the art supplies. Bingo! I grabbed one and was already rinsing my mouth out when Nina appeared with a towel turban high on her head.

"Guten Morgen mein Lieber."

"You look better this morning, Nina. Did you sleep well?"

"Most excellently, Luc.... Yuk! Something stinks in here."

Oh, no!

"I have to get ready for the 10:00. I'm late. See you later?" I handed Nina La Ruuuuuueee her pants, shoes, AND cellphone and practically shoved her out the door. Waiting for me in the hall was the silver-domed tray of breakfast food, no bread, croissants, rolls or butter, extra yummy scrambled eggs, plus two pieces of navy luggage, the finest I'd ever hoped to own.

"Open the windows, Luc, air it out, get that stench out of there in a hurry," Nina shouted from down the hall, tossing her wet curls as she evaporated like dust into the elevator.

I ran inside, threw open the balcony door as wide as it would go, brushed my teeth vigorously: up down, side-side, tongue, roof, tongue, roof, tongue, tongue, roof, grabbed the bag of barf and my room key, put up a placard stating Ne pas déranger, and ran down the stairs to dispose of *that stench*. I ran until I found a rubbish can and buried the treasure deep within. Somehow I ate and held down my breakfast, (eggs, yogurt, fruit, juice), made the bed, tidied the room, and organized the art supplies in time to greet Ralph, the Bellman, for his ten o'clock. I opened the door with a phony-baloney relaxed air.

He wafted in fresh as the breeze off the balcony.

"I'm excited to have be here," his broken English charmed me at once. I could tell this would be an excellent sitting. The day was off to a good start.

The next three days were chock-a-block. When I stayed busy enough, I didn't have time to obsess over Luis Fernando and his family. What would he be doing now if he were still alive: learning to read, A is for Argentina, B for Brazil, and C for Colombia? Finger painting? Riding a two-wheeler? Would he become an architect, professor, inventor, or chef? Who might have been his spouse and would they now be partner-less until death, children unborn?

The eyes of Luis Fernando's unborn son and daughters - three girls - haunted me like a Greek chorus, arms crossed, feet tapping, tisk-tisking my every move... unless I was too busy. Yet even while smearing a line of charcoal on a sketch of the dark brown beautiful brow of a bright Bahrainian, these thoughts clawed and clamored their way in, never letting me forget.

Was the entire world changed because of an untimely text? Who would text next and cause more distress? IF I lived, (this was still up for grabs), I had visions of staging a global campaign against cell phone usage while driving. It was easy to be brave in my head.

Mostly though, at the Hôtel Plaza Athénée, I was Lucy, the artiste, not Camille, the killer. The sitting with Ralph was a delight, as I'd expected. He has a predictable crush on me, and why not? I was the mysterious, talented America, a Bohemian, emotions playing vulnerably across my face like rainbows dancing through a crystal pendulum hung in a window at midday. Though he's twenty-four, just a few years younger than me, he seems like a child: sheltered, innocent, and boring. It was flattering though to have male attention. I missed that nearly as much as I missed my cat.

The next eight sittings were all with wealthy, international guests spanning five continents; they booked the guests before the rest of the staff since their stays were short. One client, a clever award-winning British film actor, arranged his schedule to stay an extra day to have me draw him. I wasn't sure how to capture his charisma on paper. Some extra golden tones perhaps? Whatever I did worked. He tipped me five hundred American dollars, gave me his phone number, and told me I had a "coltish" quality that he'd like to see on-screen.

"Look me up," he said with his trademark wink; "We'll get you in the movies."

There was a buzz around the hotel about my portraits. I grew concerned there might be press coverage, as if *that* would help my anonymity! As it was, I half expected someone to ask, "Are you Camille of Bertrand et Camille?" Regardless, I had the time of my life, yet the thought of the brown scarfed boy tempered every ounce of joy. When I spoke to the concierge, there he sat on the desk, legs dangling down, scowling sorrowfully at me.

My haircut appointment was a success; I looked styled. Bangs long enough now to sweep over my forehead, hair tapered, draping just over the nape of my neck, my chestnut cheekiness restored. I floated like a fairy princess through this Parisian paradise lobby.

"Bonjour, Lucy, you look lovely. I can't wait to have my portrait done."

"Bonne après-midi, Lucy. It's so nice to see you. How is your day going?"

"Guten tag, Lucy, how are finding your room, is your luggage acceptable?"

"Oh, Mrs. Van der… erm, Maria. I love it. It's so elegant! You shouldn't have."

"It's the least I can do, dear, I appreciate that you keep an eye on Nina. She adores you."

"Bonsoir, Lucy, your hair cut suits you. It delights us to have you in our midst. You thrill our guests with their portraitures. We welcome you here at half-rate anytime."

"Merci, Mr. Maynard."

"Jacque."

"Jacque."

"Hey, Luc, wait up! I have to tell you about the last call from Jabori!" Ugh, Nina.

"Not now, Nina, I have a 6:00."

"I'll see you tonight then?"

"Will you give me until midnight? I have to get some business done first."

"Já. Kiss-kiss, Luc; stay loose. See you!"

In between appointments, I ran for hours, bought groceries to put in my room fridge, and opened a bank account to stash my cash. I was getting rich! Ha. One muggy afternoon I walked Avenue Montaigne and then along the Qua to Shakespeare and Company for tea and to browse the books. The manager, named Pierre, oddly enough, asked to sit with me.

"Oui."

"You are American?"

"Yes."

"I can tell by how you walk. Determined, like you are going somewhere."

In a parallel life, I would flirt shamelessly with this man. He worked at the store while getting his doctorate in Philosophy. He had a glow.

"What else can you tell about me?"

"You carry a secret."

"Oh!"

"But it's your turn. What can you tell about me?"

I can tell I might fall in love with you, if not for my secret. Did I say that out loud? I wasn't sure.

He put his hand on mine. "Think about it. How long are you in town? Perhaps you will come back and tea with me again."

"Yes. I would love to."

He lifted my hand and kissed it. "Goodbye, Belle."

When he said this, all I could see was Bertrand. I broke down crying. Pierre hugged me right there. He held me, rocking me in front of his customers, without hesitation. Then he kissed the apple of my cheek and handed me a card with his number and work hours.

I was nearly late for my six o'clock sitting. "I have to go now."

I could fall in love anytime, anywhere, and that's how it was in Paris with Pierre, but he wore so much scent it sucked up all the fresh air. I had to say something as he fluffed my newly styled hair.

"Pierre, do you have perfume on?"

"Perfume?"

"Ah.... ahh... achoooooo.... Like a flowery smell."

"Ah, this is my aftershave. You like it? I wore it for you." He seemed so proud.

"Ahh... choo. I think I'm allergic to... ahhhh... chooooo!" My eyes stung.

"Here, Lucy, tissue… your nose. It's... dripping."

"Thank you. Umm, I have to go, ummm, Pierre. I can't... achooooooooo, achoooooo... breathe."

"We meet tomorrow. I won't wear any flowers smell."

"I work tomorrow."

"Monday, I'm off on Monday."

"I work Monday." Tears dripped down my eyes in attempts to extricate the histamine from my sinuses. "I'll talk to you later."

"Aurevoir beauté." He waved at me like I was departing on the Titanic. I half expected him to pull out a linen kerchief and flap it like a house cleaner dusting crystal. I had no business bringing anyone into my life anyway, even a painfully perfect, (though heavily perfumed), Pierre, the sweet, strong, sensitive doctorate in Philosophy candidate, who loved Dumas, Ibsen, Chekhov, Shakespeare, Muddy Waters, and, apparently me, even when snot slowly dripped onto my upper lip.

Exit Shakespeare and Company, stage left.

A few more sneezes snuck out fifteen minutes later while I was surreptitiously purchasing Amiero brass combination luggage locks to keep Nina's prying eyes out of my sordid stuff when I was showering. The surprised clerk looked at me like I had tried to poison her children. I then swung by my post box to see if my credit card had arrived yet (it had) and headed round to stake out Brigitte's house.

Brigitte lived in an upper flat with her older sister Lorelei. The mustard-hued building needed a fresh coat of paint for years now. I sat cross-legged on a prickly patch of grass across the street, preparing myself for a lengthy stakeout. I opened my notebook and worked on my life review, lifting my eyes like an international spy with intervals of a minute or two in between. Luis Fernando, my constant companion, laid tummy down on the grass and waited too.

I'd spent the few nights prior setting up my Wi-Fi and, using the pseudonym Lille Belle, becoming an online stalker of my former friends. I'd set the tablet on the desk in my suite, a plate of hummus and vegetables nearby, while I surfed uninterrupted in two-hour shifts (10:00 p.m. to midnight) until Nina would show up and crawl feline-like onto her side of the bed like Natalie Mouskers used to. She purred out her escalating psychodrama with Jabori, Jeremy, and Jabori's wife, Jemma, who seemed finally to be catching onto things, which interestingly was a relief to Nina. "Secrets," she said, "can kill you."

You can die while you're alive. I did.

Soon before I left Lille, Theo came into the twin's room one morning to check on me. Tanu had been up for an hour; it was the first time she was up before me. He sat in lotus pose on the edge of the tiny bed.

"How are you, Lucy?"

I lay scrunched in a fetal position, shivering, romping through escape plans: an anchor knot, high bridge, and bloody bathtub. None of these suited me. I couldn't even hurt a fly and there was no fleeing, especially seeing that I was with child. How was I? Not well.

"This isn't a human experience. Losing my parents was devastating. When Pascal died, I went numb, yet I always recovered me, but Theo, I exited that car in a different realm than I'd ever known. There is no healing. There are no words to explain. I am obliterated."

"Well, you're human, Lucy, and you're having this experience so it IS a human experience."

He turned rapidly around. "What?"

"Don't you see him?"

He sat silent, present with my anguish. "Refugees, POW's, victims of genocide, victims of rape, newlyweds, Olympians, Nobel Prize winners, all humans. Human experience is vast. You didn't have intent to hurt anyone. Come on, it's time to get up. Humans need to eat, Lucy. You are still alive."

"Camille is dead."

I had no intent to hurt anyone, but I did. Guilty. Guilty. Guilty.

"You're human... so this is a human experience." Theo's words rolled over and repeatedly like Natalie Mouskers when she wanted me to scratch her belly.

"What should I wear?" Felicite repeated her question. I snapped back to the lobby, the sconce lights, high ceiling, piano keys tinkling in background waves, I couldn't catch the tune.

"Whatever you're comfortable in."

"I mean like, what color?"

"What do you look good in? What color do you like?"

"Jade?" She seemed unsure.

"Wear something Jade, then."

"You won't be too tired to start my portrait at 8:00?"

"Not at all. I'm a night owl."

"Are you sure you don't want the housekeeping service? It won't cost Mrs. Van der Heffelin anything. It's what we do for our guests."

I squirmed, struggling to keep my face immobile. I disliked when people mistook my vulnerability for stupidity. I understand how a hotel works. "You're human. This is a human experience. You're human... human..."

"No thank you, just the fresh towels and sheets will be fine. I enjoy making the bed myself."

She turned and looked behind her. "What?"

"Nothing. See you at 8:00. Don't be late! It'll be great!" I winked and walked towards the music, *Surry With The Fringe On Top*. Cristoff, the piano player grinned and nodded at me. I smiled sweetly and vaguely wondered if I remembered how to tie the anchor knot.

Relationship: It's complicated. That's what Brigitte's Facebook page said. Was she referring to me, had she forgotten to update, or already fallen in love with someone else? Tragedies can trigger trenchant, transformative changes to one's life.

She'd cut and pasted - not shared - one of those lists of silly Facebook questions.

-Ever started your laundry at two a.m.? YES

-Ever gone hang gliding? YES

-Ever gone bungee jumping? NO

Her Instagram feed ended with the now infamous picture of me at the skating rink.

Comments - 7

"Fun night! Love you!"

"Love you more"

"Oh, no, what happened?"

"Is Camille okay?"

"Did you read the paper today?"

"And *POOF* she's gone."

":(!!!"

I'd only waited an hour that day. No movement in or out of Brigitte's flat. I left to go running. I planned to wait round the clock if I had to. I needed to be assured that Brig was okay.

-Ever fallen in love with someone you didn't expect to? YES

"Camille?" Sebastian stood, feet planted fifteen inches apart, a stance I associated with the physical strength of Graphene. He was practically in my lap, breathing into my Salade niçois, yet I averted looking at him like one avoids gazing into the sun during a solar eclipse. Nina and I were out to a late lunch to celebrate our blossoming friendship and a week of portraits.

"Luc, who is this?" Nine LaRue looked like a momma lion ready to pounce on this intruder, interrupting our precious time.

Sebastian is a sweet guy. We had a fling the first month I arrived in Paris. I now had the advantage of three years maturation altering the shape of my face a bit. In one's mid twenties, features seem to settle into their final structure, reflecting a finely ripening character. He looked surer of himself too. I had no choice but to float down the river: De Nile.

"Excusez-moi?" My voice a half octave below normal, enough to fool Seb, but not enough to alert Nina to the change in tenor.

"Camille, it's me, Sebastian!" He pounded his chest to prove to me he was INDEED himself; his tone revealed its bright innocence. Sebastian, I would guess, was one of the few Parisians who had not heard the news about me. He shunned public news; believed much of what it spits out is fake and preferred to keep an, 'ignorance-is-bliss' outlook on life. "The big things, I will hear, the rest I tune out," he told me on our second date. This is one reason I broke it off with him. I wanted to be with a man engaged in the world-as-it-was, not floating along in a surreptitious fantasy. Now I could have kissed him for being so removed.

"Désolé, je ne..." I began with a terse smile, took a crunch of lettuce in my mouth, and leaned in towards Nina to show that our conversation was *so* scintillating we had no time or interest in being sidetracked by strangers.

Sebastian walked away confused. In my peripheral vision I saw him glance back towards me three times as he paid his bill. He was in company of a young raven haired bohemian, likely another new age anti-establishment no news-er living in the slats between Namaste and Nirvana, nowhere near the intersection of killer Camille and poor Luis Fernando.

I would miss Paris, but it was time to turn myself in or leave, one or the other. "Do your business or get off the pot," dad used to say.

Paris wasn't perfect: there was pollution, predatory politics, stereotyping, terrorism, yet for all its foibles the city addicted and entranced me to its magic. Friends warned me before I left the Northwest for Europe the French could act snotty, aloof, and superior, but I hadn't found that to be the rule. I lived in a warm, welcoming, creative world here. I reflected on the Eiffel Tower, wrought iron goddess, guarding her citizens, like a prominent nose on the staunch face of this most spectacular city who had been so good to me, and could not help but smile.

"Luc, are you going to finish that? You have Moritz at six." She held my hands in hers, "Promise me you'll come and stay in Brooklyn. You're always welcome in our guest room for as long as you need or want, no questions asked." Nina sensed something was amiss in my life and we flit around the issue like dancing a silent tarantella. I respected her for giving me space around this. I even grew fond of her regardless of the Jeremy / Jabori gymnastics, her snoring, and daily melodramatic meanderings.

Her phone rang. "Ooh, Luc! I think it's Jeremy... *Hello?*"

"It's JaBORI," she mouthed. She slipped napkin from lap to table and sashayed out of the Café with the classy sass of a wounded, spoiled German American on a perfect day in Paris.

Saved by the bell. I finished my salad as shadows of Sebastian, the boy, his mother, my parents, and Brigitte, played ring-around-the-rosy, making me dizzy. Or perhaps oscillating pregnancy hormones were responsible for the whirl.

Glad to be out of the crowded din, I made my way back to the hotel past a busker in a bowler hat singing, *Fly Me To The Moon*. At some point in our lives, ghosts may outnumber the humans, I just didn't think I would hit that tipping point at twenty-seven.... erm... twenty-six.

GO - GO - GO

I hadn't seen my benefactor, Mrs. Van der Heffelin, all week and now I knew why. She rose whilst the sun was rising in Riga, a peaceful hour in Paris; a time in which I was normally soaring deep in astral bliss, rapid eye movements transporting me to more reasonable realms, hence our schedules were at cross arms.

"Oh, Lucy, dear. How lovely to see you. What are you doing up at this enigmatic hour?"

Without the piano player, the hotel lobby unmasked a mundane but mysterious muteness; a silent side of its personality those tucked tightly in bed at three a.m. were not privy to. I took in details of Maria, the first face I'd sketched this week, perfectly coiffed and made up, lipstick just so, brows drawn on in a slight inquisitive arch.

"Sometimes I like to walk the streets here at night," I stooped to re-tie my left runner. "Oh, ha, that didn't come out right," I popped back up, eye level with Madame again.

"Well, this is an ideal time to thank you for all you have done."

"Thank me? Maria, I owe you the world! You've been much too kind and generous with me. How will I ever thank you?"

"You already have tenfold, dear." She broke into an entitled smile reserved for the likes of the uber-wealthy who can buy themselves gold-laced shirts, silver-threaded skirts, mansions on a hill, non-medicinal pills, and friends as needed, by will. "You were a good investment, raising the spirits of our patronage, creating for me a portrait worthy to frame as a legacy, and most vitally, you are a stabilizing wunderkind for Nina. She adores you, you know."

Just then, a slight kerfuffle erupted at the front desk as Josene told an inebriated man that no, she might not give him money for food every night, and if he didn't leave the premises immediately, she would have to call the police. Feeling sorry for the man, (and not wanting to see the police), I hurried over and offered him my snack: a ripe, rosy apple and small sack of almonds. He 'mercied' me and disappeared into the naughty, nepenthe night, the character of the city, uplifting and frisky at this stoic hour.

Returning to Mrs. Van der Heffelin's side, I had an unexpected wave of nervousness, talked a tangerine tangent about the Cinémathèque Française Film Center, which I'd hoped to visit before I left town, the lovely weather we were having, and the bliss of my silver bulleted breakfast tray each morning. I hid behind any superfluous chitchat to avoid exposing my desultory situation, deceiving and dissembling like the cast of Hamlet. She did not seem to catch on. Blinks of my doe's eyes might fool even the most wise. In fact, she grew impatient; a glow of an industrialist on the go replaced her gregarious grin.

"Let's get back to business, shall we? Now, we have had a death in the family and are leaving by 11:00 a.m."

"Oh, I'm so sorry to hear..."

"Danke. It's a distant cousin from my husband's side. We will depart earlier than planned. I paid your room for the next two nights. This gives you two days free in town, if you stay. On the off chance you leave earlier, I've arranged for you to get the money refunded, in cash."

"As I've said, you've been much too generous with me."

"I hope that you and Nina remain in contact. She tells me she has invited you to New York."

"Yes, but..."

"I hope to hear good news of your visit there."

"Yes, thank you. Thank you for everything, Maria."

She leaned forward with an awkward hug, whispering, "Please help my granddaughter in whatever way you can. She's spinning like a top pulled by a two foot cord. I assume you have heard she's having a black baby? Not that there's anything wrong with it, but it will be scandalous in terms of her marriage." Her eyebrows arched an impossible inch higher.

"Yes... of... course..." I was at a loss, relieved to spill out the front doors where the homeless man eating my apple grabbed my hands in thanks, starling me into a sweat.

Life, as it is, is unfair. A wave of early morning morning sickness took hold as I wondered whether I would land in Nina LaRuuuuuue's guestroom in Brooklyn, or a Parisian jail next? The Eiffel Tower stood up straighter and beckoned me to do the same. I ran off in search of a toilette, grateful for the night, grateful, as always, to Paris.

The rumble of the rail, so familiar, like a mother rocking her babe to sleep, accompanied me thither and yon on that last day in Paris. The city was both a darling destination and Draconian slayer of my dreams. Like sheep herded onto boxcars, my fellow patrons sat and stood, sharing sweet and sour saffron smiles to the lurch and stop of the metro.

I had no time to waste. I'd opted for door number two: the cash. The seven hundred twenty-three euros would come in handy and carry me more than an extra day of roaming through familiar neighborhoods with only a haircut, new clothes, and sunglasses to disguise me.

The growing life inside me beckoned me swiftly onward to stable grounds where I might study the cycle of gestation, touch base with a midwife to guide me, and plan our future. Somberly salvaging the remnants of my soul and providing for the child, (growing in character as yet unseen), affected by my every thought, every breath of secondhand cigarette smoke, every sit up, slouch, satiated sleep, Salade, squash, or sardine I consumed.

I set my schedule for the day based partly on the maze of the map: here to there, leaving two tasks strategically for last. I hit the pavement early, blasting through slightly moist fog. With little time to think, actions encased me like a hot leather vest zipped tightly on a warm day. I cleaned the room, packed my bags, and closed my new post box. I'd given Theo's address as forwarding reference, perhaps a mistake? Natalie Mouskers and I shared a can of smelly fish and a goodbye kitty kiss only one of us knew was final. My heart pounded in anticipation of seeing Nikos, I don't know why. I left with a sigh, not even a Parlene sighting to titillate me.

This was all accomplished in the early morn; it's alarming what one can get done when rising well before the sun. My aim was to get to Brigitte's by 9:00 a.m., the hour she walked Prince Harry, her Siberian husky. I just had to see how she was doing. I must have looked like a junked up druggie jonesing for a fix, nervous, pacing, shaking my hands out like they had cooties, deep inhales like a bobsledder before competition, exhales like a horse with hay fever.

She didn't show. She didn't show. She-did-*not*-show. The door remained closed; it was like watching a streetlight at the slowest damn intersection in the world, then BAM, the gate pushed open, and a thin, haggard version of my friend oozed slowly behind a bounding bouncing dog. The hound dragged her along. This accident episode wrought her inside out. Brigitte looked like she wished to still be in bed and slumber forever, never deigning to open her sweet eyes again. Twenty-five years young, but she looked much older, well beyond her age.

I followed her, stalked her, soaked her in with my cells, dear Brig, my prize Amie, I could see without speaking with her she blamed herself, hated every ounce of her own beautiful soul. How I wished I could approach her, pet her pup, hug and comfort her, and her, me. I watched her pick up what her dog left as a gift on the walkway, wrap it in shiny cellophane and shuffle back home in thin slippers she barely lifted off the ground. This image would haunt me and make me reconsider my next moves, but onward I went, on autopilot. Go. Go. Go.

Bertrand and Leonard's apartment was next en route and one act before the last. I hoped I wouldn't see Leonard. I didn't. An old man swept rose petals from a tiny garden next door, and a young woman pushed a comically big-wheeled poussette, reminding me of how happy, healthy, normal new mothers appear taking a baby for a walk in the neighborhood.

I'd made a condolence card, a portrait of Bert and Leonard dancing together on the ice, a likeness of Bert's guitar rested in the lower right corner of the page. It was one of my best works; I'd captured it on an iPad picture, becoming more computer literate as the days drew on. I folded the page eight times over, devaluing the total effect, yet yielding a package small enough to stuff in a side nook by the back door. I left it like a time bomb then rose like rosettes, not a moment to spare until the sound dinged that it was done. Once again, Camille was on the run.

She clasped my shoulder deeply enough to bruise it, but not deeply enough to work out that darn knotted acorn lodged an inch under my right scapula. A silver name badge caught the sun in a blinding ray, 'Officier Rousseau', I read.

"Excusez-moi, qu'est-ce que vous faites ici?" Sounding like Charlie Brown's teacher, what I heard was: WAH-wah-wah, wah-wah-wah, wah-wah-wah. Three more times someone asked, "What are you doing here?" I snapped back into my body. A box-faced policeman with hangdog eyes, badge flashing 'Joubert' trotted up as Rousseau's reinforcement.

"What's the problem here?" the Barney Fife of Paris queried.

"I left for lunch an hour ago, and here she stood, I come back from lunch, and here she stands like a statue. Catatonic."

"Hello, hello," she waved a patronizing hand like wiper blades in front of my face. This was not a kind woman.

Maybe they will only file civil charges. Involuntary Manslaughter. Ah, no, but I fled the scene. I steeled myself to the idea they might lock me up. It would be best for Luis Fernando's family, his mother, father, and handsome grandfather who was the spitting image of the man I'd seen in Leonard's Uber.

"Hey you," Joubert snapped between my eyes as I tiptoed and stumbled through a field of emotional explosives puffering in my face. "I must give birth to my baby in jail," was the leaden weight that nearly sank my ship. Maybe I'll get a short sentence? Maybe no one will kill me - a child killer - in jail? Maybe Nikos will raise our child while I'm away?

"Maybe Baby," played in my head as if Buddy Holly had risen from the crash site and set up a soundstage in front of the police station.

"WAH-wah-wah, WAH-wah-wah, WAH-wah-wah. Maybe baby, I'll have you. Maybe baby, you'll be true. Maybe baby, I'll have you for me."

A third gumshoe, Girard, slid up; they caged me between them. Cop versions of Barney Fife, Stan Hardy, and Marilyn Monroe stood staring at me, their goldfish in a bowl, nowhere to swim but in circles; my future, the clockwise swirl of the toilet.

Oh, no! If Nikos gets custody, that strumpet Parlene will have a manicured hand in raising my kid. Oh, no! I made a mistake. I made a mistake, mistake, please universe, take two, I changed my mind. I need to go now!

"Is it against the law to stand here?"

Big bad brass badged Girard, surprised to hear the barmy March hare speak shook his head, "No." Joubert looked confused and said nothing. Rousseau removed her rough hand; she was as hard to get a read from as if I attempted to read Urdu upside down.

I brushed my shoulder off where she'd grasped me to show to passersby how she had physically violated me. Oh, now I could get a read from her; she wanted to kill me, or at least make me suffer sufficiently.

Adjusting my sunglasses, smoothing my styling bangs and straightening my seersucker shirt, I, Luciana Petrokov sauntered away from le poste de police and headed back to Hôtel Plaza Athénée to collect the one set of navy bags and €700 + room fee and head somewhere safe.

I'd planned for nearly a week where I was going next.

I made this journey so many times with Pascal, Brigitte, Jacqueline, or combinations thereof, I could have done it blindfolded after being twirled in dizzying circles in the dead of night. I'd also trekked it alone for solo art soaked seminars. Paris to London via the Eurostar is as familiar as looking at the back of my hand, so why was I so confused?

The Gare de Nord was as I remembered, gargantuan and gritty, yet the galvanic effect on me of leaving France was greater.

I did my best thinking in a crowded city. London was all that and a bowl of cherries - or cheerios, perhaps. Other than my tearing moral anguish, the past week drawing portraits as the consort of Mrs. Van der Heffelin's granddaughter was one of the grandest in my life. So jam-packed though, I'd barely had a moment for reflection. Before figuring my next move, I would need to study this cheeky chessboard and craft a survival strategy.

"Ello luv, need some company in the coach?"

He seemed affable enough, harmless, charming; his line was not one of the creepy ones lurking males in travel stations had used in the past. I was about to say, " No, thank you," when a tiny, translucent figure tugging at his trousers caught my eye.

"Hi," she said through slurps on her sucker, which I was sure would rot her nice baby teeth.

"Hi…"

"Sid," he said, "Short for Sidney. I'm Simon."

"Lucy."

"Hi, Lucy," her innocence shone like the North Star at night on the ski slopes back home and elevated my mood considerably.

"Cheers, Sid," and this is how four-year-old Sydney Langencamp came to sit squished next to me on the train, clasping hard my hand through the forty-five minute trip through the dark Chunnel tunnel, an esoteric transition from France to Britain, eliciting the natural nurture-nature in me. I would need every bit of that for Nikos or Camille Junior and myself.

"Are you a mummy?"

"What?"

"Are you a mummy," she repeated like she was a grown up and I was a tot.

As an American, I think of a mummy in the Egyptian term, as a deceased human or animal preserved through layers of chemical wraps, or more directly as Winona's worst Halloween costume that had fully unraveled by 8:00 o'clock.

I giggled. "I'm not a mummy, but I have a baby in my tummy."

Simon looked surprised. I offered this bit of information for him in case he fancied me as the new mum-in-waiting for the sweet girl leaning on my knee.

"Where's your husband?"

I find it rude when strangers ask such personal questions, but as a person of integrity, I tell the truth, ya know, whenever possible. That is to say, in any context other than the accident.

"The child's father is in Paris."

"You're not married?"

Surely he could see my choice to avoid the issue, yet had the gall to press ahead in this direction as the train flew out of the tunnel at Dover, rode through green and rolling countryside less flat than France, and hit the south London suburbs at Bromley, a sore, sad sight, though less so than the scattered refugee camps we'd seen outside Calais at Sanpete.

We hit the six-lane expressway spilling us into London proper at Hither Green, Lewisham, and Peckham. Simon pushed for personal details as we crossed over the Thames at Southwark. I owed him nothing but kindness to his dear daughter. We would soon part ways at St. Pancras, which is peppered with chic boutiques not found at the grim Gare Du Nord.

I knew my destination like a homing pigeon. The Penn Club, the most reasonable spot on the block between Russell Square and Bloomsbury Square. £82 per night for a single with a sink, shared bath, and full breakfast included. The Quaker accommodations perfectly suited my needs: no tellys in the rooms to distract me, and a common TV and shared reading room. This fun spot was the reliable getaway for Pascal and me before he took ill: a week's stay there would cost less than the refunded room charge from Hôtel Athénée.

Hopefully, they had a room available. I desperately needed a bed on which to lay my weary head. Hopefully, the staff wouldn't recognize me. It had been a while.

"Gaudí."

I didn't notice him come in. He puffed in like air and sat himself in the chair opposite me as I took a look at the book on World Architecture Theo gifted me in Lille.

"Gaudí is my favorite. Y tu?"

"Same." I beamed on high watt at the marvelous memories of traipsing through Barcelona slurping in the titillating, shiny tiled, multi-tiered works of the Spanish genio Antoni Gaudí.

He moved and sat himself beside me. "Are you familiar with this guy, SunRay Kelley?" I pointed at the page.

"Sure. SunRay is a spectacular world builder: Harbin Hot springs Temple, Hobbit like tree houses. Anyone who's anyone is hip to SunRay."

"I never heard of him before."

"Well, I hail from Berkeley. Anyone who's anyone in the Bay Area knows of the Vesuvian, adroit ingenuity of Kelley's creations."

A weak, "oh..." escaped from me. I didn't wish to give away I had a fake B.A. in design from The University of San Francisco and knew little of my supposed alumni environs.

"The artist reaches into the recesses of their mind and ratchets up two-dimensional magic. The architect, infusing geometry into the artistic creation, manifests 3D dynamic, circumambient chock-a-block interactive art." He snatched the air from in front of my face with such finesse that I expected a white rabbit to hop through the reading room and led us off on a Looking Glass Adventure through Neal's Yard in Covent Garden and onto the moon.

"How many dimensions have you traveled to?"

"Me? Dim... um... just the basics, I guess. Ya know the three and, well, th… the fourth ya know like astrally when we sleep, or... or kind of like music, like I've heard about th… the circle of fourths and fifths, like musically." I wanted to disappear into an unseen dimension where pain and awkward pauses were a thing of the past.

Tom Haines was his name. He riveted me like a Rainmaker, only he wasn't selling me, conning me, hitting on me, or wasting my damn time. Tom was the real deal.

"We have a lot to talk about, kid. You are hip to the bliss of making art?"

"I am."

"You have artist written on your sleeve, kid. You've got a sky writing over your head," here he moved his hand a foot above my crown like a sweeping sideways blessing, " Artist - Lives - Here."

"It's that obvious?"

Tom Haines smiled. Lithe, he sported a South American drawl. I'd guess he was fifty but he looked much younger.

"What about you?"

"I'm a writer. I weave words like wisterian wonders ebbing and flowing into the time-space continuum of that which cannot be named."

"Wow."

"Yeah."

"I also teach high school English in Lebanon."

"Wow."

"Yeah. How long you in town for kid? I'm here a week for Spring break. London has never been more vibrant, irascible, chock-a-block full of shows and theatre from the best to the most brilliant of artists who will take you to dimensions never conceived of before. So, what do you say?"

"To what?"

"To what? To whit. To wit. To woo. To accompany me, comrade, as my artistic partner in crime. I'm headed to see Hockney tomorrow at noon."

"David Hockney has an exhibit in town?"

"Meet you here at 11:00. I have an extra ticket. Stefanie came down with the flu."

"Wow. Okay."

"Yeah."

A peek of sunshine snuck through the curtains like a sliver of Parmesan expertly shredded onto a Caesar Salad made with fine French finesse, waking me much earlier than planned. I sensed something was different, but wasn't sure what. I carefully considered while I dressed: white tee, jeans, a bit of lip-gloss, done.

The change, once realized, ought to have been welcome, but I was filled with fear. The morning sickness had stopped, just like that. I'd become attached to the new life growing within me, without which I would have no good reason to continue to run. I needed to find a health center, have a pregnancy test, ask my mass of prenatal questions, and prep for birth rather than lounging with pictures of I. M. Pei, whose work is too angular for me.

I love Hockney and wasn't happy to stand Tom Haines up at the last minute, but once I set my focus, it was impossible to reset. I did a quick search and found a clinic nearby called Womenscare. Hmm. That name didn't bode well. When I rang they told me they could fit me in Tuesday next. I raised my voice with such "oh-my-gosh-I-may-have-miscarried-I-need-to-get-in-today-panache"' that the curmudgeon, Natalie, relented and squeezed me in at ten.

On the Tube I was unluckily sat next to a terse, amateur technocrat. She was in a tirade over the gerrymander pandering that is so perversely present in politics these days. Her ashen-faced partner clasped a briefcase as though he was protecting a homemade bomb or a delicately glazed ceramic vase made by his slender fingered eight-year-old. With each stop he looked around suspiciously to see who might rush in to grab the boxy brown bag.

The one hip-to-hip with me was ruddy faced with a raised red rash she kept scratching like she was sanding a shelf. Her shrill tone pierced too close to my dread-filled morning head.

I swallowed hard, looked about with distrust, and tried to think louder than their chitter-chatter. I replayed the note I'd left at the front desk for Mr. Haines three times over.

"Dear Tom. A medical need has arisen this morning, nothing life threatening, but I must attend to it at once. If I don't make it back in time to go to Hockney, please don't wait for me. I'm so sorry for the short notice. I hope I can make it up to you. Perhaps we can take in another exhibit together or I can draw a portrait of you if you'd like. Sincerely, Lucy."

These few lines had taken me an hour to write and used up eight pages in my life review notebook. I hoped I hadn't blown a friendship with Tom, an eminently interesting, educated fellow with fine taste in art and much to teach me.

I studied the Tube map posted opposite me. The Northern Line, shown in black, is my favorite. It shot straight up like Cupid's arrow piercing the heart of London with love. Piccadilly Line was Tom's choice serving many of London's top attractions including Harrods, Hyde Park, Buckingham Palace, Piccadilly Circus, Leicester Square and Covent Garden. Ah, I love London. After living so long in Paris, it was a bit of bliss to hear English crisply spill from the lips of so many. Why is it we Americans have such a natural pull to the language; our language sounds better when spoken by the English, Scots, Irish, and Welsh?

Antediluvian Ash, Radical Ruddy, and I all stood to exit at once. The early morning crowd jostled us. A stout mother with a crying child clasped firmly in hand pushed forcefully past. I landed in the lap of Ash, directly on his case, "So sorry, Sir," my voice dysphonic with fear.

"No harm done, luv. Cheers then," he pulled himself up and escorted me from the car like a real gentleman. We may never be aware of the kindness that lives behind a brittle exterior beaten down by the bullshit bourgeoisie.

I found the Womenscare clinic two blocks away, shabby on the outside, antiseptic inside, with a perniciously packed waiting room.

"Have a sit. We'll get to you as soon as we can fit you in."

Stacks of magazines and a few battered books covered a tan coffee table. I picked up Ayn Rand's novel, Atlas Shrugged; it was heavy as a block of brick red molding clay. How long exactly do they expect this wait to be? The door opened and three more people trooped in.

I opened the book and randomly pointed at a passage, reading it with the same seriousness reserved for a fortune cookie scroll hidden in a tasteless triangular treat. An oracle it was.

"Who is John Galt," I read. "In bed," I added with a laugh that roused the bushy eyebrows of the fellow across the way. After another two hours that included a trip to the toilet with a key that hung from a ceramic cervix, they called my name.

"Luciana Petrokov."

Perfect. Lu ciana PET ro kov, Twenty pairs of eyes lifted from Page Six scandals and enviously followed me as I disappeared behind the door from purgatory to the scintillating land of cold metal scopes and tongue depressors.

After another twenty-minute wait, a tall nurse clipped in, "I'm Beatrice, what brings you here today, Luckyanna?"

Seven a.m. on a solitary Sunday, I shuffled ironically past prostitutes prepping for Paphian dalliances like I was in my flat passing the telly to go to the loo; short on pomp, hold the circumstance, jonesing for sushi, salivating for Sake. It was not a good time for me to drink.

The tintinnabulation from St. Anne's echoed in my head; just a month ago, dressed up in my blue Burberry best, celebrating the elegant passing of my last University test, I texted Brigitte when the car skid on the road. Now, wondering how to face the rest of my life, hungry and hankering hard for drink, I turned into a shoppe that flashed, FORTUNE TELLER, dug out some coins, flipped one in the air for flair, and upturned my petite palm with charm.

"Your future is bright," the savvy psychic slyly said, "They left you for dead, but better times are ahead." Gong. Gong. Gong. Let's hope she's not wrong.

My life was a Humpty-Dumpty scrambled mess. I adopted the indomitable spirit of the Arauoconos, who fiercely resisted the Incas and Spanish when they attempted to colonize them. This solid symbol is what I set as my guide, and it allowed me to move forward: my pregnancy hormones were stoic and heroic – fixated on protecting my child.

I had things to do on this fine day, which left no time to ride the London Eye high in the sky, though I winked at the Eye as I rode by, admiring her grandeur. In a jam-packed Book Shoppe, I submerged myself in a sea of birth texts recommended by Womenscare. I bought a manual by someone called Pippa, as much because her name made me grin as anything else.

Next, the purchase of prenatal vitamins was another dog-and-pony show. I stood for an hour reading ingredients with the same concentration I might use to translate an ancient alchemical text for saving the world. Though I had enough cash socked away for a down payment on a diminutive house in Idaho, I'd become a frugal minimalist. Without money coming in, price mattered. I bought the second best, less expensive brand.

I took the Piccadilly Line to Heathrow Airport to check out a possible plane ticket to lift me off the continent. Along the way, I stopped to listen to the pint-sized, salsa-dancing singer, Sammie Jay. Sammie brightened everyone's day with a voice big enough to rearrange atoms. If I have a daughter, I shall name her Sammie Jay; a son will be Luis Fernando, come what may.

"You're guileless, Lucy," Tom Haines murmured like a heart skipping a beat when we met up at Wembly SSE Arena for the Bob Dylan concert that even a fresh frugal minimalist could not turn away. Once again, I got the unused ticket of Tom's sick friend, Stefanie. Guileless he had called me the night we met. I longed for lack of guile, lusted for it. It had been a while.

"I am under no illusion that I am guileless, though I used to be. You seem to be through."

"What are you, then?"

"Green, young, naïve, caught in a game I can't possibly play. Hey, it looks like someone wants your attention," my mouth curled in merriment.

Tom turned. Standing behind him were twelve high-energy high school sophomores, his students from Beirut, in pairs of two, in tow for the concert.

We filed into the arena. I sat next to a fearless, chatty young woman called Adeline. She leaned in to whisper her delight to me throughout the night. It was good to have a girlfriend with to share this special affair.

An outstanding acoustic launched this auditory odyssey by the Nobel Laureate extraordinaire, then regally rolled into a revelatory *Desolation Row*, tangled up in nothing but the sheer syncopated prowess of my father's favorite songwriter. Charles "James Julian" Portraro shared his passion for lyrical music, in particular one Robert Zimmerman with me, his daughter Camille, from the earliest, elemental moments in my life. He'd hum *Blowin' In The Wind* as he rocked me to sleep in the nursery at the top of Boise's' haunted hill, where we lived. Though I was born ten years after *Slow Train Coming*, I inhaled Dylan with my first breaths, nourishing me alongside a bottle in dad's arms, safe then, from any harm. I looked to my left and there was my father clapping along. I looked to my right, and there on Adeline's lap sat Pierre.

"Tomorrow," I promised myself between encores, "I will spend the day alone in Hyde Park and watch the idealists bold and brash enough to get up on their soapbox, those who get mocked, trifled up, or unfairly labeled as crazy by narcissists that continue to annihilate all-that-is-good in this world. I'll sit with my journal and fill in the two hundred seventy squares I drafted for myself. I will answer my inventory honestly and set my course from there."

As Dylan soared into his final song of the evening, dad and Pierre, old and young, had snuck off to sleep with the spirits as Shakespeare's Scottish play niggled away at me.

"Tomorrow, and tomorrow, and tomorrow,
Creeps in this petty pace from day to day
To the last syllable of recorded time,
And all our yesterdays have lighted fools
The way to dusty death. Out, out, brief candle!
Life's but a walking shadow, a poor player
That struts and frets his hour upon the stage
And then is heard no more: it is a tale
Told by an idiot, full of sound and fury,
Signifying nothing."

Dear Theo,

I'm sitting on the grass at Speakers' Corner in Hyde Park, London, pictured on this postcard, and cracking open pistachios. A barefooted, bespectacled Irishman in a turquoise bowtie is making all the sense in the world in a well-mannered tirade: the greed, lack of accountability, and general manqué de respect humain pour les gens de ce monde. I have a searing desire to draw chalk flowers at his feet as a gesture of respect for his common sense of word and choice of neckwear. The turquoise, you see, prettily picks up the green in his eyes.

It's my twelfth time to London yet she is still a mystery. Each turn of a corner is a new discovery. Carnaby Street, for example, while no longer swinging, is peopled with an International crowd immersed in the hustle and flow of their ever-promising young lives. At twenty-seven I feel old and disillusioned in contrast, yet my ability to fall head over Thames for London has not diminished in the least. Falling in love with a city other than Paris feels like cheating, but the humor, history, and high tea make it next to impossible not to.

I'm here for a short time, not for a holiday, but to regroup as I await my ticket away, final destination as yet unknown, multiple stops planned. Today I filled in over fifty squares of my life review, and am pleased to report that until the Paris predicament, I was doing an upstanding job of honoring the integrity James Julian taught me.

I follow your family on Jon's Instagram. Harquint lost his wobbly tooth, I see! If I were there, I'd make certain he masters the art of spitting a waterfall through that space since the time of missing only one tooth is precious and fleeting. I expect he's under fine tutelage with you, Captain. I shall keep close watch to see when the other gives way, leaving him looking like an old man until the incisors and canines arrive and give us a glimpse of what his grown appearance will be: handsome, no doubt, as he takes after his papa.

Is Bub still reading Babar or has she moved on? The way she gobbles up words, I expect she'll be breezing through the classics in no time. Does she still shadow the footsteps of her hero, brother Gilberto?

I'm hardly alone on my journey. Pierre is a constant companion, playing hide-and-seek with my psyche, can't say as I blame him. He's quieted down some, but determined to ensure I'm ever aware of him. I am, and forever will be.

It's confirmed that you will be an uncle, Theo. They have given me a clean bill of health and a due date of November twenty-seventh. An adventurous Sagittarius; I can live with that.

I had a full go at the architecture book you gifted me. The book brought a new friend, Tom Haines, into my life. He took me to see Dylan at Wembly (a concert of a lifetime), though I had to forego his invite to Hockney in lieu of a date with a speculum. Lucky me. Tom and I plan to visit the Portrait Museum, a must for a Portraiture prima donna such as myself. You and Tom, kindred souls, would adore each other. Note to self: introduce you two.

Oh, good news! No more morning sickness! I'm OBSESSED, however, with guessing the sex of the baby. Today I've settled on boy, but what does it matter as long as it's healthy, happy, and bold enough to stand up for its beliefs on a box in a turquoise bowtie?

All my love, Lucy

A staccato blast awoke me in the maelstrom of a dream. "BEEP. BEEEEP BEEEEEP BEEEEEEEEEP!"

Confused, covering my ears like Ms. Mouskers after New Years firecrackers, still in my dream body, I crouched, cowering in a corner.

"Stay woke! Stay woke!" Hyper-vigilance rushed in undaunted and saluted, "On duty, Sir!"

Where am I? The puzzle pieces reassembled. It's 4:00 a.m., frosty window, slight sag to the single bed, new navy suitcases half zipped... I'm in London! But why am I here? Where's my rooster clock? Where is Miss Mouskers? A lock of hair on my crown stood straight up, Alfalfa-like. I slipped a large, round wooden pajama button in the wrong hole, fastened as it was in the fast of night. I spit down my bed head. The ceiling spun. Something was not right.

The dream... I tried to reel it in. The life review had subconsciously pummeled me like a pissed off prizefighter in a rinky-dink dive in Sioux City would, unrelenting and low.

ZING - *"You stole a book on ESP when you were twelve."*
ZOW - "But I returned it the next day! I stole nothing again."
ZING - *"But you were old enough to know better. Stealing is a sin."*
ZOW - "Zounds! Cut - me - some - slack, I've been a good girl, a really, really, good girl..."
ZING - *"You lied to your parents, your poor, sick parents. Every night you snuck out of the house to have drunken parties and sex with Hayden."*
ZOW - "I was fifteen! This is what fifteen-year-olds do!"
ZING - *"No, some lay tucked up to their chin in bed. You rebelled during their last year."*

The whirling continued. How was I to know they would get sick? I stepped up and took care of them both. I was the angel on the haunted hill, everyone said so. I loved my parents. They counted on me at a time I needed to count on them. At sixteen, I was nursemaid for mother and father, working round the clock, five lousy hours of sleep a night, and I graduated as valedictorian! Dad said his greatest gift, his grace, was me, his daughter. I did well!

"BEEP. BEEEEP BEEEEEP BEEEEEEEEEP!"
The wind whistled, rattling the heavily curtained pane.
ZING - *"You stole a life!"*

Guilty. Guilty. Guilty as charged, but I didn't mean to. Please, oh, please understand, I didn't mean to; it was an accident. Brigitte kept me on the phone. "Did you get my letter? Do you love me too?" She would not let me go. The car skid, I wasn't clear what was happening: the pole, the awning, the boy, the alley, and the scissors. I'm sorry. It was AN ACCIDENT.

"BEEP. BEEEEP BEEEEEP BEEEEEEEEEP!"
Blood trickled between my legs. Oh, no, the baby! Am I losing the baby? The fates have been fickle with me. I felt faint, opened the door to the shared bath. Serendipity sent Adeline, my bathroom mate, to the loo too. The unhinged honking half a mile away awakened her.

"Lucy..." She was tiny but caught me in her arms as I fell. "You're bleeding."

I laughed as she set me, sweating, on the floor, one pillow under my head, the other propped beneath my knees, as though the whole thing was hilarious rather than terrifying; a ten-year-olds slumber party instead of jellied breath and a queasy quagmire concerning Sammy or Luis Fernando and I. I was pitched into momentary darkness like a blackout on our block in Boise after a thirsty thunderstorm downed the wires.

"Hello, Taxi? I will need a ride to hospital." My Dylan concert mate kept a level head.

"No, no, no, no," I cried inside, but no words came.

Legs elevated higher than my heart, head propped up on two, too plump pillows, torso sunken down, the bed in hospital contorted into an impossibly uncomfortable *S*. My arm bruised like they'd put me through the blender on high. The cavalcade of yellows, greens, and blues made me long for a watercolor set so I could splash those hues onto a canvas, distancing them from my person and magically floating away from this insidious dream.

My crotchety mood tempered somewhat when who should come into focus but Tom Haines and Theo sitting like old dear friends casually chattering away?

"A person tired of London is a person tired of life, yeah?"

"Absolutely agree, Tom."

"Have you made it over to the White Cliffs of Dover?"

"Yes; brilliant day trip, that. Spectacular views. How about the North Country?"

"North and West..."

"Theo?"

"Bonjour belle. You gave us all quite a scare."

"How did you get here?"

"Eurostar. You owe me £60."

They laughed. I froze.

"I'm kidding, love." He came over and kissed me on the forehead. Tom Haines mirror-imaged him on my right side. They like boyish bookends made me blush, amazed at my great fortune for attracting these caring, artistic, articulate wunderkinds.

"But how did you find out?"

Adeline, who I hadn't spotted yet, stepped forward. "I found the Hyde Park postcard on your desk. I searched for Theo's name and address on the internet."

Oh, no! My mind spun like a whirly top. What did I write on that postcard? How much of my situation did I give away? My head dropped back down, and a nurse with a badge that read 'Marlene' offered me water from a pink plastic cup with a straw crooked just like the bed.

I took a long, slow sip.

"How much is this hospital stay going to cost me?"

"Nothing, you're covered for emergencies in England. Let's get you up for now."

Mahogany-haired Marlene lowered and leveled the bed with a buzzy button and hoisted me erect. She hooked my arm like walking her granny to the grocery store and led me to the bathroom. I was weak and woozy. Once in the tiny toilet, I noted the IV, a towering pole of infirmity attached to my left hand, covered by bloody gauze.

A chill rippled down the thin gown that was Velcro-ed in the back. Stupid paper clothes are humiliating to patients, but sky blue *is* my color. I leaned in to the mirror to assess my condition. I was pale like momma's favorite china tea set, the one inlaid with pink roses laced with gold, but since I looked good, I figured I might be okay, but what about the baby?

Back at the bed, there was activity to get me discharged.

"It's early, but we did an ultrasound, anyway. There is a good likelihood you will see your pregnancy to term but your hematocrit is low. You must change your diet and take supplements. Do you understand?"

"Yeah, sure." I didn't really. My confusion cracked through.

"More steak and kidney pie for you, kid," Theo chided.

"I don't eat meat."

"Well, the babies want something they can gnash their teeth into and grow strong on. Hamburgers, liver, bangers and mash."

"Babies?"

"It's early to tell. You'll need another ultrasound in a few weeks so we can be sure. Does your family have a history of twins?" Marlene, pretty and patchouli-ed, pulled the needle from my arm with the same yank I used to dislodge the pump at the petrol station."

"Ow!"

"You're fine."

"But I... I was just bleeding..."

"Women sometimes spot during pregnancy."

"Can I still run?" I couldn't process all of this information.

"Ease up for now. Walk instead. Get yourself a good doctor when you get home."

Home? I looked panicked. Theo patted my un-bruised hand to help ease my mind.

"It will all sort itself out, Lucy. Come on then, we'll step out so you can get dressed. I hope you're still up for the National Portrait Gallery. I didn't come all this way to sit in hospital. Let's go see some art."

My friends filed out, Marlene handed me a pen for my John Hancock, and I slipped back on my tee and jeans: one leg for Luis, another for Sammie. Twins! What would Nikos say!

"Tanta Lucy! Tanta Lucy!"

Three small humans encircled me like bees buzzing around Queen Ann's Lace. Bub, with a new stuffed elephant clasped to her chest, motioned with an open-close, open-close of her three free first fingers for me to pick her up. Though I was weak I scooped her up. Little summer-sanded legs encircled my hip and casually crossed at the ankles as though she was in a recliner. "Babar," she grinned, nose kissing the blue fuzzy on my face.

Gilberto held my free leg as if he were hugging an oak for stability, and Harquint, dear Harquint, smiled wide to show me where his new big boy tooth was poking through the pink of his gum. How is it that kids can look so much older in just a few weeks!

Theo crinkled cutely at my surprise, "The family insisted on seeing you."

Jon came round shyly to claim his hug. He held on tight, belying his crisply controlled connection to me. Only we two knew of our parting in Lille. Our secret.

Two of Tom's students, Dani and Imad, wiped sleep from their eyes and enervated our group. We walked en masse to a classically British pub at an hour so early it was obscene. They all huddled around me taking selfies as I picked fussily at a Steak and Kidney pie. The days of soft scrambled and French yogurt seemed far-gone so swiftly.

We arrived at the National Portrait Museum just in time for the doors to open on a new day. Swedes, Chinese, Irish, Americans, Australians, Israelis, Pakistanis, and Romanians all moved forward in one cooperative push to soak in the artwork on display. Oh, if only the Governments of the world would take a cue from our queued masses. We were tired, poor, huddled together, yearning to breathe free, teeming, tempest-tossed into the golden door where we longed to get lost in art, or more. We held high hopes of touching the celluloid sky on a magic carpet painted by the brilliance of lives gone by.

They could barely tear me away from the Chandos portrait of Shakespeare, so named after The Duke of Chandos who owned the painting. I would have been content to stare at it all day, winnowing my way repeatedly through the tottering throngs also enthralled by it. The British are a brilliant mixture of crass and class. They are better literature scholars than my American counterparts, and their wry, dry humor suits me. I could easily live in London, the city as my lover without ever wanting for another, if I didn't need to hot tail off the continent.

I studied every stroke of chin, eye, nose, and the earring that adorned the Bard. Tom, Adeline, Dani, and Imad recited sonnets and soliloquies in a round robin and debated the Shakespeare authorship question as I fought indigestion from the meat pie breakfast.

As I finished my performance of Sonnet 90, *"Then hate me when thou wilt, if ever, now, Now, while he world is bent my deeds to cross..."* Tom, who *never* tired piped up.

"Hey kid, how about meeting us for drinks and dinner at the St. Pancras Renaissance Hotel? Bring your friends. Are you up for it?"

I was not, but hanging out alone in the room where I'd nearly bled to death was too grim, so after a nap, I paired Tanu's hoops with the emerald crop top from the fantabulous Fabien photo shoot and hopped in a cab. It was the first time I dressed up since the accident. Theo, Tom and I all arrived at once. With the pomp of Dorothy skipping down yellow brick, arm in arm with the Scarecrow and Tin Man, I entered the hotel.

"Ahh, ooo!"

The moment we stepped inside, my knees turned to rubber upon sight of the loveliest staircase in London, which exposed in me a tender chord. Pascal honored my penchant for climbing stairs used to bring me here to regally march The Grand Staircase like a Deb at her debut. I bewailed his absence, as one might miss their shadow on a sunny day.

Scarlet, burnt umbra, and rust unfolded like Japanese fans greeting the Imperial Family, stairs stacked like a heart-shaped house of cards from here to there to the moon. The cream on the walls, aqua ceilings, and blues underfoot harmonized, high notes over low, in rapturous rolling rhythms like tenors singing to the sea, gulls swooping and soaring overhead.

I swooned. My two unsuitable suitors, one gay, the other twice my age, caught me. "Hold on, Camille, still thy fluttering heart, radical, ecstatic beauty exists." They said this in unison.

Moments like these where steps ascend to the hemisphere of heaven in an innocuous place such as this carpeted hotel in London, swallow the atrociousness of the world. If you haven't been, I suggest you go. Leave your mind locked in a trunk and enter the angling elegance architects dreamed up for you, lose your virgin doubt, and allow your inner spirit to fly out.

Jon had shepherded the children back to their friend's flat hours before. Tom Haines excused himself back to his guests gathering in the lobby, giving Theo and me time to spend alone.

"How is Tanu?"

Theo deflated, a punctured balloon wisping and whistling its way down from the sky. "Not well." I steeled myself for some announcement of cancer.

"What is it?"

"Heartbreak."

"Oh, no, what happened?"

"Me, Lucy. I happened to her. Three children later and she has yet to recover She can't hold a job, doesn't take care of her house; hits pits of depression. She's returning to Greece."

Captain Fun collapsed into my breast. He buckled and we sat together as one on the top step of the spiraling stairs; people swished past, some stared, sobered by Theo's tears. Others didn't care and sniffed in disdain as if we were stones to kick out of the way. I held my friend, as he had held me in my hours of need. When no words come, friends hold on and hum.

The children loved their mother. I was ashamed I'd been so swept in my drama I hadn't been available for Tanu who remained an enigma: sweet in a moment, sour the next. Patient at noon, then tempestuous at one – but which of us hasn't had our own roller rides in life?

My body decried it was past time for me to go home. Tom slid up to say good night. "We leave town tomorrow night, Lucy. If you're free, meet us at breakfast. My group has grown fond of you and would love to spend our last day in your company."

"I'll see you back," Adeline appeared as though she were a genie misting out of a chalice.

"Oh, no, I can make it on my own, Addie, stay on if you want."

"Right," she laughed, led me to the street and hailed us a taxi for the second time that day.

Europe had been my home, an unbridled playground, for the past three years. The thought of leaving frightened me. I needed to ground and focus. Back at my room, I took out the notebook, divided a page into two columns and in my best printing wrote out the following questions. Blue ink for Camille; black for Lucy:

What is your full name?
Any nickname?
How old are you?
When is your birthday?
What is your family like?
What are you good at?
What are your hobbies?
Who is your best friend? Why?
What are you attracted to in a mate?
What would you die for?
What are your goals and dreams?
What is your biggest fear?

My answers are below.
WHAT IS YOUR FULL NAME?
CAMILLE: Camille Lisette Portraro
LUCY: Luciana Petrokov (Lu ciana PET ro kov)
ANY NICKNAMES?
CAMILLE: Cammie, Cam, Camster, Belle
LUCY: Lucy, Luc, from Luciana. Belle
HOW OLD ARE YOU?
CAMILLE: 27 and a half
LUCY: 26
WHEN IS YOUR BIRTHDAY?
CAMILLE: October 23, Scorpio
LUCY: April 8, Aires
WHAT IS YOUR FAMILY LIKE?
CAMILLE: My parents, Charles James Julian and Marissa Sabine, were da bomb. Mom died of melanoma and dad of pancreatic cancer. I was their caregiver beginning at fifteen. Mom said dad and I were "Two pickers in a pod." We played folk guitar, loved art, and read anything from CD covers to encyclopedias. We understood each other without words. My mother never thought she fully belonged to us, but she did. She was our opalescent abalone; dad and I wrote seven songs about her - five of them while she was still alive. Aunt Molly abandoned dad's care to me when I needed her the

most. She's skis, quilts, manages a Credit Union and likes to wear red, which indeed looks good on her.

LUCY: Uh-oh. I really need to figure this out. Oh, and I'm pregnant with a nebulous forecast of twins.

WHAT ARE YOU GOOD AT?

CAMILLE: Taking care of others, rescuing cats, drawing chalk portraits, school, skating, and singing.

LUCY: Normalizing an insane situation, living a camouflage life, drawing portraits, and posing for artsy calendars.

WHAT ARE YOUR HOBBIES?

CAMILLE: Art, ice-skating, travel and languages, music, and flirting.

LUCY: Art, architecture, life review. Hmm, I ought to figure out more.

WHO IS YOUR BEST FRIEND? WHY?

CAMILLE: Brigitte. She's my perfect BFF. She spins like a soft cyclone on skates, her laugh is like a mourning dove song, her M.O. was to grab my arm and say, "Come on, Cammie, we GOT this!" She loves me.

LUCY: I have three friends so far: Theo, Nina LaRue, and Tom Haines. Theo is my rock.

WHAT ARE YOU ATTRACTED TO IN A MATE?

CAMILLE: Truthfully, I think I still love Nikos, the twin's daddy. He's irascible, unpredictable, soulful, brilliant, and intense.

LUCY: I don't deserve to be in a relationship. I killed a five-year-old.

WHAT WOULD YOU DIE FOR?

CAMILLE: To see my father again, if that afterlife stuff really exists.

LUCY: I don't want to die. I have children to bear and nurture. My maternal instincts are succulent and ripe.

WHAT ARE YOUR GOALS AND DREAMS?

CAMILLE: To work as a chalk artist in front of the Louvre with Bertrand, the blues busker, as my partner. To travel the world, rescue kitties, and feed the homeless.

LUCY: To raise a healthy child or children, to avoid being harmed in jail, to make amends to the family of Luis Fernando.

WHAT IS YOUR BIGGEST FEAR?

CAMILLE: That my loved ones will continue to be torn from me.

LUCY: 1) Being caught or found out.

2) Never being able to make things right, not that I ever could.

"Mind The Gap," the reaching rumble reminded us in rapturous repetition not to fall into the abyss between coach and platform as we stepped from the train that stunk like white vinegar being poured into skunk kettle stew. Tourists all headed in one direction - our direction - flooded Waterloo Station. This did not bode well for our wait times in the sweaty snake-like queues forming to get to the World's tallest cantilevered observation wheel.

One hundred and thirty-five metres high, the fourth highest construction in London stood proudly next to the sparkling River Thames, alongside the former County Hall, and crickity close to the Southbank complex of elegant theaters and quirky art galleries.

"Mind The Gap," the audio echoed in a solitary statement like a pesky little brother no one pays any mind to, persistently tugging at one's jumper, "Let me play too!" And so we minded our steps as we cruised our way under the crushing sun, swept in waves of foot traffic towards the shore.

I wore the blue and white rawhide stripped cotton peddle-pushers I'd bought in Paris, my lilac crepe scarf tied like a pirate's bandana around my skull, knotted at my neck, long wisps hanging down my sweaty back. Adeline, in mahogany pants, a white tee and a cute cornflower hijab, which protected her head from the sweltering sun, was giddy, spinning in Sufi circles. The men and children of our group, who were comfortably casual too, formed an eclectic, international crowd that made my heart swell like the violins in Vivaldi's The Four Seasons. Enjoying this outing in this most iconic International city drove home the point that London would always be a regal, rallying point for the world, and come what may, Londoners will Keep Calm and Carry On.

As feared, the hook-shaped snarl of the London Eye line posed the question, "Do I want to stand in this uncharacteristic heat with small, hyper children all day?" I looked round at my comrades; no one but me seemed concerned. All were chatting gaily in Greek, French, English and Arabic.

"You see there, Gil." Jon squatted to kid level and pointed skyward with as much excitement as his monotone could muster; "We're going UP in the EYE where we'll have a view of the entirety of London!" The children gaped.

Jon was growing on me, showing dimensions light years from the stuffy pedant with the obsolete, superannuated ideas.

"Will we see St. Paul's Cathedral?"

"And The Palace of Westminster, papa?"

"Yes, we will: so right, Gil, exactly so, Harquint. Also Shakespeare's Globe, the Tate Museum, HMS Belfast, the Tower of London and Tower Bridge and Canary Wharf."

Little Bubindina, usually obsequious for a toddler, stared at Jon blankly, eyes crossed. Her comeback was to hold the stuffed elephant up towards my face and crow, "Babar!" I leaned over so she could rub it on my nose; the tenth Eskimo kiss of the morning.

Something about Bub's honeyed smile caused a chain-like reaction in me and, ever the opportunist, I chose that moment to pass Theo the postcard I'd written for him. "Read it later." He hugged me with such love I choked back sobs.

The Eye spun round, and my head spun with it – perhaps because of anemia, pregnancy hormones, or the paralyzing Paris predicament; in any case, I had to sit down stat. I plopped on the ground and the kids joined me. Our giggles attracted three Shih Tzus. One padded over to piddle nearby, which ended our little pavement party in quite a hurry.

The hours in line passed in fast and slow moments, hanging out with me mates, even sharing in the proposal of a man from Slovenia to a woman from Slovakia. Each of Tom's young students looked as though they were astronauts climbing aboard the first spacecraft to the North Star, as with awe and wonder, we filed into our capsule.

The ride up was magnificent; we marveled, ants looking to earth, at the statuesque sights shrinking in size. I peeked over to Tom. The view enraptured him, nose pressed forward, steaming a spot on the pane.

"I've never seen such beauty in the clouds," Adeline squeezed my arm.

"I hope to see London once ere I die," Tom Haines looked at Theo who replied without skipping a beat like a mirror self talking to himself, "Ah, I might see you there, Davy!"

The pink clouds parted like the red sea. I felt this viscerally as though they were opening within me. I had so much to experience, and at every turn, there were new companions to share with. Whether low, or riding high, our friendships ground us and allow us to soar. "Babar," yelled Bub as I bent down and got my twelfth Eskimo kiss of the day.

"Is that supposed to be me?"

"Yes."

"It's good."

"Thank you."

"It's a little too..." His eyeballs shifted side to side, carefully considering his words. The trees in St. James Park swayed in unison, waiting.

"What? Too what?"

"It's a little too flattering. I'm not that lush."

"Um, actually you are. I'm an excellent portraitist."

"May I purchase it from you?"

"No." I ripped it out of the sketchbook. "You can have it. A gift."

"I insist." He handed me £25.

"Thank you."

"Will you be here tomorrow?"

"I can be. What time?"

"Same time, half three. My wife will be miffed if she doesn't get one too. You'll have an easier time with her, she's much more tidy than I."

Word spread, and for the next week and a half I ran around London morning and mid-day and drew portraits in the park until the last light of day. I had to stay in Europe longer than expected until the leave date on my ticket. I was neither in a rush or resistant to the passing of time, but the days flew by: Bow Bells, Beefeaters at Buckingham, British Museum, Big Ben, and bargain theatre tickets in Leicester Square - I even got to see the brilliant Mark Rylance, whom I adore even though we clash on the Shakespeare Authorship Question. For goodness sakes, Mark, Shakespeare wrote Shakespeare. Leave it.

I window shopped Oxford Street, Foyles books, Notting Hill and Harrods, fed the pigeons at St. Paul's, and traipsed on the Dickens walk. And — the BEATLES! I visited St. John's woods to see Paul McCartney's house, posed on Abbey Road, and saluted the Trident Studio where George recorded *My Sweet Lord*. My dad would have loved it. We always planned to go on a tour of the U.K. together.

Everywhere I went, Luis Fernando was there; no Sundays off or late night chill out sessions. He sat across from me as I ate every type of sausage, steak, or hamburger I could find. I grew stronger, red blood cells robust, cheeks orchid pink, lips kissed with cranberry. The strength from the sun energized me too. The nausea was a thing of the past, hopefully gone for good and I threw away the soda crackers and ginger water. I walked - not ran - for hours a day, did push-ups, squats, leg lifts, slept soundly. Honestly, I'd never been better.

The tourists and Londoners were generous with me; they'd give me hugs, pecks on my newly flushed cheeks, braids of flowers, oranges, and once I got £100 pounds for a portrait. My income wasn't close to what I made at the Plaza, but that was a once-in-a-lifetime experience. The portrait money from the park was enough to pay for my room, meals and outings in cash. I spent it all so I wouldn't have to explain my income at customs.

I was so happy that guilt overcame me. The happier I was, the worse it got. I put my hands on my belly and sang a Spanish lullaby to the babies before bed. Then I sang to Luis Fernando.

>Cierras ya tus ojitos.
>Duermete sin temor.
>Sueña con angelitos
>Parecidos a ti.
>Y te agarrare tu mano.
>Duermete sin temor.
>Cuando tu despiertes,
>Yo estare aqui.
>
>Da, da... Da, da... Da... Da, da... Da...
>Da, da... Da, da... Da, da...
>Da, da... Da, da... Da... Da, da... Da...
>Da, da... Da, da... Da, da...

Close your eyes.
Sleep without fear.
Dream with angels
Similar to you.
And I'll hold your hand.
Sleep without fear.
When you wake up,
I'll be here.

Da, da... Da, da... Da... Da, da... Da...
Da, da... Da, da... Da, da...
Da, da... Da, da... Da... Da, da... Da...
Da, da... Da, da... Da, da.

THAT TODDLING TOWN

"Your ticket please," the cultured crackle of the upper crust Londoner landed like a lit cherry bomb, unnerving my pre-flight reverie, her forehead forced immobile as though overly botoxed, but no, it was part of the job, the faux smile, enjoy your flight, enjoy your flight, tension in the air, regarding everyone as suspicious. This was the last checkpoint to weed out me, the wild card from boarding. "Luciana." My shoulders locked, neck stiff, my own false smile lobbed back to her. They might catch me without warning. This was no way to live.

April in Paris, Chestnuts in Bloom, played in my head as I got settled in seat 15A, suitcase squeezed between my knees like I was exercising my adductors at the gym for a bodybuilding competition. Ella's finger-snapping rendition played robustly as though a phonograph sat at the rear of the plane, needle scratching in old-time charm, accompanying the choreographed machinations on each flight.

The gentleman with four-foot monkey arms stuffed a beat up berry blue case into the overhead bin for the bent grandma with lipstick bright as the August sunbeams over a caking hot cornfield in Iowa. A mother burped her baby, laden with a blankie peppered with big-eyed sheep jumping over misty moons, a broken pacifier, and purple polka-dotted squeeze-toy. She was eyed by every passenger already seated, "Please don't sit next to me," they telepathically told her, not a good message for me, a mother-to-be.

The tanned couple in matching shirts cooed constantly, foreheads together, forcing all within earshot to share in the afterglow of their ten days in paradise - Majorca, Spain perhaps? The location didn't matter. They had holed up in their honeymoon hideaway to explore every position and possibility as though these were the last days on earth and tantric bliss was their ticket to everlasting union with the divine. When they get home and struggle to pay the mortgage, their car breaks down, and his mother smothers her son with unwanted affection, the couple will pull out pictures from Shangri-La, and this will keep them going through winter.

No one gets off this earth without joy and sorrow was my takeaway from observing the parade of people filing past: a pretty girl, long chestnut curls like I used to have, clutched a guidebook and waved a tiny Union Jack, a souvenir from her week away, Russian accent flowed like red wine, lush, intoxicating. An obese man with kind, sad eyes sat next to her and her happy chatter stopped. My heart sank for him, "There's still time to exit the aircraft and hop a train back to Paris," I thought as much out of rote expectation than honest desire.

Eight out of ten people spent the last moments before departure buried in their phones, communicating with friends or strangers more compelling to them than the present.

The greatest prison is to live in a mind that doesn't quiver with curiosity from the crack of dawn until the last drop of black velour swallows the sky. "How does a quarter-inch turn change a profile, does dialect affect perception, in what ways will I contribute to the world?"

Gentle, funny, charming, unaffected by himself, Felipe from Lisbon sat in 15B. He held tight a book of crosswords and peeked at my drawing. "It's very good. You are an artista?"

"Yes."

"Where are you from? Where are you going? Have you thought of doing this for a living?"

Simple questions I could not easily answer.

"What is a ten letter word - the sixth letter is a G - that means fascinating?"

I wasn't sure if he was hitting on me. I looked at his puzzle book. "Oh! Intriguing."

"That's it! Obrigado!"

"De nada."

Buckle up, Camille, the ride has begun.

Ding. Ding.

"Ladies and Gentlemen, I'm Erin speaking to you on behalf of your flight crew. For your safety and comfort, please remain seated with your seat belt fastened until the Captain turns off the Fasten Seat Belt sign. If you're moving about the cabin, please return immediately to your seat. We won't be able to collect your…"

CHHHHAAAHHHH.

"Ahhhhh! (Ahem.) Put your food trays in the trash bags in the seat pocket in front of you so the contents don't fly about the cabin. We're going through some heavy turbu... turbulence and I apologize for the..."

RERRRRRRUUUUMMM.

"We apologize for the...."

KERRRRRUUUUUMMMMMMMMM.

"On behalf of your flight crew...."

CH… CHHH… CHHHH... UUURRRRRUUUMMMM.

"Just stay seated, and err, whatever happens, thank you for flying with us today!"

Erin sat, buckled herself in. Damn the passengers. She gripped the armrests, seat in upright position, tray table locked, as the aircraft seemed to slow to a molasses pull like an eighty-year-old man climbing out of quicksand with his grandchildren grasping hand over hand on his spidery forearms. A-one-two-three-heave-ho.

The moment she settled solidly in her seat, our attention was engaged by jaw-dropping jolts and lurches like a teen on her first day out to drive in papa's old stick shift pickup, only we weren't on a wide country road with plenty of width to wander in, we were high above the swirling turquoise sea. Sharks looked skyward, smacking their salty lips.

"Whatever happens," What kind of flight attendant says, *"Whatever happens?"* What might happen, I wondered, beleaguered, as images of deploying a bright construction cone orange inflatable vest, while plummeting deep into the Atlantic played on a loop through my brain?

"This seems p... p... problematic," Felipe turned to me with a false, quixotic grin, his voice cracking like a boy who just dove in the ice cold Arctic Sea. He'd been a fantastic seat partner for the first two hours of the flight; we chatted passionately about art over the chicken masala and then he asked if I would "mind terribly" to "have a go" at sketching him.

"I'd be happy to," I responded, and I was.

The light, quick beginning strokes formed the outline of his face, and just before the 'whatever happens' remark suggested a pummel to earth headfirst like drops from the Pha Pheng Falls spilling back into the Mekong River, I'd picked out a royal purple to use for his shirt, which was really a muted plum. His features were perfect for a portraitist: strong, squared chin with a slight dimple, (not enough to be a caricature, but enough to buckle a schoolgirl's knees), high cheekbones, symmetrical, wise-looking eyes, a scar over his right brow, adding intrigue and dimension, and a plush of hair so black it shone blue, swept over and back in a wave.

I summonsed all my volition to keep from screaming; the cabin seemed to close in on me like a hand closing around a fly. Felipe's perfect features pinched in, his caramel skin turned mustard, then lime and finally olive. He reached for the airsickness bag, but...

KERRRR-CHUUUUUUMMMBAKET.

...The plane shifted sideways a good twenty feet when down he dropped, eyes closed as though to the *sleep* snap of a stage hypnotherapist. His seatbelt cut into his slumped neck, inhibiting his intake of air.

Our eclectic group of passengers reacted rapidly as though we'd rehearsed for six weeks to perform *The Scottish Play* to a full house. I put away the purple and unsnapped the belt. The pragmatic mother, Bethany (whose little one, satisfied by her breakfast of breast milk, baby-snored through the whole ordeal), helped me lay him on the ground, so the blood could return to his brain. The man with the monkey arms slid a pillow under Felipe's head, hair tousled just so. I wished I could draw a picture of this scene. Was that wrong of me? I stamped the sight into my memory for later, hoping there would be a later.

From her seat, Erin, legs still in table pose, still gripping the armrests, barely turned her head, yet yelled in reprimand. "All passengers STAY SEATED!"

The cooing couple answered her back in perfect unison like a synchronized swim team. "We've got a man down here!"

The elderly woman, arthritic fingers hardened by sclerotic arthritis screamed, "We're poached!" The Russian girl unbuckled herself and rushed to the vacant seat next to her, interlaced her supple fingers with the crooked, shaking hands of the petrified lady and softy sang a Russian folk tune, *The Birch Tree,* to her. The melody had a calming effect on the lot of us. Felipe bolted up before anyone realized he had even come to.

"What's happening?" His wise-eyes now lost.

Then a BLAAAAKKKAHHHHH-KKKKKK, nearly knocked him and Buckley (the tall man), to the ground. They grabbed the tops of the seats. This woke the baby who burbled with joy and played pat-a-cake with the ten-year-old lad in the seat in front of her.

"This is your Captain, Nelson Nelson," crackled a voice that reminded me of the principle at our middle school calling for an emergency drug assembly that had no effect whatsoever on our irascible, loaded student body. "We've hit some bad turbulence. It will be a very rocky flight. We need all passengers to STAY SEATED. I repeat, STAY SEATED, remain calm, and God willing, we'll make it." He sounded shaken. Not a good sign.

"God willing? Whatever happens?" Who trained these people? The captain's message immediately agitated everyone. Alyona restarted the lullaby. It worked. It washed over us like a sedative. It jarred my cabin mates and me from side to side, up and down, with booms and hisses as though the wings were being ripped off by stegosaurus, for the next four hours.

We managed as a group of strangers in an emergency do. We introduced ourselves, taught each other songs and played peek-a-boo with little Olivia until she conked out again. When the flight emerged from the wrathful rocking pocket of cumulus quaking, I finished the portrait of Felipe.

It was the best flight I ever had.

Ding. Ding.

"Ladies and Gentlemen, for your safety and comfort, please remain seated with your seat belt fastened until the Captain turns off the Fasten Seat Belt sign. This will indicate that we have parked at the gate and that it is safe for you to move about. Please check around your seat for any personal belongings you may have brought on board with you and please use caution when opening the overhead bins, as heavy articles may have shifted around during the flight. We thank you for flying with us today and hope you have enjoyed your flight."

Hyped from airplane adrenaline, in that floaty time warp mist of intercontinental jet-lag, and having gotten no sleep, the light show in the O'Hare airport tunnel buzzed me along in my cranberry Abercrombies like a zombie. I was nearly paralyzed from processing American again. After three years abroad, American accents sounded harsh and flat, a mite malignant, lacking melody. The movements of my American counterparts were archingly ambitious - not always a bad thing - yet on this day they showed am impatient side. More than anything I sensed the absence of the depth of history that permeates European soil, a grounding grandeur, which endeared me to the land and her people.

    I was most grateful that the luggage Maria Van der Heffelin bought me wheeled so smoothly: not a squeak, a blip, or a burble. I decided this was my favorite airport.

    I was not, however, in a good mood. Our bumpy plane ride, anything but expeditious, arrived an hour later than expected. The airline personnel were not helpful, as my connecting flight - which I'd missed by thirty minutes - was with another carrier. I couldn't get a decently priced ticket out for four days; the timetable stuck me in Chicago, a city I had always desired to explore, albeit under more auspicious circumstances than this calamity.

    After the in your face, intimate imbroglio with the agents about my missed flight (an impuissant interchange) and the labyrinth of lines through customs, I spent fifteen minutes waiting in a busy bathroom. I crowded into a dirty stall with my bags to honor my ever-increasing bladder needs. Then, at long last, I spilled out onto the street without a cursory clue where I would take shelter.

    Lo-and-behold, serendipity sashayed her way into my lane, landing into my lap the ebullient Buckley, a hero on my flight from the moment he stuffed that beat up bag in the overhang.

"Lucy?"

"Yes," I turned to face him in full.

"Buckley Blakely," he held out his lanky right arm and offered me his hand that featured a fine set of elongated, perfectly formed fingers, an artist's hand if I ever saw one.

"Do you play guitar?" I gushed, unable to monitor the sophomoric statements came out of my mouth because of my serious lack of shut-eye.

"Mandolin."

"Oh!" I knew he was a music maker. I knew it! I could spot them miles away.

"I heard the argument with the agent about your predicament."

"Oh." How embarrassing! If he only knew about my real predicament, the one precipitated in Paris.

"Look, I'm hungry. I plan to stop and catch some Chicken Sichuan, my treat, if you'd agree to join me. Some friends of mine run an Airbnb near me. I hope you don't find this too forward, but I already made a call on your behalf. They have an opening."

On the ring finger of his articulated left hand sat a plain wedding band. I didn't want to lunch with a married man. Buckley caught the glint of the gold reflecting in my eye.

"I'll introduce you to Justine, my wife - she'll love you."

"Okay, thank you, Buckley. Let's go. Only don't expect any intelligent conversation from me, I'm zonked out."

"That makes two of us," he opened the door of the cab as the driver grabbed my bags.

"Ah. Wait! I'd like to sit with those, please!"

"You'll be much more comfortable without them, Miss."

"I might need... I... ahem... I..."

"As you wish." Buckley Blakely, my easy-going escort from the fiasco of flight 1515, intercepted like an All Star.

"My name is Inigo Montoya," I daintily stepped into the yellow cab, (glad it wasn't an Uber), and sat with one heavy bag on my lap and the other pressing precipitously into my side.

The cabbie turned around and looked me dead in the eyes, "You killed my father..."

Buckley let himself in on the other side, "Prepare to die," he completed the *Princess Bride* sequence setting the three of us off into fireworks of laughter as off we lurched into the Illinois Springtime, the best time, my father always told me, to visit Chicago.

Sandburg was right: Chicago is the city of the big shoulders. Wide too, like a Panama hat built to shade you on a scorching day. Sinatra was right too: you can lose the blues in Chicago, that toddling town, find 'em too at the Kingston Mines on Halstead, where maybe, just maybe, you'll hear snap-your-fingers, slap-your-knee, be-bop till you drop blistering blues. Wear your dancing shoes, I double dare you to listen and try not to move.

Like a tour guide toiling for tips, my father repeated this so often I had it memorized verbatim and would recite along with him in loving mockery. I loved the toddling town through his recollections. He had attended Northwestern as an undergrad, while living on the lakeshore in friend-filled Roger's Park. Two parties per weekend were the norm.

"If you ever get to Chicago, Camille, promise me you'll go to the Museum of Science and Industry, The Art Institute, and most of all, enjoy the nicest people this side of the Mississippi. Spring and fall in the Midwest are spectacular. Winter is wicked windy, and summer is hellish hot and humid. And take a boat ride. You got all that?"

"Yes, dad. I promise I will."

He'd settle back then, take his pain medication, and seem content. If his little girl made it to Michigan Avenue, he could die happy.

I arrived to an Airbnb in Evanston atop the Arnold-Applebaum estate. Evanston is the home to Northwestern, so my father's presence was even stronger there than at the Dylan concert.

Mr. Applebaum was Roy, the Mrs. was coy, they had a spunky little boy, and several pets. The first eve, they introduced me to their friend, Adam, a charming young filmmaker from North Carolina who knew how to clog. Jane played the piano, and I juggled apples, which excited Buddy, the Arnold-Applebaum dog.

Their house was a beauty, old but not ancient, clean with quirks and loaded with perks: a hot tub, workout room, large yard, easy access to public transit, piano, washer and dryer, housekeeper, and large kitchen. I had the third floor "suite" to myself. The suite = wooden beamed attic rooms, and a private bath with old-time separated sink spickets. I had to splash hot and cold together like I was clapping my hands for an exquisite ballet.

It was only half an hour commute to the city. Not bad at all. The A-As were generous. I would cook, or Jane would bring home grilled Soba tempeh and veggies from a health food restaurant in town. If we dropped something, Buddy would rush in and wolf it right down. They gave me a key and let me come and go as I pleased, all for a reasonable rate.

"Thank you Buckley Blakely!"

"Didn't matter if you were seven or seventy," Roy recounted, "politically charged Chicago in the 60s, awash with the Vietnam War, pulsed with patchouli worn by wayfarers walking above the Wabash waterway; for them, Woodstock was just a wish away."

The Illinois of today, a salt-of-the-earth blue-state anchored on the Windy City, was a melting pot of Polish, Irish, African Americans, Hispanics, Jews, Asians, and other races and ethnicities semi-assimilated by the thousands along Lake Shore neighborhoods and drier inland communities. Monoliths of modern architecture, jazz, blues, sports, hearty immigrant-influenced cuisine, and the arts provided a palate-with-pizazz for the tired, poor, huddled masses yearning to breathe free, and everyone hoorayed for Democracy.

The building that rocked my world was the multi-dimensional Museum of Science and Industry dad recommended where you can see chicks hatch, study the stages of an embryo, daydream by Colleen Moore's Fairy Castle, and spend days enjoying Chicago's best. I stayed only four hours since my time in town was scarce, then I headed over to the Magnificent Mile to window shop and explore the toyshops.

The Midwesterners went above and beyond the call of duty to help me out. One elder gentleman, probably late sixties, took two busses out of his way *just* to escort me onto the correct route. I asked him directions at a north side bus stop. I expected him to draw a map or point out landmarks, but he got on the next bus and motioned me to follow him. I did.

"Get a transfer," he put coins in the slot for me.

"One transfer, please."

He was not obtrusive; he gave me space by sitting rows away and looked out the window, minding his own business. He again sat through an entire twenty-minute ride, tapped me thrice on the shoulder, "We get off here,"

THE PARIS PREDICAMENT

when it was time to disembark. After pointing my way to the museum, he blessed me, and turned around to get on a bus headed back whence he came. This kindness knocked me out.

As with many places I visit, I fall in love with the people and surroundings and imagine I might happily live there long-term. It's a curious love affair I have with the world. At that moment, the culture and cacophony of Chicago had me hooked.

What I missed was Pierre whose steady presence had been conspicuously absent for days. I longed desperately to see him. Without his presence, I was nothing, an empty vessel without a conscience, lacking value. I looked for him everywhere, amongst the billowing crowds on Michigan Avenue, in the museums, on busses, trains, toyshops, and in each reflection of April sunshine lilting off revolving doors and glinting off freshly washed windows.

As I exited FAO Schwarz spinning from toy utopia, I spotted a girl of Luis Fernando's age with waist-length pigtails. She clasped a stuffed lamb to her chest. A man yelling fi-fie-fo-fum obscenities leaned over her. He smelled of vodka, an odor I was familiar with, having mixed it with boxed freshly squeezed orange juice early mornings behind Win Co. when I was sixteen. The burn of the liquor down my throat took the edge off the smothering grief from the loss of my mother, and the wretched melancholy of nursing dad in his last days.

"You're a piece of crap, Zara. You don't listen. You cost me money. You got your shitty little lamb, and that's all you're getting. Stop bothering me; I'm interested in your mom, not you."

Zara bit her lip and whimpered. She looked to me for help. I jumped right in; scooping her in my arms. I wiped back her tears. "You're strong and wonderful, Zara, and have a lot to give the world. Where's your mother?"

With one finger in her mouth, she pointed, "There."

I set her down, and she ran to her mother who was gabbing and laughing with another woman down the block, oblivious to the bullying of her daughter by her jerk boyfriend. When I turned back around to face him, he grabbed my neck, pressed his thumbs into my epiglottis, trying to crack apart my hyoid bones. As Michigan Avenue spun and went dark, I finally spotted Luis Fernando - at last he came back to me!

"There's some leftover Soba on the stove, Lucy, help yourself!"

"Thank you!"

"How was your day?" Her rosy voice reverberated from the living room.

"It was great," I lightly fingered my bruised neck and gently swallowed a few bites of the cold, sesame flavored noodles, testing, testing, testing to see if I could still swallow.

Diane sat grandly at the piano, Buddy snored sloppily at her feet, Roy and Jake, I assumed, were already in bed.

"Sit. Tell me what you did today."

"How about a rain check for tomorrow? I'm exhausted."

She clicked her drink down on the piano: white wine, two glasses a night. The melody of *For No One* poured magnificently from her hands onto the ivory and ebony keys.

I sat. She turned her body half toward me. We sang.

My mind did break and ache, just like the lyrics said.

Her form blurred into the Magnificent Mile milieu: the two policemen who asked my name, took a report. "Are you okay" the man who had pried Jacob off of me wanted to know. Ew, he had a name. The creep. The asshole. The bully. The girl's mother screamed at him, "Jacob, fuck you, Jacob, no more. No more!" The girl cried and eyed me with sorrow, Luis Fernando just behind her, like her shadow. A crowd gathered. A reporter showed out of nowhere. A microphone thrust in my face. They called me a hero. They called the man who saved me a hero. I'm no hero. I killed a boy in Paris. I don't want my name in the paper. Officers cuffed Jacob and took him away. All I want is to be low-key, but life keeps crashing around me.

The song pulls me back.

"... La la la la la la la LA."

I cry. Diane stops playing. She positions herself next to me and gives me a sideways hug, lays her shoulder on my sore neck, unaware this hurts me. She stinks of wine and garlic.

I drag myself to my room, splash hot and cold together to wash up. Soak a thin washcloth in icy water and hold it over my eyes to calm the throbbing in my temples until it's warm from the heat of my skull. I fall asleep on my back, knees propped with a pillow. All night long I dream of texting Brigitte, the pole toppling, Nikos kissing me, Tanu in her tousled apartment packing for Greece, a girl in pigtails, innocent as the dew looking to me to help her, hands choking me. I awake with a start. The lingering image is of my father dying.

"Take a boat ride."

"I promise, dad, I will."

"Lucy? Lucy, are you okay?"

I turn the clock towards me. It's 3:00. I'm not sure if it's day or night until the light peeks through the shades. I slept for nearly fifteen hours. I needed it.

Ding. Ding.

"Ladies and Gentlemen, for your safety and comfort, please remain seated with your seat belt fastened until the Captain turns off the Fasten Seat Belt sign. This will indicate that we have parked at the gate and that it is safe for you to move about. Please check around your seat for any personal belongings you may have brought on board with you and please use caution when opening the overhead bins, as heavy articles may have shifted around during the flight. We thank you for flying with us today and hope you have enjoyed your flight."

Liftoff and landing were right on schedule this time. The four hour thirty-five minutes in between was smooth like a Snow Valley ski run on perfect powder with a side of sun cups.

I sat in a middle seat between Mel, a sedate octogenarian from St. Louis, and Marcy, a politically swarthy, cantankerous woman, a few years his senior, from the near North side. Her cri de coeur was that American healthcare was going to hell in a handbasket, and I agreed. For the full length of the flight, a slim hardcover book, *How To Cook A Quince*, lay opened on her tray table.

My seatmates, well acquainted with the town, insisted on hearing my perspective as a visitor and so I talked an easy, fast flow like the guy on the soapbox at Speakers' Corner.

"What's the best part of Saint Louis?" Mel asked like a seasoned 1950s comic in the Catskills.

"What?"

"Chicago!"

It took me, a non-native, a few minutes to get the joke, but Marley brayed with laughter. Then it hit me: ninety-two-year-old Marley was flirting with Mel, using me as the conduit! I asked if she might want to change seats with me but she ignored my question and asked me about my windy city experience as though it was of the utmost fascination.

They leaned so far over me, conducting their shy little budding romance, that I angled my seat back right into the lap of the large man behind me who was none too happy about it.

I was in a chatty mood. I described the breathtaking boat ride on Lake Michigan as a pearly ode to my father, James. I waxed lyrical about the Buddy Guy tribute at B.L.U.E.S on Halstead, enough to make the head of an Idahoan soar among the stars. I tried to explain the pull a voluptuary painting by Georgia O'Keefe had over me at the Art Museum, but words failed me. I had been fixated like super glue to those five-foot perfect petals.

I even sang the praises of my daily six mile jogs through Lincoln Park, weaving on and off the waterway, soaking in the city in the way I loved: with pavement, dirt, and grass under foot, allowing the energy from Illinois earth to enter my body and call my soul alive.

Upon arrival, a tall man with angular arms kindly retrieved my bag from the overhead compartment; I flashed in a sudden sweat back to Buckley Blakely and my other cabin mates on the Cuisinart blender flight into O'Hare.

"Hey Marley."

"Yes, Lucy?"

"How DO you cook a quince?"

Mel laughed so hard, I thought he would split in two, his grey face blushing like bottlebrush; bushy brows jumping up and down like Groucho's. I steadied him under one arm, Marley under the other, as I leaned in and whispered in his good ear, "Did you get her number?" Well, this set him off into hysterics again, this time bent over in a coughing fit, as the flight attendant looked up to see if we might need to call the paramedics.

Arlo Ricoco, the notorious mystery writer, had invited me to stay as his guest if I ever made my way to San Francisco. Arlo was the Nom de guerre for Jim Bushinell of Rochester, New York; his name change helped him rocket to stardom, Ricoco sounded more enigmatic than Bushy, his former pen name. The fans took to it like dry ducks to wet water. He and his wife were some of my favorite portraiture sessions at the Plaza, though she, Donalise, had slight narcissist tendencies, they weren't enough to make friendship with her a deal breaker.

She had plenty to be proud of: the daughter of a Wall Street mogul, she eclipsed nepotism and founded her own iconic perfume empire, *Freaking Fragrances*. With a certain amount of distance, there is no one so imminently entertaining as a mystery writer from Nyack with a marvelous Manhattan maven by his freakin' side.

After a limb-lengthening yawn, I emerged from the airport into the dew soaked, rain soaked, sun-touched air. I became one with the Petricor, the sweet, musty fragrance of the nourishing natural world that gave off enticing earth pheromones that stimulated my grunting, just-getting-going, game face. Boarding the Bart train with my bags, the lyrics, *California Here I Come*, seamlessly replaced, *We will dance the Hootchy-kootchy, I will be your tootsie wootsie, if you will meet in St. Louis.*

A sun-kissed maid said "'Don't be late!"

That's why I can hardly wait.

Open up that golden gate

California, here I come.

I sung aloud as I headed for my stay with the Ricocos.

MATSAKO AND MATT

Her lava orange Porsche careened street side ten feet past me, revved and reversed and, like a shaken baby, gave a double forward and back bobble before coming to a full halt. How is it that with my lifetime of safe driving, one minute of texting ended in tragedy but all the yahoos out there who drive like drunken stallions were fine? Donalise leaned over like she was stretching in sun salutation, pushed open the passenger door, and lowered her Saturn-sized sunglasses to size me up.

"Welcome to sunny California, Lucy. Throw the bags in the back."

She shifted aggressively into first gear and shot up to the top of Lombard Street, one hand on the steering wheel circle-wiping her way up the winding roads like a window washer giving final polishes on the Empire State building lookout glass. Her other hand tapped on her lap, a la finger dancers doing a French gavotte, high on cocaine, the extra energy needing discharge through any available appendage.

She left both bags for me. Perhaps she didn't want to break a nail by helping; as an artist, I noticed how beautifully done they were. Tiny palm trees, perfectly arched rainbows, and twinkling sparkles in the sky. Kudos to nail crafters; I'll stick to sidewalks.

Framed in the foyer, the first thing I saw were the 'his and her portraitures' from France. I set down my bags to stare. They looked great! I did this! I am the artist! Art is a superpower, a corporeal gift, something not everyone has. The pictures, hung so prominently, reflected the bright afternoon light; I cried tears of joy.

"Emmylou," a Japanese girl who looked to be fifteen, (but later told me she was nineteen and that her given name was Matsako), handed me semi-warm ginger water overflowing with fizz. Who serves ginger water? Were they aware of my situation? I quivered with paranoia until I saw Donalise sipping a glass too. She launched into an espousal of the benefits of ginger for the alkaline balance of the body. I agreed though I found Donalise to be preachy. She seemed full of herself, a quality I'd noticed in Paris and sneaked into her portrait.

We three sat for a chat in the living room.

"Matsako is such a lovely name. How did you choose the name Emmylou?" I was familiar with the complexities of choosing a nom de guerre.

"Miss Dona choose it for me."

I looked to long nails for an explanation.

"Emmylou Harris is Arlo's favorite singer."

Wow! The nerve! Matsako shifted awkwardly and sat coyly on her hands as though stifling the desire to take a punch at Miss Dona for imposing her husband's name choice upon her. Just as I was going to ask if Matsako wanted me to call her by her *actual* name, Arlo's voice boomed in the front door followed by a blast of his energy like a tropical storm.

"Welcome, Lucy! How was your flight? You honor us with your great presence in our humble abode!"

Humble? Their stately house sat atop an awe-inspiring serpentine street in a state with a golden gate and a shy servant who bites her lip as she serves ginger water.

He approached and bear hugged me for an inappropriate count of five one thousand.

"Your future is bright," the soothsayer in Soho had said, "They left you for dead, but better times are ahead." I thought back to life with Bertrand. I could not afford the luxury of that too often because it opened up a sinkhole and I, like a wooly mammoth stuck in a tar pit, struggled to pull my way out. If redemption was ever coming for me, I didn't see it happening here in the lap of mendacious spiritual materialism.

When I needed to feel grounded, I counted to myself, annunciating each number with deliberation accompanied with slow breathing in and out, in and out. One. In. Two. Out. Three. In. Four. Out. Each breath striving for an ideal that would move me forward with meaning: complex as an azimuth, wild as midnight wolves, and fundamental as my father's love, though I so rarely feel his presence during these heady, unsteady days on the road.

They set me up me in the room next to the Ricoco baby, Rocky, who I hadn't even heard about until I got to their crooked street with the hairpin curves, Gamelan gongs, amethyst-laded altars, and phony New Age nonsense. In France, Arlo and Donalise paraded through Paris like rock stars for the signing of Arlo's, *The Silent Staircase*, (which shot to number one on five international lists), leaving young Rocky in the care of a morose Matsako, who suffered severe sleep deprivation as his sole charge.

Ten-month-old Rocky Ricoco was a poor sleeper. He napped well during the day and began his shady shenanigans at night coming to life about midnight and not settling down again until sunrise, by which time I was discombobulated - insomnia-by-proxy. From the next room over, it sounded like he was presiding over high court, practicing to be a helium-inhaling cartoon voiceover artist, or was being eaten alive by a posse of possessed lemmings, as a cavalcade of screeches and hyena type screams ricocheted off the walls, grabbed me by the tootsies and tossed me like a flapjack in the most comfortable King-sized bed I'd ever made the acquaintance of.

The first night I stuffed Kleenex in my ears, set a pillow atop my head like a pillbox hat, and finally fell asleep by 3:00 a.m., only to awake again by six a.m.

The second night, (after a stolid daytime snooze), I sat up sketching amaryllis, the delectable belladonna lily in particular. I spontaneously signed the bottom with a poem:

"To darling, daring Matsako,
flowers from Luciana to you,
Belladonnas pink, sky so blue
I suggest you tell Dona you're through."

I did not give her the drawing.

The third night I tiptoed in and tried to soothe the rambunctious Rock. I sang the poorly parented miscreant the Mexican lullaby, bounced him on my shoulder, played hide-and-seek, and spun playful pirouettes with no luck. Rocky stood in his crib cooing and applauding, pleased to have a private one woman show come to entertain his highness.

I had to do something. I was in town for business, had no interest in touring the Bay Area in blurry-eyed delirium; frankly, I'd had enough of this ridiculous Rocky Ricoco rigmarole. I purchased a pretty piccolo in the Haight and played it for him like the Fairy Queen in a Midsummers Night Dream. Rocky slumbered on his side as though a sleeping dart had pierced his heart, one knee tucked up, thumb in mouth, bamboozled by the beauty of the dulse melodies. Getting him to run in circles around the ample-sized nursery first, I'm certain, did the trick, but I like to imagine music charmed this young man, whose life I did not envy.

"Oh, such sweet sounds last night!" Matsako poured us freshly squeezed juice made with oranges picked in the backyard.

"Thank you, Emmylou," Arlo sipped his with a straw, a red woven Guatemalan napkin securely on his lap.

"What was that crap?" Donalise slid in her seat, barely a glance at her baby. "Lucy..."

I turned as though shot.

"Would you like to come see the *Freakin' Fragrances* headquarters today?"

Seven hours of sound sleep had restored a juvenescent joy to me. "Yes, that would be lovely," I jangled out without forethought.

Ah, well, curiosity killed the cat too.

"Lucy!"

Matsako ran to catch up with me. She pushed a hyperactive Rocky in a pale yellow stroller, all four limbs moving as if he were an octopus doing interpretative dance, high on ecstasy.

"Lucy!"

"What is it, Matsako?"

She bent over holding her ribs. At first, I wasn't sure if she was laughing or crying.

"Are you okay?"

"Yes, it's a pain, here, it will go away in a minute."

I paused, reverently taking in the view; moisture from an early morning rain ladled pretty puddles on the ground reflecting a kaleidoscope of fern, viridian, and pink taffy hues onto the water. San Francisco from up high was an artistic inspiration. I zeroed in on a piece of pavement that a furtive couple walked on, which I was keen to chalk on. I would ask the neighbor later if I might draw a washable mural there. It's hard for people to say no to art.

"Lucy," she began again. "Let me go with you. If I have to stay alone one more day in the house with," she nodded at Rocky, who stretched like a bear upon awakening from his winter hibernation, "I'll go mad."

"Emma. Up. Upa."

"No, no, no, Rocky, not yet." She handed him a raspberry rubber ring to teeth on; he chewed contentedly, with a slimy drip of drool running down his chin.

The couple clipped past, heads averted, looking as though immersed in a clandestine consociation and hoped to be invisible. I made a mental note that when trying to hide, it's best to stand up straight and bold.

"Matsako, I have business in the city today," I touched the map in my pocket and coughed out my wormy words. I did not have a solid plan other than to buy a wig and traipse around taking selfies, photo bomb a few people so it would look like I'd had friends in the town where I got my design degree.

"Please," she squatted and zipped up Rock's plaid jacket, pulling the hood over his ears to ward off the wind.

I was stuck in mire. Matsako needed adult company and I could use a companion.

"Okay. You know what? Today is your day. You choose where we go. Anywhere."

She squealed with jubilation as though I'd handed her a winning lottery ticket. "Oh, thank you, Lucy. Arigatou gozaimasu," her hands in prayer pose. Rocky, imitating her, clapped and crowed.

"A companion and a half," I corrected myself silently.

Luis Fernando appeared behind the stroller, he in a hoodie too. Make that three. It was a full house today.

Matsako kicked into gear with a kinetic energy verging on mania until we got to the Steinhart Aquarium in Golden Gate Park where she finally relaxed. We spent the day luxuriating in a breathtaking array of beautiful sea life, including a polka-dotted stingray and hungry piranhas, in a building that stank like spoiled sushi. We concluded the day viewing a vibrant Philippine coral reef and lush tropical rainforest.

Our last stop was the gift shop where I dropped fifty dollars buying Bub, Harquint, and Gil rubber alligators. I had a great time with Rocky, and even given his nighttime hi jinx, being around him brought out my maternal side. I was getting excited about becoming a mom!

The day unfolded so well I had forgotten about Donalise Ricoco and the scent factory field trip planned for the following day. As we walked by a group of ten hippie jugglers in the park, a wave of longing for Bertrand and Brigitte swept through like a warm wish.

On the way back home, Rocky and Matsako slept on the bus as I fretted over the ground I would have to cover by cramming a supposed four years of University into a compacted tourist trip. An African American man holding a djembe drum got on at Webster Street and winked at me. Things could be worse. I think I will like San Francisco.

I had a headache from playing Pachelbel on the piccolo for Rocky Ricoco at three a.m.

I had a headache from trying to speak Japanese with Matsako.

I had a headache from the fumes at the friggin' *Freakin' Fragrances* factory.

The perfume making process combines natural ingredients with distillation technology. It dragooned raw chemicalized substances, blended them with ethanol, and turned out as mist sprays for palms, or perfumes dotted behind ears and rubbed on the nape of one's neck to make one smell enticing. I never appreciated the appeal of cologne; I like my men smelling of sweat and pheromones rather than being doused in eau de anything, and I didn't want my growing fetus exposed to this sneeze inducing, alcohol laden, cinnamon, citrus, musky, animatic, flowery, or woody wunderkind concoctions that made me wither, not wish to come hither. He or she would need to develop a histocompatible antigen to fight the autoimmune challenges from pulsing perfume toxins.

Donalise is an accomplished businesswoman with acumen, who sadly lacks ethics. She launched a production warehouse, which yields her a lucrative living, allowing her to live in a big house on the hill no matter whether her husband's novels tank or bloom; his books have done both. She treats employees like lowly peasants blessed to be in the Queen's perfumed presence. I think she would be happy with a harem of He-men fanning her face and Greek-like gods dropping grapes into her mouth. Her cooked books would show malfeasance, and yet she mistakenly believes her financial windfall sets her highness above reproach.

Why does someone who chants Namu Myōhō Renge Kyō make chemical potions for people to slap on their bodies that cause one's temple to pound?

I had to get out of the scent factory.

I had to get out of the Ricocos roost.

I had to get a large allotment of legwork done in town and could not judiciously complete my tasks while playing Pied Piper to a child abandoned by his parents and left in the charge of a teen on overwhelm. I wanted to save them all, but it was beyond my scope or schema.

I considered calling child protective services but had no grounds to report them. The agency's superficial perusal would please them: Rocky has a spacious, clean, toy filled room in a house in which he is eats and dresses well, and get a nightly bath. There was no overt abuse. The agency would be powerless to step in and take action regarding the crimes against his heart. He is an afterthought, a part of the package to present to the public, not the apple of his globetrotting parent's eyes. Rocky, I hoped, might develop compassion in his older years, heal his sleep problems once the lap of luxury gave way to knock knees of a nobler reality.

Since Nikos so kindly bestowed me with a degree in design from the University of San Francisco, I had come all this way to build background credibility. By the time I left the Bay Area, I intended to inhale every nuance on all the stones that cobbled together the grit and girth of the city. Each glint of the sun rays that fell on the local architecture from the Golden Gate Bridge bike lanes to the cocksure 1888 Bayview Opera House that obstinately survived the 1906 earthquake to The McElroy Octagon House emblazoned itself in my memory. I'd become an expert Bay Area Archophile in the time required to plant cherry tomatoes.

Arlo, though gregarious on the surface, was garrulous in his home. He and his wife interspersed bouts of praying and genuflecting to their guru with disagreeable paranoia aimed at anyone in shouting range: Donalise, Matsako, Rocky, me, the dog — in no particular order. The Ricocos knew Maria Van der Heffelin well, so it was imperative that my departure be politically correct - bridges un-burnt, and false friendships intact.

"Good morning, Arlo."

"Morning. Have you seen my coffee? I set it down here not ten minutes ago."

"No, I'm sorry, I..."

"Are you drinking my coffee?"

" No, I..."

"Well, a cup doesn't get up and walk away by itself."

"No, it doesn't."

"Oh, never mind. I set it over here by the orchids."

I rousted my bravado.

"I will move myself over to Berkeley today. I wanted to... um... thank you for all your kindness."

"Berkeley?"

"Yes, sir, Arlo... that's where my primary work will be. It will save me a commute."

"What work do you do, dear?" Donalise adjusted her hair as though it was a crystal crown.

"I... well..."

"We set several of our friends up to have portraits painted by you. Were you planning to travel back to do those?"

"You... you... what?"

"They've seen our portraits and everyone wants one."

"It is how you'll pay us for your stay here."

"Oh."

"You didn't think we were just putting you up for three weeks for free, did you?"

"Dada! UPPY!" Arlo's son screamed like a train whistle.

I had a headache. I had to get out of the Ricocos.

I picked up Rocky and carried him out to the garden to pick oranges with me while I sorted out my thoughts. The air was cool, the sky clear.

"Lucy," he said. I turned and saw Luis Fernando. He was waiting to see what I would do.

"Why so silent?" I apprehensively approached the deceased five-year-old, almost expecting he would offer me a à propos aposite; I would appreciate even a suitable admonishment to take under advisement. "I can use your advice at a time like this."

He kicked an orange around like he was in the world finals of a Hacky Sack championship.

Perhaps I was losing my mind. I'd have to deal with that possibility later. Just then either the baby or me got the munchies. I shuffled back inside and cooked up fluffy broccoli, red pepper, and green onion omelets for everyone, drizzled with toasted sesame seeds, and garnished with avocados and sunflower sprouts. Breakfast was a work of art too pretty to eat.

"Rick and Laurie are free this evening for their portraits. Will that work for you?"

No.

"Yes, sure, what time?"

The beauty of Strawberry Canyon was bold and untamed, like a Behemoth lion sitting squat in the Sahara. Being in nature notched down my angst, which had run amok at Arlo's, and brought back an appreciation of the alchemy of daily life. The light in the canyon was as luminous as I recalled from the childhood visit with my father. While hiking an incline and taking in the glorious glitter of the leaves above, I stepped wrong on a rock, twisted my ankle, heard a snap, and fell to the ground to shift the weight bearing load off of my joints.

It was a Monday morning; few people were crawling up and down the pass. I picked myself up and tested my gait for pain and balance, hobbled to a ridge that had some smooth rocks to sit on - so far so good. Just a twinge shot up my leg; it didn't seem broken.

I sat on the lookout amidst a loneliness that loomed as large as the Grand Canyon and as solitary as a American Indian soloing on a vision quest, only my quest was for a clean, quiet short-term room rental in Berkeley. Ultimately, I was searching for my life's meaning and purpose, especially regarding the changes of the past few months, but first things first. I had to cut loose from Lombard Street.

Rick and Laurie were respectable people. They wanted a tandem portrait, the kind I have such a knack for and often used to draw in chalk. The gods of creativity were with me even though I was running on adrenaline and a weird sleep pattern thanks to Rocky, the precocious, cherubic-by-day, cranky, hanky-panky sleep-stealer by night.

I did portraitures of three other Ricoco clan couples: Lou and Marylou, Johan and Robley, and Petra and John. All filthy rich, none of them tipped, not so much as a cent. Stingy bastards. Now that I'd fulfilled my duty in San Francisco, I was ready to move on.

Ominous clouds rolled in from the South, blotting out the sunrays; the precipitation suddenly palpable, portending of a dour downfall. I pulled out the paper I'd printed at the Ricocos with listings of room rentals. I had a one p.m. appointment to meet with Kasey.

Available Now

Enjoy a spacious first-floor bedroom and private full bath to rent in a large private, deluxe, hilltop home with spectacular views of the Bay Area and a stone throw away from miles of hiking. The house is 2500 sq. feet, in a safe residential neighborhood. Lots of privacy! You're on the first floor. I stay up on the 4th floor of the house.

This rental includes:

Furnished Spacious Bedroom
Full Bathroom with Shower and Bathtub
TV with basic cable, Utilities, WIFI
Lots of street parking

Shared use of:
Chef's Kitchen
Large balcony
Shared living room space
Washer-dryer
Outdoor kitchen
Close to BART and gas station
Daily: $100
Weekly: $500
Monthly $1,200

Kasey opened the door with a smile that extended wide like a harp bow and heralded me inside just as the wet catharsis from the brooding skies beat down at my heels. The house was spacious, as advertised, and beautifully designed.

"The stairs have a good geometric cadence."

She looked at me either in awe or to size me up as an alien. I must have passed the test because I got a twenty-minute chatty tour of the grounds. The bedroom had a bed, an arched 1920s mahogany dresser, one plastic plant, and a Peter Max poster of a butterfly.

"Would you like to sit in the living room and talk?"

"Sure," anything to get off of this ankle.

We settled onto an oversized ivory coach with cheerfully bright hand-woven throw pillows.

"So, Luciana..."

"You can call me Lucy." I had used my full name because it sounded more ostentatious.

"Lucy. What brings you to Berkeley, how long do you plan to stay, and what are you looking for in a temporary house share?"

Wow, a woman who communicates clearly. I could live here!

"I studied at USF. I'm here to see friends and catch up on some art and architecture. I'm looking for a clean, safe, and compatible house share for a few weeks."

"You saw my rates?"

"Um-huh."

"Is that okay with you?"

I'm certain she wasn't aware how much money I had socked away, or how tightly I intended to hold on to it.

I hesitated. "Yes."

"It's cheaper if you pay by the month. I like you. Perhaps you'll stay that long?"

"I might. I was thinking more like two weeks. How about $1,000 for three weeks?"

"Do you like cats?"

I brightened up. "I love cats! I have a wonderful cat named Natalie Mouskers."

"Natalie Mouskers," she laughed. "Where is she?"

I had not prepared for these personal questions.

"Kasey, may I use your restroom?"

"Of course."

My reflection showed a woman with a beet-red face, hair that was softly growing out, a blend of Camille-Lucy, a person I was growing fond of.

"You're limping."

"I twisted my ankle pretty badly on Strawberry Canyon."

"Does it hurt?"

"Quite a bit."

"I should take you to get it X-rayed?"

"NO!" The baby / babies wouldn't like that. "Thank you for offering. I don't think it's broken. I can walk on it. Do you think it's broken?"

"I'm not qualified to say. You seem to be able to walk okay. Would you like some ice, Lucy? Have you heard of RICE?"

"Oh, I'd love some rice, if it's brown. I don't eat white rice."

She laughed again, a welcome sound to my ears. "RICE: Rest - Ice - Compression - Elevation. Here," she set one of the pretty pillows on the coffee table for my foot, "Put it up here and I'll get you an icepack and something to eat."

"Thank you, Kasey."

"I have three cats. Would you be willing to take care of them when I go out of town?"

"Oh, yes, I'd love that."

"Purr-fect. When will you be moving in?"

"Tomorrow." We shook on it.

The tremendous loneliness lessened as I fell asleep on Kasey's couch. She left me alone there for a precious hour. I woke up to a tan tabby purring on my lap; two other cats curled up nearby. Lentil-vegetable soup sat in a pale green ceramic bowl by the foot cushion. This was the first time I felt at home since Paris.

"Onegai shimasu, Lu-cee. Onegai. Take me with you!"

Matsako followed me like a duckling shadowing its mama to remonstrate her desire for me to save her. If she thought I would agree, she was mistaken. I have a soft heart and a great deal of compassion, but my pragmatic nature keeps me from melting into a puddle like butter.

"Matsako, you are welcome to come visit on your day off."

I folded my freshly laundered white tees and tucked them neatly into my bag.

"I don't get a day off, Lu-cee! I'm stuck: room, board, and crying baby! I send home the small pay I get to my parents." She panicked, her emotions on the verge of pandemonium. I looked outside. The moon was full with a navy three-ring halo. An overwhelming desire to sidewalk chalk struck me, but this wasn't the time or place.

There was a parallel arc to Matsako's journey and mine: we both were alone, without family support, with the welfare of a child, (as yet unborn or already a boisterous boy), to put above our own. Her mother, though still alive, was sick with heart weakness, ankles like water balloons, unable to work or even garden. Matsako's father, decades older than this wife, pushed himself in sanitation, ticking off the days until he would retire. Three younger siblings were still in school. Sending Matsako to America as a nanny with the wealthy couple she met at one of Arlo's book signings had seemed like a way forward to a better life.

Struggling to balance boundaries and responsibilities for self and others, I closed my eyes and recited the pedantic, yet firm and fluid foundation my parents instilled me with:

1) If someone gives you a compliment, thank him or her.
2) When you ask for help, say "please," and have no expectations.
3) Wear layers - the weather may change unexpectedly.
4) Shop at a Farmers Market or on outside aisles of the grocery store.
5) Take risks, but not stupid ones.

6) Avoid trouble.
7) Listen and offer your presence rather than trying to fix someone.
8) Buy nothing from someone out of breath.
9) Dive into your bliss and splash joy onto others; people are thirsty.
10) You can't help others unless you put your own oxygen mask on first.

I ached for Matsako. The temptation to bundle her into my suitcase between the architecture book and my art supplies quaked through me, but I was like a fish out of water gulping for air and my own oxygen mask was nowhere in sight. Nothing I could say or do would remedy the situation for this young woman, or for Rocky.

We hugged in silence, our tears mingling as tributaries tricking together back to the stream. Rocky crawled over and reached up to us from his knees as though he was a Sundancer praying to the heavens for rain. I picked him up, and we had a group hug. When in California, do as the natives do.

Before heading out, I remembered something. Setting down my bag, I foraged for the piccolo. As I showed Matsako how to play it and told her where she could get one. Rocky curled up on the floor, one knee tucked up, and fell asleep.

"Promise you'll come see me in Berkeley - we'll go hiking when my ankle heals. We can figure something out for you, Emmylou." She slapped me and slipped three gigantic oranges in my bag.

I'd cunningly planned my departure for early evening, a time when the Ricoco's were out. Apparently I dawdled too long with my goodbye and as I exited, Arlo's car rounded the bend. I thought of firm and fluid pedantic rule number six: "Avoid trouble," and so I hid in the bushes until he disappeared inside.

I, Lucy, the girl with kaleidoscope eyes, cruised down Lombard Street lugging two suitcases filled with plenty. Halfway down I sat curbside, pulled out an orange and ate it under the bountiful overhang of a bright pink Crepe Myrtle. Life, however trippy and tragic, was good.

The ivory picket fence whose waist high peels cried out for a fresh coat of paint, the apple tree that graciously offered her small golden fruit, the Peter Max psycho-delicious butterfly poster which read, "We see the earth in its true light and realize that we are all one," and Kasey Kaufman's uneven, quirky smile quickly became symbols to me of home. My being relaxed each time I approached the peach door with arched lavender moldings, winsome wind chimes, and doormat that proclaimed 歡迎, "Welcome," in traditional Chinese.

A Women's Studies professor on sabbatical, Kasey was home most of the time, which I liked. At night we made meals together, (dinners of tempeh, quinoa, and purple and green cabbage smothered in a chopped parsley-minced garlic-oregano chimichirri sauce that oozed with flavor), watched foreign films, and had heart-to-heart talks reminiscent of the tête-à-tête's Brigitte and I had when we met. Knees pulled under us on the couch, heads bowed together, we held mugs of warm Sleepytime on cool nights and sipped on chilled Hibiscus Cooler with spearmint when it was still hot, evening hot, global warming why am I still sweating at 10:00 p.m. hot? We discussed everything and the kitchen sink. Kasey was refreshingly open about her life and ditto for me. Well, except The Paris predicament and all the events touched by it.

Kasey was a wild child who ran away from San Diego to San Francisco, arriving in the Summer of Love. She had endless tales for me of political idealism, rock stars, free love, and drugs. I had grown weary of portraits and yearned to draw a mural illustrating the era.

"I love the idea! Where will you draw it?"

"On the pavement in front of your house, in chalk, if that's okay with you?"

"Oh, oh, oh," she hopped up from her staid position and clutched her heart like she was Nebuchadnezzar celebrating a pyrrhic victory after overthrowing the Egyptians. "Oh, oh, oh, that would be... oh, yes. It would honor me."

After finessing the details of the chalk walk, (yay!), I confided in Kasey about my pregnancy and THAT part of my predicament.

"So you'll be a single mother?"

"Yes."

"You don't know where you'll live or how you will earn a living."

"That's right."

"The father loves you, but has been unstable in the past, and he now has a young girlfriend who you think might cheat on him?"

"You're very good at active listening, you got this all right."

"Do you see yourself marrying Nicholas?"

"Nikos. Hmm. I don't.... I... No. No, I can't imagine it right now."

"Have you considered abortion?" she asked with the casualness of, "Would you like honey or lemon in your tea?"

"No. It's not an option for me to think about or discuss."

Kasey and I leveled like a moonbeam on this. She sensed that neither religious fervor nor fear instigated my reaction. I emitted a calm certainty about this matter, an unshakeable decision I made for reasons that were no one's business but my own. She dropped the topic and never revisited again. I retired to bed exhausted by my life, ready to chalk it out in a parade of 1960s proportions beginning as soon as I could. Art, as always, is my prayer.

The next evening I had my heart set on asking Kasey's advice about the pragmatic, physical concerns of pregnancy: how do I keep my iron count up, what should I eat, how intensely can I exercise, and what tests might I need? Just then an enigmatic eruption of sorts blew in from Biloxi, Mississippi. His luscious, languid southern drawl gave it away. The minute he saw me, he stared like the eye of a cyclone circling its target, and said, "Hey."

"Hey."

He hadn't used a key. I stayed silent for clues as to this young man's connection with decades-older Kasey.

"Matt, this is Lucy. Lucy, Matt."

"Hey, Lucy."

"Hey, Matt."

Kasey, wary to interrupt the slow cadence of our budding chemistry, gave a lithe explanation, "Matt is my stepson. Lucy is my new summer roommate. It's the light on the back porch, Matty. The one that the mourning dove's occupied last month."

"Gotcha — nice to make your acquaintance, Lucy. I'll catch you later."

Yes. Yes, you will.

"I'm good with my hands," Matt Lamoureux laid a large, calloused palm on my knee at Sproul Plaza. Coral-colored cuts covered the knuckles on his fingers; his wrists and forearms beautifully sculpted, like Michelangelo's David, only more muscular, tanned, with silky smooth skin like the gods had gifted him an extra pint of creamy collagen. He told me later it was the effects of a healthy diet, daily loofa, and pink sea salt scrubs.

A drum circle surrounded us, followed by a trio who played the best Spanish guitar I'd heard since Bertrand. The afternoon was exquisite: clear, bright, and mild. We'd spent the day with Matsako who'd managed a day off to soak in some East Bay nature with us. We hiked in Tilden Park up to Inspiration Point where we drank in prodigious panoramic views, twirled in Sufi circles blessing the sun, and ended by riding the Carousel — twice.

"Rocky would love this," Matsako declared with such adoring love it made me wonder if she could ever pull herself from that situation.

"He'd sleep well afterwards too!"

"Without the piccolo!"

"Ha. The pied piper piccolo!" I was grateful to have a quiet room in which to sleep at Kasey's, far away from the Ricoco boy's night bellows.

"Next time I bring him for horses and shinrin-yoku."

Shirin-yoku was Matsako's word for communing in nature, translated to "forest bathing," a chance to stroll through nature and take in the atmosphere for one's well being. I always found wandering among trees, shrubs, and flowers to be an invigorating, angelic assassination of the senses. We relished the sweet smell of California lilacs, thrilled to the choir of Phoebes, Robins, and Goldfinches. The gracious click and squish of boots on rocks and grasses sprinkled with wildflowers grounded us, and cooling Berkeley breezes washed away the heat of prior days. I percolated on these pieces to pour into the peace mural.

The plaza stunk of pot. No longer illicit in California, marijuana still smelled like skunk. After Matsako took off, Matt and I walked to People's Park and sat on an empty bench.

Aside from being a master woodworker, Matt was an obsessive, encyclopedic storm of English literature, astronomy, mathematics, geography, ethnography, anthropology, human physiology, zoology, botany, agriculture, horticulture, pharmacology, mining, mineralogy, sculpture, painting, and precious stones. His wealth of knowledge impressed me. He was only three years my senior; what had I done in life while Matt gulped in the universe?

"Matt, I will only be in town for three weeks and likely won't ever be back."

He seemed unfazed, so I continued.

"I have secrets and I don't want to talk or field questions about them." No response.

"I'm pregnant, possibly with twins," I blurted out, "I don't want you falling in love with me."

"What makes you think I'd fall in love with you?"

I wasn't sure if that was an insult or a challenge, but it was then he leaned in and kissed me. I inhaled his essence for those moments. The fecund assault of the day: the drums, flamenco guitar, spinning, birdsongs, and strong, velvety hands all sloshed through my brain as we traveled to an exalted galaxy far away.

The first thing I saw when I opened my eyes was how the sun highlighted the copper in his brown hair. The next thing I noticed, more distinctly than before, was the third-degree burn covering a third of his face, continuing down his neck, and surreptitiously disappearing under his shirt. When the time was right, I would ask him about it.

"Do you want an orange? I have two."

"Is that code for something?" the most mature man I ever met beamed, becomingly boyish.

"No." I took out the oranges, handed him the larger one, and we slurped on them together in silence.

"Hey, why doncha work with me as a woodworker while you're in town?"

"I've never made moldings or carved desks, Matt."

"You're an artist, right?"

"Yeah."

"You don't want to do portraits anymore."

"Someday I do. I just need a break right now."

"Are you independently wealthy?"

"No." While paying for my seven-dollar salad earlier that day, Matt noticed I was reticent about parting with my money.

"I'll teach you."

A stray basketball rolled our way. Matt jumped up and sunk a two-handed behind the back shot from the far end of the court. The iridescent Sunday afternoon crowd bustled with Friday playful vibes. The scene overflowed like warm, fizzy ginger water: three children spun cartwheels to our right, and on our left, an acrobatic, slightly aggressive Ultimate Frisbee game featured a white disk that whizzed past our heads like an Olympic javelin, close enough almost to cut nick my ear, and not one bellicose bully in the bunch. Two teens cheered vigorously for Matty's shot, which made my heart soar.

"Great shot, dude."

"Hey, thanks, man."

I didn't want to ruin the moment.

"I have so much to do while I'm here. I don't want to get sidetracked."

He passed me the ball — fast. "Your shot."

I made an over the shoulder throw. It banked off the backboard and jiggled the hoop on its way in. Matt gave a two-pinky whistle. The teens clapped.

"You set your own schedule. Twenty dollars an hour, cash. It'll pay your expenses in the month you're here."

My mind calculated: twenty dollars an hour, say five hours a day, five days a week would bring in five hundred a week, two thousand a month. Not too bad.

"I'm just going to be here three weeks."

"It would be better for Kasey if you stay a month - or more - until the college students come back to town."

I shot again and missed. One kid returned the ball to me.

"Unless you're in a hurry to be somewhere."

"I want to get settled before the pregnancy advances too far."

"Lucy, rushing things can set you back. Take the time you need to think about my offer and let yourself settle in the home of this wonderful woman. It might do your soul good."

This guy knew psychology. If you push me, I topple or run. Give me space; I am drawn into your sphere. He grinned with a smile so sultry it made me swoon. This smile ought to be illicit on a public playground. He lifted the hem of his sweat soaked tee and wiped his face in a circle like he was drying a windshield after a soapy wash — this gave me a look at the burns, which cover one side of his torso, and disappear below the belt line.

I handed him his water bottle. "All right. I'll consider it," I said with finality. Subject closed for the day.

"All right. Hey, you're good with the ball. What's your sport of choice?"

"Volleyball. MVP in high school."

"Oh, for the love of humanity!"

"What?"

"We have a game going Wednesday nights. You in?"

"Heck, yeah!"

"What's wrong?"

"Nothing," his tone, grievous.

"What is it?"

"Nothing. I'm not falling in love with you. You're just a volleyball playing artist who is passing through for three weeks."

Awkward pause, awkward pause, awkward pause, awkward non sequitur... "Can we go to the art store now?"

"Sure." He put his sweaty arm around me as we walked to the car. His pheromones make me giddy.

When he dropped me back at Kasey's, I chalked the mural on the walk until a sliver of moon rose above the trees and my enlarged pupils could no longer adjust to the lack of light. To begin my 1960s mural, I drew a psychedelic VW bus, and a stoned, cheering crowd at Woodstock. This would be my Masterpiece. I hoped the neighbors wouldn't smudge it before I finished. I prayed it wouldn't rain. I love the unpredictability of sidewalk art, so tentative and fragile just like life. Two hours of impassioned drawing did not erase the sight of Matt's burns or the sound of his words, "I'm not falling in love with you."

Shit. Neither was I.

"When is the last time you saw her?"

"I..."

"Let's try again. It's not a difficult question. When is the last time you saw Camille?"

"I didn't see her."

"You didn't see her, when?"

"At Bertrand's funeral, in Brussels, in March. Margaret saw her."

"Bertrand, that's her partner?"

"My partner."

"Your partner or her partner?"

"Yes."

"Yes? I asked you a question with a choice."

"He was Our Bertrand." Leonard broke, sobbing in episodic spurts as though short on oxygen and trying to gulp it in up from the floor. "It was murder! Bertrand, he was murdered!"

"By Camille?"

"What! No! By Rémy Jacquard, that two-bit bartender with a hardcore heroin habit."

Officier Rousseau unbuttoned the top clasp on her collar though it wasn't hot in the station. "Are you aware of her whereabouts now?"

"No. No. No," he recited emphatically, an incantation of sorts, and then with pellucid irony, "I don't even know where Natalie Mouskers is. She has disappeared."

"Who? Another disappearance?"

"Her cat. Bertrand, Camille, and the cat, all gone."

"Joubert, can we get some tissue over here?" Rachelle was grouchy. Making a man cry wasn't her forte. She handed the box to Leonard in a grand gesture. "I'm sorry for your losses, Mr. Latourelle. Thank you for your cooperation. Here is my card. Please call me if you have any further information."

Leonard didn't move, he sat in a catalytic trance staring at her silver pin. Joubert helped him up and escorted him to the door, gave him three pats on the back and a little shove outside. Leo's eyes squinted to slits in the sun. A hand grasped his shoulder. Brigitte on her way into the station, trembling and translucent, trilled, "C'est incroyable, Leonard, toute l'affaire, c'est incroyable."

They hugged. The streetlight changed to green. They kept hugging. Yellow. Red. Green. Yellow. Red. Green. Yellow.

"Bertrand, Camille, and the cat. All gone," he stumbled into the crosswalk as the light turned red. A car screeched on its brakes, as did the four cars in line behind. A lone finger jerked out the window. "Hey, watch where you're going! You want to kill someone out here?" Leonard jumped back on the curb as the door closed on Brigitte.

"Miss Paquette?"

"Oui."

"Step in here, please."

Young Brigitte held her head high like a steadfast noble Satyagraha standing in peace while entropy raged around her. She planted her feet on the floor and interlaced her knuckles in her lap. She looked Rachelle Rousseau in the eyes and answered queries for half an hour.

"You are best friends, but you have not heard from her since the call on your birthday, the day of the accident?"

"Yes, that's right."

"Who else was in her life?"

"Just the school friends I told you about, her landlady, Leonard and Bertrand."

"She has no family?"

"None that I'm aware of. Her parents died."

"No boyfriend?"

"Pascal died too. It was he who left her the car."

"And the cat?"

"Excuse me?"

"What happened to her cat?"

"Oh, Natalie Mouskers! I don't know."

"No one else knew her?"

Brigitte crossed and uncrossed her ankles. Beads of sweat dripped down over her ears, a drop splotched on her jeans and it wasn't even hot. She sipped from a glass of water."

"Who - else - knew - her?"

"Ummm..."

"Who?" Rachelle leaned in like a lynx.

"I... I don't know. Maybe Nikos? I don't know. They hadn't talked for a while."

In the next room sat Madam Trouli, legs crossed gracefully like a queen, hands rested on her purse, sweat dripped down her brow.

"I don't know who took the cat. She was a good girl; my best tenant, very artistic. Helped me in the garden. A good girl."

"Yes, you said that already. Here," Joubert handed her the tissues.

"Merci," she grabbed two and honked out a handful of mucous, while in the next cubicle over, Joubert asked Brigitte, "How do you spell his name?"

Brigitte, mouth pillowed in cotton, reached again for the water. "N - I - K - O - S."

"Breathe... Breathe... Breathe..."

Bowing my head down, I could see my toes, feet dangling from the edge of the bed - nails clipped and polished a shimmery tangerine from Kasey's collection. She held a lunch sack over my mouth the same size mom used to pack egg-salad and celery in for me when I was in grade school. It seemed like she was trying to turn me into a Platypus with a brown paper bill. She rubbed circles on my back like I used to do for mom and Pascal when they got sick from chemo. Dad had refused treatment he called poison. My mother, Marissa, also did soothing massages for me when a reading of *The Gingerbread Man* upset me.

Mom had tried everything that night when I was three: she sang *Blackbird*, gave me warm milk and honey in my cute kitty mug, which I spat out like a baseball player up to bat, and together we counted jumping sheep. The sheep didn't make me sleepy at all - each one had a different colored, numbered vest, some emboldened with flowers, others with stars, and the elaborate ones festooned with intricate paisleys. The only antidote for the sad demise of the gingerbread man was when she rubbed gentle clockwise circles on my back.

"You had another bad dream, Lucy."

Ah, so I did. On nights I wasn't too physically exhausted to dream, I often had a recurring nightmare about the crash and the aftermath: running, cutting my hair in the alleyway, hearing Natalie Mouskers' mews, and flashing in and out of a police station scene where my friends filed in and officers grilled them. Brigitte, Jacqueline, Nikos, even my joy, my deceased partner, genial Bertrand was there. When I awoke, Luis Fernando was as realer than real, staring silently, his big brown eyes were gloomy like the gingerbread man's.

These moments arose in me a cloying existentialism in which I pondered my freedom of choice and responsibility for the consequences of my acts. Though I wasn't religious, a guardian I took to be an amalgam of the three Magi, Balthazar, Casper, and Melchior, periodically stood behind Luis Fernando in a protective stance. The angels seemed not irate or vengeful nor compassionate towards me, but their presence was solid. They were there to prop up Pierre, meek and vulnerable as a baby gazelle that lost his life to a wild hyena.

I pushed the paper bag away. "I'm sorry to get you up again, Kasey."

"It's okay, I was already up. It's almost time to catch the train to the city. Today we have The Asian Art and Cable Car Museums." I wiggled my tangerine toes in excitement.

Matt couldn't go; he had a home repair job. I'd miss him but could use a day away without toying whether to have sex with him or not. Rocky and Matsako, (who had big news for me), would meet us at ten o'clock. On the way, Kasey and I guessed what it could be.

"Arlo is being sued for plagiarism."

"Freaking Fragrances caught fire."

"Donalise is pregnant with the mailman's child."

"Matsako is leaving to go back to Japan and study the flute."

Rocky was bouncing up and down in his stroller when we arrived. Matsako waved at us like she was calling a lost ship in from sea.

"Lu-cee! Lu-cee!"

"Konnichiwa, Matsako!"

"Lu-cee! I did what you said. I went to Japanese market and met people. I am hired for a new family. I begin in two weeks. Tonight I will tell the Ricocos."

"Congratulations, Matsako! How do I say congratulations in Japanese?"

"Omedetou."

"Omedetou, Matsako."

"Thank you!" She picked up Rocky and nuzzled his neck. "I will miss this one, but I need to go."

"Yes, I think you do."

"Omedetou, Matsako," Kasey group-hugged them, and I joined in, glad I wouldn't be there tonight to see the fireworks when she gave notice.

"Lu-cee, Mrs. Dona says for you to come tonight. Bob and Nancy will come to have their portraits done at seven."

"What? No. I did six portraits for them already."

"She says you stayed a long time. She says you owe them."

My face flushed raspberry and my tangerine toes became cold. "I have a date with Matt tonight."

"She says you owe them. We're going to the bathroom. Be right back. Thank you, Lu-cee. I got a new job." She danced away.

I looked at Kasey. She threw her arms open, "Group-hug?"

"Put it down."

"What?"

"The phone. Hang up."

"My client is on the line."

"Pull over."

"Why?"

"Let me out."

It was our first fight.

He was faux gregarious in his delivery, "Is it okay if I text you back in a few minutes? .... Okay, thanks, bye. Lucy, I was in the middle of..."

"I've told you before not to text and drive. Let me out, I'll walk."

"Calm down."

"Whoa. *Ne-ver* tell me to calm down."

"It's no big deal, I'm only going thirty miles an hour."

"It IS a big deal. Someone driving on surface streets and texting killed a kid! A FIVE-year-old." His client call was a cyclonic catalyst for me. I was fanatical and furious. I drew my demarcation line. "I don't *e-ver* want to repeat this. Do not *e-ver* minimize me by telling me to calm down. PULL OVER. I will walk!"

He pulled curbside, and I scrambled out like a hamster; I could not exit that car fast enough. To his credit, and the saving grace of our friendship, Matt ran after me and caught me in his arms as apoplexy turned to tears.

"I'm sorry. I'm sorry. I'll never text and drive again. Do you want to tell me about it?"

"No."

Shit. He was a keeper. My pedant pragmatism juxtaposed with rosy romanticism; Do NOT fall in love with me, Matty. Do NOT fall in love with Matt, Cammy. Then an inkling of a rhyme and limerick popped to mind:

"There once was a girl from Par-eee,
A man blew into her life like a breeze.
He dropped to his knee and said, 'Will you marry me, please?'
'But I'm not in love with you, can't you see?'"

Oh, no! Where did that come from? I hit the side of my head as if to dislodge an earwig in the ear canal and shook my head like a wild stallion startled by a cannon shot.

"Lu-cee," he imitated Matsako, "After we finish this job today, can I stay over? I think it's time."

I walked three circles around him, squatted down and patted the ground with both hands, then got back into the car. He turned on the ignition, looked from me to the road and back, then slid smoothly back onto University, while his phone sat silently in the cup holder.

I stared straight ahead and propped one leg up onto the dashboard like I used to do when Noni drove us to Sun Valley to ski. "Sure," I said in the most casual manner I could muster.

Kneeling on cold ceramic clay flooring, Matty leaned in to me and stared as though nothing else ever existed or ever would exist.

"I need more light. I need to see you."

I reached behind me and flipped up the switch. A soft ivory light flooded the room.

"Ow!"

"Shh. Hold still. Give me your hand."

I was timid in turning my palm back over to him so he could poke at my middle finger with the sharp silver-sleuthing needle.

"Ow!"

"Shh. We passed the nadir, almost got it, lifting off again, Lucy."

Everyone realized, (me, Matt, Kasey, customers, strangers on the street, Matsako, and even Rocky Ricoco), that this harmless, cheeky, rapscallion captivated me. The guy who stuck a tweezers sterilized blue-black from a match out of a decades old Hotel de Anza matchbook into my delicate artiste's hand enamored me, and that was a difficult position to be in.

"I hope I can work on the mural tomorrow. I have a motley crew of characters to get back to drawing."

"You'll be okay," he cooed as he dug in further.

"Ow!"

"Shh," seemed to be the ubiquitous response to the plight of wood in flesh. "You've been doing a great job. I admire your pluck in learning to use the saw and sander."

"Thanks. Ow! Did you say pluck?"

"What did you think I said?"

"Nothing."

"Duck?"

"No."

"Muck?"

"No," I put on a playful, vacuous veneer.

Getting a sliver taken out had never been so sexy.

"Got it!" He held it up like he had discovered gold in the 1949 gold rush.

I turned off the light, leaving only the glow of a flickering white tea light, and we celebrated like our tongues were salsa dancers.

Matt broke the salivacious spell.

"I have a question for you."

"No questions."

"You pique my curiosity."

"What?"

"Why don't you have a cell phone?"

"I do."

"Why don't you ever use it?"

"I'm not into the sanctimonious use of electronics. I'd rather be present."

"Yeah, but we could text. I could call you. You could get directions instead of getting lost."

"Yeah."

"Yeah, what?"

"I can dig it out, turn it on. I'll give you the number later."

He took out his phone. "I'll punch it in now."

"I don't recall the number right now. I just got it in Chicago."

"You were in Chicago? I love it there."

"Yeah, it was a layover. I wanted to see the art and where my dad went to school — Northwestern."

"There's so much I want to ask you."

"I understand."

"I respect you, but I can't help but wonder what your secrets are. I hope you'll trust me enough to tell me one day before I'm a crotchety, old octogenarian."

"Maybe."

"I have some secrets too."

"About getting burned?" I'd been dying to ask, but didn't feel right prying when I asked him not to inquire about me.

"Umm, no," he took his shirt off. The scar, white-pink, raised and mottled, looked painful. "Let's get back in bed, I'll tell you."

I rubbed my hand lightly on the deep crevices, "Does this hurt?"

"Not when you touch me. In some places the skin is dead. I can't feel anything. I have terrible shooting nerve jolts fairly constantly though, and the pulling from the contractions of scar tissue feels like a crane is ripping me. People think burns look bad, but they don't consider the long-term damage and how difficult it is to endure unrelenting pain."

He wrapped me in his arms. I was used to being with Nikos and Pascal, fit men, but of normal to small stature. Matt was a weightlifter, with stormy, husky, brawling, broad shoulders like Chicago.

"I was ten, sound asleep, four in the morning. The neighbor's shed caught fire. Faulty wiring. I woke up, smelled something, thought it was a Southern barbecue, but no one barbecues at four in the morning. I could have woken my parents up, but I fell back asleep. The fire spread. My bedroom was next."

He pulled me closer. I was silent, full focus on him, imagining this young boy in bed in Alabama, dreaming of ribs on the grill, while flames engulfed his house. Waiting for him to tell me what he chose to, unfurling the tale in his own time.

"I remember little after that until I woke in a hospital two days later. Damaged my lungs too."

Don't fall in love, Camille.

"I can tell you more about it another time. I'm getting sleepy."

"Okay, me too."

"That's not my secret though."

"No? What is it?"

"I killed a man."

"That's not funny."

"I ain't joking."

He fell asleep in my arms, looking as innocent as a newborn babe, pink and downy fresh, laid on its mother's breast.

NIKOS

He rose and dressed this morning like any other, only the hour was earlier than usual, earlier than he preferred. He splashed his face with cold water, the coldest the tap had to offer, patted dry his skin with both hands on the white cloth, not the finest cotton, a bit too scratchy, he noticed on this day. The razor glided sharply against his cheeks, chin, and upper lip as if the early morning brought with it the sensitivity of a baby lamb, delicate and soft, not yet in need of shearing. He gave a yelp as drops of crimson blood trickled down the side of his face; he'd nicked himself badly, something he hadn't done since the day Camille left France and any hope of a romance with her evaporated much as the droplets dried from his forehead. He had blown his chance with the captivating, creative beauty that he shared rhapsody in and out of rain with.

If a med-tech had hooked his heart up to a tachometer, it would have shown it was spinning fast, too fast, in protest, avec résistance, but willing or not, he had an appointment to keep. Next he brushed his teeth with precision, up, down, back, spitting the white paste in the bowl, glad for the satisfying spearmint rush that tickled his nose. Tiptoeing into the bedroom, he slid one leg than the other into starchy tan trousers. Opening the top drawer, he picked the most unblemished undershirt he had. On top went his finest shirt, tailored perfectly to fit his trim form. As he tucked in the back, she awoke — pretty Parlene, sassy, smart, self-centered and xenophobic regarding any foreigners in Paris, including him.

"Where are you going so early? I don't want us to have any secrets between us. Please tell me, or I will lose all of my trust in you."

He stammered in response to her yammer, "I... it's... I have to go somewhere. I can't explain. It's private. I'm sorry. I shouldn't be long." He took her face between his hands, tucked her under the chin, and tilted her head back for a long, slow kiss, the whole time wondering, "Is this the woman I want to have a child with and share my life legacy? She is, after all, not my Camille."

Last to go on were his shoes now outfitted with new matching black laces that stood out against the permanent scuffs roughly ingrained along the outer soles.

Parlene sat up in bed and watched him adjust his watch, check the time and, like the white rabbit, scurry out the door. A jealous zealot who wanted to keep track of where her man was going, she moved with haste, used the same spearmint paste, enjoyed the same minty taste, and in two minutes flat she was out the door behind him.

The street, though close to Paris proper, had a bucolic ambiance in the sunrise. He walked with a determined clip, his wingtips clicking in tap dancer time on the cement. She had to hustle to keep him in her sight and hide to keep out of his. The long blocks to the metro passed by in a flash. Down the stairs, through the turnstile, and onto the train he went. She did the same, bending down to obscure her face when he looked her way.

There was a station change, and another ride to a destination she was not familiar with. The commuters crowded off in such a rush they jostled him and she nearly lost sight of her guy, her own heart now racing like a ticky-tacky tachometer. She scurried several meters behind as he turned right up a main thoroughfare and vanished through the doublewide doors of a police station. She exhaled, her fresh breath hot against the cool air.

"Nikos?"

"Oui."

"Officier Joubert. Thank you for coming. Come back here, Officier Rousseau is in charge of the investigation. She'll be questioning you. Would you like some coffee?"

"Please."

"How do you take it?"

"Black is fine."

THREE CATS AND A TIGER

"Brussel sprouts for breakfast?"

I looked up from the book, lost in the delicious fictional world of unicorns, barleycorn, and metaphors, and returned momentarily to this one, "Yeah, lots of iron."

"What's that on top?"

"Goat cheese."

"Umm, my stomach is grumbling for some now." She was teasingly sarcastic. "What are you reading?"

"Hemingway. *Old Man and The Sea.*"

"You're making your way through my bookshelves, I see."

"You have good taste in writers."

"And you have good taste in men. Matt stayed here last night?"

"Yes, he did. Is that weird for you?"

"Not at all. I'm happy to see you together. I think you guys are a great fit." Then she scrunched up her face, "You..."

"What?" I stabbed a half of a sprout and stuck it in my mouth so I didn't have to answer.

She patted the back of her head. This action confused me. Is this how she passively expressed her discomfort about me and Matt getting close? Her eyes shifted to the back of my head, which I pat with my hand. The hair on my crown was standing stick straight up. Yep, I had an embarrassing case of first-sleepover-date-elflock. I poured water on my palm and tried to flatten down the defiant loop-de-loop locks.

"Has he told you his story yet?" She poured herself more steaming coffee. The smell bothered me perhaps in part because of my pregnancy, but more like because I don't share the universal love of bitter java as everyone and their brother does.

"About his burns?"

"About whatever."

"He told me about the fire, and then he fell asleep."

"It was terrifying for a child, the crackling of the walls, the scorching heat and tenebrous smoke, no way out, screaming out but getting no response. His mother was an evangelical Baptist; he thought the rapture had come."

"Oh, my god."

She spooned Scottish oatmeal into a deep clay bowl she had thrown during her hippie phase as a potter.

"He made it sound so casual."

"He downplays things, Lucy. Matthew has been through a lot. I was engaged to his father. As a boy, his road to recovery was grueling and nothing short of heroic. We formed a lifelong bond. He trusted me."

I wasn't sure what to say. I wanted to hug Matt, my lover, the mysterious murderer. Surely he'd had some reason to do what he did. I wondered if he killed someone when he was a child because of the fire?

"What happened? What was he like then?"

"Withdrawn, rebellious, and incorrigible until age twenty. He thought god was being vindictive with him."

"Why?"

"He blamed himself for his parents' divorce."

"Why?"

"Kids do."

My mind was still on the other thing Matt told me, just before he dozed off. I skewered another Brussels sprout and steered my focus onto the vintage nickel fork as I searched for a less upsetting, countervailing thought.

"Here's my daughter's number in Connecticut, here's the Vet's number, the Plumber, you have my cell, and Matt's close by. Call anytime day or night if you have any concerns, or even just want to talk. I'm sorry to leave you with Calypso when she's like this. Hopefully she won't throw up again. It's hard to watch my sweeties get old and sick. So, you going to be okay while I'm gone?"

I felt to see if my hair was still misbehaving. It was. "Kasey, don't worry about me."

"Don't you and Matt burn the place down while I'm gone."

I looked at the book and read the same line four times over without comprehending a thing, pretending I hadn't heard her.

"It's a joke, Lucy. A joke." She hugged me. "It's up to Matt what he shares with you. He likes you. I've never seen him like this with anyone before. He's a good man."

I nodded on automatic.

"Call me for any reason. Any time."

"Thanks. Have a great time."

While Kasey said goodbye to Calypso, Cassia, and Cleo and attended to last-minute details, I got busy too, excited to have a house to myself for three days, time to take care of business, and hopefully, some space to think. I cleaned my room, ran the dishwasher, did an hour of hot yoga - without the heat, laid out on the deck and soaked in those almost-summer rays, washed my hair with the new apricot shampoo until it shone and laid flat. Then I took out my notebook and spent the better part of the afternoon knuckling through that life review I started in Paris - so far, so good. No vindictive gods need knock me down for my existence before the twenty-fifth of February when the accident shattered lives.

I can't imagine how people with cluttered consciences deal with a blow of this magnitude. Fighting with one giant marlin per life is enough and I'd already had at least four. Three were laded upon me. It helped me compartmentalize the Paris predicament as its own entity and proceed through that minefield with a fixed focus.

I made a baseline calendar of events, details to come later ~

Paris, Feb 25 - 28 (got pregnant Feb 28)
Lille, Feb 28 - April 14
Brussels, April 14
Paris Hotel, April 15 - 23
London, April 23 - 28
Chicago, April 29 - May 4
San Francisco, May 5 - May 12
Berkeley, May 10 - May 25 (so far)

I was three months pregnant!

I made lists: things to do, places to go, people to contact. I gathered names and numbers of my new friends and put them in my phone: Tanu, Theo, Jon, Fabian, Felicity, Larch, Ralph, Maria Van der Heffelin, Nina LaRue, Pierre, Tom Haines, Adeline, Felipe, Buckley Blakely, Bethany, Roy and Diane, Jacob, Mel and Marcy, Matsako, Kasey, Matt, and twenty-five portraiture clients. Wow — busy girl, Camille.

I made a list of the roads I might take... or not. Being a pragmatic person, I approached this logically.

1) Finish business in the states, return to Paris and turn myself in.

2) Finish business in the states and kill myself. This was on hold, perhaps permanently, because I would be a parent.

3) Finish business in the states and move somewhere to live the best life possible as Luciana Petrokov, doing my best to make amends to Luis Fernando and his family, though I don't have a vision for what that will look like yet.

My energy was wan. I had one more thing to do: check my ColourfulCamille email. I hadn't had the moxie to tackle this before now. I imagined thousands of rogue emails, and a range of messages from my Parisian friends.

My cell buzzed, startling me as though I'd been struck by lightening. Up I jumped like a jack-in-the-box, adrenaline cruising through my veins.

"Oui." Old habits die hard.

"Hello, Lucy?"

"Yes, it's me. Hi Matt."

"Hi. I'll finish with work at seven. Do you still want to get together this evening?"

He said still. Do I *still* want to get together? He knew I was on edge by what he told me, before he left me hanging.

"Sure. I just have to eat and feed the cats."

"Great. I'll swing by when I'm done."

I looked for Calypso. Oh, poor kitty! She had gotten sick all over the carpet in the living room. Gross.

"Okay. Um... Matt?"

"Yes?"

"Can you give me until seven-thirty?"

"Sure thing."

"I called the Vet. He's expecting us. Help me get her in your truck." I whipped him through the door with barely a hi, hey, hello, hola, or Salut.

"Hang on. Slow down. Who's sick?"

"Calypso. She's not eating or drinking. She's been throwing up. She was languishing earlier, now she's not responding at all."

"Where is she?"

"In the living room. Near her bed."

Matt strode over. His boots sounded like a funeral march. He squat down, pet her with a smooth glide from head to tail, stood up and squared me in the eyes. "She's dead."

My head fuzzed up and my ears buzzed, drowning out my rapacious heartbeat. Apparently I collapsed onto the couch, but I barely recall that. The thought of telling Kasey her once vivacious, sassy cat was a dead duck was repulsive and devastating. I hadn't planned on a kitty crisis; I had planned to find out how such a conscientious man had taken a life.

I hankered for solid sleep, yearned for the dramas of life to sloooow down; I didn't want to fight even mini-marlins anymore. When was recess? When could we play ball again: sweaty shirts, cartwheels, and Frisbees? I desired to finish my mural to show I could see something beautiful through to fruition. I'd gathered historic pictures of peace marches and protests by the generation I idolized who were into hugs, VW Bugs, and mind-altering drugs. Art is my prayer, and I required to worship at the chalk alter, but you can't always get what you want, though sometimes, if Jupiter aligns with Mars, you get what you need.

I willed myself up, picked up Callie's limp body, and cradled it - her. I peered around the room for her spirit, desperate for a sign, a bell ringing, bird singing, anything. The world was silent but for my cries. The considerate killer consoled me; his massive arms warm and supportive in the weirdest group hug since mom died and dad and I clung to her for an hour like waifs on a deflating raft floating, or rather sinking, fathoms out to sea.

Though I longed to release my grief into his capable hands, my resistance against him persisted. You don't just tell a woman you killed someone and then fall asleep.

I had just met him. Kasey said he was a good man, strong, heroic, the real deal. But she is an enigma to me too. She left me to take care of her dying cat! I then flashed on Natalie Mouskers sitting on my lap, gobbling up sardines on the street directly caddy-corner from Nikos' flat. Shame blew through me in circles like a typhoon over Lake Tanganyika, skiffling the cool, calm waters into tidal waves. It's way too easy to judge others. I needed to reel my attention back to how I might make reparations to those I hurt, rather than making superfluous assumptions about those who were kind to me.

"Have you eaten dinner?"

I blew my nose. "No."

"I will lay her back down. We'll cover her with a pillowcase. After we eat, I'll bury her in the yard and call Kasey for you. Then we can sage the place. We'll have a ceremony when she gets back. Give me the Vet's number and I'll call him for you now."

He was grounded. He would take care of everything. I never had anyone do that for me before. I was famished, but how could I eat? It didn't seem respectful. I sighed, "I can't."

"I brought some fresh greens. I will go wash up and make a salad. Why don't you do the same and come help me?"

"When are you going to finish telling me what you began last night?"

"After supper. I'm sorry I fell asleep. You can trust me. I'll expose everything. I never met anyone I wanted to tell before."

Oh, lucky me.

He scooped me up with the tenderness and protectiveness of a tree kangaroo flyer safeguarding her pocketed joey.

Don't fall in love, Camille.

It was a double pink or purple full moon in Scorpio or something. Three planets were in retrograde, which means they seem to move backwards like a slow train next to a parallel one that moves faster, yet they look like they are going in reverse. The decrease in longitude and change in angles as viewed from earth create these illusions. Anyway, apparently retrogrades can make you feel like a tar baby stuck in a muddle of molasses. When I heard this I promptly nicknamed myself 'a renegade in retrograde' and resolved to some day draw a mural as an ode to forward moving rebels who seem to be regressing.

The moon appeared violet on the horizon, constellations danced against a deep Pacific blue backdrop as the cicadas gave a three hundred and sixty degree concerto like a Greek choir serving as accompaniment for the odyssey of his paroxysmal past that Matt unraveled. A barely there wind blew, ruffled up our hair, completing a panoply of perfection.

"My mother moved out to Albuquerque..."

"From Alabama?"

"Yes."

"Why?"

"What do you mean why?"

"It seems like a random move. She leaves her kid in Biloxi and moves to New Mexico? There must have been a reason."

"She got a job, she met a man. She had her reasons. Do you want me to continue with the story?"

"Yes sorry. I just didn't want to miss anything."

"We'll have a question-and-answer period at the end. How's that?"

"That's fine, sorry." I felt like a nincompoop. Truth is, I was slaphappy from my lack of sleep and sidelined by the unexpected loss of Calypso; I was ripe with emotion. 'Bonkers in Yonkers,' as my parents used to say. They were fun, silly people, and I take after them.

Then, as if on cue, a wild wind whipped up and blew over the sunbrella. The fear I might get the giggles overcame me. Fits of laughter come at all the wrong times: when Noni and I were getting the fifth degree for painting on the side of the house when we were seven (that was when mom bought me chalk to fulfill my need for drawing on large surfaces), when cops nearly arrested me for being drunk out in the back lot of the supermarket after I learned of dad's hoodwinking, hooligan doctor, and when I sat for my college entrance exams. After months of preparing for the GRE's, I arrived early fueled by buckwheat, grilled zucchini, and tempeh, locked my earrings, hair tie, and water-bottle in the cubicle assigned to me, and before I sat down, a cascade of hiccup-like eruptions burst forth. This annoyed the moderators and garnered death-dagger glares from other test-takers. Yeah. Giggles are not always amusing. I have laughed so hard I thought a rib might fracture or funny bone break.

"I was nineteen, on a summer break from college, it was my third time visiting my mother out West."

"What school did you go to? What did you major in? Can I see a picture of you from that time?" I struggled to hold back my queries. I just didn't want to hear what was coming. I craved popcorn and a red velvet chair with armrests worn a quarter inch.

"The stress emaciated me. I was stick-thin, depressed, and completely lacked confidence. My mom and step-dad lived in a rural area. Neither of them had good night vision, so they didn't drive past six. I flew in on a red-eye and took a cab to their house from the airport."

"You sat in back?"

"Yeah. I said it was a cab."

"Just checking." I'm a visual, empathetic person, so I was right there with him as he sat his gangly self into the back seat of the cab.

"The driver wasn't friendly. Most people weren't in those days. I was so timid, scared, and ashamed of my scars I seemed to give off a sour scent. I might as well have stuck a sign on my forehead that said, 'Kick me.' Most people wouldn't even have bothered to ask, 'How hard?' they'd just have complied. This guy though, he had an evil aura."

"An evil aura." It was more a statement than a question.

"Oh, yeah. I never saw anything like it. He had on some vile hang-banging music... don't ask me what, I don't remember."

I smiled and swallowed down my inquiries.

"The cab stunk of B.O., Camels, Strawberry air freshener, and something foul, like a dead skunk. Perhaps some drug he smoked, or just his sinister soul."

"Wow."

"It was dark and deserted in the desert, and hot, mother-fucking hot. Triple digits, I'd guess one-twenty."

I bit freshly cut nails. The suspense was killing me.

"This piece of crap human, this asshat, sped in the wrong direction. 'Give me your watch,' he says. I had a nice watch, a Casio Databank, it was a graduation gift. 'Fuck you,' I said, 'you are not getting my watch, where the fuck are you going?' 'I'm going to rob you and kill you,' he said. He adjusted a cracked rearview mirror and stared at me with his beady eyes, enjoying the hell out of watching me squirm. 'No one will miss you. Look at you, not even a mother could love that face.' 'My mother loves me,' I protested. This asshole had me right where he wanted me, defensive and vulnerable. 'No, she doesn't,' he spat. 'Trust me, she doesn't.'"

"Oh, my god!"

Matt was up on his feet now, pacing back and forth like a caged tiger, rage ricocheted through him like a ball in a Medieval Madness pinball game. It scared me. I'd never seen this side of him before. My pussycat had turned carnivorous, fangs flared.

"What did you do next?"

"I knew he would kill me, Lucy. I took off my belt."

I thought I would wet my pants. "Excuse me a minute, Matt. I have to pee really badly, you know, being pregnant and all. I'll be able to listen better after I go to the bathroom."

I tripped over the braided mat and spilled into the house where I saw Cleo and Cassia curled up like a yin-yang symbol in the opposite corner from their cat beds. Normally the three felines all religiously lay together in the area where Calypso had died not more than an hour before.

The minute I closed the bathroom door, I doubled over. The giggles got me. When set free they bubble and fizz in streams of audaciousness, 'joyeux audace,' Brigitte effervesced en français. 'Awesome,' I would respond through upheavals of hee-hee-hee-ho-ho-hos."

"Oui, Camille, son impresionante, oui, oui!" I could hear Brigitte cry out through her own glorious gales.

After I wore myself out tumbling around the toilette, holding silent my uncontrollable guffaws, I steadied myself to go hear the second and third acts. I picked up Cassia and laid her over my shoulder both to comfort her and myself. With her white paws draped like a boa around my neck, I stepped back out onto the deck. Matt's back was to me as he looked out into the dark night, his mind light years away.

It was just an occasional thing at first. The neighborhood kids would gather at our kitchen table a few times a week, a bowl of eight fat broken crayons sat in the middle, our chubby fingers grasped at the waxy red, purple, green, and yellow, to draw pictures. We colored whatever captivated our three-year-old worlds: apples, family, trees, clouds, houses, a horsey and ducky, like that. Sometimes either Noni's mom or mine gave us a glue stick that had silver sprinkles in it; the sparkly goop became as much part of the picture as anything.

The next year I got a gorgeous black chalkboard easel bordered with a cheery cherry wood trim that seemed ginormous to me then, and tiny to me now, with a ten pack of chalk and an eraser, and for my birthday they gave me a royal blue bell-shaped dress that had paintbrushes embroidered as if they were sticking out of the pockets. I'd stand at the board for hours scratching out my four-year incandescent masterpieces — teachers and townsfolk whispered that I had IT, the creative touch.

In nursery school, we progressed into play dough, clay, spin art, yarn puppets, and face painting at the Renaissance Faire. Once art got a hold of me, it never let go. When I look at the world, it is rampant with beauty. I study patterns in nature, fabric, and faces. Scenes arise in shadows; a sidewalk crack thrills me to my toes. My folks were lenient with what I wore and I dressed like an artist, people said. I paired plaids with stripes, orange with purple, and if I wore socks (which I preferred not to), they were argyles from England, or candy-stripes, or spouted whales swimming round my ankles. The community called me charismatically colorful and laughed at my raucous rayon rebellion; there was no reforming me, but then there was no need to. I rebelled against the status quo, mediocrity, the mundane, monotonous, boring bits of life.

I was fun to be around; I liked to be me and soldiered on through a minefield of mockery early on. Once my classmates saw how delightful it was to drape oneself in delightful apparel, they all wanted in on my merry-go-round. After a play date at my house, kids would go home with pink hair, tie-dyed tees, and fringed jeans, much to their parent's chagrin. Art is an attitude, a heaven, a haven; I crave it, love it, lurve it. I am an art addict.

As Matt continued his story about the nefarious nihilist in that god-forsaken arid wasteland outside Albuquerque, I had to pull myself back repeatedly from the chalk mural I was dramatically drawing in my mind.

"Let me out here, and we'll forget this ever happened," I said. He sniffed at me and floored the gas pedal. I thought of opening the door and rolling out on the road, but my head meeting concrete at that speed did not bode well for a functional future, so silently I lifted my belt and waited for the right time when we passed by bushes. I expected the car would veer off the road as he lost consciousness and I had to plan well for the crash."

"How fast was he going?"

"Over a hundred."

"That must have been terrifying!"

"You're a monster," he shot back to me. "I'll be doing you a favor by ending your life."

I wanted to give Matt a hug, but this wasn't the time. His delivery ramped up.

"I had been suicidal before. I hated what the fire did to me emotionally, socially, and spiritually. My left profile still showed the handsome boy I had been, the right side of my face melted like a candle flickering at wicks end, my arm withered, face pale, appetite gone. I had lived like a ghost for nine years."

"Coast?"

"Ghost."

"Ohhh."

"'Tell me about yourself, what brings you to New Mexico?' I asked him."

"Why did you ask that? He was crazy."

"I'd heard that madmen act from a wounded place. I thought I might make human contact. Save him from himself. Save me."

The violet moon hypnotized Matt away from our here and now. I endured the dramatic pause, my foot tap-tapping like a dog pawing at the door to go for his Sunday stroll.

"What happened next? Did he answer you?"

"He turned the music up as far as it would go. The windows rattled from the fucking feedback spilling from the speakers. I lifted my belt and slipped it around his neck."

La la la la la la la. I'll draw a demonstration against the Vietnam War at the corner, the Chicago Seven, and a Picasso peace dove...

"It happened quickly, he gasped, lifted his hands from the wheel to his throat..."

LA LA LA LA LA. Flowers, mushrooms, a psychedelic acid trip...

"I jumped into the front seat and barely steered into a soft embankment. I expected another inferno, waited for the can to burst into flames, my worst nightmare, but after a bumpy mile or so, we bucked to a stop."

LA LA LA... "Was he dead?"

"No, but he was barely breathing."

"And?"

"I finished choking him with my hands. I did him a favor. No ill will intended. I just suddenly wanted to live. He gave me back my lust for life."

That was the time to hug him. There was so much more to his story, and I wanted to hear it all, but I'd catapulted way past capacity for the day.

"Let's go out."

"Where?"

"I want to dance."

"It's Thursday night. I just told you how I killed a man, and the cat died."

"All the more reason."

I scampered off to put on the green velvet crop top. Pierre stood by, seeming to question my attitude, which may have come off to him as irreverent. I needed some new tops, all clothes, actually; my pants were getting tighter as I approached my second trimester. When I came out, Matt handed me the keys to his car.

"We're going to San Francisco. I'm tired. You up for driving?"

I hadn't driven since the incident in Paris. It was time to get back in the saddle.

"Oui, mais bien sûr."

A succulent stash of groovy Telegraph Avenue vintage clothing store finds: wraparound skirts, rope-tie pants, blousy jumpers, and even some tie-dye, a stylish, arty wardrobe perfectly pragmatic for the predictable pregnancy changes ahead, billowed my bags full. Every pouch and pocket crammed to capacity.

"Belle journée," a halcyon voice rang out from the kitchen just below my room.

Kasey! I ran to greet her like she was a long-awaited refreshing serein, washing away the suffocating heat of the cruel crucible that Calypso's death levied upon us during her short sojourn. We hugged like the sisters in Frozen, arms encompassed in a 'we-are-one' circle, heads laid gingerly, then passionately, on each other's shoulders. She sobbed for her cat, came up for air and indulged me in French, which she did periodically, "Tout va bien?"

"Oui, bien, and crazy too — I'm so sorry about Calypso!"

"No worries, she was old and sick, I considered canceling the trip to stay with her, but I knew she was in your capable hands."

"She died peacefully, K."

"All your bags are packed?"

"I'm ready to go."

"Why now?"

"I finished my work here." The impression of Niko's email, (I finally mustered up the courage to look at my emails), seared my mind. "Cammy, we all are being questioned about you. Call me when you are able. Love, your Nikos."

"How are you getting to your next destination?"

"In my truck," Matt strode in the room looking taller, wider, and more heroic than ever.

"You're loaning Lucy your work truck?"

"I'm going with her."

Kasey swiped away tears of grief for Calypso to confront this new loss, "How long will you be away?"

"As long as it takes. I'll secure some of my projects in the flatbed and work on them there."

"Where is there?"

"Idaho. My parents have an impressively sized, solidly stacked storage locker bourgeoning with stuff and I'm the sole person responsible. I plan to liquidate everything, or just burn it." I cringed. Did I just talk about burning down a shed in front of Matt?

"What about your regular clients?" Kasey, cloaked in concern, unconsciously circled the kitchenette like she was training for a speed walking contest. She shot a protective 'I don't want you to leave me' pout Matt's way.

Matt picked up the cue as he always does and softened Kasey, his still-surrogate mother, with a bounty of soft sawder. "You're the best, Kas, I won't be able to stay away from home for long. I have to hit the road and be with Lucy right now though."

After one more loop around the kitchen, she slowed as my phone rang. Who was calling?

"Oui?"

"Konnichiwa Lu-cee. My new job did not work out. I have nowhere to go!"

Holding my hand over the receiver, I mouthed the news to Kasey and Matt.

"She can rent here this month, and we'll see how it goes. Perhaps it will work out long-term. Matsako and I get along well. I might be able to help her with a job and papers."

"Oh, I heard! Thank you, Miss Kasey. When may I arrive?"

"When are you two leaving?"

"Now. Right after the ceremony."

"Tell her the place is hers and to come as quickly as possible to take part in celebrating Calypso."

Before I hung up the phone, Matsako appeared as though she was a rabbit in a magician's hat. "I was just down the block, waiting to call, hoping you'd invite me in, missing Sakura season in Kyoto; I am miss my home, cherry blossoms, but not so much family. Does this make sense to any of you?" She shook her head, confused.

"Oh, hell yes," Kasey got it.

"I ain't ever put on the Ritz to rush home to kin," Matt did too.

"Matsako, your feelings are normal. I feel this too." Me three.

We had a group hug, picked fresh oranges and cumquats to chop with almonds into our oats, and fuel us to dig a Calypso sized grave. Clea, Cassia, and even Hank and Lilly next door came to pay their respects. There wasn't a dry eye in the house as we overturned the last shovelful of dirt in her sweet, little, kitty grave, and placed stones and trinkets on top. Those tears gave me an excuse to cry throughout my goodbyes. Matt practically had to pry Matsako off of me, Kasey looked lost. She handed me *The Complete Works of Ibsen, Strindberg, and Shaw,* for the road.

"I'll mail this back when I finish it."

"Don't be silly. Book loans are gifts. You'll get more mileage from them on the road than I will here."

"Will I see you again?"

"You better."

Now Hank and Lilly were crying too. Matt kept packing and fixing small things around the house for Kasey until he herded us outside. I'd finished my mural. It was time to move on. Barely smudged from wind or rain, we got group pictures of everyone encircling it flashing peace signs and smiles. Matsako took some of me alone with my creation.

"Time to go. Bye, everybody!" Matt led me to his truck laden with our gear, a tent, and three woodworking projects covered by an olive green tarp. I turned and waved until they were out of sight. As we rounded the corner, a lightening bolt lit the sky. I counted aloud, "One one thousand, two one thousand," and the cymbal crashed above. The empyrean ether flooded the land as my peace mural turned into rivulets of runny dye flowing over cement and spilling into street gutters. I trained my eyes to look ahead and did not turn back. Well, none but that one time I looked over my shoulder to whisper, "Why?"

THE NINTH HOLE

Driving Matt's truck on un-crowded roads, warm wind whipped cross current through open windows, set up high like on her majesty's throne, bug guts splat on windshield. We cruised past lines of Mack tracks, waving "Hi" to fellow drivers. Singing *Five Hundred Miles* in mezzo-soprano, sweet harmony to his tenor, I'd found my bliss. Matt stole a quick kiss, but I wouldn't let myself get sidetracked while behind the wheel. Been there, done that.

Our Berkeley to Boise drive was off to a great start — the route took us Easterly over to Sacramento, Southeast on US 20, then onto 184W, ID, ID 55, then US 95 S passing through Nevada and clipping the corner of Oregon before heading towards my home zone, if I can legit call it home anymore; Idaho didn't resemble the place I'd grown up any longer after the death of my parents and others of their generation who lost their lives too young or moved in a Westerly direction to Vancouver, Seattle, or San Jose.

The trip would only take a day, not nearly long enough to be on a road trip with Matt who is as much fun in a truck as in the woods, the park, his workshop teaching me to saw, or doing crosswords and consorting in bed. Once or twice I sighed and thought of how lovely it would be to head back to live a semi-normal life in Calif-orn-i-ay.

We played *I Spy, What Do You Like Better, This Or That,* and *What Do You Love*, and *What Do You Hate*. I went first.

"I hate it when people are faux spiritual, passive aggressive, put up platitudes instead of admitting they want to punch someone's lights out, are so sickening sweet and cloying while they psychically stab you in the back. Behind their screens, windows, or shades they give the finger, the middle one, tallest and most urban of the bunch, bent or straight, that finger means business, and it doesn't mean, 'God bless you,' which is what they say when signing off on their letter, insinuating that *you* have the problem, *are* the problem, *caused* the problem by standing up for yourself after they flat out used, abused, and insulted you, citing then, 'You have no sense of humor.' I hate it when one needs a phone call, meal, hug, or conscientious voice but someone instead waves the religious flag of non-pragmatism and the penultimate pacification, 'I'll pray for you,' before the final robotic, pre-programmed propaganda, 'God bless.' How about you?"

"I hate sushi."

"That's all? I poured my heart out."

"I hate medical commercials on TV."

"Good one."

"I hate first dates."

"Have you had many?"

"Yes."

A wave of jealousy ripped through me, so green it threatened to fester and infect our whole trip if I didn't reel it in.

"Try having a blind date with half a profile like this," his tone was hard to read sometimes. His struggle with degradation obvious, yet overtaken by a resolve to move on and as he said, 'Just do him and let the judgmental, speculative bastards hang themselves on their own words and putrid actions.'

"I hate people that start saying something but then cop out and when you confront them they say, 'Nothing.'"

"Matt?"

"Hum?"

"What happened after you...?"

"After we crashed?"

"Yeah. How did you get out of there? What did you do with the cab? What about his body? Did anyone see you? Do you ever worry they might find you?"

"I stuffed the old boy in the trunk. Drove to my mom and stepdad's house that night. Needed to eat and sleep. Parked in back. Threw a tarp over the cab. Next day, drove his body to the woods and burned him. Good riddance. Deflated the tires and took them and the motor to the dump. I spray painted the frame then sautered it apart and used it in art projects all summer."

"Didn't anyone report him missing or suspect you?"

"An asshole like that? Not a soul missed him. No one suspected me. I was the sad, artistic kid with the weird face that people avoided looking at or laughed at. No one suspected anything except that I was doing my weird thing."

"Wow."

He smiled as though he'd just told me he won the Kentucky Derby.

I considered his honesty with me and decided to reveal my truth too. It would be hard to explain my life in Idaho and goal of getting rid of all my folks' stuff if I had to keep dancing around the truth. Being transparent is easy; lies are merciless. As we crossed over two state lines, I worked up the manner in which I'd broach the subject. Finally, during his turn behind the wheel I ahemed and began, "Matt, there's something I want to tell..."

Just then a light frost beige Jeep Cherokee with a flattened front left fender swerved into our lane and back out, in and out, in rhythmic motion like the Queen's wave.

Matt hit the horn full palmed, full blast, red faced, eyes flashing for a good thirty seconds. HOOOOOOONK. HOOOOOOOOOOOOOOONK. HOOOOOOONK.

"That fucking bastard, did you see him? Jackass is wearing sunglasses at night! Been dark for two hours now, right? Two hours. He could kill someone. I hate bad drivers who risk the lives of others. Someone might want to shoot that guy! This could persuade me to pull a Lizzie on that dizzy jerk hole." I guessed that was an allusion to Lizzie Borden and her axe. He took three long, calming breaths, put his hand on my knee, and picked up where we'd left off. "Sorry, now, what were you saying?"

I didn't want to piss off the guy who strangled a cabbie, burned his body in the woods, good riddance, and used the cab parts for welding projects, so I hid behind an Alcazar of yellow-bellied, morose placidity, "Nothing."

He laughed.

"Yes, sir, officer. I sure will." Contrite and humbled in front of the policeman, Matt mumbled an expletive under his breath, "God damn him," the minute the badged one got in his Charger and cruised away to the south, headlights blazing to catch another sucker. There was a preponderance of cops along this stretch of highway whose sole job was to make money for the state by catching unsuspecting visitors driving through speed traps.

"Fucking sign said forty, two minutes later we're in a 20 MPH zone with no warning!" Matt popped a steaming hot French fry in his mouth. He chewed painfully as though it was blistering in his mouth. I thought to ask him why he would burn his tongue rather than his hand, but edited myself for once.

"It's totally messed up; they set these traps to catch the tourists. It's an awful scam. Why didn't you tell me?"

"I'm sorry, I forgot. I haven't been here in years and I was distracted by the beige beast." I picked at my pesticide laden iceberg leaves with no appetite, worried that our honeymoon was over. I zoned out the window wildly wishing for a bitty beacon of hope, or at least an organic salad and a swig of strawberry kefir instead of this roadside crap. I pictured a quainter life full of mystical serendipity, beds of red roses, and children spinning circles and yodeling in the Alps. Ah, if only I could paint my life with half the skill I could create an enticing art scene on cement.

"Are you going to eat, or should we get going?" His words brought me crashing back to reality.

"I'm gonna eat." I dug into my scrambled eggs with bravado, needing the sustenance of a good meal to fuel me on. I even ate the fake wheat toast with honey on it, polished off the tasteless tomatoes, watery skinned cucumbers, and that limpid white lettuce.

"What were you going to tell me back there?" He eyed the check with disgust.

"Where?"

"In the truck. When you said, 'Nothing.'"

"Nothing," I delivered the words, my dimples showing. He was having none of it.

"Okay, fine, be that way. I bared my soul to you. Told you things no one in the world but Kasey knows, but you're still on this fucking trip of hiding from me. You don't trust me yet? You think I'll hurt you, Lucy? What could be worse than strangling a guy and burning his body in the woods?"

I looked around to see if anyone was eavesdropping. Waitresses clanked down plates heavy with sausages and greasy hash brown potatoes, the old time cash register rang like a sick songbird, trucks sped by on the highway. I had to pee something terrible.

"I'll help you get set up and head back to California tomorrow."

"I thought you would stay a few weeks."

"I changed my mind."

"Why?"

"Oh, it's nothing."

The ambiance in the dive Cafe bathroom was titillating: the walls were a rainbow wash of lavender, rose, and turquoise blue as though a pack of half-melted Schmopsicles had exploded out of the sink and sprayed over all the surfaces in sight. Plaster of Paris angels formed an arch over the changing table where I laid out my tiny travel toiletries. Spanish guitar gently piped in through speakers in the ceiling. It made no sense — seemed misappropriated in this environment. I wanted to move into this room and cocoon forever.

A bottle I pulled from my pack supplied the water I resolutely poured over the soft-bristled brush to clean my teeth, cheeks, and tongue. I used the same water to smooth my matted cowlick. Peach flavored lip-gloss transformed my mouth from matte to a lip-smacking sensuous sheen, and I stepped into my new-used tie wrap pants with shrub shapes on them. My favorite is the upward braying elephant. I'm also fond of the curled up cat that reminds me of my feline friends, whether French speaking or recently deceased.

Finishing my operose changes, I slipped on a fuzzy, light lemon cropped jersey, causing my just-combed hair to crackle with static electricity. Behind my reflection in this restroom haven with sparkling faucets, stacks of pristine white toilet paper and not a shoddy, silver buttoned hand-blower in sight, stood Luis Fernando, his face peaceful, though I'm unsure why. Puzzled still by his intermittent presence, my soul stained from the predicament.

When I stepped outside, Matt's eyes softened. I could sense he wanted to rush over, lift and twirl me in celebration of our still budding love, but he had to hold his emotional distance position from me. I've been there.

The sun broke overhead. When he lifted his sweater off up over his head, his shirt rose over his waist. I was on the scar side. The length of his torso was a pale whitish-pink, the contracted tissue, vulnerable in the light of day. I tried for a moment to look at him as a stranger might. I was vividly aware of the repulsive looks shot to him from passersby every day. I plainly saw that it bothered him, but he dealt with it well, better than I surmised I would; he turned his charm full force on the contemptuous cavalry, cleansing them with his clarity and courage. When he got angry, he lifted weights, his upper body massive now, biceps and pectorals well defined under his white tee shirt.

He swept his hair fringe up off his forehead touching his right eye, (the one that was partially closed because of the burn), unconsciously, unceremoniously, fingers lingering as a blind man reading poetry, taking in each distinct dip and rise, his lip curled up almost in a smirk on that side of his face. I tried again to look at him with judgment, any kind disgust or disdain, but all I saw was that I lo... I lo... I lo... Oh, no. No, no no no no no no!

I loved him.

"Do you want to drive?" he asked.

"Do you mind if we walk first? I like the air here. I need to move. The sun is out." I squinted up at the sky.

"No, I don't mind. There's a trail over there," he gesticulated towards a grove we had passed down the road.

"Great," this time he caught my dimpled smile in a mitt he brought in towards the heart.

The nearly summer shimmer of sunlight through trees touched the tops of our heads like light laughter, nature doing her thing, sung to us softly in a dazzling display of a drizzly Spring, her glory reflected on us like a meteoric mood ring. We strolled, then sauntered, pranced, skipped and ran. Matty picked me up and twirled me around. The honeymoon was back on and I hadn't told him a word about my past, and on our outing, he didn't once ask.

Matt drove the rest of the way. Our destination was a campground twelve miles from the *Ernest Elves Do-It-Yourselves-With-Extra-Shelves Self Storage*, facility. Blame the long, frenetic name on me. My folks were friends with Myra and Morrie, the original owners. The handle was my idea and I painted the sign when I was nine. Matt laughed when I told him the name, which bode well for us. If he denigrated it, it would have precipitated a fight. *Ernest Elves* was my first succulent brush with fame.

We covered twenty miles in lush, awkward silence; the soulful singing of Leadbelly, (*Where Did You Sleep Last Night*), was the only sound besides the rolling, bump, bump, bump of the road as it passed underway. Finally Matty turned off the music. "You don't have to tell me anything you don't want to. It doesn't matter to me. In fact, I don't want you to tell me. Just be you. Just do you."

"Okay... thanks." Exhausted, I settled back, making a pillow by balling up the skirt I'd worn earlier in the day. A man with good taste in music is essential for a relationship to work; his love for Leadbelly, lightening quick wit, and tender compassion formed a perfecto trifecta of traits that could capture my heart and mind, and spark passion forever. I turned the music back on, softly closed my eyes and drifted off, hypnotized by the steady motion of the truck and the cracking of the old blues recording.

When the song ended, Matt turned off the music again. I opened one eye to survey the scene. It was pitch dark out, no moon, and few other headlights on the road. He looked at his watch like the white rabbit, querulous and remote. "Two more hours till we're there."

"Do you want me to drive?"

"No. You can barely stay awake. Get some rest." He brushed my bangs to the side before sweeping his own hair up over his forehead again, fingers tacitly touching his right eye. His back arched in a stretch, the limited sort that the driver's seat of a truck allows.

"You look uncomfortable. Are you in pain?"

"My back hurts a bit," he looked at his watch again, "An hour and fifty-five minutes ta-go."

"Are you mad at me?"

"Why would I be mad at you?"

"Because of what you said before. You think I don't trust you."

"I'm over that, Lucy. Life's too short to hold onto grudges. Truthfully, I don't want to know. I don't think you should tell anyone something you're not comfortable with. Don't think about it again. It's done." He yawned and rotated his stiff shoulders.

I wondered what he was thinking, tried to crawl into his mind, and flip through the pages he had shown me so far of his life's book: His early childhood living in white privilege in Biloxi was fairly carefree, filled with a preponderance of prank-playing friends, Frisbee, and frequent baseball games. He had cereal for breakfast on weekdays; eggs and pastries, church, and mini-golf on weekends. Took special trips to the Lighthouse, Ship Island, and Mardi gras in New Orleans. Raffia ribbons with curled edges decorated birthday presents of monster trucks, books, and six-packs of white socks — all conventional trappings of Southern suburban life. His young parents fought for civil rights and eventually fought with each other. When they divorced, his mother married a member of the Tiwa nation she met at a peace rally and left Matt and his brother with their father in Mississippi. Kasey became their stepmom, and the abandoned boys didn't take to having a new woman in the house. Then the fire happened and changed everything. He and Kasey bonded as he endured several terrifying skin grafts and unrelenting rounds of bullying.

Bump, bump, bump went the road.

Years of hiding in agony followed. The outgoing boy transformed in his head to a monster. He got good grades, but missed dating and prom;

it attenuated the social scene of being a teen for him. While I was rousting our winning Volleyball team as the lauded captain, juggling three boys at once, traipsing with friends to the mountain for each fresh snowfall, and being groomed from grade three to be Valedictorian, Matt holed up inside, withering away, reading *Moby Dick* and *Call of the Wild* instead of experiencing nature directly.

Curiously, the carnage in that Albuquerque cab catapulted him back into the stratosphere of life. His capability to contend with danger and protect himself transformed how he comported himself in the world. Though his love of reading never waned, the sickly boy pumped iron, regained his appetite for life, and moved forward with moxie. This attracted people, regardless of the straggling detractors who stare, gasp, or cover their eyes in a reflexive, often unintended reaction.

Now here he was, driving me - a woman he fully connected with - out to Idaho for some secretive reason he could only speculate about.

"Truthfully, I don't want to know. I don't think you should tell anyone something you're not comfortable with," he had said. Well, that was the wrong thing to say to me. If you tell me not to talk, then for one hour and fifty minutes on a road so dark it made black look light, you will hear me spill my beans, show my hand, give an uninterrupted disquisition without time to take a breath. Both of my eyes were now open and my mouth moved at warp speed. I laid out the basics of my life-book: my hippie-dippy mom and dad, hedging, unhelpful Aunt Molly, my childhood BFF Noni and our elfish escapades, the encapsulating charm that chalk held over me, and the stereotypical turn from a good girl into a troubled, rebellious teen who became a caregiver without having a word to say about it otherwise.

I told him how I had to sell the house on the hill to the bank for peanuts, after which I hit bottom, rebounding by literally drawing my way out, line by line. I drew an open door in the contentious cage I was caught in and flew fast as a hummingbird to Paris for graduate school. I touched on meeting Brigitte and Jacqueline and had time for a quick mention of Nikos, Pascal, and my partner, the best blues busker this side of Brussels, at which point I was so tired, I burst into tears at the mere utterance of Bertrand et Belle.

We turned into the campground as I mumbled the words 'Paris predicament,' and 'Pierre.'

The minute Matt set his feet on the ground he grabbed the small of his back and bent over moaning with a bellow frightful enough to scare the coyotes.

"What is it?" I ran to his side. Sweat wept like sideburns past his ears. "You're burning up! What should I do?"

"Nothing," he mopped his brow with his shirtsleeve, "Nothing."

A smattering of serene, stars winked in the moonless sky to illuminate my way. Light years distant, their phosphorescence was filmy by the time it reached me scrambling on shaky knees over treacherous terrain to find rocks weighty enough to anchor the tan tent. Matt lay squirming on a pad I set for him on a prickly patch of grass, the softest surface I could find. A ruffed grouse peeked from the bushes in wordless wonder at our hapless human antics, so oddly out of step with the rational rhythm of nature: a sac-religious, slapstick satire.

Like a chef stirring and seasoning five delicate dishes at a time, a juggler tossing an apple, hard-boiled egg, and machete, or a mother with eyes in the back of her head trained on two taurine toddlers and a newborn babe, I, like a creative cyclone, multitasked too. I soaked Matt's fevered forehead in water from our dwindling supply using the skirt I had slept on as moistening material, while he mumbled something about Froyo and Dr. Brown's Cream Soda, cool treats from his boyhood. I called on the Komani, the lion-dogs to guard us safely through the night. I pounded stakes into the ground hitting impenetrable hard spots, peed twice in the bushes, and calmed my friend in a voice smooth as satin.

"How are you, sweet? You're less clammy now."

"A little better... Ow." His eyes squeezed shut. "Ow..."

"Shhh. What's wrong? What can I do?"

"Lucy?"

"Yes, love?"

"Could you massage me for a few minutes?" His face scrunched up. "Ow."

"Yes. Where does it hurt?"

"Here, on my side where the flesh burned away. It shortened the tissues where the scars are; it constricts my whole body."

"Like this?"

"Ah, yes. Thank you. I'm sorry I have to ask."

"Ask me any time. How often does it hurt like this?"

"I'm in pain every day, but at home I stretch and get bodywork to keep it at bay. The driving was too much for me."

"Oh, no. Why did you come then?"

"You need support. You're strong, Lucy, but no one should have to go through this alone. Whatever you're going through."

The grouse drummed his wings in agreement; a playful pitter-pattering that began slowly and built to a climatic crescendo, a percussionist practicing for Carnegie Hall.

"What was that?" he sat up.

"A grouse."

"He concurs!"

"Apparently." We laughed.

"I have something to ask you."

"Can it wait until morning? You're burning up again. I still have to arrange the sleeping bags and get you settled in the tent."

He head dropped back down at the thought of moving.

"We have to keep our strength up. Can you eat?"

He nodded.

"I'll go get food from the truck."

Pierre stood behind him mouthing, "Don't fall in love."

"Too late," I mouthed back.

I could tell Pierre liked him too.

A tantalizing wooded wonderland was an idyllic place to hang out for a week — there were only a few other folks in our quiet camp, our favorite by far was 'Andy the Amphibian Guy,' a bundle of bright energy, who taught us about the intimate mating details of Tiger Salamanders, Rough-Skinned Newts, Great Basin Spadefoot Toads, and Northern Leopard Frogs. Andy, a student/researcher, was a rugged outdoorsman who spent most of his days hiking and collecting specimens.

THE PARIS PREDICAMENT

Up before the sun, he washed in his own portable shower at dawn, and in the evenings, piped Allman Brothers songs from his car stereo and swigged kick-ass homemade blue agave tequila, which Matt sampled and I got the slightest taste of when I kissed him — Matt, not Andy.

Andy was not simply a talker, but also a teacher; if you gave me a test, I could tell you that the Coeur d' Alene Salamanders are small and grayish-black with light-colored speckles, an uneven dorsal edge which sparkles yellow or gold, and a yellow patch on the throat that distinguishes them from the Long-toed Salamander, which lacks this patch. Salamanders and the smell of tequila will go together in my mind forever.

Were you aware that a study of the salamander brain has led researchers to discover a hitherto unknown function of the neurotransmitter dopamine? I do. In this study, they show how in acting as a kind of switch for stem cells; dopamine controls the formation of new neurons in the adult brain. "Their findings may contribute to new treatments for neurodegenerative diseases, such as Parkinson's," Andy excitedly relayed to us on a Saturday night over a crackling orange campfire.

My contribution was to sketch out a colorful family tree of Idaho amphibians, a gift Andy said was the sweetest thing he'd ever received. He ran to his car, supposedly to put on *Soulshine*. After a few minutes, we heard a slight kerfuffle, then a crash. This apparently was Andy rummaging through his trunk for Kleenex and then slamming the hood shut. The sight of his beloved frogs drawn so beautifully made him weepy. I marvel at the power art has to move even the toughest individuals.

On the third day, we left the campgrounds in search of massages. Matt and I both desperately needed one. We lucked into a hole-in-the-wall Chiropractic Center called, *Cracked and Unscrambled*, a branding so hokey, I could have made up myself. Bonnie, a brilliant body worker with a blue streaked bob (and a certificate ironically in a frame of frogs and flowers next to her tulip shaped tip jar), kneaded the knots right out of us.

She gave what Matt said was a 'heroic effort' to lessen the tautness surrounding his scars, leaving the pair of us refreshed like we'd had a year's holiday. While he was on the table, I wandered down the block and got vegetable soup and salad at a diner with a boring bathroom. During my turn, Matt did the same. We brought gumbo back for Andy only to find that he'd packed up and left.

With Andy gone, we had more time to get to connect deeply with each other and figure out a plan. I soaked in more details of Matt's story and fitfully spilled out my past in Paris that placed the predicament in the needle's eye. I feared Matt would abandon me, and rightfully so. He killed a psychopath in self-defense; I killed an innocent child out of stupidity.

He took it very hard. It upset him for my sake and he mourned heavily for the lost life of Luis Fernando. I wish Andy had left behind his Kleenex because I caught sight of Matt blowing his nose into his favorite light blue tee shirt, which got so gunked up he finally threw it in the fire.

"Let's honor him as we did with Calypso."

"Yes. Let's do that."

This suggestion touched me; I was ashamed I had not thought to do this yet. It took several hours to prepare. We each wrote a short speech, in the solemnity of silence.

We held the ceremony for Luis Fernando under a sweeping Magnolia tree, flush pink in spring splendor. Pierre attended his own service looking like a zombie, unsure of what was happening. Between Matt and I there wasn't a dry eye in the house. When it was over, the drumming of the grouse serenaded us in a deep slumber, depleted and drained. Only the boy stayed awake after his wake, watching me, ever so closely.

The ninth hole was the one that most often messed up my score. As a kid, I could cruise along, blowing Cathy and Noni out of the water, while I rocked my kinetic hand-to-eye coordination, until I tilted at the windmill of that hole. I'd waste four or five strokes on those few yards of stained, synthetic greenery made to resemble grass. This course was one I'd been to when I was a kid. Time-space realities merged as images of the past superimposed themselves onto the present. While there, I worked to reign myself in from concern about my future conundrum; the angst wasn't good for the babies or me.

It was Matt's idea to play. I wanted to ice skate like a 1960s go-go-dancer to corny old rock music, sock a volleyball, or shoot hoops in the park after dark, but I had a great time, just us and two-dozen other misfits, swatting balls in Mike's Mini-Golf Park and Playground. My nifty yellow ball, a perfect yolk, teased me to not overshoot the cup again.

"Ooh, so close!"

Matt took his turn. He stood, feet apart, silver club lined up to his tangerine ball just so as he gauged the geometric rebound needed to land his shot. He strode up the carpet and down with a silly grin to make me laugh. It worked.

The plastic orange globe rolled three times around the rim of the cup and clattered in. Hole in two! He was winning. "Yes!" his fist clenched and pulled chin-to-waist like an old-time train conductor ringing a bell and shouting, "All aboard!"

Matty was my jewel, my gem, my Zen Rinpoche, who always brought me to the here-and-now. "Ah-mazing shot!" I threw my arms around him and hugged him for no reason, because I could, because he was what was good in my life.

Earlier that morning we'd trekked to the *Ernest Elves Self Storage* and sussed out the state of things. The situation was I had a two hundred square foot unit crammed full of my parent's furniture, clothing, books, dishes, family photos, my childhood toys, and god knows what else. My first bicycle, a red tricycle with pink, yellow, and blue tassels sat atop two now-moldy mattresses. Facing this mass of memories would be my encounter with Goliath. I shiver to think how it hard it'd have been without Matt's enigmatic empathy.

Matt checked his watch and scratched his forearm. I scratched mine. We both felt itchy for days. It was time to bid adieu to the grouse and find a temporary house. Our plan was to find a rental where he could set up his commissioned woodworking projects, and I'd have a base from which to brave my sessions in the storage shed. Aware that our work would soon begin, we eked every bit of pleasure from this day off.

A whirring sound shifted my focus up above. A dirigible flew overhead, ominous, obscuring the sun — like a warning of dark things to come. I shuddered and turned to make eye contact with Matt. He was on the ground. My heart stopped. I thought he'd fallen, slipped on a ball, or was in paralyzing back spasms like before. He was down on one knee on the tenth hole, his eyes too turned towards the sky.

A biplane passed east to west — trailing behind it was a banner that read, "Lucy, will you marry me?"

Two tear-eyed couples, three goofy groups of friends, a buoyant, big-boned blonde, a Finnish family, and seven rowdy eight-year-old boys at a birthday party, (making ferocious fake farts under their arms), gathered from the seventh to twelfth holes when they saw the marriage banner flutter by in the sky. The statistical supposition is I would say yes to such an exotic (for Idaho), tantalizing, public proposal.

This was Matt's moment. He looked up at me with tangible purity; a supplicant seeking approval, waiting entrance to the rest of his life. My heart pounded as molecules expanded before my eyes, galaxies were born, and exploded and reborn, gods offered sacchariferous ambrosia to one another, libations of life and liberty.

I briefly thought I might feign a faint, my head was hot like a cystic eruption; Matt, the man, was as vulnerable as Matty, the young boy, who was burned in the fire. Twenty sets of eyes - attached to a soda pop slurping, sundress and khaki wearing crowd - grilled him. I knew the "No" was coming, but I couldn't form the "Nnnnnn" on my lips. Matt saw it in my eyes. He saved himself, saved me, stood and dipped me in a carbon-copy clone of Eisenstaedt's iconic soldier and nurse in Times Square photo. We kissed.

The cluster of kids whooped and hollered, the adults clapped with glee like they were calling for a third encore at a rock concert. The men patted Matt on the back and congratulated us with winks. The women gave me quick hand squeezes and wide crescent moon smiles. We played the remaining eight holes in silence. Matt won by ten strokes; I was glad for his elegant victory. It was the least I could do.

We ate a late lunch of spelt pancakes, eggs over easy, and freshly squeezed orange juice, my favorite drink. Matt raised his glass in a toast.

"Here's to us."

I lifted my glass and touched his, scratching the nape of my neck with my free hand.

"We have poison oak, kid."

I cried. Matt got up and came to sit on my side of the booth.

"You haven't given me your answer yet." Perhaps it was the late afternoon glare glazing through the window, but it looked like his eyes were moist too.

"I don't have a normal life. I'm not normal. It's not fair to you. I can't... ummm... I can't bring you into this... this... crazy life."

He swirled his orange juice, took a long, thirsty look out the window as five more star clusters erupted and collapsed. He up tucked my chin like Nikos used to do.

"I'm already here, Lucy, and I hate to break it to you, but there ain't no normal."

PANDORA'S BOX

One does not know the prodigal tide of life until total body poison oak sweetens the kitty. We were inflamed - hot and bumpy head-to-toe. We lay next to each other like sunburnt sardines, raw, temperamental, and unable to sleep. The inside of my nose itched, Matt's throat swelled. That soft patch I situated the tent on was an anoxic Toxicodendron.

It was critical we find a place to live, so we barked out of the gate like a bombastic tornado, swirling in on any opportunity. We talked to everyone, even stopping people on the street. We littered bulletin boards and poles with pretty fliers, and searched online seamlessly and relentlessly. We toured seven places a day for three days until we settled on a tiny turquoise trailer on the back lot of Jospehina and Finn's lush twenty acre estate.

Madam, a Tarot card reader with a pink rose emblem on her calling card, moved with a sensuous sashay, and Sir, an ex-politician from Ireland with chipmunk cheeks and a space between his front teeth, had an impossibly confident handshake as though he were on a whistle-stop campaign — possibly a corrupt couple hiding behind a cosmic veneer, but who were we to judge? They were kind and generous with us.

These eccentric landowners gave us free rein to set up Matt's woodworking studio, full use of a washer in the shed, and access to a bitty, bubbling creek, a bissel of heaven right in our own backyard. The victory was pyrrhic; we celebrated with an ironic chuckle as we scratched each other's backs in dogged desperation and triple-washed everything we owned with Borax to rid our lives of the curse of the itchy oak, which is no joke.

For several weeks we settled into our venturesome version of domesticated bliss. Having a tiny refrigerator and stove in a mini-house was a vast improvement over buying almonds, gogi berries, and red peppers on the fly. When we were packing our campsite, we ran into Andy the amphibian guy. We invited him to visit our new home if he was ever in the area for his frog finding missives. Andy was always ready with a dirty joke, implausible-but-true tales of his trippy travels, a helping hand, and a sip of home-brewed tequila for Matt.

When we weren't hanging with Andy, Matt and I were solitary and inseparable. He rarely brought up marriage, playing his cards close to his chest. As a team we sawed, shaped, sanded, finished, and shipped his three commissions from Berkeley. No sooner were those done than locals placed orders. As artists, we were fortunate.

Two days a week we cleaned and organized the shed. Going through my parents' history wore on me. They got sick so suddenly, they didn't have time to thin through their possessions or prepare me for what lie in between comforter covers and the ceramic wheel.

It was Matt - clamoring through my family's stuff like Sisyphus' steady soldier - who pulled the box from between the piles of cloth. On the left was the baby blue blanket that kept me warm on chilly nights as an infant, and on the right, the crocheted afghan, black background, brightly curled, florescent flowers stitched in a foursquare pattern, which was a ghost from my mother's girlhood in the patchouli-ed psychedelic sixties. This jumble of bedding served as a parental divide that separated dad's sports gear, musical memorabilia, and math periodicals from mom's clay pots, finger puppets, and poetry of Poe.

Andy and I were outside finagling the reconstruction of a child's wooden step stool / chair that had been my mother's, then mine. A blue, yellow, and red merry-go-round stood was painted on the base and the poem on moveable-hinged step read: "Wash hands and face and do them well, when you step on this carousel." I imagined my mini-me climbing on the shoe-scuffed bottom and soaping up at the sink, tiny toothbrush at the ready.

"Lucy, come see this!"

I ran inside breathless with positive anticipation. The thing at first appeared innocuous, but as I dug though the sizeable, sage scented, sandalwood box, a complex story arose. I pawed through dog-eared love letters and stamped, sheenless state documents. The lot within boosted bits and bobs of a secretive puzzle. Guarded, yet curious, I decided I better return fresh and fortified another day before pondering this perplexing Pandora.

We passed a park on the way home, a park we appreciated from afar each day along our way, but had not yet played in.

"I'll see you at home, okay? I need a few minutes alone."

Matt hesitated. He wanted to buoy me with a non-religious supportive sermon to rise above the salacious melee, but my love knew better than to spout platitudes to me. He held my hand, lingering one last poignant moment, kissed me lightly on the lips, and disappeared.

I climbed on a beat up leather swing, it's seat shaped its structure to my now bodacious body; hips swelling with the pride of pregnancy. I pumped my legs back and forth as I watched a little girl, three-years-old, making patty-pies from wet sand in the box. My stomach dropped with each forward glide. I hoped the babies had as much fun as me.

The little girl looked up and smiled at me.

I stayed through four rounds of sand pies, pumping hard. My elbows cocked, head bent, and fringe fell across my forehead. I looked downward like a bull ready to ram, then released and kicked my legs out, as though I was three, feeling free, "wheeeeeee!"

"Come on Sadie, it's time to go. Say goodbye to the nice lady."

"Bye."

"Bye, Sadie."

I hoped my children would like me. A lot. They too would one day find a pithos of Pandora's containing Paris and a predicament. It takes a lot of love to wade through the muck of our ancestors and judge them not. I hoped the babes would love me when the light of truth blinded them in the weariest, wee-est hour of night.

"Bye, bye, Lucy." My heart swelled when her toddler's lips formed my name.

By the time I got back to our turquoise sardine can, it was pitch black out like a hole in a coalmine, the crescent moon just pushing upward past the sunflowers and heliotropes. The inside of the trailer was more roomy than the outside let on: I climbed the three shaky steps, opened the squeaky door and turned right to face the bedroom which was a queen-size bed in a cubbyhole. Fake wood flanked the walls in this spot with nary enough room to walk round and change the sheets. Overhead cupboards that didn't close properly housed our scant wardrobes, neatly folded and arranged by color hues, by me, Camille the chalk artist.

I immediately sensed Matt was not alone. I was correct. Though the dim shine provided by that rising sliver of moon was not bright enough to see, I heard her breathing.

"Is Sheila here, Matty?"

"Yes."

Then she herself answered with "Urmph, urmph" and a sneeze. Sheila, Sir and Madam's knee-high Pug, who had cockiness and charisma enough for a litter of pups, was curled up like a June bug on Matt's right thigh. We'd struck a bargain early on we would share him. Well, I proposed the bargain; Sheila barked along in delight.

"Urmph, urmph, grrrr." She wore her heart on her waggely tail, now swatting a mile a minute, paws pitter-pattered to reach me, and on tippy-toes, put her paws around my waist as if we were entering a peasant Minuet marathon. She squinted at me, her squat, wrinkled neck in terse traction and tried to elongate herself the length of a giraffe to lick my face.

I picked up our girl, "Cchew, humph, cchew, mcheeew, grrrr." We communicated through eye contact and scratches to her head. This was a soul thing twixt she and I — we got each other. My role was the gregarious girlfriend, confident and welcoming, but still claiming rule over this roost. Her role was to be the life of the party and finagle back pats, head scratches, and as many naps on Matt's broad, warm body as she could.

I lit a stout vanilla candle and turned my attention to Matt who - stretched out diagonally with his arms crossed behind his head - took up the length of the bed. He looked unsure.

I broke the silence. "Hi. That's the longest we've been apart in weeks."

He seemed to search for words. I was shy; concerned I'd said or done something wrong. Maybe he would tell me he was leaving since I'd rebuffed his proposal.

"Did you eat?"

"I had wild rice, lettuce, and avocado. There's some for you." He pointed his chin toward the narrow kitchen counter on my left. I looked as per reflex. There on the drop-down table it sat — The Box. Two-foot wide, a foot and a half deep, it glittered like a Pirate's prize, decorated in rich, patterned material from a mysterious world far away. On it were situated three drawers on the front with round brass rings attached that one could stick one's finger through to open the compartments. I turned back to Matt. It seemed clear he had spent his time alone perusing the contents within this chest. I tried to read the results in his eyes.

"Come here," he sat upright, and patted the mattress next to him. I encircled my arms around the box, lifted it, and clutched it to my breast. It was heavier than I'd imagined. I took a step towards the bedroom, or in this case bed room, but Sheila beat me to the spot.

"Urmph, urmph, yip, yip, grrrr."

"Aren't you going to open it already?" Matt scratched Sheila between the ears; she gave a little grrrr of approval.

"Going by the look on your face, it looks like I'll need some nourishment to deal with this monstrosity."

I took a few bites of slightly burnt rice and settled cross-legged on the quilted comforter with the Cowboys and Indians on it Madam provided us with; hard to tell if she was undereducated, racist, a Xenophobe, or going for a campy effect. We weren't acquainted with our landlords well enough yet to make that call, and one could make arguments about the Tarot goddess that veered in any of those directions.

Her husband, the ex-politician-always a politician, seemed a right wanker though. It's not like he was a tyrant or anything — they were fair enough with us, didn't overcharge, and gave us roaming space on the land, but then we were excellent tenants in return. We were clean, quiet, paid in cash, helped with the pruning, fed their menagerie of animals while they were away, collected the eggs, and even milked Sophie, the spotted cow — it's just that he had a bad reputation in town for being a bit of a jerk and I'd noticed a snarl to his lip. Madam Pruitt walked with a limp that seemed more to do with injury than her purple varicose veins, and I worried out loud about abuse, but Matt didn't see cause for concern.

The whole mystery box scenario felt oddly exciting like I ought to wear a Zorro inspired domino mask and a flowing Spanish cape.

"Is it good or bad?"

"I'm unsure how to answer that."

"Is it monumental? Will it traumatize me?"

"If you've told me everything you know about your family, it's monumental, yes. I barely had time to scratch the surface since I found it yesterday."

"I thought you just found it today?"

He shook his head. I could see he had his reasons for waiting to show me, and I trusted him enough not to question.

"Okay," I closed my eyes and laid both hands on the lid to ready and steady myself. "Uh-hah. Okay. Here goes."

I opened the box. A jumble of pictures, postcards, passports, letters in my mother and father's writing, and envelopes stuffed with official-looking documents lay in wait. My first pick was a photo of my father and I dated the week of my birth. "Camille Lisette and I," read the back in his scrawling, ornamental cursive. I'd never seen this picture before, which was odd because we had several albums full of photographs from my childhood.

The next picture I picked up showed my father cradling a baby in each arm. Dog-eared in the corners, they dated it the same day. "Camille Lisette, Kristína Alicia, and I." I looked closely. Kristína Alicia looked identical to me. I assumed I was the one on the left, only because they had written my name first. But I had no sister, definitely not a twin. It filled my head with a noise like that of a roaring of a jet plane about to break the sound barrier.

I looked up at Matt whose eyes were wet with compassion.

"They told you in London you were carrying twins?"

"Yes, but it was way too early to tell. I don't know who this is. I've never seen these pictures. I'm an only child, Matt." The cowboys seemed to mock me on their brown and black animated horses.

"There's more, Camille."

"Lucy," I croaked out involuntarily. "I'm Lucy, and I don't know who this other girl in the picture is."

Piece by piece I sorted through the marrow of this arcane family heirloom my parents shrouded from me, keeping truth at arms-length throughout my life. During the flagging dark hours, knee to knee with this kinetic version of me, cognizant of each poignant pang, Matt was my rock. He is the most selfless person I've ever met, or a quixotic mesh of man and mirage. He heaved heavy sighs as I sifted through lies.

Matt heroically sang sad or slaphappy songs with me when I sought solace in the flute I'd bought to resolve Rocky Ricoco restless nights. We rolled into a celestial groove as the planets peeked through the waxy window: *Venus and Mars Are All Right Tonight, Drops of Jupiter,* and a tip of the hat to Bertrand, *Fly Me To The Moon.*

Picture after picture that emerged showed two adorable, identical enfants with my father and a woman identified only as "Jónína." She bore a rousing resemblance to Kristína Alicia, my other half, and I. My mind spun like a widow wrapping wool, round and round, tighter and faster, to dizzying depths of despair, delight, and near derangement.

"She must be my mother. My birth mother."

"She has your eyes - huge brown globes - your nose, set square on her face like a queen, your hair, the cowlick and curls, your smile, enticing and exotic as sweet sassafras."

"I'm not that beautiful!"

"You are. You're the spitting image of her."

I stopped to kiss him, my poet, supporter, and the love of my life. It was past five a.m. and after a rousing recreational interlude, we plumaged through the mire as the sun rose higher.

Sheila long ago trotted out to romp through the fields in the fresh Idaho air thick with rooster crows and cow bellows. We didn't miss her. We needed the space to sort out piles of paper and piece through my parental puzzle. Here's what we had:

I was born an identical twin.

I was the older of the two, by twenty-two measly minutes.

My birth certificate read Camille Lisette Portraro.

My twin's birth certificate read Kristína Alicia Jónínadóttir.

My birth mother is Jónína Johanson.

My mother, Marissa Sabine, was not my birth mother.

My father raised me, Camille Lisette Portraro; Jónína raised Kristína Alicia Jónínadóttir.

My father and mother met at least by the time I had my first birthday.

My father, mother, and Jónína kept in touch, at least superficially.

My mother's journal, which I'd barely riffled through, details her struggle to figure out how and when to tell me of my birth.

My mother's journal, with a purple paisley cover, repeats a theme: guilt. It wracked my parents for not being forthright with me.

My parents had plans to tell me when my mother first got ill. I was twelve.

Her decline and untimely death overshadowed their plans.

Jónína and Kristína lived in Iceland.

There's more, much more, but unable to bear a morsel more on that morn, I picked up the flute. Before it touched my lips, I fell solidly asleep. I dreamt of the house on the hill, my marvelous mother-not-my mother, an adoring father doting on me with the fervor meant for a duo of daughters, two toddlers took first steps, learned oopsy-daisy, Patty cake, Patty cake Baker's Man and slapped together mud pies, continents apart, sharing a heart, but traipsing through the ecstasy and trials of life alone.

I never had missed what I had not known to exist.

Now I had heaps of unfinished business on my parsed plate. I wanted to hate my parents, but didn't have the energy. They must have had reasons for doing what they did. I had mine.

I not only had to atone for the death of Luis Fernando, but now had to find my family among the fairies to allow my parents a chance to rest in perpetual peace; they who had given me so much, they who withheld my birthright from me.

I must find Kristína and Jónína; I was to be the mother of twins. My children needed a clan.

"Whoa."

"What?"

"I finally checked my Camille email."

"And?"

"There are, let me count, da-dada-dada, forty-four, forty-five messages from Brigitte, da dah, seventeen from Jacqueline, one from Molly, my mock jolly but macabre aunt. One, two, three from my favorite professors. Hmm, let's see, some assorted friends, art customers, fans, my bank, uh-oh, Tanu, whoa! Noni, an art society, and ugh, spam about penis enlargements. Ah, too many! How am I going to get through these? I can't handle this. Oh, and this one from Nikos."

I disappeared for a few moments looking out the window onto Idaho's spectacular scenery. Side roads of red ochre rumbled past as summer leaves new-growth-green lit up baby blue skies. This was equine country. I marveled at the slender legged, silky maned, brown, red-brown, elegant, spirited, powerful beings that strode the field just feet from my gaze. A white nosed colt, crooked on her new legs, ran circles around her mother, then toppled over, lithe limbs akimbo, cute as Natalie Mouskers when she was a six inch kitten.

"Spam from Nikos about penis enlargements?"

"No. Ha ha." I swatted his arm, "It's intense. The whole thing is like some harsh hashish hallucination; trippy and terrifying."

"Lucy, you'll get through it, one message at a time. I have faith in you."

Ding! Ding! Ding! My digital device like a dragoon kept firing as more messages shot through. I oughtn't dawdle or I'd be swaddled in another set of paralyzing virtual prose.

Matt merged onto I-80 from US-20 W. We headed to Boise to see my old house and hood and pay my respects to my folks, a mish-mash of love, loss, and at that moment, loathing, at their modest gravesite on a peaceful parcel of land near to town.

"You wanna read it out loud — the one from Nikos?"

"Sure," I fluffed my cowlick nervously, (that way I do), as I interpreted the words from my phone, translating his Greek inflected French out loud into English. Waves of nostalgia for Paris and my lost life there struck me like a six meter serpentine wave.

"Cherie Cammy, I think of you every day. Words cannot express my shame for the despicable way I behaved when we were lovers and also this night you came to me in need. I won't again ask forgiveness, as that would be an insult to the situation. I hope I have helped you with the papers I bought. I long for news of you, more than the scraps I get now, bits of torn bacon that enhance my hunger like a homeless dog. Tanu, IF she hears from Theo, refuses to tell me much. Those who love you are protecting you.

I write you now to tell you some pieces of news. Miss Mouskers and I, we are now great friends. She gives me much undeserved joy, though naturally it is you she misses. When I show her the picture of you in gregarious pirouette, she cries as a babe lamenting the loss of her mater.

Parlene, this young woman you saw me with, she is pregnant. This is my mistake because I don't take enough for protection and she has telled me, hmm, told me, she was taking birth control. Now she is planning to have this - my - baby. I am not prepared to be a patéras, Cammy. I am no interest... I have no interest in marrying this woman. It's time I clean my mistakes and be a man my parents and I can be proud of.

The police are looking for you. They say to us, to all of us, they have information for you. I ask them what they will do with you. They tape their lips and reveal nothing, just say to tell you to contact them immediately. If you contact anyone, please, agápi mou, call Brigitte. She seems to ail without you. Then call me. I would appreciate your advice about this baby.

I am considering going back to Greece to finish a degree; I'll make something decent of myself yet.

I am always here for you.

S'agapo, Nikos"

"S'agapo?"

"I love you."

"Does he know about your pregnancy?"

"No."

"Are you planning to tell him?"

"Yes."

"That's just dandy. This man, this... boy... this child... will have a litter of children."

I said nothing. There was nothing to say. I fought against saying, "He's a good person," my heart and mind still confused.

"Do you have a picture of him?"

"Yes, I have a lot of pictures."

"Show me. I'd like to see what he looks like."

I slid through several sets and held them up for Matt to view.

He was quiet for an uncomfortable length of time.

"What's wrong?"

"Nothing."

"Nothing!" I couldn't believe he was *nothing-ing* me!

"He has a nice face. An extremely nice face."

A tear rolled down his unblemished cheek, the right side; the side I saw from the passenger seat.

It was undeniable. Nikos had chiseled cheekbones, wide set chocolate eyes, the nose of a Greek god, a square jaw, regal forehead, naturally quaffed brows, and that gorgeous grin.

"What do you like about him, this... this handsome man? Is it just his looks?"

Noni always warned me not to talk about ex-lovers with current ones. "He's electric."

"Go on."

"He's smart, supremely well read, creative, and wild. There is never a dull moment with Nikos. He made me feel like the most special person on earth. He lives from his heart."

"While he was impregnating other women and taking advantage of you?"

"He's a good person." There, I said it.

"It's a sickness to love this type that hurts you."

"He's better now."

"That's what they all say."

"Have you ever loved someone you had mixed feelings for?"

"Yes." I was afraid he meant me.

"Who?"

"Rebecca Marie. We were together for nine years."

It stung to hear this. Why can't love live in the ardor of acceptance, without the whiff of unwelcomed envy?

"Why do you even want to be with me, Matty, I'm a mess?"

"You're exquisite. You notice everything — every shape, color, shadow, shimmer, and every nuance of a noctilucent sky. You're the kindest person I've ever met. I notice the small, selfless things you do for others when you think no one is watching. You light my fire, and I don't normally dig fire. You're the Alpha to my Omega, the dot to my i, the because to my why, the nuance in my nascent sky." This is where he could have added, "I'm not a martyr, and I won't wait for you," but he didn't.

"I have an incredible need for you. It's terrifying," I replied.

"Is this why you keep me at arm's length? Is it a pre-emptive thing?"

"Protective."

"Who are you protecting?"

"You."

He pulled over. "You drive now, this is your country. You know the roads from here." He got out, stretched in salutation to the open skies, and got back in the passenger side. I looked over at his face, the scarred side. It was the loveliest sight I had ever seen.

"Allô."

"Allô, Brigitte."

"Qui est à l'appareil?"

"C'est moi, Camille."

A mesmerizing gurgle and splash of bath water ran in the background. It was eight p.m. in France, noon in my mountains. I sat on a mound of sparse grass peppered with pale purple Western mountain asters arranged by chance, by nature, in a five-starred stelliform pattern facing my parents' headstones.

Matt, a workout zealot, was doing calisthenics just a few meters away. He knocked out fifty alternate knee crunches in the time it took for her to respond. Still anti-social, he was just doing his thing, sneaking satisfying gulps of Acerola juice in between sets, as I undertook this potentially troublesome, surely costly and catalytic, call to dear Brig.

"Camille?"

"Oui. C'est moi."

The bath tap cranked to a squeaky stop. I focused on a blemished spot in the upper right corner on my father's freshly swept grave. Using a hand broom, rags from a torn up maroon Maroon 5 tee shirt, and a jug of water in the truck, I maniacally cleaned and polished the plaques I had picked out years ago, nothing pricey, just simple and classic. My mother's stone emblazoned with her favorite quote: "*It is only with the heart that one can see rightly; what is essential is invisible to the eye.*" ~ Antoine de Saint Exupery, and my father's, his: "*In matters of style, swim with the current; in matters of principle, stand like a rock.*" ~ Thomas Jefferson.

"Give me a moment," I imagined her now thin, still pliable body bent perpendicular over the spout, cheeks blanched, wild hair restrained in a ponytail, shining eyes, sad. I missed my friend.

"Mais bien sûr."

"Okay. I'm back. My belle, is this really you?"

"Oui, Brigitte. Oui, oui, c'est moi, c'est moi!"

"Oh! I'm worried sick about you. How are you? Where are you? What has happened in your life? How is Natalie Mouskers? They asked about her. They had me come in twice, Belle, twice! I'm so sorry. I did this. I killed the boy."

"What? No! You did nothing, I did! I killed him, Brigitte! Don't talk like that."

Matt gave me a stern look alerting me to notch down the decibel; there was a mourning family of nine nearby.

"I pushed you, asked you over and over if you love me. I'm so ashamed. I'm being punished for this."

"Brigitte, no. It was a horrible accident. I was behind the wheel and I alone am responsible. The car slid out of control from beneath me; it was the same sensation as when we skated on that unsalted icy lake and the wind spun us around."

"He is dead and gone, lady. He is dead and gone; at his head a grass-green turf, at his heels a stone."

Nikos was right: Brigitte was unraveling.

"How are you getting along daily, dear Brig? Tell me about graduation? You must feel so accomplished! What are you up to next?"

"I dropped out Cam. I can't focus, can't sleep. I lie awake at night; shadows come alive and haunt me on the wall. I take never-long-enough naps during my nervous days. I have no appetite or ambition. The doctors suggest medication to me, but I don't believe in such things. I say no and they get angry with me, they say I am "non conforme," as though taking care to do the right thing for myself is criminal rebellion. I am depressed, I miss you terribly, and grieve non-stop for Luis Fernando and his family."

"I'm sorry that life is so hard at this moment. I feel terrible. I'm responsible for this. Do you work? What do you do with your time?"

"I walk the dog, sometimes two or three times a day. I watch movies in bed. I force myself to eat. Once I thought I saw you on the lawn across the street. My family nearly got me locked away for that. I am crazy, they say."

"Oh, no! C'était moi! It *was* me!"

"Oui. I thought so! I wasn't sure though. There was a young boy with you and you did not greet me."

"You could see him?"

"Oui. I saw a boy. I thought it was Luis Fernando, but my sister told me I was having hallucinations. It couldn't have been him: He is dead and gone, lady, He is dead and gone."

We spoke for half an hour. Once, not so very long ago, we were twin purple asters sailing free, high on each other, gliding glissade after glissade, propelled by music and mischief, each step leading nowhere, closer to the dream, the world was our oyster, but it slipped from us at the close of last winter; each flower, now separate, struggles for meaning.

"Je t'aime, Camille, please stay in touch with me. I need you."

"Je t'aime, Brigitte, please take care of yourself."

"Au revoir."

"Au revoir pour le moment."

"Someone's home. Let's knock."

"Oh, no, I couldn't."

"Why not? You want to see inside, right? Do it! You might never come back. I'd like to see the house you grew up in."

"It's not the same with someone else's stuff. Someone else's family."

"When I visited my childhood house in Biloxi, it was a dang good thing for me; it stopped the obsessive dreams I was havin' about the fire, but you're right, I reckon you have to decide for yourself. I'd get it while it's good though." Matt winked his good eye. He rarely winked.

The House On The Hill sat silent, radiating an effervescent majesty over us. We'd lived large with our prolific social life on the hilltop, the three of us creative extroverts, people magnets, and celebratory folk. I estimated we threw over a hundred parties here, BIG to-dos, in the years until my parents' health problems got serious, and even then some after that. We were infamous for hosting the spookiest Halloween fetes; mom, Noni, and I would canter about, decorating the place with fairy wings strapped to our backs, while dad wobbled on a ladder speckled with paint drippings, nearly giving mom a heart attack as he rigged up brilliant blinking lights, strung streamers, and hung ghosts from their heels.

On Thanksgiving we had bountiful pot luck gatherings that welcomed friends, neighbors, and any lonesome or wayward man, woman, or child in the county. Winona's mother and other first Idaho natives, including Cheyenne, Sioux, Crow, Arapaho, Nez Perce sang and told stories that spanned back to their great-great-great ancestors. We heard about medicine men and the great buffalo herds and bald eagles that once stretched across the Great Plains.

We rang in each New Year with fifty of our closest friends, half of my school swirled sparklers and had water balloon fights on our grounds on

The Fourth of July, as American as apple pie, and popped a cork for Martin Luther King Day, blaring Stevie Wonder and crooning along, "Happy birthday to you."

Constantinople, Boise was not, but we reigned with pride from our perch on high for what, to our town, was the closest architectural wonder we might ever wish to see there. The porch, wide and welcoming, showcased a requisite white swing pillowed with fern green, lemon yellow, and light tangerine flowery cushions that saw us through our birthday party pizzazz. Mom was born February 14, a Valentine's baby. Her celebrations were chock full of cherubs and Chantilly lace, swinging Sinatra tunes, and ice cold champagne. Dad's day was April 16. We celebrated springtime with volleyball and cricket games on the front lawn, showing off our glorious garden, gladiolas and all. October 23, my birthday, so close to All Hallows Eve, was a costumed blend of dress up and art themes. I made chalk, paint, clay, and paper mâché available to each guest who stepped in our door.

The townspeople knew us as eccentrics, and why not? Why not live with luster? "Why not, forget-me-not," mom would sing, fairy wings undulating to unheard songs. Why not offer a double-seated swing from which lovers, on our dry-as-a-bone chatty summer evenings, could sit and watch fireflies? My first kiss when I was twelve was on that swing; we pretended to search the sky for Jupiter, but spent our turn searching each other instead.

Go inside? Yes! Why not?

"There's a doorbell."

"No, no. Knock Matt. It seems more appropriate."

The rapid, rhythmic tap-tap-tap-tap-tap rung hollow throughout the house, a scuffle, light footsteps, and a tiny person stood in the entryway. A girl of seven, barefoot, with sparkles on her inquisitive nose. She could have been me twenty years ago making pictures with glue stick while reciting Alice Through the Looking Glass on a sultry summer day.

'Twas brillig, and the slithy toves
Did gyre and gimble in the wabe:
All mimsy were the borogoves,
And the mome raths outgrabe.
'Beware the Jabberwock, my son!
The jaws that bite, the claws that catch!
Beware the Jubjub bird, and shun
The frumious Bandersnatch!'
He took his vorpal sword in hand:
Long time the manxome foe he sought —
So rested he by the Tumtum tree,
And stood a while in thought.
And, as in uffish thought he stood,
The Jabberwock, with eyes of flame,
Came whiffling through the tulgey wood,
And burbled as it came!
One two! One two! And through and through
The vorpal blade went snicker-snack!
He left it dead, and with its head
He went galumphing back.
'And hast thou slain the Jabberwock?
Come to my arms, my beamish boy!
Oh frabjous day! Callooh! Callay!'
He chortled in his joy.
'Twas brillig, and the slithy toves
Did gyre and gimble in the wabe:
All mimsy were the borogoves,
And the mome raths outgrabe.

I still remembered all the words.

"Hi. Who are you?"

"Hi. I'm Camille. This is my boyfriend Matt. I lived here when I was your age. Are your parents home?"

"No, but Brandon is. BRANDON!" she hollered hard like Tarzan whooping through the trees.

A seventeen-year-old in white socks slid into view with the joie de vivre of a pro snowboarder lifting lightly over billowy drifts.

"Hey. 'Sup? Who are you?"

"Hi. I'm Camille. This is my boyfriend Matt. I grew up in this house."

"Cool. You want to come in and see it?"

"Fiddle-dee-do, little Cammy Lisette, is that you?" I turned from showing Matt the wall where Noni and I painted a teddy bear mural on the side of the house to see Andrika Arshling, the glass shattering shrilling shrew who would go down in infamy as the zealous, jealous, nightmarish neighbor through my teen years, greet me like her next of kin.

"My word, you have grown from a sassy, skinny Minnie into a bodacious Bohemian beauty. Come here, let me get a look at you."

"Andrika!"

She exited her side door like it was a grand proscenium and she was channeling a resplendent Carol Channing on the Great White Way. I half expected her to burst into a rousing verse of *Hello Dolly*, full of black stocking-ed half kicks, shoulder shimmies, and garter grabs.

My sagacious soul man gave me a second quick wink of the day, telepathically transmitting to me, "Any mischief from this diva, and I'm on it."

When she saw Matt, she struggled to smile like a blue tufted titmouse opening a shelled peanut. She stared directly at his face in disgust. I could hear his biceps twitch in anticipation of a turbulent interaction. I try not to hate; I meditate and have love in my heart, but Ms. Arshling is the embodiment of evil. Seeing her brought back the trauma of dealing with my father's death, a hard event made a million times worse by her wickedness.

"What good are you doin' with your life, Cam Cam? Tell Auntie Andrika everything."

I was speechless for a minute. Ha. This was such a balm for me! If I'd had any doubts about how operose she made things for me in those treacherous years, they dissipated instantly like a good shaking of an etcha-sketch erases all the shapes. I had no tolerance for bullshit. I stood tall, neck elongated, and looked directly into her heavily mascaraed, red-hued eyes, "Why did you break that glass in our driveway? My tires deflated when I was taking my father to the ER. I was always kind to you, I did nothing to cause you to act in such a way."

"You ungrateful little bitch. I see you haven't changed, always making up taaaaalll tales." She took a good, long disapproving look at Matt and then swung her hinny around and re-entered her horrible habitat where I imagined angry bats flew in anarchic angles. The door slammed, and that was it — she vanished. Brandon heard the sound and ran outside.

"What was that?"

I pointed to the Arshing estate.

Britney approached and scrunched her angelic face in revulsion, "Oh... her." She flipped the bird in the general direction of the house. I felt her pain; this house trapped the innocent girl just as I had been. For all the talk of loving thy neighbor, some make it impossible. I had repeatedly appeased without being a doormat. I sought to compromise when the Arshling lady refused to meet midway; she flushed my clear words like dirt down a toilet.

We washed the taste of the wench down with the delish honey lemonade I kept in a cooler in the truck. We toasted to a new friendship and a fine day. Britney and I drew crayon portraits of teddy bears to celebrate the long-gone mural. The boys played a fiercely competitive game of pickup basketball with some guys from the neighborhood in the same hoop my father had erected on that woe-some, wobbly ladder that so worried my mom.

After hugs goodbye, the kids asked to exchange social media information. I wanted to stay in touch so I gave them my Lucy Petrokov accounts, and Matt gave them his.

"Why did you change your name?" Britney was curious, rightfully so. "A rose by any other name would smell as sweet," fell from my lips. "*Romeo and Juliet*," Brandon flashed with excitement, "We just studied that in school!" They didn't ask other questions of us. Matt and I could have been Bonnie and Clyde for all they knew. "Eskimo kisses," Brit insisted as she inadvertently rubbed sprinkles on both of our noses as we headed out.

I turned and took in one last inhale of the House On The Hill as we drove away. Andrika's piercing eyes spied at us from her crusty curtained living room. The kids ran outside and waved like windmills on a stormy day. I gave my best *beep-beep-beep* as we rolled away. Matt and I touched the sprinkles on each other as though to say, "Focus on THIS."

The names Jónína Johanson and Kristína Alicia Jónínadóttir roared in my head as I wrestled with the fact that my lovely parents kept such a secret from me. As I turned the sharp, steep corner with a smooth panache, I glimpsed Pierre. "You're a superb driver, Lucy," Matt observed.

"Ironic, isn't it?"

I wondered what Matt and I would tell our kids about our pasts.... OUR kids? Oh, no, what am I thinking? Do NOT fall in love with him! My sagacious soul man seemed to read me again — for a third time that day, he winked.

"I need a good soak."

"What do you mean?" Matt smashed a plump, burly blueberry onto a crescent shaped cashew and popped it in his mouth. We'd stocked up on a few things from the WinCo where, in the back lot by the blue dumpsters with the yellow and black writing and a tiddley-bit of my graphic graffiti, I'd numbed myself sick with liquor several times during my juvenile detention Senior high school days phase.

"I miss having a bath." The quaint tiny turquoise trailer offered us only a tiny tinny shower, not quite the sanitary, soul-satisfying satisfaction of a blissful finger wrinkling submergence in a tub. "Water is my thing, it's like being back in the womb, warm and welcoming, my heart steadies. Steaming in springs in the fresh face of mountain air is my drug of choice — in those moments, oneness IS, beyond even any thought of being... Skinny-dippers Hot Springs is just up the road. We still have a few hours of daylight left."

He matched a purple-blueberry with a golden-red almond the shape of Natalie Mouskers' eye and laid it gently in my mouth, open in anticipation like a featherless fledging mourning dove awaiting his first worm. Matt was elegantly egalitarian in his match-up of fruit to nuts. I crunched down. The juice exploded against my cheeks as nourishing nectar ricocheted off my taste buds, confusing them with a combination of sweet and tart signals.

"Skinny-dipping sound insidious."

"Oh, and then some."

"Sounds ludicrous."

"It's magnificent."

"How long till we're there?"

"About forty minutes."

"Drive on Belle, you're my heroine."

"Heroin?"

"Heroine."

"Ah," I opened up for another Nut Sandwich, this one blue-blue, received perfectly on the palate. The road twisted left in a sensuous curve.

"Cashew originates from the French word, acajou and from the Portuguese word, acajou, fruit."

"Acajou... mahogany, oui. How do you know this?"

"From years spent inside avoiding people, reading, Lucy. Books were my mistresses."

"The cashew is not a nut or a legume, it's a seed."

"You are correct! The cashew..."

"Bless you."

"What?"

"Cashew — bless you."

He leaned in to kiss me, his luscious lips stained violet, tasted of berries.

"I can pull over, we can da-da-do it in the road, but I have to focus on driving." The road now veered right in a rush.

"Let's say you were confident about how I feel. Would you marry me?"

"Oh, my god, Matt, I'm maneuvering hairpins here. Me, the Lizzie Borden of the road, and you're distracting me. If you want my thesis on matrimony, we can pull over. I can't have this conversation while I'm steering a one and a half ton truck."

"Watch out for that deer."

A fawn poked her nose through the bush, startling us. It's hard to say who was more awestruck, Matt and me, or the young thing unsteady on her legs, eyes big as bowling balls.

"There's a place to pull over up there. I'll drive. Thirty minutes till we get there, talk can wait."

"Cashew."

"Your welcome."

"No, cashew."

"Oh, bless you."

"No, cashew." I opened my mouth. He tossed a cashew in for a perfect shot!

If I wasn't concerned about dragging him into my drama, taking a perfectly sane man, (well, except for the killing thing), and wrapping him up in my peculiar Paris predicament, I would say, "Yes, yes, a thousand times yes!"

Thermogenic groundwater bubbled and steamed. The heat, like magic fingers, kneaded our stiff worn muscles pliant as the gurgling burble like a momma's lullaby eased our worried minds. *Skinny-dippers Hot Springs* exceeded even my most sumptuous memories of it. Matt sat aside me, astride me, for mere moments, and then removed himself for a respite, his skin thin in spots and sensitive to constant contact at such elevated temperatures.

There on the impeccable grey, granite rock, Matt splayed himself bulky and brilliant, naked as an erudite jaybird, confident, unselfconscious, wearing his burns like a jaunty hat. The few folks who stared soon looked away when they didn't receive an apoplectic response.

I closed my eyes, hair wet, head tilted backwards, memorizing the moment, the smell of sulpher, eerie call of the coyote, and even the line of hardworking acrobatic ants marched in a meandering, yet perfectly planned formation. We moved a far distance from them after appreciating from three paces back how the roving red insects hold their abdomens above the rest of the body as if they were pirates carrying their bounty on their bellies.

"I'm open, Luc, to living wherever you want. Idaho, Iceland, Poughkeepsie, or Paris."

"Oh, no, not Paris."

"We can't predict anything. You may go back."

"Where did Poughkeepsie come from?"

He let out his deep, delightful laugh, sat upright, and pulled THE RING out of his backpack pocket. I hadn't gotten a look at it when the "Lucy, will you marry me?" biplane banner flew overhead. He handed it to me to examine like he had bought a perfectly smooth collinarare pearl from an atomistic, mystical, abalone angel.

The band was sterling silver, a good move by Matt, as this is my metal of choice. I find gold too glitzy, not necessarily narcissistically so, but just not for me. "Don't gild the lily," my ma used to always say, keeping my artistic tendency for painting my face at bay. This also hushed the sensual side of me from spritzing Ylang-Ylang in unapologetic puffs to snare the laid-back boy of my thirteen-year-old dreams. "Uh-uh," mom would shake her head, while dad held his nose as if he were a scuba diver getting ready for a deep-sea dive.

But this was no ordinary band given me by this extraordinary man. On the top left lay a lady, a bit Botticelli, *Birth of Venus*, a bit Joni Mitchell, *Ladies of the Canyon*; a Bohemian beauty for sure, belly bare, naked, leaning languidly on her elbow, legs outstretched as if on a red velvet chaise. The main stone was turquoise. The luscious crackling hues were bright and bold, not bawdy. This was the lady's lake; she was at home here as saints in heaven. Next to her head, a small stone, a ruby, more pink than red, utterly perfect, representing a rose, was close enough to her nose that she could smell its sweetness.

"This is beyond compare — it's the most elegant, peerless, flawless, piece of jewelry I have ever seen. It's exquisite. Did you make this?"

He nodded twice, lips pressed closed, quiet.

"When?"

"The day we met, Lucy..."

Now, my lips closed, processing; I licked them as all moisture had evaporated, more so from emotion than the sapping steam of the springs.

"...Sometimes you just know."

I rose from the water like an injured Phoenix, destroyed by a raucous, ashen flash, and struggled to find resolve, wings wildly unfolding, reaching for a life worth living. I would need to own up, make amends, though I couldn't see how in the diminishing light of day.

As I reached for my towel, a pure voice echoed out, "Camille, is that you?"

"No! Noni? NONI! Oh, my goodness, Noni!"

"Baby Bluebell!"

Winona and I hugged and high-fived in fierce Idaho style.

"This is Matt."

"This is Gregg."

"Hey."

"Hey, man, 'sup."

"When did you get to town? You look great! Short hair! You didn't tell me you were coming? How long are you here for?"

"Spur of the moment. Came to go through that behemoth storage space at *Ernest Elves*."

"No, finally? Ah, that must be so hard - all those memories. I can come help if you want."

"Oh, thank you, Non, I'm almost done."

She seemed miffed. "How long have you been here?"

"Just, a... bit."

"Were you going to call? You haven't answered my e-mails."

"Umm..." I looked to Matt for help. He nodded nearly imperceptibly, "Go on. Tell her."

Winona moved her long black hair in front of her right shoulder and petted it like she was shucking corn.

"I thought I might call another time. I... It's a bad time for me. Umm... I'm pregnant." I touched my belly with both hands. Realizing I only had my towel sheet covering me, I pulled on the sapphire blue wrap pants and a white tee.

"Congratulations." She laid her warm hands on me in a V welcoming the babies, as only a childhood friend can. "Congratulations," she hugged Matt like they were old chums.

"It's not his."

"Oh, I'm sorry... I mean..."

"It's okay, it's a long story."

"I just lost mine — miscarriage." She sat hard on the rough rock, knees up, and planted her face in her palms, sobbing for all parents who lost babes before birth, a cruel and crusty slice of life's pie. I squatted behind and enveloped her shaking body until the hiccups quieted. The dark swathed us in silence until the sky cracked and warm rain fell in large plops on our heads, rolled into our eyes, dripped down our wrists, and splashed on our toes.

"Will we be able to spend time together before you go?"

"We're camping here tonight. I have to go to a prenatal check up tomorrow in town. I'm leaving soon after."

The rain, louder, fell in sheets and caused us to run for the cover of our cars.

"You're not camping in this. Come stay with Gregg and I. We live just up the road. Here." She hopped in the cab, got a pen from the jockey box and wrote her address on my arm, Gregg turned the engine on with a hum and they disappeared into the night's horizon in a jeep engineered to fly as fast as a fifteen foot hummingbird over mountain roads.

"She's lovely," Matt marveled. It was good to have him meet my first bff. "Baby Bluebell?"

"I painted bluebells on the side of the house. The nickname stuck."

"Well, Baby Bluebell, I have somethin' for you." He pulled out a delicate thirty-inch long silver chain, like a magician making coins appear from a child's ear, threaded the goddess ring onto it, and slipped it over my head. I tucked it between my breasts, and we walked, small hand in large, drenched by the mountain deluge, back to the truck.

"Ooh! Look at this one of us spinning around in our butterfly wings."

"Ha ha, we were dancing to The Spice Girls. Girl Power, baby!"

"So nostalgic!"

"It still mystifies me why we loved them so much."

"We were five, their target audience."

Greasy-haired Gregg, chomping gum or tobacco, I'm not sure which, put his chin on Winona's shoulder to take a peek. "You were cute,

Nummy." This guy was getting under my skin. He rubbed me the wrong way like a fly in my soup, dust in my eye, a sliver in my finger. I did not trust him.

"Nummy?"

"Like Noni and yummy... Nummy. Can I have this one? Cam?"

"Sure."

"Why did you change your name to Lucy? Wasn't that was the name of the coach's cat? We all adored her, but I don't think of you as a cat."

"It's a long story, I'll tell you sometime, just not now, I promise."

"Is it okay if I still call you Camille? I really can't grok the Lucy thing just yet."

"Call me whatever you want, just don't call me late for dinner." I tried to slough it off with a joke, but I regretted having Non and her clingy, demanding guy along to go through my stuff. I should have been stronger, should have said no, but it was so damn good to see her.

"Your mom used to say that."

"Yeah."

"It's mysterious to change your name to the name of a cat, like you are undercover or something. Who did you kill?"

Matt was outside moving a couch, his eye was not there to catch for silent support. "Your boyfriend calls you Nummy and you're quibbling about my luscious name, Luciana?"

Adam clambered in and tripped slapstick a la Charlie Chaplin on a flowered dustpan in the doorway. "Are you okay?" Noni touched him on the shoulder. I thought I detected an electric charge like when you stick a wet fork in a light socket, but sizzling hot. Gregg stepped outside to spit.

"Adam, you guys can take away the furniture now. We're pretty well done here. Here's some cash — a tip for you." I held out a hundred-dollar bill.

"'Nah, keep it. You paid the truck rental, it's a favor."

"Wait! Gregg and I will take that reposeful chair, the one your dad used to watch Larry Sanders in. We'll get it reupholstered. We can use the Aspen pattern from the couch, hun."

"That'll sizzle, sweet-lock."

"If you ever want it back, Cam, it's yours."

"I don't think I'll want it back, but I'm glad it will get a good home with you."

Matt stumbled in, catching his foot on the darn dustpan. "Who keeps putting this fucking thing here?" It was Gregg, but I said nothing. I jumped like spring lightening to move the cleaning tools to the back of the shed.

"Check this out, Halloween when we were thirteen."

"You look nefarious, Lucy. A naughty fairy." Matt took the picture from my hand.

"A harbinger, Matt, of what was to come."

"Oh?"

"Yeah, she became a wild child."

"That she did... Whelp, we'll see you ladies later. Lez GO guys, get this load hauled before the sun sets. See you at the homestead," he kissed me in a PDA uncharacteristic of him. I was conscious of Nummy and her half-wit honey trying not to rubberneck a hole through his face.

I was relieved when the men left. Winona and I finally were our silly selves. We reminisced about our last French journey together to the turquoise shore and sandy beaches of Théoule-sur-Mer. We chit chatted, gossiped, and giggled about everything from our eccentric classmates to Native prophesies to pregnancy, avoiding the most important thing - Luis Fernando, a smart boy who recoiled at the sight of Gregg.

We piled the sentimental treasures I couldn't bear to part with: two of my dad's favorite flannel shirts, mom's jewelry and ceramics, some of my folks folk albums, photos, natch, my baby book, school essays and artwork, and a stack of Shakespeare, Ginsberg, and Dylan Thomas, into Non's car.

"I make a great quinoa - spinach salad. I coat the grain with egg, then brown it in virgin coconut oil, add grilled garlic, onions, grated ginger, and boiling water, cover it and cook it for seven minutes. When it cools, that goes on top of the spinach, cucumber, grape tomato, avocado, and seaweed salad. There's a store up the road, all I need is more garlic." I slammed the trunk.

"It sounds great to me but Gregg will go ape shit without meat."

"Do you think he'd be okay if we just buy him a hamburger or something? I don't want to cook meat in the trailer. It's so small, once you get a smell in there, you can't get it out."

"We can get him tacos. You don't mind the place stinkin' of garlic?"

"Matt and I love garlic."

With her signature toss of her tresses from front to back, she shook her head like a horse, I thought in reaction to the dinner conversation. "I can't believe you're an identical twin. Another Camille! I can't wrap my head around any of this."

"I don't know if I want to be a twin. What if I don't like her? What if she doesn't like me?"

"Ooh, I can't imagine that. I think she'll like you. You're very likeable. Everyone likes you. What do you think of Gregg?"

"Wha... what type of tacos does he like?"

"Yeah. I thought so. He's a jerk. I want to break up with him, but he was so supportive when we lost the baby and he needed my support too. Now I'm financially dependent, I'm barely back to bookkeeping yet. Boring life, Cam, not like you."

I couldn't fathom still living in Idaho, beautiful as it is. Idaho to me was a place to grow up in and retire to. My folks were happy there though. I think. I hope so, secrets and all.

"What are your dreams, Noni?"

"Right now? To get some stinkin' garlic and wash off in your tiny tin stall and get them cobwebs out of my ears. Dib's for the first shower."

There was only enough hot water for one warm shower. I'd be stewing in filth for hours. Such is the price of friendship. "You got it, Winona."

"Nummy," she made a face and tore out of the lot.

A cacophony of booming bass rattled the car windows reverberating through our bodies before we were halfway down the gravel road home. Some head banger band kicked out-of-key ass like they were taking names. My hopes for a lackadaisical evening died.

"This place reeks of wrongness," Noni looked at me in alarm, "Look, There's a pug cowering behind the Canary Grass."

"Pull over... Sheila! Sheila, come here, sweetie. Come here, Sheila."

Sheila snarled low and wild and stayed put, "Grrrr."

"She's not usually persnickety like this."

Noni cruised three feet forward moved us into a BAD olfactory zone. The stench was nauseating. Where were the freaking *Freakin' Fragrances* when you needed 'em?

"Oh, my gawd!" Noni held her nose. "It smells like a dead animal." She jerked the emergency break up so hard I thought she'd fracture her wrist. We dashed inside. The boys had propped the teeny tiny door open with a spoonbill-shaped spatula. The teeny windows were ajar, a small step they took to circulate out the foul air. An mélange of pot, tequila, and burnt popcorn gut whacked us like Rock 'Em Sock 'Em Robots.

"Hi Beautiful." Gregg greeted Nummy.

"Hi Beautiful." Matt imitated this jackass.

Adam, the only one with a wee bit of sense hopped up like one of his frogs to turn down the music, if one can call that non-melodious mishmash music, and cleared the settee of dirty guy-gear so we could sit. We did not.

"What in tarnation, Gregg!" Noni's third stepfather, Earl from Alabama, used that term with us often when we stood up on the swings and swung so high the whole set toppled over, nearly killing us and Buster the cat when he came to get Non after we made the marvelous mural at my house. He cried, "What in tarnation," when we got busted for making out with some bitchin' boys up on Quail Ridge when we were eleven, and when we dyed our hair, hers purple, mine pink, the year before. "What in tarnation?" was Earl's inchoate cry before grounding her, taking away her skateboard and deflating any joy out of her next week.

"What were you thinking, Matt?"

"What? We're just having a good time."

"I'm not talkin' to you, Gregg. Matt?"

"Sorry, Lucy. We got the munchies and Adam burned the popcorn."

"Adam burnt the popcorn? Adam burnt the popcorn? You think this is the biggest problem here? It's stinks to high heaven in here. I'm pregnant, queasy, we're filthy, famished, and exhausted and we come home to this? Where am I going to sleep tonight?"

I fingered the ring around my neck, searching for the love that was there an hour ago. It vanished in the sobering stench of this sickening smoke, which he knew I couldn't tolerate. I rummaged through the cupboard for a paper bag to heave into.

Gregg sat smirking like a Yoo-hoo on Yohimbe. "I wasn't going to Bogart my stash..."

"I just gave 'em a taste of that tequila, Lucy," Adam sheepishly hung his head, "I didn't mean any harm by it."

"Give me your keys, Gregg, you're not getting behind the wheel tonight. Look at you, spittle dripping on your shirt, you can barely stand up."

"I gotta ga-home... ummm... ahhhh... work ta-morrow."

She snatched his keys from his jeans. "You're not driving. You want to kill some kid out on the road? Not on my watch, buddy."

Matt and I exchanged the look.

"Hey, CALM DOWN!" He slapped her.

Matt, on his feet in a flash, towered over Gregg and grabbed him up by his collar. The guy, on tiptoe, cheeks ruby red, lips pulled forward like a puffer fish, had a wild look in his eyes.

"That was the WRONG thing to do, man."

I was afraid he would kill him. I wasn't sure what he was capable of.

"Are you okay, Noni?"

"I've been better."

"Do you want to call the police?"

"No."

"What do you want me to do with him?"

Gregg's grey-green eyes darted from one to another as they decided his fate.

"Let him go. He can sleep in the tent. We're through Gregg. After I drive us back tomorrow, I'll pack and move out by the weekend. You're a bad egg. I deserve better."

Matt shook him once for good measure before he let him go. "You bastard."

Adam, wanting to help and get the heck out of there, offered, "I'll get the tent," and slipped out the door. I followed closely behind him and threw up for five minutes in the bushes ten paces away. Matt came out to talk to me; he rubbed my back and brushed my sticky hair from my face. "We were just having fun. I was in pain. I thought the weed would help."

"If your back hurts, get a massage, don't just cover up the pain with drugs. I thought you didn't get high anymore?"

"Not regularly. Look at how you've grown in the months that we've been here. "

"Don't change the subject. When did your back start to hurt again?" I didn't really care to be honest. I'd just barfed in the bushes and I was not in a cooing, compassionate mood.

"It always hurts, Luc, but the pain is in my finger."

"Your finger?"

"I got a paper cut," he held his right index up like a little, bitty child with a boo-boo, and cried. He broke me; this grown man with a terrible paper cut sobbed like an abandoned boy burned decades before. I held him in my arms.

"I want to sleep with you in our own crappy bed with the mattress that feels like cottage cheese and the sloppy dog with the dastardly breath who is as jealous of me as the day is long, but I'm going with Noni to that divey hotel up the road so we can shower and sleep this off. We'll pick up some lentil soup or something on the way. Did you eat?"

"Burnt popcorn."

"Get a good meal in you, okay? Tomorrow we have to pack up and get out of here."

This set off a new round of tears. "I will miss you when you're in Iceland."

"Me too, you." Maybe.

NINA LA RUE

Fresh off a flamboyant filibuster with my effulgent Southern boyfriend, I hoped to realign our hearts at the departure gate. The pot and popcorn party still made my pulse race though Matt had been the poster child of a supportive spouse over the past day: he moved my stuff from Noni's car to his truck to transport it for safekeeping at his Berkeley flat, arranged with Sir and Madam for Non to move into the trailer after us, and called her three times to make sure she got home safely in the company of that capricious chowder head, Gregg.

Living on the edge suits me. Traveling internationally, soaking in new cultures with delight gave me insight into the human condition. Frequent and spontaneous globe-trotting is on my list of favorites along with: the trapeze class I took in Helena from Marcello, the ex-Trappist monk, truffle oil spinach-porcini risotto with shredded beets red and yellow beet garnish, and picnicking in the shade of an autumnal crabapple tree, pink-white-and-coral, after swinging like a truffle-filled ex-Trappist trapeze artist through its springtime branches.

The thought of crab apples, CRAB apples, however, triggered the worst aspect of traveling while pregnant for me. I'd developed a gnarly case of nosophobia rendering me helpless to worries about catching everything from a common cold to crabs on the plane.

"You don't catch crabs on a plane. If you didn't catch crabs from that creep Nikos, I'd say catching crabs is the least of your concerns. Do you have to go to the bathroom again?"

"Yes. I'll be right back and please... stop calling him a creep — he's the father of my children."

"He's the sperm donor who forced himself on you. I don't understand your delusional idealization of this guy."

We had this fight three times that week. I pulled Matt aside, out of earshot from the leggy lady reading Vogue and the mousey man munching Nachos, licking his salty fingers after every bite. "Listen, Matt. I was barely over the shock of Pascal's death, which threw me into this mess. The car skid happened so quickly. I wasn't even driving fast. I had control one minute, Brigitte asked me if I loved her, and the next thing I knew, I ran down the Montmartre steps and cut off my hair. Nikos HELPED me. He got me my new ID and hired Tanu to take me to Theo and Jon's. I owe him a great deal."

"He had sex with you against your consent."

"Shh." The Nacho guy looked up mid-lick. "He did not. I didn't say no. I was in shock."

"Exactly, Lucy! You were vulnerable and he took advantage of the situation." The woman shifted in her seat, kicked off her Kenneth Cole silver ballet flats, sensible for a cross-country flight, and ruffled the magazine like she was shaking sand from a beach towel, sending us a signal she heard our hullabaloo. She mouthed to me, "Me too."

I pulled Matt a few feet further away. "This isn't how I planned my life. I feel sorry for myself and I don't even have a right to feel this way." I lowered my voice drastically. "I killed a boy in Paris. He has no more life. I don't have energy to be mad at Nikos. He had a terrible childhood. He gets in his own way. He meant no harm. I'm mad enough at myself."

The expression on Matt's face pulled it to the side signaling to me I wasn't the only one working hard to align. "I don't understand why you make excuses for him, he's a predator."

"He's not. Stop it. I want him to be in the twins life, and I don't want you talking like that."

"I say what I feel, Lucy. He abetted your flight from France."

"Hoah," I could barely breathe. His words made me feel like a common criminal. Thankfully, my phone vibrated, saving us from an ugly escalation of that moment.

"Excuse me. I have to get this."

I stepped out of earshot from everyone, past a toddler and her mother singing, *Toot, Toot, Tootles the Tugboat, goes toot, toot, toot all day,* over to the window with a wide view of our plane being checked by a mechanic in shadow grey coveralls and tools the size of Tootles, which was not reassuring at all.

"Oui, hello."

"Bonjour, Luciana?"

"Oui, c'est elle."

We spoke for ten minutes. A flight attendant announced that all passengers were to board and we talked for two more.

"Who was that?"

"Theo's lawyer in Lille."

"What did she say?"

"She doesn't think I'll get jail time if I come back soon, show remorse, and do community service. Maybe a few months max in a reasonable jail, whatever that means."

"What about the after-shower lipstick scrawl scandal?"

"She thinks it plays in my favor that I apologized and showed contrition with pangs of conscience."

"Naturally you have pangs of conscience, you..."

"Shhh!"

"... killed a kid." He whispered, his breath hot in my ear.

Matt had no pangs for his murder. Lucky guy. The line was moving. I had to get out my camouflage passport and board the plane with Nachos, Tootles, and Silver Slippers.

"Has she spoken with the police? Does she say why they want to find you? "

"No. They probably want to find me because... ya know..."

"What are you going to do?"

"What do you think I should do?"

"It's up to you. I hate that you're in this position. You don't deserve this."

Who really deserves bad things in life? People banter about karma, but I'm not a fan of the concept, not in the limited way the human brain catalogues it. I don't see any victim of genocide, violence, natural disaster, or the caustic, greedy, sycophantic form of capitalism as 'deserving of it.' Did I deserve for my wonderful, *secretive* parents to lie to me?

Why does there never seem to be enough time to say goodbye before the final boarding call?

"Do you think she'll like me?"

"Who?"

"Kristína Alicia."

"You're very likeable."

"Are you okay? Does your back hurt?"

"I'm okay and my back hurts. I'll get a massage before I hit the road."

"Did I do something wrong that karma is crushing me?"

"You did nothing wrong. Shit happens, Lucy. I was a good, sweet, compassionate kid, and I was burnt. I did nothing wrong. Quick, come here. Now, go."

I swirled the ring through my fingers as he gave me a kiss that would carry me to Iceland. "Are we okay?"

"We are. Why do you ask?"

"I need to take childbirth classes, buy diapers, and nest. And I have to pee. And we just argued about everything."

"Last call for flight 3201."

"Is he here?"

"Yes." Pierre waited for me by the entrance to the plane.

"Why was it his karma to play by the pole that day?"

"FINAL call."

"Go. I love you."

"I love you too."

"Call me from Brooklyn." He winked or cried, I couldn't tell through my tears.

Text to Matt - The plane was packed; I sat in back, my backpack on my knee. I looked around and didn't see the leggy woman who had mouthed "Me too" at me, but then the lavatory door burst ajar, I could see an uncomfortable conversation wasn't afar. They sat me on the aisle for access to the toilette since being pregnant is difficult on a jet. She plopped down right next to me with verve and vigor. When she saw it was me, her already large eyes grew bigger. I was on the iPad looking up the taiga of the lowlands in Iceland, when Nacho guy across the aisle shifted nervously like he was packing contraband. Silver Slippers, with no introduction, leaned in and began yakking with fervor. She interrupted my concentration. The nerve of her!

Text, Matt 2 me - Hey ma belle! Luv the rhymes! Lol. I got yr boxes shipped, and then reloaded the truck w/ table, chairs, & bookcases. They look sweet! I'll send yr $ soon as the checks clear. What happened after that?

Text to Matt - She was socially critical, her arguments sounded like a little girl. As I fastened my belt, she kept on bitchin'...

Text, Matt 2 me - ... and for a fight u were itchin'?

Text to Matt - That's where I was going with it, yep, you know me too well.

Text, Matt 2 me - Go on, get it off your chest then tell me where u r

Text to Matt - Matt, I need to go for a long Sun Valley mountain run. Being cooped up for seven hours on that plane was NOT fun. Had enough of her arguments, so arcane, in my ears they sounded like Sheila's non-stop barkin' in the rain. Could REALLY do with use a festive soiree... I miss you already, mi eterno Amore.

Text, Matt 2 me - Miss u 2

Text to Matt - At least she wasn't reading *How To Cook A Quince*. That would have made me wince.

Text, Matt 2 mw - How To Cook A Quince?

Text to Matt - Remember, I told you about Marcy from my Chicago flight to S.F.?

Text, Matt 2 me - The lady set up with Mel ??

Text to Matt - Yeah. Ha ha. In trying to evade her, I was tenacious, but Silver Slippers would NOT let up, she was rapacious!

Text, Matt 2 me - Where r u now?

Text to Matt - JFK. It's a zoo and I'm being followed by the Tootles the Tugboat mother too... Hey!

Text, Matt 2 mw - What?

Text to Matt - She's waving a sign with my name! She looks more pregnant, otherwise exactly the same.

Text, Matt 2 me - Who?

Text to Matt - Nina LaaaaaRue!!!!

Text, Matt 2 me - Oh, great! Call me when u get 2 Brooklyn. I <3 u

Text to Matt - Will do! I love you too! <3 <3 <3

"Velkommen, Luciana!" She stampeded in place like a trapped racehorse unable to tear around the track; her eyes closed tight as if to keep out ice water from a frozen tap. Her free fist - the one not holding the sign high - clenched and pumped as if a favorite quarterback just threw the winning pass after a season of sleeper scores. "Luciana, guten abend! Velkommen to New York! Welcome! Ah, so, finally you come visit!"

A kiss on each Plum Perfect lipstick-stained cheek reminded me of the fun (often frustrating) force that IS Nina LaRue. Her devoted brilliance, a bastion in my sordid storm; we'd formed an unlikely alliance. I relaxed in her presence and kiss-kissed her back.

"Nina! You look marvelous!" And she did: red, green, and yellow beaded bangles jangled on her tanned wrists artistically juxtaposed by flushed pink cheeks and baby blue sundress. She rocked a short haircut:

pointed in front, pixyish in back. Pregnancy suited her. She glowed like the archaic Lite Bright set Noni and I made our first mini-murals on.

"I planned to take the air train. You didn't have to drive here to meet me."

"I didn't drive, I'm taking the train with you." She grabbed the handle on my bag and walked. The wheels spun round in that squeaky surrealistic way they do after a dehydrating flight. "Do you have to use the bathroom? Are you hungry? I've missed you. The wrap pants are rad. Are you pregnant too? Wah! Where did you get this EXQUISITE ring? She lifted Matt's Lady On The Lake from between my breasts and stopped us in her tracks. "Ooh, that's a nice amethyst too. This Lady is the most splendid silversmithing I've ever seen! Where did you get this?" She seemed suspicious.

"That's a lot of questions at once, Nina. Yes, I have to pee and brush my teeth. I need water and gloss. My lips are dry. I'm hungry, but I can wait until we get to your place." I hugged her again and a gritty flood of grief poured from my irises onto her tasseled book bag.

For once Nina was quiet. She pulled me aside from the bustling walkway and rocked my head as though I were a day old preemie. In the hustle and flow of the airport Nina let me cry for Kristína Alicia. She didn't pry and let the gusts of tourists pass on by.

When all my tears were shed, she was back to business. "Jabori's band *Paolo Paradis and the Psithurism Paupers* are playing tonight. You up for some music; dance off the flight?"

I felt like a party-pooper. All I could respond was, "What does psithorium mean?"

"The sound of the wind in trees and rustling leaves." She shimmied around me thrice and clapped her hands like a bullfighter rousing the crowd of the Coliseum. It was wonderful to see her. How many people burst full of life?

"That's an interesting name for a band." Interesting was my way of saying I didn't get it. It sounded jazzy, beyond my musical aptitude.

"They're super popular in these parts. I'll take you to see them while you're in town.

Great. I... umm... couldn't wait...

The rest of the passengers from flight #3201, Boise - SeaTac - JFK, exited the terminal on their way back to their workaday lives, to sleep, perchance to dream, greet lovers with lust or disdain, or walk in the drizzly rain, while I stood with Nina LaRue and wiped sleep from my eyes, close enough, I surmised, to grab my bag, my prize, from the turnstile.

Several meters away, tensed like a fascicle tiger ready to pounce, paced Nacho guy with an insane grin on his face; the same man who so loudly and crudely asked Bronx flight attendant Jeanine for another brewski and more measly peanuts.

"Hurry, the service in this joint stinks."

I'd exchanged an eye roll with the mother of the Tootles-singing cherub, a plump pastry chef from Queens. Jeanine simply plumped his pillow as she passed by; a real saint.

Silence — a stand off.

Then a clunk... clunk... and out came my bag!

Wait...

TWO blue bags spun slowly round the baggage claim carousel like twin yolks in one egg.

What are the odds? Two blue bags. Both three by two, a tad battered, with silver accents, indistinguishable in any way. There spun our prey.

The man stepped forward. I could feel a fight. We had a moment of opia, a pair of wild beasts vying for territory, "Don't touch my stuff, I've had enough," I thought, but didn't say.

Sensing my dismay, he stepped back; let me pick up my case on the second go-round.

He tipped his hat, gave a gentile, "Have a nice day."

I swear, Nina LaRue could talk an Eskimo into buying snow. After traveling down Ocean Avenue, past Q Street en route for Coney Island amusement park and seaside resort, we dropped my bags at the handsome Brownstone where she and Jeremy existed in the final turfs of their marriage. She convinced me - Woo- whooo-whoooooo - to find a second wind and see *Paolo Paradis and the Psithurism Paupers*.

Brooklyn at night brought to mind a bright bowl of multi-hued cherries. Lights flash fast on cars and streetlights, licked candy red, amber, burgundy, and gold; auto exhaust, sweet summer sweat, a light breeze off the water, baby's cries, children's giggles, and ships bellows round out the satisfying sense-around. My *LOVE* sign clicked ON as infatuation began with this fresh frontier and her sticky air, so alive at night. I devoured the fleshy fruit of Brooklyn leaving only stems and pits on the plate.

"Come on, let's go dancing," Nina twirled my ring and me around her forefinger like a cat playing with a mouse's tail.

"Yeah, okay, let's go." I wanted to hole up and sleep like after too much Thanksgiving turkey, but I put on my ballet flats and followed her like Mary's little lamb.

The lighting in the joint was moody, almost morose. Teal and black paper lanterns shielded dim bulbs. The band did a sound check when we arrived. A husky voice purred in the microphone, "Pruebas, pruebas, a-uno-dos-tres." A diverse crowd trickled in, a melting pot of America ready to unwind with a beat-beat-beat of the drums to beat the blasted heat.

"Bop-ba-da-doo," the drummer slapped the drum skin palms flat, and then fingers fanning the edges lightening quickly, blink and you missed it, "Bop-ba-da-doo-doo-doo." Maybe it was jetlag, the warm air, protein drink, or Nina twirling me ten times round, but baby I was high on this sonorous sound. I dug every note the swift-hipped singer sang.

"Who's that on drums? He's fantastic!"

"That's Jabori!"

"I thought he was a jazz pianist?"

"By day."

"Wow." I had new respect for the quandary Nina was in.

The music lifted us away. We boogied the colors of the rainbow with strangers con amigos, and danced until dawn. When the second set was over, I turned round and Nina wasn't there, in her place, the lead vocalist, dark, intense and seductive, zeroed in on me.

"Hola! Yo soy Rrrrraaathththththth-ah-mon." As Ramon pronounced his name, he lifted his hand from waist to eye level on the first thrilling syllable - *Rrrrraaathththththth* - like Maestro Yuri Termikanov directing Itzhak Perlman on Tchaikovsky's 1812 Overture at the Leningrad Philharmonic; the movement fluid like a swan's neck rising to greet the morning sun. On the second syllable - *ah* – he swiveled his wrist inward, like a daffodil twisting in the wind. On the last syllable - *mon* - he pinched his fingers onto his thumb like a sock puppet of a rabbit, lips closed, ears drooping, ready to open wide and let loose a sonata.

Our connection was instantaneous; if I wasn't pregnant already, his rakish look alone might have fertilized me. Against my wishes, he pulled me into his juicy web. He was a Cuban Nikos with allure that melted me far beyond what the ninety-degree humidity already had.

"Rrrrraaathththththth-ah-mon, y tu? You rrrrrreaaally are rrrrrthththav-ishing." Hmm. Ramon was an artiste rrrrrreaaally into alliteration and intent to pick me up.

"I need some ice water."

"How about a Rum punch?"

I shook my head, "Water," and squeezed my father's amethyst and The Lady On The Lake tightly in my right hand.

"Your name, please?"

"Lucy." I didn't want to say.

"Gin and Dobonnet with a slice of lemon, and a water… you sure, Loo-cee?" I nodded yes, "Water for the lady."

"Same for me, water, twist of lemon on the rocks," Nina chimed in. We pregnant ladies really knew how to party. Where did she come from? Last I saw her, an overly amorous Jabori pinned her against the wall; a man who was a husband, father, her lover, the baker of her bun, and the greatest drummer I'd ever heard.

"Make that two Dobonnets," a man of forty with the vigor of a twenty-year-old, a face carved by Michelangelo, and a set of beautiful, bronzed hands, leaned over to order. Jabori. My heart skipped a beat. Charisma has that crushing effect on me.

We hung out with Jabori, Ramon, and Paolo, the guitarist, for an hour. I was quiet, taking in the flavors of their various dialects, charms, skin tones, and perspectives. They talked the breadth of Broadway plays and Democratic Socialism as they downed Dobonnets. I wished Bertrand were there to hear this music and soak in the scene. He'd love it.

Nina and I straggled out, the last to leave. We sat on a bench to look at the stars, where she promptly fell asleep. I waited, hoping she was resting. After ten minutes, she snored.

"Wake up. Let's go home to sleep," I jostled Nina's shoulder. She was out. The REM cycle had to run its course. I didn't have her address. I considered getting a hotel room, but couldn't leave her there alone. I laid my head in her lap, just for a minute. My eyes closed. I dreamt of meeting Kristína Alicia in Iceland. We played mirror-mirror in pantomime; even I couldn't tell who was who as we morphed from one to two.

Nina shook me awake. "Come on, Luc, we have to go home." For a moment I was disoriented — we could have been Martians on Mars for all I could figure.

"Yo soy Rrrrraaathththththth-ah-mon," I responded accompanied by the full lift, swivel, and pinched bunny puppet. She shrieked with laughter. Water flowed from her eyes causing black mascara to drip down her jawbone like a clown. Her cachinnations were contagious. I doubled over convulsing with such intensity I thought I might miscarry.

We hailed a cab. Every few minutes, one of us would lift, swivel and pinch, "*Rrrrraaathththththth-ah-mon*," and we'd roar again. It was a great first night in New York.

The town was abub when I awoke. 2:12 p.m., just after noon Mountain time. I lay curled around a Labrador-sized downy pillow, another between my knees, and a third, drool soaked, under my head; unusual for me, the drool, not the pillow propping. The last thing I recalled was the glowing Brooklyn brownstone at dawn. Now, midday, light laid shadows on homogeneous eggshell blue walls with tasteful teal trim in need of a Camille mural.

My phone lit up. It was Matt.

"Hi, I miss you already."

"I'm not good for you." I blurted out.

"Let me decide what's good for me. Where's this coming from?"

"I'm messed up, tortured over Luis' death. I have to make it right in the world somehow. I have to atone. It consumes me."

"You're lovely, Lucy and deserve someone to love no matter what your burdens are."

"I don't understand how you don't feel remorse?"

"I feel anguish, sadness for his life, I didn't want to kill a man, it's the most painful thing I ever could imagine, but I don't regret my actions. He was an evil rat bastard and a slubberdegullion to boot. I did what I had to out of self defense."

"You don't seem consumed by it."

"I was tormented for ten years. I struggle, but now live my life. That experience doesn't define me. I've shared this with you often. Where are you? I thought you'd be marching merrily around Manhattan today. What are you up to? How's Nina LaRuuuue?"

"I'm not sure I'm a monogamous type."

"What happened? Are you and Nina having an affair?"

"Me and Nina? No." I threw the coral and grey sheet off and got up. "My bangs are at that stupid place. They're in my eyes no matter what I do," I tucked a wetted brush under the fringe, pinning it severely back with a bobby pin decorated by a six-pedaled lime green crystal flower. Harumpff. I looked like a messy two-year-old. "I'll grow my hair out. I can't stand it anymore."

"Did you sleep with someone?"

"No."

"Did you want to?"

Sleep tee off, dusty blue paisley print shirt on.

"No, but I was... tempted, and I feel terrible about that."

"So did I, it's natural."

"What! With whom?"

"Bonnie, the massage therapist."

"With the matted hair?"

"Yeah."

"You think she's cute?"

"Hell, yeah, and brilliant with her hands."

"Cuter than me?"

"No."

"Why would you tell me that? It's hurtful."

Paisley blue patterned shirt off, tee back on; I would go for a run before heading out wherever. I needed to clear my head.

"You had her massage, you said the same thing."

"I didn't say she was cute or I feel tempted to SLEEP with her. Honesty is overrated sometimes."

"Who's your guy?"

"No one. He's not MY GUY."
Runners laced up and pulled with tight double bows.
"What's his name?"
"Ramon."
"A musician?"
"Yeah. Why do you say that?"
Toothbrush loaded up with paste.
"You went to that club last night."
"Oh."
"Did you hook up?"
"What? No!" sheet tucked in, ivory summer quilt pulled up, "I'm in love with you."
"What are you going to do today?"
"I might get a haircut."
"But you just said..."
"I know. I don't know. Whatever." I pounded the pillows to fluff them. I didn't drink, but I could have downed four martinis along with a red bell pepper, scallion, and goat cheese omelet.

Matt milked me for more information, "What did his face look like, describe the features."

I sat back on the bed, "Oh, Matt. It wasn't half as beautiful as yours. It's a stupid conversation. We've just hurt each other for no reason."

It sounded like he was crying.

"What are you up to today?"

"I delivered the bookcase to the gnostic church, I'm headed to bring Scooby his cupboards and then go see Kacey."

"Give her a hug for me." This surprised me. I was homesick for some place other than Paris - me, rambling, rolling stone Gallophile of the rough road.

Nina blew in the doorway like a Biscayne Bay breeze, lip primer on, coffee in hand, bangs perfectly coiffed. "Hep, hep, hep, what's this sleeping away the day? Let's go get some Coney Island on. We'll storm troop the City tomorrow."

"Hey, Matty, Nina is here. I have to go."

"Is that the man? There on the phone?"

I nodded.

"Give it to me," she pulled the phone from my hand, "Bonjour, soleil! Félicitations, c'est un oiseau assez libre que vous avez attrapé."

"Oh, my god, he's not French. Speak English to him... well... don't speak to him at all!"

"Oui, she is a free bird," His faraway voice sounded weakened by a windstorm, but assuredly strong at the core, "She'll need a goat cheese omelet, Nina," he commanded, "Can I count on you to make sure that happens?"

She looked stunned, "Ja, sicher, natürlich."

"Ausgezeichnet, Nina LaRue, ich spreche mit dir zwei nach Coney, also bis dahin, auf Wiedersehen."

I don't speak German that well, but he just said, "Excellent, Nina LaRue, I'll speak with you two after Coney, so until then, goodbye."

She handed me back my device; her cage rattled a bit. "Most impressive man. You did good, Luc. I'll pop over and get some goat cheese. You want to come?"

"No. I need to go for a run. Is there a park nearby?"

"Ja. Hurry, though at this rate it'll be midnight before we get there. Oh, and Jeremy wants to tag along."

"You look disappointed." She did.

"We have little time, you only gave me three days and we have so much to talk about."

"Well, I'm eager to get to Iceland. I don't want to troop around for my whole pregnancy." I placed a protective hand on my growing belly.

"Ja. So much to talk about."

"Nina?"

"What, darling?"

"Will you get some broccoli and red and yellow bell peppers?"

"Yes, my portrait queen."

"I dreamt I had a talking dog."

"What did it say?"

"I don't remember?"

"What kind of dog?"

"Doberman."

"Male or female?"

"Um. I don't remember."

We inched forward in line toward the Wonder Wheel. My moment was overlaid with images of Bub and Harquint laughing on the London Eye, and riding the wheel at The Idaho State Fair, feet dangling, my mouth stained goobley grape from an icy-ice; Noni's stained cheeky cherry. Dad's was green from the lucky lime and mom's full, upturned lips bright from the orange crush. I wondered if next time I might be happy, holding hands of my twins? If they were both boys, I'd call them Sam and Max, honest names; two girls, Rory and Sydney, unisex names so they could be whomever they wanted. If they were a boy and a girl... Jeremy's spurious tone interrupted my reverie.

"So you had a dream you had a talking dog..."

"Um-huh."

"... But the only other thing you remember is that it was a Doberman?" He seemed angry at my story.

"Well, I also remember we were on a sweltering beach, lightening cracked, a tremulous thunder echoed, and the dog put on a polka dot raincoat."

"So, why didn't you start out with that?"

"I just remembered as I was telling you. Hmmm, maybe I put the coat on him... or her." I thought he might kill me.

"Hallo!" Nina's joyous German salutation saved us from further trite talk. She was back from the bathroom, a place pregnant mums are used to. Six months along, she was a bodacious goddess. Jeremy gave her a tickle on the small of her back with sex on his mind. She winced, muscles tight, her face instantly older, eyes dulled. I wanted him to unhand her, her to leave him, and Nina and I to have time to talk alone.

"He has the arms of an octopus, and the tenacity of a tiger, but he's a boar and a chore," she'd whispered in my ear on the bus to the park.

"Why is he coming today then?"

"I have to be civil with him until I work out the details. I don't want to lose my house along with my mousy spouse."

In Paris she filled days detailing how unparalleled their unity had been at the beginning. He rocked her world and she, like Sally Ride, was up for an ultramodern adventure. I tried to see him through a compassionate lens, understand what turned a good guy bad, but the effort wearied me. I had Jónína Johanson and Kristína Alicia Jónínadóttir on my mind.

A girl of about seven with strawberry braids and freckles flecked across her nose like a midnight meteor shower tugged at my pants. "Can I see?" She pointed to the ring necklace around my neck. I held it out for her to examine. "Ahhhh, it's beautiful! Look Sammy!" Her friend ran over to see. He was Filipino, compact, brimming with curiosity. They smiled at me - one mouth grape, the other cherry red.

"What's your name?" I asked the mini Pippi.

"Cammie."

"Sammy and Cammie. That's cute."

They giggled. "Well, thanks. Bye!"

"Bye!"

They disappeared in the crowd's swell.

"Bye!" Sammy and Cammie. Those would be fine names for a boy and a girl.

"When a talking dog is in a raincoat, that's the bit you lead off with." Jeremy's brow furrowed still over my silly dream.

"Okay, next!" A young man working his first job as a Wonder Wheel assistant beckoned us forward with the seriousness of an elementary school crossing guard. Nina did me a solid. She sat between her soon-to-be ex and me. The ride chugged backwards slowly. As we neared the top, I spied Sammy and Cammy climbing on the carousel. Something made them look up. They spotted me and waved their arms like mad.

"Jeremy doesn't like you."

I flipped responses through my head faster than a slight-of-hand-furtive-fingered magician shuffling a fixed deck of cards. I could have blurted out, "Well, he's a jerk," or "How is it you married that guy — what made him so absinthian?" or "Why are you telling me this, to make me feel bad?" or, "I didn't remember the dog was in a raincoat until I talked about it!" Instead I settled on, "I'm sorry to upset your household. I'm usually a welcome guest."

"You are welcome, it's wvunderbar to see you. It's a badge of honor to elicit any response from him; this means he sees you as a strong woman."

But I didn't care how he saw me. I was strong enough as is and not dead yet. I just wanted to enjoy my stay and rest up for the trip of a lifetime to meet the monozygotic me.

Union Square Greenmarket was buombinating with energy: white-tented stalls showcased burgundy beets the size of bears. Parsley, sage, and rosemary sang under the punishing Manhattan sun. A man on a red beach bike rode alongside us. He glanced up and down our bodies; when he saw the baby bumps, he moved on. A stout, ruddy-faced woman grabbed my elbow; she handed me a card that explained she was mute and would appreciate money. I flattened a ten-dollar bill and held her hands for an awkward moment as I gave her enough, I hoped, for a good meal. 'Life is unfair,' life consistently reminded me. An off-leash German Shepherd in a blue-and-white checkered bandana poked his nose into our private parts. The feckless bicycle man straddled the seat and laughed.

"He says you're hiding something. There's no trace of you on the Internet except your new social media. No art portfolios, resumes, references, addresses, genealogy, embarrassing college pictures, nothing. He thinks your lack of transparency is conspicuous."

"What? Is he stalking me? Gathering Kompromat? What's his deal?"

"Did you look me up?"

We had a nice day. I bought a frosted blown glass vase for Kristína Alicia; it was three inches in diameter. On the outside two women faced outward with their hands clasped together. I'd played tourist several times before in The Big Apple. This day was a chance to take a bite of daily life in LaRue style. We avoided the tourist traps - no Statue of Liberty or Times Square. We ambled haphazardly and picked out trout, lettuce, avocados, and sweet potatoes for supper to prepare for my flight to face my doppelganger.

"I looked out of curiosity, sure, but not to judge you. I wanted to learn more about you and your Aunt Maria, who is so kind to me."

"How would you have reacted if you didn't find a trace of me?"

"I... didn't have expectations."

"Yes, you did. Everyone is traceable. We wanted to see your art portfolio. I want to know you too. Who is she, this mysterious artist? I have many contacts, Luc," she chomped on a Persian pickle squirting a peppery punch of juice in my eye, "I could be Stieglitz to your O'Keeffe. If you stayed longer, I could set up sittings, but you only gave me three days!"

"I don't have my work online. I like to keep a low profile. I love the picture of you in the serpentine boa and top hat popping the champagne. Where was that taken? I'd like to draw it if that's okay with you."

"No, not that one. It was at Mardi gras the day Jeremy proposed. I don't relish that memory," she popped the last bit of pickle in her mouth and licked her fingers like Nacho guy. "How are you going to become famous if you hide?"

The mute woman walked back by, this time contentedly eating a black sesame seed bagel smeared with apricot flecked cream cheese. She didn't notice us. 'Life is beautiful,' life constantly reminded me.

"I'm not hiding!" I disliked lying, especially to a friend. "Nina, not to change the subject from this pleasant interrogation of me, but what are you going to do about these men? You're pregnant! Prepare for the baby and take care of yourself." This didn't come out with the finesse I intended. Out of concern, I sounded accusatory and defensive.

"Let's go. We have a lot of catching up to do. There's a quiet place we can chat."

We walked for miles and ended up at Strawberry Fields, lushly lined with tall elm trees, shrubs, flowers and rocks. My parents revered John Lennon; they would have loved this homage to him. I felt their presence here. Go figure, they had nothing to say in Idaho, but perked up in a public park in Manhattan. We gravitated to the spotted shade under the overhang of a maple tree, plopped ourselves down, and talked for four hours.

Nina wanted to leave Jeremy, break from Jabori, and exit New York altogether. First she had to figure out details about real estate and legalities regarding co-parenting with a man she wished she hadn't fallen for, so hard, so deep, so fast like jumping off the Empire State building into the ocean on a drunken double-dare. In her time of marital despair, he was the only one who had seemed to care. Jammin' Jabori, a dashing

Arthur swishing a magical Excalibur, led her up from the depths to a burgeoning bliss with their very first kiss.

"'To infinity and beyond,' he cried the night he plunged me into my current fertilized plight," she rubbed her belly like a mama-bear. "To complicate matters, he's still my accountant and has access ro every corner of my coinage."

"Oh, my god," was about as much wisdom as I mustered in response. I was a failure as a friend.

"Tell me more about Matt."

"I don't deal well with a long-distance relationship. He feels like my soul mate, whatever that means, but am I supposed to miss him every moment of the day when we're apart? If that's love, I don't feel it. I mean, I want to share everything with him, but I also feel complete on my own. In quiet moments I miss him terribly, especially at night. Every evening he'd lay his warm hands right here and sing to the twins. I feel they miss him too."

"Twins?"

"I thought I told you."

"Oh, girl," she shook her head and pulled me up off the grass. "Time to go back to Brooklyn. Lucy, you got some 'splaining to do and all you give me is three damn days." She marched ahead of me, past the Strawberry Fields memorial, shaking her head. The word IMAGINE winked up at me.

KRISTÍNA

The first thing I noticed was her black pilled socks and how the straps of her flower embossed brown sandals stuck between her big and index toes. The latter, in her case, were a mite longer than the others. Her clothing confused me. Why did she make this footwear choice? Her hair was half-shorn, shaved on the left and swept over past her right ear, the side I sat on. I didn't get an aisle seat on this flight because I booked too late. Beggars can't be choosers; she sat on the aisle with ample room to stretch out her sandaled soles.

"Halló, I'm Cadence."

"Halló, I'm Lucy."

"Is this your first time going to Iceland?" Her pronunciation was soft, yet crisp. I imagined the word halló spilling from Kristína Alicia's mouth.

"Já." I had been practicing my words.

She laughed. "Your pronunciation needs work." She ran her hand through the hair on the right side of her head. "We have long summer days and midnight sun now, everything is green and lush, the weather predictably unpredictable, you will want to wear layers," she wiggled her toes. Ah. "The highland roads will be open to raw and somewhat untouched lands. Have you ever seen a midnight sun?"

"Nei."

She laughed again.

"What would you like to drink?" A male attendant with a gelled widow's peak and warm eyes asked.

"Hot water with lemon, vinsamlegest."

"And for you?"

"The same. Visam-la-gast."

Candace pressed her lips together and tried not to laugh, but she giggled, then I did, then the flight attendant did, and soon half the passengers too, though they had no idea why.

She sipped her drink and closed her eyes. I did the same.

Then later...

"Lucy, Lucy, shh, shh, shh. You're having a bad dream." Cadence squeezed my shoulder in a reassuring and desperate way.

"Uh, Pierre!"

"Who is Pierre?"

"Pierre? He's umm..." I wondered how many nights I dreamt of him but when I awoke the more-real-than-real visions vanquished before recognition, like flakes in the snow globe of Paris my parents bought for my seventh birthday from the fair in Montreal.

"It's all right, you need not say, Lucy, but tell me, what would a perfect day for you in Iceland comprise?"

It would be an ecstatic day IF she liked me and I liked her. Would she? Would I? Tension accumulated in my body: my jaw pressed tight, almost off-kilter, scapula pulled sharply back as if hogtied, and my calves knotted like gnarly oaks. If she doesn't like me, at least I will get to see the Northern Lights, I thought. It scared me. I was suddenly shy and insecure — she was a part of me. I invested fully in making this meeting a success.

The hours from New York to Reykjavík seemed short. Not nearly enough time for me to wrap my head around the imminent greeting. From the air, colourful red, yellow and blue rooftops whirled closer like a palette when I mix paints. I couldn't believe we were landing already! My heart pounded and salty beads seeped into the indent above my lips.

"On a perfect day I'd go to the Blue Lagoon, have a captivating, creative conversation with my companion, and eat anything but one of your shark or whale delicacies."

"Yes, but you mustn't say this in Iceland. We like our food there, this is normal to us."

"And a perfect day for you, Cadence?"

"Today is a perfect day, coming home, and meeting you."

Cadence kindly guided me through customs arm in arm as if I was a blind Venusian just landed on Planet Earth. Though I'm a wayfaring lass from way back, the commotion in the airport played upon my dysphonic distress. The thought of meeting my twin with nary but a fifteen minute phone call exchanged between us seemed not much to go on.

"You want to meet your sister, já?"

"Já," came out as more question than answer.

"Why are you waffling?"

My head wasn't working right. I suddenly craved waffles with thinly sliced strawberries and whipped cream spiraled high into a towering frothy point. I wondered if this was a pregnancy craving? This was some time to find out. I thought I'd faint if I didn't get some waffles — stat.

Landlocked on an iceberg at the edge of the Arctic with cliffs ascending over furious seas, the people love their fermented shark, pickled ram's testicles, singed sheep head, and blood pudding. This diet was shocking in comparison to my timid vegan palate. And what of their elves who hide in the hills, frolicking amidst Huldufólk? They seem suspect too.

"I need to eat." I sat on a bench, woozy.

Cadence, with the staid patience of a summer gardener pruning peaches, offered me a sip from her water flask, "Here. What do you need?"

I sipped sullenly. "I'm sorry to bother you. You must be excited to be home. You should go." She worked as a history teacher in Hoboken and hadn't been home in four years.

"Don't be silly, what do you need?"

"Carbohydrates. Waffles. Protein. I'm not sure."

Her laugh had a charming ring I was growing keen on. "I can't find waffles here, but I have a sandwich. Tuna fish."

I hate tuna fish. "Thank you." I devoured it like a cannibal chewing a crisped corpse.

"Why did your sister insist on meeting so soon. You just connected, já?"

"She said we have too much to catch up on - twenty-seven years - and it would be best to do so in person."

"And you think this is a good idea?"

"I do, já. We have a complex past."

"Do you have a photograph? How will you recognize her?"

We both looked up. A synchronistic swivel of our heads landed our gaze upon an incandescent woman — kona in Icelandic. Our piffle puffed out. Cadence looked from her to me, me to her, her to me, and sat entranced. "Ah, so."

There, seven meters away, stood Kristína Alicia, my Nordic reflection; her chestnut waves crested over her shoulders like autumnal leaves teaming, tossing, tumbling over a butte. She wore dragonfly dream catcher wellies with paisleys on the toes, a succotash scarf, and an off-white fuzzy beret for it was puddly and windy out, though noontime bright at eleven p.m. She twisted her hands like she was flattening cauliflower pizza crust dough. Clearly we developed from the same zingy zygote.

My body froze. Iceland turned me into a statue. Twenty-seven years of lost time – climbing trees, pillow fighting, and more – shuttered through my inner eye. The Looney Tunes epilogue, "Beda bida that's all folks," played through my mind.

Thank goodness for tuna fish without which I surely would have passed out.

"Camille Lisette Portraro." Kristína Alicia Jónínadóttir held onto my shoulders as if expecting me, like a helium balloon, to float fast away into orbit unless she, my rock, anchored me to the earth. Choked up, we stared at each other, our minds not believing what we saw. She laid a hand gently on my cheek and I wrapped my arms around her waist, smaller now than my burgeoning belly, one of the few physical differences between us. From there we fell into a hug, souls reuniting, moments ticking into eternity.

Cadence, wiping tears from her eyes stepped forward from her spot twenty paces back where she'd retreated to give us space for a private reunion. "Stop fiddle-farting-around, you'll be best to get acquainted in a good warm home instead of this drafty airport."

We stared again and fell into a round of giggles at seeing the spitting image of ourselves come to life, in flesh, before our eyes. I like her! She liked me! A prehistoric twenty minutes older, I was protective of my little sis, but on her home turf, she grounded me.

"Well, I'm going. Gaman að kynnast þér, Lucy. Gaman að kynnast þér, Kristína. I'll be in touch, Lucy," she whispered in my ear, "I hope I didn't intrude, but I snapped photos for you and your sister." Then she, her socks and sandals, disappeared.

Kristína handed me a pair of brown rubber wellies with white spots on them the size of the poker chips. "Here, you'll find these useful. Just your size." She winked. I love winks; along with freckles and dimples, they are human details I find friendly. Kristína had all three, but then so did I and Nikos did too. I thought of him as the twins chose that moment to kick me for the first time. They too were excited!

A hard rain hammered down on the car; the slow ride home was silent but for the whoosh of the windshield wipers, which barely whisked the water away enough to see the road. We stole sideways glances at each other trying to work out the quick turn our lives had taken.

Her hair looked exactly like mine did before I'd cut it in a panic in the alleyway in Paris; it was an iconic length for our facial features, flowing to mid-back just before the bra strap. Our waves took kindly to a trimmed yet unkempt libertine, no bangs. Her front locks blended blissfully into the back, as mine had too, while I had the rakish bangs that waged an insurrection against my forehead. I hadn't worn the hair clip because it looked silly and I wanted to make a good impression. I had a similar task as the windshield wipers swooshing hair away from the field of my vision at regular intervals.

Many rooftops in Reykjavík, (pronounced Rake-ya-week, I'd learned from Cadence, or Raykjahveek, as nearly as I could make out), shone like a jumble of shiny buttons, an artist's dream town; Kristina's house had a deep periwinkle blue roof, a consummate cap to a quaint cottage. The aroma of a Birchwood hearth fire wafted over to welcome me home.

A round white couch over three metres in diameter settled into a sunken spherical area over to one side took up the living room.

"What's that?" I pointed to the metal slope from the second story spilling down to the edge of the chaise.

"What does it look like?" Her eyes sparkled.

I inspected it more closely. "It looks like a slide!"

"Já, so it is. Our móðir was a renowned architect. Together we designed a one-of-a-kind house. Tomorrow we will climb the mosaic steps on the side, open the hatch, and take a ride on the slide; it's a soft landing, but I warn you, it's addictive." I tilted my chin up to check out the carved, cut out hatch that sealed the slide from the outside. "I can't draw for the life of me, but I'm a carpenter. I'm handy with tools and have an artistic eye."

I noticed her hands, identical to mine except for callouses and clear polish. I wore none. This is the first I'd heard about our mother. I'd been too afraid to ask. "Is she still alive?"

"No. Sadly, Jón died earlier this year. This is when I sought to find you."

"You sought to find me?"

"Yes, I'll tell you all about it tomorrow, and you can tell me what you wish about your life," she stole a sideways glance at me, this time at my belly.

"Come, let me show you the stairs."

"Ahhhh!"

There were two sets of identical staircases, each formed a double helix, and led past stained glass windows into a loft. The panes interwove golden, carnelian, red, lavender, Kelly green, bright baby blue, and orange into the most brilliant formation of Scorpio and Libra Zodiacs — our birthday was on the cusp.

"You made these?" I marveled.

"Jón designed; I sautered."

We spiraled up the left staircase and she led me to the guest room.

"This is your room. It's been here waiting for you forever. You're home now, Camille."

A banner greeted me, "Velkominn, Camille!" I flashed on the "Will you marry me, Lucy?" scroll in the sky in Idaho. I couldn't wait to tell Matt! He would love Kristína — maybe too much! She looked just like me but was more capable with woodcutting tools than I. A pile of neatly folded sea green towels and a washcloth sat bedside. The homemade quilt had a star pattern; the energy pulsed out in positive waves. On the wall above the bed was a delicately framed picture of our mother holding Kristína and me as babies. The same picture I had found in the mystery box at

Earnest Elves! The caption in perfectly swirled calligraphy read, "My girls ~ may they always be happy, may they have innsæi."

Then I saw it. To the right there was a wooden table made by stacking a plywood board over maroon bricks. On top lay paints, brushes, crayons, charcoal, colored pencils, paper, scissors, glue, and bottles of sparkles. Next to the table was a four by five foot chalkboard, with all the best brands of chalk. The caring details buoyed my spirit.

The midnight sun shone sweetly upon the simple fineries Kristína Alicia had lovingly prepared for me. The time zone changes caused my body clock to go cuckoo. After we said good night, I messaged Matt, "arrived safely! I love you!" I didn't wait for an answer — before I closed the blackout curtains, a double rainbow arched angelically over the town. I fell solidly asleep and dreamt about Pierre.

It was nearly eleven when I awoke disoriented and hungry; I opened the curtains with three sharp tugs of the cord — the damn sun was blindingly bright. "Give a girl a bit of darkness, will ye?" I lipped as I slipped a leg into my trousers, nearly toppling over. My foul mood tainted what I'd hoped would be an ambrosial first morning in Reykjavik.

Sometimes pregnancy hormones create seesawing emotions, but I pegged the boorish flotsam and jetsam of a gypsy-fugitive's life for upsetting my apple cart. Running from the scene of a crime was illegal and blasphemous. It was not emblematic of my behavior and I was incredulous about it. I would have to right my wrongs my whole life, and if future lifetimes exist, I'd atone then too. All I did was wish Brigitte a happy day. I'm an excellent driver, everyone says so — patient, prudent, and aware. I was careful, but for one moment when that damn pole jumped out of nowhere. It happened fast like careening bellyside down on a slip-and-slide spread wide on the grass on a blistering hot day.

Kristína was in the bucolic backyard doing sun salutes. She undulated her body, palms on the grass, in plank position so her head rose like a serpent. "Good morning, Sleepy, join me?" I wanted to go home, but didn't have a home anymore; it was no longer in Paris or Idaho; it wasn't in

Helena; Berkeley didn't feel like home though Matt was there. This super sunny city didn't feel like home though I couldn't help but wonder if it might have been if I had not been a byproduct of immigration from Iceland, taken by father to the United States before I had a say, details of which I hoped would be filled in on this day.

Kristína noted my sour countenance right away, leapt up and hugged me, smoothing my ridiculously unruly bangs from out of my eyes, "What's wrong, Camille?"

I began blubbering, a sorry contrast to my buoyant sister. Snot made several resilient runs down my lip like the New Years snowfall in Sun Valley. I used my sleeve to wipe the dripping from my nose. "I just read that The Blue Lagoon averages 37–39 °C, but I'm pregnant. I can't goooooo." I wailed. "I want to gooooooooo. I've always wanted to goooooooooooo."

My sister flew into the house and returned with a box of soft white tissues, aloe added. "Many pregnant women go to the hot springs, perhaps they don't stay in too long, but you have to decide and do what's right for you." Her distress seemed to unravel the effects of her slow, sensuous yoga stretches. "How far along are you? When I made the reservations, I didn't realize you were pregnant. We don't have to go."

"Just over four months. Oh no, I want to experience The Blue Lagoooooon," I fell into another round of languishing laments.

She disappeared into the house again, this time for fifteen minutes. She returned with two bowls of piping hot Hafragrautur, a thick, gooey oatmeal, garnished with blueberry Greek yogurt, gogi berries, and roasted pumpkin seeds, moistened by a splash of goat's milk. We greedily spooned up the mush, slurping the end bits from the bowls. It was de-licious and settled my body in a way it hadn't been in weeks.

"How did you sleep?" I asked.

"I tossed and turned and woke early, unable to go back to bed. I'm too excited to have you here. I planned this since I was twelve when Jón first told me about you — about us."

This almost set me off for a third round, "Why didn't they tell ME?"

"Twelve-years-old. Twelve. That was the age they decided they would tell us, but your mother got so sick then and we all waited."

"You all? Everyone knows but me? Who 'all' decided this?"

"Jón, his wife, Aðalborg…"

"His wife?" This confused me.

"She - Jónína, our móðir was, how do I explain, not born in the right body. Jón felt trapped in a woman's body, but more than that, Jón identified as human."

"Are you saying she was transsexual?"

"Ah, well, people thought he lived as a man, a straight man, but Jón didn't identify with any gender. Jón has a wife, Aðalborg… so, Jón and Aðalborg, your mother, your father, and me. I have much to tell you, and I can see you have much to tell me."

"Já." I turned and headed back to the house. I couldn't think straight.

"Where are you going?"

"To get ready for the Blue Lagoon."

"WAIT!" Her yell startled me.

"What?"

"Don't you want to use the slide?" She grabbed hold of my hand and led me to the right side of the house. There, we climbed a flight of thirty steps patterned with stunning Gaudí-esque tiles. A weighty black combo lock sat on a maroon barn-style door, which opened outwards like wings.

"You first."

"My pleasure," I set my legs on the silver slide with the eager anticipation of a two-year-old in big girl pants going down for the first time alone.

"Wheeeeeeeeeee!" I plopped softly onto the couch, rolled over, and yelled, "All clear!"

"Wheeeeeeeeee!" Kristína Alicia plopped next to me. She pressed her lips together, suppressing laughter, her dimples dipped inward. "Want to go again?"

"Do I!" I popped up like a jack-in-the-box.

"Wheeeeeeee!" we squealed for nearly an hour, playfully pushing each other out of the way as we ran out the front door and up the side stairs, giggling like we were at an elementary school slumber party, the very kind being separated robbed us of having together.

"How do you close the door from the inside?"

"Like this," she uncoiled a rope that looped around a hook on the kitchen wall.

"This — is — the — best — house — EV-er!"

"It belongs to both of us. All of us," she nodded down at my swelling belly. "Now, I will go unlock the lock." With that, she loped away leaving me to wonder what combination my twin chose. I flashed on the numbers 867 - 5309 from the Jenny song, Theo's post box number. I'd been out of touch with him for too long. I missed everyone. When, I wondered wistfully, would I have time to catch up... especially with Matt with whom I was growing more and more attached? I yearned to hear about his day and tell him about mine.

While I wished for more time, the sobering thought hit me like a wallop of snowball-fight ice, the hours for Luis Fernando's family might seem too long — each moment pulled painfully from one end to the next like a torture board of taffy wrenched to the snapping point. For those who have lost a child or any precious life, seconds may stink; minutes may be miserable, and hours agonizing. Luis Fernando's mother would not be celebrating today.

I reached for my phone to message Matt. A text from him awaited me. "Lucy, Kasey is in the hospital, she just had an emergency appendectomy. I think she's okay, but I'm a wreck. I may be out of touch for a bit. I can't wait to hear how y'all are getting along. XO."

"Ready?" Kristína Alicia leaned her limber body into the doorjamb, hair pulled high in a ponytail.

"Yes!" I smiled brightly, concerned about Kasey, and unsure how transparent about my life I would be with my twin. I yearned for courage to come clean, to be forthright about my plight, and do the right thing, whatever that might be, rather than perpetuating more Jónínadóttir-Portraro clan secrets. The hush-hush of half-truths dulls the natural light within. Piecing ultraviolet rays streamed down in agreement, quickly replaced by thunderclouds that blew in with more bluster than I'd mustered when I rolled out of bed.

"Boom, boom, boom," said the sky. *"Do not tell your twin a lie."*

The grey-green moss on the Reykjanes peninsula was otherworldly and strangely soothing. Kristína was more of a bold driver, to put it mildly, than I am: she took turns faster, hit hills harder, and shifted like speed racer fueled by triple lattes from Peet's, yet she was caffeine free. I had made my mind up to tell her the truth — I hoped she wouldn't think I drove half a bit as recklessly as her. I was a careful driver; the car skidded and slipped! I still could not fully maneuver my mind past the denial surrounding the blatant, idiotic deadly destruction I'd caused. Cognitive-frickin'-dissonance.

I found Iceland to be heady and wild. The weather again changed from blustery to sunny in the snap of a one-two blues beat. We saw a geyser erupt with the speed of a torpedo, and my twin had a carefree streak that mirrored the rugged seas rushing to explode in shimmering shades of blue and green kablooey onto monumental cliffs hang-dogging above. I needed this uncivilized, untouched, untamed energy to free me from the crushing capsule of captivity. I also needed her, and she, it seemed, needed me.

From the moment we sat our behinds in the car on the way to the hot springs, Kristína spouted verily like a volcano in her own right: words, words, words — she couldn't spit them out fast enough. She too waited none too patiently to tell me stories of our birth, our vibrant mother/father/human, whom she called Jón, and the split family she was privy to for fifteen years, while I had blissfully carried on as if no Icelandic double existed. Her focus jumped, disjointed, like a hen on hot cement.

"I suspected something was up. Jón dropped hints like birdseed when, as a child, I questioned him about my father. 'Who is he, where is he, why won't he come to see me?'

"What did Jón say, did he... Jón lie?" I wanted to hear all about my mother, who he was, how he lived his life, and if he regretted giving me away — did he think of me? Why did our parents have us and then split us apart? My emotions ran together like watercolors, which splayed in a parade of hues. Anger appeared first, a red wash on a white page; love next, golden, silver, soft pink like billowing cotton candy, and the sweetest translucent baby blue like a five am sky. Righteous strength struck in Tropical Rain Forest green in bold, vertical strokes; despair, black; doubt crawled in like a sickly grey snail; denial is a mousy mustard, and finally royal blue and a rich, regal violet brought the assurance of a phoenix surveying the scene from on high.

"He loved you, Camille, yes. Once Jón gave me the gift; that's what we called it, "The Gift," when I turned twelve, my life changed. We talked of you all the time and closely followed your development. I became obsessed with meeting you. Jón made a seven-foot shine to you, alter of adoration, which Jón refreshed with each new photo your parents and later, Aunt Molly, sent. What about you, how was it to grow up in Idaho? Did you travel much? You ski and play volleyball, right? I ski too."

"I'd love to go skiing with you sometime, here, in France, or Sun Valley, which is spectacular. I ice skate too and run. But how are you in touch with Molly? We rarely spoke with her." We two barely knew where to start. So many questions! So much to catch up on!

"For two years when your father..." ahem, she cleared her cottony, dry throat. "When *our* father was so ill, he gave Molly letters, packages, and photos to mail to me. She has been loyal and constant with us, now me. She wanted to help you, Camille. She respects how you took care of your father, your parents, and yourself."

I remember! She would come for short visits with a shopping bag in hand, ask for a few minutes with my father alone, and leave with it full. "But she didn't help me — hands on. I was drowning there by myself. She abandoned me. I resent her."

"She couldn't stand to see your father so ill. She said you were strong enough for it, but seeing him like that gave her gripping stomachaches. Her job, she said, was to help pave the way for us to connect; this she did with all her heart."

Cognitive dissonance reared its head again. I'd seen Molly one-way and one-way only: it would take time to accept she meant well. I hadn't even looked her up when I was in Idaho.

"Did anyone call Jón Jónína? What was he like as a father, and... was he called a husband? You said Jón married?"

"At first his family was resistant to letting go of calling her Jónína, but Iceland is aware and tolerant of LGBT rights. Jón was an advocate and eventually the community came to see Jón as Jón was. People adapted to using neutral pronouns. I wish you could have met Jón — you would have loved each other. Jón did not marry, but that doesn't mean so much to us here. Jón has a loving partner, Aðalborg. I call her "his wife" for your understanding."

"Oh, yes, you mentioned her. Is she still around?"

"Yes, Aðalborg and I are close. She's excited to meet you; she feels she is your mother."

"Hold the horses," I thought, "*My mother* was my mother, yet a biological mother, dead now, who gave me away at birth and his (or Jón's) 'wife' both claimed the honored mother role? No. My mother is and always has been the one and only."

"Marissa Sabine is my mother."

"Oh, I mean no disrespect to her. I hope you don't take us the wrong way; we have loved you for so long and want to welcome you completely into our family. We have cousins, aunts and uncles. We are together now." She kissed me quickly on the cheek. As she slowed the car to make a turn, she flipped me her phone, "We're here. Check and see if it's safe for you to go in the springs. I don't want to cook my nephew or niece."

Device in hand, I checked my emails. There was one from Tanu, whom I hadn't heard from in months. "Hi Lucy," was all it said. "Hi Tanu! How are you? Great to hear from you," I shot back, as I snuck messages in between my conversation with Kristína.

"Twins."

"Twins?"

I clicked through five emails from Brigitte. "I have to get out of France for a while, Camille," the first one said. "Perspective - I need to distance myself from the city, even for a short time," By the fifth message, she was ready to hop a plane and join me wherever in the world I was. "Cammy, just for a few weeks to clear my head, I have to leave. Get in touch soon, ma belle, where on this great globe are you now? Please say I can join you."

"I'm having twins."

Then, I kid you not, Kristína screamed a blue streak as though she was being murdered or had won the lottery as she skidded into an empty spot in the tourist-trafficked parking lot. The shriek bubbled buoyant, breathtaking, and butterfly blue. I covered my ears and added this hue to the psychedelic palate I already had mocked in my mind.

The smell of algae and sulpher from the steamy blue waters slipped up my nose as I stepped from the car. More blue. The soothing mountains surrounded us as steam puffed off the water like melted marshmallow curls from a childhood cuppa cocoa on a below zero February day after tobogganing in Hailey. Fresh air, magical skies, more blue still, danced with pinpoint polka dots. The land, the air, and the stench of rotten eggs and green slime cradled me deep. Finally, I was at home where I belonged.

"I can go in the water if we find a cool spot and I don't stay in long."

Kristína stood and smiled as if Jupiter and the moon hitched up the corners of her mouth.

"What?"

"Welcome home, Camille."

"Hang on, let me take this off." I pulled off the forest green wool sweater I'd borrowed from Kristína with a static Pssst, leaving my hairs dancing in the air. Most shades of green complimented our auburn hair and the slight smattering of freckles on our noses.

"Okay, one, two, toss." I led with my dominant right hand; she, my mirror image, led with her left, which was her solid side. Blisters along her lateral palm, well earned from being a hardworking craftsperson were the only differences in the appearance of our appendages.

The lemons flew in an up - up - cross-catch flow; a magical meditative rhythm took over. What are the odds, we both were capable jugglers! The spaciousness of her two story open ceiling allowed us the vertical space to get some juicy height from the fruit.

One, two, toss, "I like to eat lemons plain, Jón couldn't stand it."

One, two, toss, "Me too! I love lemons! Strawberry mint lemonade!"

One, two, toss, "Yum! Apple, ginger, lemon juice..."

"Umm, great combo!"

One, two, toss, "Can't stand sauerkraut though."

One, two, toss, "Sauerkraut, och, can't stand it either."

One, two, toss, "Are you in a relationship?"

One, two, toss, "On and off. I had a boyfriend, Sigurður, for five years before I realized he was a bit of a pebble-headed narcissist."

"Oh, not good, even a bit."

One, two, toss, "No. Then a girlfriend, Kristín; we're unsure now if we want to stay together. People cycle in and out, you know?"

One, two, toss, "Yes, they sure do. Kristína and Kristín."

One, two, toss, "Já. Confusing, no? Tell me more about Matt."

There's an early phase of love, sometimes enduring to those lucky few that encompass the outpouring of passion, playfulness, and potential so poetic it sends me soaring like a barn owl in the dark night. For all we've been through, I was in that potent place with Matt. Speaking of him energized me. The thought of his jocular, uneven smile, his wink, and strong forearms elicited effervescent elation from me.

One, two, toss, "It's transcendent with Matt. He's a good man. I think you two will get along. He's a woodworker too."

One, two, toss, "Já, you mentioned that. And how did you meet?"

One, two, behind-the-back pass, "His stepmother was my roommate in Berkeley. The moment we met, love mitosis exploded under our nose."

"Tricky shot let me try." One, two, behind-the-back pass, "Love mitosis. You're a poet too."

"Ha! Well done the loose caboose shot! I've never been one to look - or not look- for love or family..." One, two, toss, "I just set my chalk down and followed the lines; Bertrand called it *The Beingness of Belle*."

One, two, toss, "Ah, Bertrand, your partner. I like this description of you."

The lemons wobbled, "You've heard of Bertrand?"

One, two, toss, "Yes. I... I have looked for you for quite some time, Camille."

I almost missed the pass, "Oh." One, two, pass.

She reached far for it, saved it from crashing into an arched rosewood bookcase, hand carved by her, serving as host to Thoreau, Whitman, Dylan Thomas, Ibsen, Shakespeare, and Hunter S. Thompson, just to name the few authors one could read at a glance.

One, two, pass, "Is Matt excited to become a father?"

One, two, toss, "Yes, but he's not the biological father."

One, two, toss.

One, two, toss. I was slowing down, like a jalopy running out of gas.

One, two, toss, "Who is the father of the twins?"

One, two, toss, "His name is Nikos. He's an ex-boyfriend. It's a long story, with lots of Picayune details." One, two, toss, "He's a bit of an irascible narcissist too, but he's loyal and he loves me. It's complicated."

She dropped the lemons. "Nikos?"

I dove after the greenish fruit that rolled and dropped onto the white sunken couch. "Yes, Nikos, he's Greek."

Kristína rounded up the other two and plopped down onto the couch. She was a plopper. "Sit down. We have to talk." Kristína rubbed the callous on her left pinky like a girl scout trying to start a friction fire. "Where do I even begin? I have so much to tell you."

"That makes two of us."

"Do you want some something to drink?" She un-plopped herself and headed to the kitchen.

"Yes, please."

"Water?"

"No thanks, something warm. I'm freezing... growing stalactites here."

I un-plopped myself too and stood, hands clasped behind me like a felon in shackles, stooped over, twisting my head this way and that, snooping at book titles, pictures in porcelain frames, and a neat row of knickknacks in the back of the bookcase.

"I'll just put on some tea."

"Wonderful. Tea with lemon, vinsamlegest." I'd finally learned to say the word.

"There's some leftover fennel Parmesan soup, do you want some?"

"Yes, please! I'm hung-reee."

"Me too. Famished."

My appetite increased as the incubating babies flourished. I craved grape leaves, Greek Dolmades to be exact, like a teething baby who flaps its hands for applesauce. Perhaps I needed iron? As eager as I was to be with my twin and soak in everything about her, I craved solitude and needed to connect with friends. Tanu, I'm sure, would have a recipe for Dolmades, and I still wondered how she was. And when would I find time to break the news to Nikos, already reluctant about becoming a papa, he had two more on the way? My hunger, thirst for Kristína-connection, and need for time alone tugged at me; I was trapped in a transatlantic nocturnal sleep cycle. A voice inside cried, "You need to nest!"

Where might I settle? How will I raise these children well, and what did I have to do to atone? It seems I had no time for *what ifs*; I was too busy with *what is*.

I picked up a photograph of Kristína nuzzling a Manx. "Was this your cat?"

She popped her head into the room, "Já. She was Snúlli. In Iceland we believe cats respond better to S sounds."

"Really? I have a cat too. A friend is watching her. There is an S sound in her name."

"What do you call her?"

"Natalie Mouskers."

"Spell it."

"Natalie, like Natalie Wood, and then Mouskers, M-O-U-S-K-E-R-S."

"Natalie Mouse-kers."

"Mooo- skers."

"Ah, Natalie Mooo-skers. Yes, that is a good S sound. What does that mean?"

I took out my phone and showed her a picture. "Nothing, it's just a silly name. Here is Miss Mouskers. Bertrand, Leonard, and I made it up one night."

"Oh, she's beautiful! You must miss her."

I had to fight tears from coming like a roofer who spackled shut a hole in the ceiling during a downpour. "Oui," I said absentmindedly. "I miss everyone."

"I'll be right back — just going to give the soup a quick stir."

I picked up two snow globes of Paris: one of The Eiffel Tower, symbolically powerful to me, and the other of Montmartre, of all places. I followed her into the living room like a newly rescued puppy. "These are lovely. I collect snow globes too. I have this same one," I shook the one of the Tower and watched white pieces swirl in the dome and then like lazy leaves falling from Aspen groves, float with a sway to the bottom.

"Father sent me this one when I was ten. It came as a mystery package. I knew it was from my father. Jón should have told me at that point. I was old enough then to be leveled with."

He gave me that one at ten too! How many times did he buy double? How many secrets kept from me?

So many thoughts like shaken snow globe flakes circled to settle in my mind; unsure which to address first, I blurted out, "The picture of you dancing with your head shaved is stunning. I always wondered what I would look like bald. Now I see. Beautiful." Was it cancer or teen rebellion, I was keen to find out?

"I teach salsa, tango, and the waltz, modern, belly, and ballet, as you know. This was my first competition, age fourteen. I won first prize." She went in the kitchen for the food.

"I always wanted to be a dancer."

"And I longed to be an artist."

"And your head...?"

"I shaved it in solidarity when I heard your mother lost her hair to chemo." I gasped.

Kristína reappeared with a tureen of the steaming seafood soup. It was a simple presentation in wooden navy bowls. Salad lit up by tiny tomatoes saturated with vermillion pigments twinkled at me. Before she sat, she walked to the bookcase and perfunctorily pulled an Egyptian blue leather-bound book, worn with care, stained with tears.

"What's this?"

"Jón kept a journal for us. I would rather wait and ease you in, however you have given us only one week before you leave to lay our foundation. We both have a lot weighing upon our hearts to share; until we do, we are two similar metals, dissimilar at the moment, intersecting in turbulent thermojunctions."

I couldn't follow what she was saying. Instead, I flashed to an image of Matt reading the poem I'd written him in Kasey's hospital room — or was she home by now? I lifted the book that sat on the long table before us. It smelled of love. In gold leaf calligraphy, drawn by the adept hand of my artistic móðir read the words, *Kristína Alicia and Camille Lisette.*

I blew on a spoonful of the lemon-tinged soup. I would need nourishment for this.

The licorice kickback from the fennel peekabooed through the sharp snap of the cheese, "Ummm. Matty would love this. I can't wait to cook it for him." I reached in the kobica-colored wicker basket and took a zebra-striped napkin to lie in my lap.

"What do you love about him?" the question, so straightforward, so simple, stunned me.

"He can put the bottom sheet on the bed in one try: top left, top right, bottom left, bottom right — on my own I wrestle with it for half an hour." She had a captivating laugh like the tinkling of brass chimes blowing in a Boise breeze. We both sat with secrets; mine, more ludicrous than hers. I counted our calm moments until our reveals. I'd give a quick quip rather than expose my emotions; not an hour earlier I had sent my love this poem:

"My love has liquid eyes that gaze upon me from the depths of his sweet and gentle soul.
Bewitched, questioning, they dance with possibility and fear.
While my small hand sits lost, cradled in his larger one -
Enraptured, radiant, I sit
Inescapably surrendering my heart."

I eagerly await his reply when my cell reception faltered. It was tough to lose our contact during such a transformative time. If I saw the glory of an Arctic Harebell or Field Forget-Me-Not gracefully tussling on this strange terrain, found out my sister had a slide from the second story down to the living room, or turned into a mid-morning Werewolf from lack of sound sleep, I wanted Matt to be the first to hear.

"Tell me more details about this mystery man." Kristína curled her legs under her. She leaned in to listen with the innocence of a child hearing their favorite bedtime story.

"*Hoah.* Matt. He's a likeable guy; he's found his niche in an easy, affable, unaffected charm. Are you familiar with the Mississippi accent?"

"A little."

"He's like this," I sat up straighter, combed my bangs up and back over my forehead with my fingers in adoring imitation, winked slyly at her, "How Y'all doing?" Then I grinned the grin of a girl in a corps perdu love.

Her sweet laughter tinkled again, "I miss this love. I had it with Kristin so recently, but the stress of my last year put a kibosh on that."

"When did Jón die? What happened? Do you think about him every day?" I'd been dying to find out. Kristína put her head in my lap, wrinkling up the striped material I had just smoothed so carefully. She curled into a fetal position as an avalanche of tears rolled in pebbles from her eyes. It was so sudden, so intimate, almost more than I could bear. I stroked her hair back until her convulsions slowed to a stop.

"I miss Jón every day, yes. Jón died last October… on our birthday."

"Oh, my gosh, that must have been terrible!"

"It was."

"What did he die of?"

"Surgery."

"Having to do with gender change?"

"No, Jón wouldn't risk that surgery. Jón saw his existence beyond conventional bounds, anyway. Jón used to say, 'Many people don't take the time to know themselves, instead they are self-justifying, manipulative puppets. It's those that explore the inner realms I'm interested in.' Routine hernia surgery was on the twenty-first. We planned to celebrate on the twenty-third, but Jón caught an infection, sepsis, in the hospital. It was preventable, that's what gets me. It was preventable." Her anger stopped her crying.

"I'm sorry I wasn't here to support you. I wish had met him."

"We celebrated your birthday every year. When Jón died, the first thing I wanted to do was to find you and tell you."

"I was easy to find on the Internet."

"Yes." There were those giggles again, "You were. I followed you on all your accounts — sometimes you disappeared."

My heart pounded like a squadron of police trying to topple down the door of a serial kidnapper. She must have figured it out. I disappeared completely from view at the end of February. I would tell her, but I wasn't ready to just yet. "I was busy and preferred to not my spend my time online…" This was true, but I omitted the truth. My face grew hot, my tongue stuck to my mouth, I couldn't feel my hands or feet.

"I wanted to meet you in person as I had planned all my life and share of this directly. After I settled Jón's affairs, I flew to Paris."

"You did? When?" I knew. We both knew.

"February twenty-first."

I hit Pierre on the twenty-third.

I had to pee. I looked out the window, wanting to flee; Reykjavík in its few hours of darkness was translucent.

She stood statue still as tourists swirled around her in dizzying, counterclockwise spirals like the fresh flurries of snow that fell while riding horseback at Thingvellir National Park the spring prior, chasing the lascivious lights of the Aurora Borealis. Those otherworldly lights that dance on the sky - collisions between millions of electrically charged particles from the sun that enter earth's atmosphere by the solar wind, reminded her that the universe was bigger, brighter, and more combustible than she could ever in eternity imagine.

Everything was going well. The last-minute flight - a bargain - flew direct with a seamless takeoff and silky landing, amidst an aura of peaceful neutrality. The cab driver pointed out iconic landmarks of the ethnically and economically diverse right bank: the tremendous triumphant Arc, cobblestone-paved streets and hidden vineyards of Montmartre, puffs of poetry and Picasso impetuously ghosting about, and the Musée du Louvre where the object of her quest spent the better part of her days kneeling on cement, creating masterpieces of art that washed away right quick, but no matter, she poured her heart into each one.

Chestnut curls poked from beneath her grouse grey felt hat as she wrapped her sapphire scarf around her neck to keep at bay the wind; the blue complimented her auburn hair and men spun their heads around to look. She still had a tickle in her throat left over from a three-day virus. Moving hesitantly through the throng, she spotted the artist. There - at last - was her extroverted other half, effervescing with the crimson full-fingered pizzazz of Aurora, the Goddess of Dawn. Seeing her in the flesh sent shivers up her spine.

From a distance, she watched her chatty twin work. Birding binoculars provided details the unaided eye would miss. Her twin's hiking shoes were grass-stained and her creamy cheeks didn't have any make-up; she was the most radiant person in the square — her graciousness with customers and tourists spoke depths of generous spirit.

The woman from Iceland took time off to gather the courage with which to approach this agile angel. After days of garnering up nerve, she returned to the Square. A petite woman with a dark tumble of hair pulled her into a private pocket in the Plaza. "Where have you been? For days, your appointments have been waiting for you. Nikos is worried sick. We heard of a hit-and run in a car registered to you. Was that you?"

"Who are you?"

The woman wore a three-tiered skirt, four-tiered silver earrings, and a silken cranberry coat that complimented her round ruby lips and smooth olive complexion with perfection. As she pulled back, her earrings tinkled like tiny tambourines. "I'm Tanu, the cousin of Nikos. Come with me, Camille. Please, we want to help you."

"Camille is my sister. What happened? What's wrong? Where is she?" Less than a day ago her artistic sister drew chalk portraits right where they now stood. Hope, the base of a reunion twenty-seven years overdue, was the batten of her bobbing boat.

"There's been an accident."

"Whaaa...?"

The world folded into an origami of nothingness; the woman collapsed onto the ground.

"Cammy!"

A man bounded in the front door, his jacket lapels flapping, knelt down, and grabbed the woman's hand; she, horizontal on a soft sangria settee, trembled; her lips were white and cracked, feet and head propped on faded green velveteen pillows. He was hysterical, "I just got your call. What happened?"

"She fainted on her chalk corner, she..."

"Cam, are you in trouble? Tell me. I will help you. Was it you? Did you do it?" He looked over his shoulder with a despairing look in his eyes, "She passed out again. Tanu, bring some tepid water, a wet washcloth, and peach Kefir. She likes that."

Tanu slid off her slinky coat and set about these tasks. She laid the damp cloth across the lady's forehead, smoothing her hair from a perspired brow. "She's delusional, Nikos. She says she's not Camille. Amnesia perhaps."

"Shh, shh, shhh," she's waking. "Shh. Here," he wet his own lips mirroring the dryness, "Take a sip." He supported her head as she weakly lifted it to obey the kind command.

"Who are you? Where am I?" Notwithstanding the expressions of concern, she felt like a nuisance. Not wanting to be an intrepid imposer, she abstemiously denied Kefir and the thick, heavily seeded crackers offered her, though her mouth watered for both.

"Eat it, you're weak and confused; you fainted," this vivid voice came from Tanu, a practiced mother of three. Reconsidering, the woman took the container and greedily guzzled the fermented liquid leaving a filmy moustache, which she wiped away with the back of her sleeve. "Thank you."

Nikos stroked her left forearm with his thumb to comfort her. As he did, he jumped back as if electrocuted. "You're not Camille. Who are you?" he commanded.

"I'm Kristína Alicia. Camille and I are twins. I came from Iceland to meet her... to surprise her. What has happened, can you tell me? Who are you?"

"No. She doesn't have a twin."

"She doesn't know about me; they separated us at birth. It's a long story."

"Ha ha ha ha ha," he threw his head back and brayed with laugher, "What kind of fool do you take me for?" Then with laser heat, "I don't believe you. That bitch lied to me, she told me she was an only child," he kicked a chair, overturning it.

"Nikos! Why would she lie about that?" Tanu grabbed him like she was trying to restrain a foaming, rabid dog.

Kristína jumped up and snatched up her jacket, scarf, and hat, and backed away toward the door. "Please tell me what has happened to my sister. Is she okay?"

"If you're not her, she has disappeared. When I checked at her flat, she was not there." Tanu pressed her lips lightly in Kristína's ear and whispered, "Meet me in the square tomorrow at two; perhaps I'll have more news then."

Nikos was still pacing, Kristína couldn't discern whether he was angry or concerned but wasn't going to stick around to find out. She escaped out the door, tumbling onto a quaint tree lined side street. Armed with an old-fashioned street map and some broken French to ask for directions, she made it back to her hotel in an hour, which seemed like ten.

Quivering from the ordeal, she turned on the bathroom tap, which exploded with a squeak. She splashed water on her still pale face and noticed two things:

1) She looked identical to her missing twin.
2) She still sported a white upper lip Kefir moustache.

Her own silly image ignited a light, tinkling laugh. Though it was only six pm, she was depleted like a grapefruit squeezed of the last drop. Snuggling into the quilted bed, she fell asleep. She dreamt of her sister, Camille Lisette. They were children playing on a slide.

"Wheeeeeeeeee!" cried Cammy.

"Wheeeeeeeeee!" She replied.

But how often do dreams come true?

The next day, the light shone dull and dreary. Tanu showed up at two o'clock, as promised. Unsure of her connection to Camille, Kristína panicked and turned to flee. A firm hand grasped her shoulder. "I have bad news about your sister."

Kristína fixated on the Eiffel Tower, so familiar from her snow globe, for strength. Flakes fell in a stream, melting as they hit her lapel. Each October since their twelfth birthday she closed her eyes, shook the globe, and made a wish. This was not how their story was to go.

A lone bird streaked overhead, squawking as it passed. A sad boy in the distance caught her eye. He looked to be about five-years-old. A mass of brown curls, olive skin, dimples, brown hoodie, chocolate scarf, tan pants, he stood still and stared back.

"You saw Luis Fernando? Maybe he thought you were me?"

"I just saw a lonely boy." Kristína wasn't catching on.

"The child, the boy I hit."

"It was just a boy with his family."

"You saw a family?"

"Come to think of it, no. He stood alone."

"Pierre."

"Why do you call him Pierre if his name is Luis Fernando?"

"Before I knew his name, I named him. He felt like a Pierre. I still think of him this way."

"Pierre, I can see that. It suits the boy I saw."

"Yes, it does. Do you hate me for what I did? What did Tanu tell you?"

We both slurped soup for a few minutes, pondering.

"She told me you showed up at Nikos'. She said she was on her way over to see you. There'd been an accident. I told her I wanted to come. She said, 'No, this is not the time, she's in shock.' She promised to stay in touch."

I churned over my meeting with Tanu. Reality shifted with this new information. How could my whole life pass by unaware of other's secrets and lies? And now I lived that way: shifting the truth, omitting facts, dancing in shadows.

I revisited those horrible moments in my psyche, "When I saw Nikos, he seemed confused. He focused on my cat, didn't want to look at me. He told me I looked good, asked me what I needed, called me a bad girl, said he'd help me 'for a price.' He seemed callous and angry with me in a way I'd never experienced from him, even when he was philandering."

"He had just seen me the day before. He thought you'd been lying to him," Kristína seemed to make excuses for him. I wanted her to be on MY side.

"I gather that now. I never lied to him, ever, except I..." I faltered. The babies kicked.

"What?"

"They're kicking. Do you want to feel?"

"Yes." Kristina shifted closer, leaned in, and cradled my belly like she was protecting a kitten from the rain. "I don't feel anything."

"They stopped."

"What? What haven't you told him?"

"That I'm pregnant; that he's their father."

"Does Tanu know?" Her eyes wide like the rings of Saturn.

"That I'm pregnant, yes, but not by him."

"When are you going to tell him?"

I ignored her question. I wasn't through with my interrogation of her. "Did you stay in touch with Tanu?"

"Yes, a bit."

"Why haven't either of you told me?" The babies kicked again, harder this time. They seemed mad.

"I waited for decades to meet you, but everyone told me it wasn't time. When you were doing well, I wasn't. When I was well, you were in crisis. I didn't want to mess it up."

I felt nothing. Everything. Confused. She had been in control since we were twelve, not me. I could have had a sister all that time. I needed a sister all that time.

"What happened when you saw Nikos?"

I hesitated, unsure if I wanted to answer her, but the flashbacks came strong and fast, like contractions. The babies kicked up a storm. I had to talk. I recounted for Kristína what happened and even acted out the parts. I bounced back and forth from Nikos to me, his voice deep and resonant with my mine, melodious, frightened, nearly frozen. I scattered a few narratives in like birdseed on the beach.

—"What did you do, Cam? What are you running from, my angel?" He seemed dark, darker than a hollow hole in hell. I was in shock. "Can't help you if I don't know." I couldn't figure anything out. I figured I did a bad thing and was being punished. He clasped my hand, turned my chin towards him, and I told him. "I was driving down..." "Driving? In Paris?" "Yes," I said. "Whose car?" "Mine." "You have a car in Paris? You - a student, an artist?" "Yes." He laughed, it was menacing. "Oh, you spoiled American girl. This is what you spend your money on?" I'll never forget those words, spoiled American girl. How dare he? That's not who I am. "I didn't buy it. Someone left it for me." "Who? Someone died?" "Yes." "A lover? A rich lover?" He insisted I tell him. I sighed. At that moment I wanted to die. I felt trapped. I feel trapped now."

I stopped. Took a breath. The story reactivated the trauma. Kristína moved close and took my hand, silently encouraging me to go on. I needed her before, perhaps now it was too late. "How did he respond next?" I wasn't sure should continue, but I did.

—"How soon after we split up did you date this rich, older, man?" "He wasn't much older. WE didn't split up. I left YOU because I didn't want to be part of your harem or associated with your illicit... activities. Are you going to help me or not, Nikos?" I begged HIM, this man who had cheated on ME and broke my heart. "The whole thing, she doesn't make sense."

I imitated his accent, mannerisms — I had him down pat. I repeated nearly word for word what I told him. Kristína remained mute, which gave me space to continue. Those moments, that world, overtook me. It was as if Iceland never existed. No slide. No double helix staircases. No stained glass. I was still an only child, a daddy's girl. I was still the same person before the world tipped upside down.

—"It makes sense, it happened! You haven't even asked me what I have done. You're fixated on the car. The stupid car I wish I never had! I met Pascal a few weeks after I stopped seeing you. We fell in love. He was everything I wanted in a man, in a partner. Everything. We soon found out he was sick. He didn't come from old money, if that's what you're thinking. He was a self-made, successful young man, only thirty years old, he worked as an avocat, a lawyer, and he died in the prime of his life. We used to drive to the country together. He left his daughter and ex-wife everything except the car which he willed to me."

I stopped. "Then what happened?" Kristína was rapt, like she'd seen Hamlet's father's ghost.

"Then I told him about Pascal and how he worked for humanitarian causes. Then..." My mouth was dry. "Then, he said, 'If you had siblings, you would call on them, right?' Oh, my god, I didn't know why he said that. He was testing me for authenticity!"

Kristína stood and walked to the window. She stared out into the night, the precious window of lightless sky in which we ought to be sleeping. "Then?"

—"Oh, course," I told him, "But you're the closest I have to family."
She turned around with tears in her eyes.

—"I will help you regardless of what you have done," Nikos said to me. "Why?" "I love you, Camille, and I know what a good person you are," he lifted my chin, he always did that, like this — I lifted Kristína's chin. "Now, tell me everything, we make a plan, and I will help in whatever way I can."

I finished. I had told her enough.

"So he believed you?"

"Yes. I told him the truth. Nikos got me a new identity, gave me money, encouraged me to leave town. He told me not to doubt him. He paid Tanu to help me. He promised to take care of my cat. He said he loved me."

"Oh, he does, Camille. He does. I saw it in his eyes. He loves you."

"I have to pee," I said. I always had to pee. These twins used my bladder like a trampoline. I hoped they would be close and confide in each other. I would never separate them. I hated everyone. It was already beginning to get light. I glimpsed Kristína's face in the mirror. I hung a towel over the glass; I didn't want to see it. In my rawness I forgot to be ashamed of what I'd done. Forgot to worry about whether SHE would accept ME.

I craved a midnight so bold that it was blue. I looked at my phone, there was a message from Matt that said, "I love you."

"Kristína?" I poked my head out the front door. She wasn't there. "Kristína!" She wasn't on the couch. "KrisTÍNa!" No sign of her in the loft. I'd been in the bathroom just five minutes, long enough to do what I had to, breathe four deep breaths in - four out, and check my emails. Kristína had disappeared. I had messages from everybody and their brother - literally, Brigitte's brother wrote me, concerned about his sister.

Matt wanted to video chat — stat.

I also had emails from:

Brigitte — "I'm miserable and aching to join you, my sweet Belle. Ring me soon."

Nina LaRue — "We need a video chat, girl! Jeremy is now thick into a chick named Brick, as in a brick house. She's a bitch, but what a relief to have him out of MY hair."

Kasey — "Thank you so much, Lucy, for the lovely get-well card! I don't recommend appendectomy. I'm as worn as if I'd climbed a mammoth mountain, but on the mend. Thank goodness for Matt and Matsako!"

Matsako — "Luc, I got a job. I take to-go orders for a Thai restaurant. Pay is terrible, food good though. I go back to Japan for a while."

Noni — "I'm totally crushed on Adam. This is a hiccup I didn't expect. He's a good dude, yeah? Feeling I need to 'find myself' outside of Idaho. Where the bleep are you? Can I join up with you? Holler!"

Adam — "Is it too early after her breakup for me to make a move on Noni? She's an amazing woman. I'm asking you because Matt hasn't been in touch in days. Is he mad at me? Please contact me. I may not wait much longer."

Theo — "Such an insightful birthday card you drew for Jon, Luciana. We all miss you and can't wait to hear where you are. Bub now has a boyfriend called Bryon. The boys approve of him because he has red racer cars."

Jon — "Thank you for the delightful card; the cartoon strip of us on the London Eye is spot on. Please drop Theo a word, he's worried about you, as am I."

Maria Van der Heffelin — "Hello dear. Would love to have you back to Paris pour un autre tour of portraits at the hôtel. Word has spread. You have many patrons waiting. Répondre with dates, tout de suite. Sincerely, Maria."

Tanu — I hadn't the heart to open that one yet. I needed to learn more about what happened from Kristína.

...and bumpity-bump-bump...

Nikos — "I miss you, Cammie. I'm confused about Parlene, about life, about becoming a father. I wish to have the benefit of your wise words of advice. I write now to tell to you we have not seen Natalie Mouskers in two days. I put fliers up, and we hope for the best. There has been no word of any cat casualties in le levoisinage. S'agapó, Nikos."

Cat casualties! Oh, no!

"Where are you?" I cried.

"I'm in here!" her voice floated in from the kitchen. There she stood with her hands, palms flat, in the freezer. Was it was an Icelandic thing? It seemed counterintuitive to me. Wouldn't hot toddies make more sense in the cold snap?

"Hi. I couldn't find you anywhere."

"I'm right here," she said plain as rain, but her thoughts seemed a million miles away.

Her refrigerator door was littered with purple plastic Icelandic letters on one side and the English alphabet on the other. In my clumsy haste, I accidentally knocked over a Y. Good question, I thought. Straight to the point."

"Why," I asked, "do you have your hands in the icebox?"

"To cool down. When I get upset, I get hot and my ears turn red. This frystir constricts my blood vessels and calms me." Her ears softened in hue before my eyes from bright maroon back to peach. Impressive! "Would you like to try?"

"Já. I could use a cooling off after hearing of a possible kitty catastrophe."

"Kitty catastrophe?"

"Miss Mouskers is missing." I stood shivering to the count of one-one-hundred: bits of skin stuck on icy patches, but the pulsing veins on my temples shrank back into a smooth brow. "We need to talk, but I have to sleep."

"Oh, I'm sorry about your cat. I hope she turns up! I can barely keep my eyes open, and my legs are buckling, but Jón always said to not go to bed angry."

Dad would say, "There are no rules, do what suits you as long as it's not dangerous to yourself or others."

"I have to sleep," we both said at once with that same-voice-same-time-twin-thing. Hard to stay mad at her, though I reserved the right.

"You want to sleep in my room with me? It's the best room in the house. Spacious. Well insulated."

"Yeah, I don't think I can sleep alone tonight."

We worked as a team, silently cleaning up from dinner until we got in her suite, and practically passed out in each other arms; our guards were up, but ready to tumble down. Her bed was as luxurious as the one at the Hôtel Plaza Athénée; the pillowed mattress welcomed me like a soft dune when falling backwards to make a snow angel.

Of all the physical, emotional, spiritual, symbolic things to dream about, I dreamt of the porous breakfast porridge with berries, roasted nuts, and peach Kefir.

We jogged through old town and over to the Harbor front where we saw whales' tails lift and disappear in the distant mist. Regardless of any uncertainty or the indomitable five-year-old, curly-headed boy that kept apace not far behind, it was a great start to the day. Kristína and I moved as one. Our shoulders lifted up and down alternating with the percussive musical beat of our feet on the pavement, *Chuh-chuh-chuh.*

Chuh-chuh-chuh, carried the same meaning in any language, on any continent I'd been to, or ever would visit. *Chuh-chuh-chuh,* we ran to that a while, both of us circumspect. Neither of us rushed to revisit the conversation from the night before.

"We have fifteen minutes until it rains," Kristína broke the reverie, nodding up to the cumulus clouds overhead; the uppermost parts reflected off a moonstone in moonlight; the lower halves heather grey like a three-day-old cadaver.

"Okay, let's head back."

"Already? I like to run in the rain, don't you?" I liked the way her freckles moved when she crinkled her nose. My nose, splayed with tiny flecks of brown, crinkled back.

"Yes, I do and so do the babies."

For me, movement tempers emotion. Discussions take on a constructive tone as air pumps through the lungs, endorphins ping the brain, and sweat tickles top lips. My questions flowed like cherry wine. "What happened after you saw Tanu that day? Why didn't you stay to see me or get in touch after that? How much contact do you have with her? Did she tell you where or how I was?" *Chuh-chuh-chuh-chuh.*

"I extended my trip for two days, then returned to my students. I was still mourning for Jón, and the combined stress destroyed my relationship with Kristín. Tanu is kind, yet evasive. She is protecting you."

"Are you still in touch with her?" Memories from Lille raced through my mind. I wonder what Theo knew?

"We are in touch, but she doesn't know you're here. I devoured any news I could find of you. I feel connected from a lifetime of longing. I viscerally feel your pain. I don't normally pray, but I prayed."

"What news did you hear?" I dreaded the answer. I knew the answer.

"The lipstick scrawl." Kristína pressed her lips closed, awaiting my reaction.

I stopped, breathless, and stood still in the downpour which flattened my hat onto my head; rivulets of unwrought wetness dripped like water pouring off a Cocker Spaniel after a bath.

"When were you going to tell me you knew this?"

"Now - as soon as I reasonably could, not on the phone or in front of Cadena at the airport."

"Cadence."

"Já, Cadence. I'm here for you no matter what. We're family."

"Even after you read about the lipstick?"

"Já. My heart broke for you, the boy, and his family when I read about the scrawl on the bathroom mirror. It was a tragic accident. I love you."

I believed her. My heart opened; a stampede of emotion rushed out like wild horses set free after months in captivity. I wanted to do cartwheels to release tension. She pulled me under a mulberry red roof to get out of the rain.

"And what about you, Camille, did you decide in advance to open up to me?"

"I had, yes, though to be fair, I didn't resolve that until I met you. My plan was - is - to disclose everything to you." I looked out over the water, no sign of whales now. "I'm Lucy now, not Camille."

It was her turn to gaze into the horizon, searching for the right response. "You never were Camille. I am."

"What?" I feared she was experiencing a psychological over-identification with me.

"Let's go. I'll show you back at the house."

Our words were silent, but my inner dialogue roared; our squishy shoes and the patter of the slowing drops were the only sounds. *Chuh-chuh-chuh-chuh-chuh-chuh-chuh.*

THE SWITCH

We sat stiffly side by side like soldiers lined to midnight march. Kristína set Jónina's blue journal on both our laps; it was large and spanned the width of one of the great gullies at Zabrinski point. Noni and I visited Zabrinski's mountains and mud hills the spring of sophomore year. While there, Noni had a fling with a married man who imagined himself king of the canyons. While they were cavorting, I stood at the edge of a cliff in front of an easel relishing a westerly zephyr, happy to capture the depths of the desert, a la Georgia O'Keeffe, my art heroine who painted bold flowers like come-hither King Kongs.

Kristína showed me photos, documents, letters, and inch-long clips of our red-gold baby hair taped to a sticky page; all alluring and surreal. When she arrived at a particular passage of a journal entry on creamy paper, she straightened her back as if a spider ran up her spine.

"Read this out loud," she asked of me.

I took a sip of water and sounded out the words, drinking in the meaning. "My baby girls, both perfect, precious, with pale pink cheeks and wet, rosy lips that curl up at the corners in gassy giggles like Pulcinella poppy blossoms, have rocked opened my heart in ways unforeseen. Somehow - but how - I am to choose which one to keep and which to let go to Charles? He will be an excellent father, I'm sure of that and am grateful he and his sweet bride, a boon to humankind, will raise my baby next to her bosom as though her own, setting aside her own dreams to welcome in little Kristína."

I looked at Kristína, confused. "I called dad James Julian."

"We called him Charles. Go on," she nodded.

"When I conceived via surrogacy..." I looked up again. Her eyebrows rose nearly imperceptibly. She gave another tiny nod to continue. "When I conceived via surrogacy, I had not considered the full platter of outcomes. Having twins weighed not in my imagination or realm of reasonable concerns, though now I see how naïve I was. I love them both equally. My heart bursts in kaleidoscope array as when I saw a double rainbow over the Norðurljós last November."

I stretched my arms in front of me like a baby giraffe extending her wobbly legs for the first time. "Would you continue?" I slid the book a few inches over to her lap and closed my eyes. Her voice sounds like mine save for the Icelandic accent.

"Kristína Alicia notices everything. She loves flowers. Her eyes trace each outline: petals, stems, and leaves. I think she will be an artist. Camille Lisette moves her bitty body to the music like a miniature hula dancer. I think she will be our Isadora. Both of my babies have excellent taste in tunes from Ella to Big Bill and Bonnie; these girls get it. They have soul."

She pushed the book back to me — my turn again.

"So, who do I choose? It's been three months now and I am clear that financially and logistically I can't give them both what they need. I blame myself for not being enough. I'm not functioning well in this situation and my wish is for what is best for my loves. When Charles offered to raise one of them, I concurred this is a gift to all. After many late night calls, we agreed to stay in touch, share photos and stories, and introduce the girls when they are twelve, no earlier, no later. Since I can't choose, I handed the burden to fate; I flipped a coin tonight. Heads for my blessed one who has a sienna freckle inside her left wrist..."

I gasped. "That's me!" I held out my arms and pointed to my beauty mark. Kristína continued reading, pressed now against my right leg, hip, and shoulder.

"...tails for my Picayune princess with the pliant grin. Heads is the one I shall keep, my Camille. Tails goes to Charles who arrives tomorrow at half-past three."

"I don't understand." Charles took me. I have the freckle. I'm Camille.

"They mixed us up. I'm Camille," Kristína said. "Nikos noticed the difference right away."

"Oh." I gaped. *The fates, the fates, they have a mind of their own.* "So, I'm not Camille."

"Well, what's in a name?" Kristína said, "You are who you are, Lucy."

"I'm Kristína?"

"Yes, Lucy, you're Kristína."

"Oh, my god. I'm so confused."

"So was our mother; the adoption happened so fast. He had just flipped a coin to see which of his babies to send to America."

I repeated everything to make it sink in. "He, I mean, Jón, our mother?"

"Yes."

"Flipped a coin..."

"Yes."

"Our mother who was a man and has a wife?"

Kristína was furious. Her words shot out with hot velocity, "No, I've told you this already. Jón wasn't a man! Jón was just Jón. Jón didn't want to be categorized. Jón believed each person is unique, not an adjective to be heaped haphazardly in a homogenous hog pile."

Wow! I felt shamed, politically incorrect, I had no judgment about how he - Jón - lived, it's just that a few weeks ago I didn't even know I had a mother in Iceland or a twin, and an identical one, except for the beauty mark on my wrist. I wanted to call Matt, my luscious, safe landing, and tell him everything, but first I needed to hash this out and squeeze credence from this story. The circumstances that followed resulted in me growing up daddy's girl with my sperm donor father, being called by my twin's name, which belongs to her, as possession is nine-tenths of the law and nearly one hundred percent of emotion.

"The coin toss said Camille, so how did I - apparently NOT Camille - end up in Idaho?"

"Our father took you. It wasn't an accident. Here, read this." Her tone was excited. She dreamt of telling me this for fifteen years —probably had the whole performance choreographed in her mind: the hot springs, the blue journal, crackling logs in the fireplace, and even the seafood soup! I took a spoonful. It was cold.

I was like that sour party pooper amid a group of playful people at ten to midnight, as they got ready to uncork champagne and holler, "Happy New Year!" I was done reading about the mishaps and meanderings that tossed my life to the fates.

I shivered. Badly. Kristína, (I call her that though she is Camille), led me through journal entry after entry, letters, photos, and cards, unraveling our intertwined, twisted tale.

They named me Kristína after Hristina, Jónina's Hungarian grandmother, whom Jón said I embodied in spirit. Jón named Camille, (Kristína), after Camille Pissarro, one of Jón's favorite artistes whom Jón admired for painting statements of pictorial truth. "I see the sea in Camille's irises; to me, her soul reflects all that is true and good."

What a lovely thing to say about one's child. I wondered what she saw in me. "What was Hristina like? In what way did Jón feel I had a kinship with her?"

"She was a hero, Camille. She was a young woman living in the Jewish quarter in Pest, Hungary..."

"Wait, we're Jewish? Hungarian?"

"One quarter."

"Isn't Hristina an odd name for a Jew?"

"Her name was Hypatia, it means Supreme Woman — she changed it when she fled Hungary." For an instant I considered taking the name Hypatia, such a beautiful name, but no... perhaps my plate of names was already full to overflowing.

"They ran her country on fundamentalist policies. Polemics about the Jewish question flared up. A Jewish Law broadened the definition of Jewishness, cut quotas on Jews permitted in the professions and business and met required quotas by firing Jews. Life got harder for Hungarian Jews. Hristina led scores of people out of Pest before the war. She saved many lives."

Kristína detailed for me the history of Hungary, of which I knew very little. Hristina was a heroine. Even if I didn't carry the name as planned, I was proud of her. My shivering increased. Kristína threw another log on the fire, carefully placed a canary trimmed quilt over my shoulders, and reheated our soup. "You need to eat, Camille," she said, her eyes reflected oceans, her tone echoed our long-gone grandmother. But wait...

"Is Hristina still alive?"

"Yes. She can't wait to meet you."

I was elated and abandoned all at once. "Why couldn't SHE help raise me?"

"She remarried and moved to Spain. She had polio as a child; she wanted to, believe me, but was not able."

I gulped in air along with my soup and let out a prolonged foghorn belch. This led us into gales of giggles, lightening the ambiance considerably. Before then, I thought I might have a heart attack.

"Charles picked up one girl and wouldn't put her down; the two bonded instantly like a pair of waltzing swans. They had their dance to do together. He called her Camille, and I thought she was until, all alone once again rocking my only infant to sleep, I noticed the error. As I rubbed my baby's wrist to comfort her, I realized I had Camille. Together my Camille, now Kristína, cried many nights for our lost little artistic Kristína. We began the countdown to year twelve. Twelve. Twelve. Twelve. A random target age medical professionals told Charles and I was the best time to reunite our family. I have never trusted professionals of any kind since. I shall teach my daughters they must trust in themselves.

I made marks in groups of five. Four stick straight lines, then one crosshatched diagonally. Five. Five. Five. Five. Five." Jón counted off the days until our reunion! I'd seen similar carvings on the walls in The Tower of London counting days until a prisoner's head was to roll. Being human is not for the weak of heart. I clasped The Lady on the Lake around my neck as though it was a life raft at the sinking of the Titanic. *I have to call Matt now. I can NOT wait any longer.*

His face came on the screen before we could say Hristina.

"You look thin, Lucy, are you eating enough?"

Suddenly it felt funny when he called me Lucy.

"I'm not Lucy, I'm Kristína."

"What?"

Kristína popped her face in to the screen with me, "No, I'm Kristína! Hallo, Matt. Nice to meet you."

"Ah — hooooo." Matt exhaled like he had just seen double. "THIS is Kristína, I reckon! Lovely to see y'all together." He got that word lovely from me just at the time I trucked off to Reykjavik. I stepped back from the screen and let them have their moment together.

Seeing his familiar face, (warm brown eyes just a few shades darker than his tan complimented his magical mop of hair he swooped out of his way), made me feel melancholy for America. I could tell from Matt's gaze the separation was as hard for him as for me. I had a hankering to reach into the computer and touch his face, to kiss those soft lips on his bright-toothed grin, which always hints at a joke, sometimes crude, always funny, never at the expense of anyone's feelings. His is a face I trust.

Kristína saw his laudable qualities too. I wondered what she'd think about him dismembering the cabbie though, wondered if she would ever find out about that episode. Would she believe in his innocence as I do? One thing was fer sure though: my Matty was so smooth and respectful to females; his feminism shines through.

Matt was self-conscious about his syrupy drawl, but I love it. "People sometimes stereotype and think Alabama is a hotbed of misogyny, homophobia, and bigotry — some are and I'll tell ya I've met assholes everywhere, but the many of us Southerners," Matt explained on our first date," are intelligent, open-minded, and accepting folks who live on what was Confederate soil and speak with a twang."

Kristína, impressed, backed out the door, fluttery, to give Matt and me our private time, which we lapped up for two hours.

"How's Kacey doin'?"

"Good. Some bumps in the recovery road, but rebounding like a Labrador chasing a Frisbee. Tell me about you."

"You first, once I get talking, it'll be hard to stop me."

"I told you about me by text. You're the one who just met your twin. Damn, you two look alike." He took out his stopwatch, "You got till 2:00 cuz I got a job. Use your time wisely, Ms. Petrokov." 2:00 there is 10:00 in Iceland; perfect timing, as Kristína and I pinky swore to keep better sleep hours.

I fit the stories together like puzzle pieces clicking in one by one, beginning with Cadence, meeting Kristína in the airport, and the she-racer driving to the hot springs. I painted Iceland in words for him: arched, open skies, effervescence of the land, raging, racing waters hissing like a roomful of tigers, fierce and fantastic.

Up and down through the peaks and valleys of my emotions Matt journeyed with me as I told him about Jónína; Kristína's trip to Paris, the beauty mark on my wrist, the mix-up of us nearly identical babies, and my father choosing me. I told him about Hristina nee hero Hypatia, our Jewish grandmother from Pest, and finished by chronicling my mum and dad's journey and how painful it was for them to wait until I was twelve to tell me everything. Yet life threw them curveballs, and they died with unclear consciences.

"Do you forgive them?"

"There's nothing to forgive. They loved me, they did their best, I love them, but it still smarts anyway. So be it." I shrugged.

"I miss you. I need to see you soon."

"I miss you too," I held tight to the ring around my neck as though I was holding him. My eyes closed and a fat tear dripped into my nose, and landed salty on my lip. When I opened my eyes, his were closed, his face wet too.

"What are your plans, Luc? What now?"

"One more stop, Matt, I can't shake it."

"Colombia?"

I nodded.

"You want me to come?"

"You don't have to. You've missed too much work."

"I know I don't have to. I'm doing fine; I'm booked with commissions that will carry me through March next year. Do you WANT me to come?"

"Yes, I'd love to see you, but you don't ha...."

"Get me the details. I'll make the arrangements."

"Brigitte wants to go as well!" I spit out. "She... it's not her fault, but she feels guilty. She wants... needs to see Luis' family too."

"Well, in that case, Matsako ought to come. She's moving back home. She misses you something awful."

"Oh, yeah, she mentioned she's leaving. I miss her too. I worry about her. Sure, if she wants. The more the merrier, though this is the hardest time in my life, not a holiday."

"A good reason to have friends surrounding you. I need to get you settled soon. We're gonna be having…" his voice broke, he tried again, "We're gonna have a family soon."

It hit home when he said it. I didn't think about present reality nearly enough. I was too busy chasing ghosts.

"Have you told Nikos yet?"

"No! I haven't even had time to consider it."

"You're over four months now, Luc?"

"Yes, I am. Oh, I forgot to tell you, the babies kicked!"

Matt looked at his stopwatch, "I'd say it's time to tell Nikos. He's the father." His simple acknowledgement of this unsettled me.

"Yes, he is."

"He sounds like a decent fellow, screwed up in his own way, but he cares for you. We're all going to get along."

"Okay." I liked this strong side of him. I needed this now.

"A week or two tops in Colombia, Lucy. You can't keep traipsing around. This is the last trip. It's not good for the babies. Or you," he added as an afterthought. "Or me."

"Okay."

"How's Pierre?"

"I haven't seen him in the past two days, I've been so busy."

"Well, he's been here with me."

I wondered if Matt was mocking me, or trying in his way to console me, but then I saw him glance to the side with the same *sigh* I heaved when Pierre was nearby.

"Bonne journée, Matt, bonne journée, Luis Fernando. Je vous aime tous les deux."

"Je t'aime, Lucy, Camille, Kristína, Hypatia. Safe dreams." He winked and his picture blinked off.

"It's not a damn vacation, this is spiraling out of control," I thought as I arranged Kristína's mismatched forks on the table for the dinner party she threw for me - for us - on my last night in town, "All these people wanting to flock to South America is ludicrous."

I sprinkled the salad with goat cheese contributed by Silphy, a best pal of Kristína's who raises her own goats. I'd never eaten cheese churned from milk of animals I knew the names of: Kazoo, Tattoo, and Gertrude. The timer dinged for the cauliflower crust pizza I'd prepped that morning. I first made this recipe with Brigitte the week we met, years ago, on a sunny, chilly, perfect day in Paris. Now she planned to meet me in Colombia to track down Pierre's parents — why, I was no longer sure. The trip truly made no sense. I didn't have a plan, it wouldn't bring back Luis Fernando, comfort the family, solve my problems, or help my babies who needed me to nest, even if that nest included a stopover in jail.

Gah! What would my parents have said about this Paris predicament? I could not even get there in my mind.

"Umm, that looks luscious," Silphy, luminous, lanky, and barefooted, with three rings on each foot, leaned over and smelled the pizza. "The vegetables are shaped like lamilin."

"What's lamilin?" I hated feeling stupid.

"A protein that holds the body together." Along with raising goats, Silphy was a research scientist.

"Oh." Lucy (or whoever I was), the misanthrope! The fractured fairy tale of Matt and I still pulsated through each cell in my body. Click and Clack, the curious trapeze artists in my belly, did flips and I knew my time to wander was ending. I would return to Paris and turn myself in. When one makes a mistake, one must own up, make amends, and work each day to be a better person. I ran from France fueled by fear and adrenaline. I forgave my initial reaction, but it was time to move forward. My morbid mood trumped the chitchat from my sister's friends, no matter how much I yearned to impress them.

Silphy pressed on anyway, "How do you like Iceland?"

"It's stunning and I love the people."

The bells on her toes tinkled as she put one foot against the counter, leaned back and took me in. "You look so similar, it's amazing, no? Except you have a mark on your wrist," she pointed to her own left arm to show the positioning of it. I mean, come on, that's an observant detail to notice on someone during the first conversation together.

"Yes, how did you know?"

"Kristína talked about this since we were twelve," she took a swig of Viking Classic, a golden amber Vienna style beer that smelled of roasted malt. My mouth salivated for some. Her tone conveyed the subtext, "You're important to my friend, take care of her heart." She knew nothing of my life.

"That's a long time to wait."

"Já," she swigged again, and wiped her mouth with her sleeve. She was judging me. "So, what have you seen here?"

"The cliffs and volcanoes, the Blue Lagoon, the harbor front, um, some galleries, history museum..."

"You saw the lights?"

"Some, from the Lagoon."

"I'll take you to a special spot tonight; we might get lucky. It's a sight you'll never forget."

"Great," I didn't care about lights. I just wanted to be alone and sing to my babies.

"Have you gotten up to the phallic museum?" Ah, a pun, perhaps she was easing up on her interrogation?

"Yeah, we went yesterday?"

"And?"

"It made me miss my boyfriend."

That broke the ice. Silphy set down her drink and with heavy beer breath kissed me on each cheek. "Ha ha. You're okay, Camille. Can I help you?"

"Sure," I handed her a pan of pizza with an oven mitt decorated with red elephants, "You want to take this out to the table?"

"Jú," she and her mariachi feet marched away, with a smug smirk as though she had soaked in something of substance from this conversation. What she wasn't aware of is that just before the guests arrived I had packed my bag for the flight just eighteen hours away. I finally threw out the Speculoos crumbs I'd saved from Bertrand's funeral. I also tossed the green crop top from Fabien's photo shoot because of the memories it carried for me. I gathered together my ticket, snacks, water bottle and Lucy Petrokov passport, charged my cellphone, re-read through my life review in the blue journal, and planned to meet up with Brigitte.

Matt was working out his plans and I had about ten other emails to field in the next day or so. Everyone wanted to go to Santiago de Cali as though we would go body surfing in Montego Bay or search for the Holy Grail. As far as I knew, Cali was sinfully hot, and not exactly the safest place. I wanted the trip to be quick.

I'd hoped to video chat with Theo while I had access to Kristína's computer, but his schedule was packed: he was taking a watercolor class Wednesdays and Sundays, the kids had colds and martial art competitions - even bitty Bub - and Jon was at a work convention in Milano. I was avoiding Tanu's messages until my fury flattened out. Kristína and I covered a lot of emotional ground in our last week together, more than I had hoped for.

I painted on some strawberry lip-gloss, picked up the salad, and straightened myself up to put on a brave face for Kristína's friends. I entered a room of ten strangers who believed in fairies with a sparkly, forced smile.

"SURPRISE!" They sang in a chorus of clapping. They had hung a Happy Birthday banner from the slide to the stained glass windows.

"What's this? It's not our birthday."

"I've wanted to have birthday parties with you since I was a girl," Kristína choked out. "My friends set this up. Aren't they wonderful?"

I looked across the room at Silphy; she raised her beer in salute to me.

"Yes, they are. They really are."

We partied for hours until there wasn't a morsel of food or drink left or any topic left untouched. Then, though Aurora activity was iffy in the summer, we drove an hour out and waited under polka dotted umbrellas in a gushing downfall until those few elusive hours of darkness when the gorgeous mystic green-gold-carmethene-blue lights bequeathed us with a visit. I squeezed Kristína's hand through it as though I was giving birth.

"I'm so glad you're in my life," I whispered in awe, with my head tilted back

"I'm glad you're in mine too. Happy birthday, Lucy."

"You must be very lucky, Camille. We haven't seen a showing like this in months. The universe is conspiring in your favor." For a scientist, she was stupid.

One good thing about Reykjavik is there are plenty of rainbows, each one brighter than all the sunflowers, bluebells, and poppies I had ever seen. I slept soundly that night and dreamt I was riding the rainbow like a rocket ship. When I awoke, I crashed back to earth. I only hoped that somehow Pierre was somewhere riding a rainbow too.

THE SIENNA SUN

We arrived in Seville an hour before sunrise; the silent, still sky glimmered tenderly as it does in that wee hour of the morning. Kristína had taught a few classes in the days before our journey, enough, she said, to stay in a good steed with the school. I swallowed my pride and wore pregnancy knickers to take part in belly and ballet for beginners and caught up on some needed sleep while she was away teaching ballroom.

Silphy would cover for Kristína until she returned, which was kind of her to do so we twins could go to our amma's house together. Between tending to her goats, growing a sizable vegetable herb garden, leading cellar studies, and now subbing for this demanding course curriculum, Silphy's magnificent talents, breadth of knowledge, and kinetic energy boggled me, and I enjoyed imagining her toe bells ringing through plies and pas de bourrées.

I'd visited Seville before with Jacqueline, Kendra, Dominique, and Brigitte, and did the usual touristy things: admired the breathtaking magnificence of the Real Alcázar palace, gazed upon the gorgeous gothic architecture of the Catedral de Santa María de la Sede, bicycled to get free tapas along Calle Elvira, and went Flamenco dancing with eight muy guapo Spanish men we had met up with — yep, by all counts that equaled two-a-piece. My lovely lot included Aarón, a twenty-two-year-old drafting student with cobalt blue eyes, kinky black hair, and an even kinkier sense of humor who gave me a tension-liquefying neck massage that left my head perched one inch higher. I pulled away from him to return to our B & B as I was in a relationship with Nikos, which had lingered on too long.

Perhaps my favorite spot in Seville was the Plaza de España, a majestic complex designed by Aníbal González, the principal building built in 1928 exhibited Spain's technology and industry. The site I remembered most vividly was the perfectly arched, yellow, blue, and orange tiled Roman bridge. The influence from this spectacular artwork lent a flair to my chalk portraitures that helped catapult me to the top; my reputation became cream of the crop, thanks to the creative splendors of Spain.

Our group of young women even traversed Triana's tangle of cobblestone streets to see the Moorish Revival Chapel of El Carmen next to the bridge and visited the Museum of the Spanish Inquisition. I was clueless that this neighborhood was home to my grandmother, Hristina, or Hypatia, as I like to think of her. Hypatia's apartment, salmon and cornflower on the outside, was cozily cluttered inside and smelled of roasted garlic, rose oil, and cat food. No less than five feisty felines roamed around our feet. I'm left to assume it was from Hypatia I inherited my affection for collecting kitties.

Crippled as a child by polio, Hristina used a hand-carved blackthorn walking stick to assist her, yet whatever limitations she had did not diminish her maternal welcome of both granddaughters. She served fried potatoes with spicy red sauce, espinacas with garbanzos, and carrot cake. I declined the sangria. It was clear by my protruding pouch why.

Hristina was all I could have hoped for. She looked from me to Kristína and back again, smoothing our cheeks with her trembly hands. "Kristína. Camille. My girls. Jónína would be so proud. 'May they always have innsæi,' she would say." Then she cried, perhaps as much for losing her child as for the gift of me.

We conversed for four steadfast hours: she regaled us with tales of her youth and a story of her trip to the store earlier that day as though each event from her heroism to her impetuous purchase of plums held the same significance. I hit highlights of my life, leaving out the latest chapters, which by then could fill a book. When Hristina left to take nap, Kristína set to work cleaning her cupboards.

Amid it all, Nikos was as much on my mind as he was during my first trip to Seville; every move the twins made pressured me to tell him about them. When Hristina settled down to sleep, I decided this was THE time to discuss with Nikos our mutual malfeasance.

"Kristína, do you mind if I go for a walk?"

"No, not at all... She's special, isn't she?"

"Oh, yes, she's exquisite!"

"See you later. Don't get lost."

"I won't." Physically I knew where I was, but emotionally my compass was arumpass.

After quick kisses on each cheek, I was out the door, a woman on a mission. I walked down the street to a store I'd noticed on our way from the bus stop — there I bought a phone card to call Click and Clack's bio dad in France. The phone rang eight times; I was about to hang up when I heard his sleepy, "Allo, qui est à l'appareil?"

"C'est moi, Cammy."

"Ahh, Salut, mon amour."

There were butterflies in my stomach with Matt but with Nikos the sensation was of a bat tearing through my intestines, slamming against my ribcage, and leaving my legs wobbly like pink rubber pegs; a dash exciting and a dollop insufferable.

"I miss you."

"How are things, Nikos?"

"Koko, who is it?"

"It's ah... it's...um…"

A woman's voice hissed into the phone, "Allo, qui est à l'appareil?"

It was *her* - Parlene! I held my words steady, "A friend of Nikos."

"Ooh are you? Wat is your name?"

"Please put Nikos back online."

"Ooh is this bitch?" I heard her inveigh before a muffled conversation in which her voice jumped indiscriminately to jealous heights, and then followed zigzagging footsteps, and finally the sound of the Paris traffic I missed so much.

A long slow horn honk faded in the distance. Nikos sighed into the phone, "D'accord, we can talk now."

"I thought you were breaking up with Parlene?"

"No. She's... I'm... We're having a baby together. I will be there. I won't be like my father."

"Your father was there."

"In body, yes, but not altogether."

His papa, a man with incandescent blue eyes that reflected the sparkle of the South Aegean Sea, had seemed an intelligent, caring man to me, but somehow could not be present for his son. It's a story of generational shortcomings, human weaknesses, and bad luck. I admired Nikos' desire to make good for his own children.

"Nikos?"

"Oui, mon amour?"

"Is this a good time to tell you some things?"

"Oui, mon amour? What things?"

"Heavy things."

"Oui, mon amour? Tell me."

"Do you want me to talk about you or me first?"

"You must choose."

"All right. I'll tell you about me first."

"I'm listening."

"I will come back to Paris soon. I will turn myself in. I should never have run. I wasn't thinking clearly. I was in shock. I was scared."

"I understand."

"You're not surprised."

"No. I expected this of you." He said this with kindness, a nod to my character.

"I want to come clean about everything. It's the right thing to do."

"I was just trying to protect you. It's a felony in France to falsify identifications," his concern momentarily shifted to himself, which was reasonable given the serious circumstances of what he had done.

"I know, Nikos. When I was in Idaho, I got my birth certificate from my parents storage unit and legally changed my name in court. I burned the USF Design degree and all the rest. I am now legally Lucy Petrokov."

"You'll always be Cammy to me."

"Nikos?"

"Oui, mon amour?"

"I don't think we ever need to mention the documents again, do you?"

"No, mon amour."

"Before I tell you about you, is there anything else you want to tell me?"

"How do you mean?"

"Think for a minute."

"About what?"

"I'm a twin."

He was silent for a good three minutes — cars whizzed by.

"Nikos. Are you still there?"

"Oui, mon amour." But he wasn't, really.

"Nikos?"

"Yes, I met her. I met Kristína."

"You didn't tell me."

"No."

"Why not?"

"Tanu asked me not to. She said you were too vulnerable."

I was silent. The street I was on was silent too.

"Cammy?"

"Yes."

"I love you and wish the best for you."

"Yes..."

"I'm worried about you coming back to Paris. I understand why you have to, but I'm sad. I'm sorry you are in this predicament."

"Thank you... Shoot, my minutes are running low. I have to tell you about you now."

"Oh, I thought that was it. What is it about me?"

"Well, I'm a twin..."

"Yes."

"Twins run in my family..."

"Now I know this."

"I'm pregnant - with twins."

"Oh, mon amour. This is surprising news. Should I be happy for you? What does this have to do with me?"

"You're the father."

"No. I can't possibly be."

"What do you mean, you can't be — you are!"

"How can this be? The night we were together, you said it was safe."

"Safe?"

"For sex."

My mind raced back to that night. What could he be talking about? I never said it was safe for sex. "I said I was scared. You asked me if I felt safe! I said I felt safe there with you. Why did you have sex with me when I was grieving and in shock? You took advantage!"

"Advantage? I WAS COMFORTING YOU! This is how I comfort you! I risked my freedom to help you with fake documents that we are never supposed to mention again."

"Oh, my god." I sat on the curb. I'd never done as much curb sitting in my life as since the accident.

"You are pregnant?"

"Yes."

"With my babies?"

"Yes."

"Will you marry me?"

"No, Nikos. You're with Parlene, and I may be engaged." And, "You were not good for me," I wanted to add.

"You are in love?"

"Yes, very much so."

"What's his name?" He sounded defeated.

"Matt."

"Does he deserve you?"

"The question is, do I deserve him, Nikos."

"I can't believe it. I will be the father of three children! How will I support them? I must go back to school. We should have stayed together. We should have married by now. I ruined everything."

"I'm not asking you to support them. Matt and Kristína will help, and I have an excellent, wealthy patronage now, IF I survive what comes next and IF they don't all excommunicate me when the truth comes out."

"What are you asking of me then?"

"Nothing. I just thought you should know."

"You have much to handle. I'll do the right thing by you, Cammy."

"Lucy."

"Lucy."

"Thank you. Has Natalie Mouskers come home?"

"No. We haven't seen her in days."

Miss Mouskers had good instincts. If she didn't like someone, she would stay away. I was sure the now steady presence of Parlene set her scarce. I needed reassurance she was okay.

"Nikos — get some cans of gourmet sardines, open one, and sit on the stoop on the Southwestern corner — she'll show within twenty minutes. Call me back on this number."

"All right, à tout à l'heure."

Nineteen minutes later the phone rang.

"Allo?"

"Someone wants to talk to you. I'll hold for her the phone."

"Natalie Mouskers, it's me, your mama. I miss you. I love you. I'll see you soon, sweet girl."

She gave me zilch at first then, after a few minutes, she gave just enough to warm the cockles of my heart.

"Meow," she sounded pleased, but pissed, and justifiably so.

After we hung up, I called Matt with my remaining cell minutes.

"Hey! Where are you?" A psychedelic jam-band in the background dwarfed his words.

"I'm in Spain at Hristina's."

"No kidding, already? How's it going?"

"It's good. I like her. You will love her; she's kind and strong and smells like garlic. Kristína and I look just like her. Where are YOU?"

"We're seeing *Open Border*. Two beers, please." The Open Border Electric Band's sound is dangerously good; I'd caught them twice with Matt in Berkeley. It's hard to stay seated at their shows as their music milks movement from even the most staid sorts. Their *Atomic Angel* is the most wakeful, rousing song. I heard it playing now.

"We?"

"Me and Matsako!"

Shit. A kettle of envy tipped off my shoulders, wiggled my hips, and spun me around like a kaleidoscope. It's so easy to be judgmental, but hard to be human. I now had compassion for Parlene. I put the Lady of the Lake ring on my ring finger and held my hand at arm's length; the ruby caught rays from the Spanish sun.

Who was I kidding? I would be jailed. I killed a boy in Paris.

"Lucy? Are you there?"

"Yeah." But I wasn't. My life whirled before me like the Victorian zoetrope my folks got for their fifth wedding anniversary — the one with the gymnasts, tigers, ballerinas, and race horses dancing in circles. It gave the illusion of motion as strips of successive pictures ran round a slitted drum. Blump - blump – blump; the years like an Icarus asteroid flew past the glisten of the hot Sienna sun.

UNLUCKY LUIS

Some people say you make your own luck, but I disagree; you can work hard, be a good person, and affect things in life to varying degrees, but luck is luck, and it was not on Luis Fernando's side that pale winter day in Paris when a pole hit him on the head and knocked him out mid-laugh.

JUAN ALBERTO

Our flight to Santiago de Cali was five notches lower than passable. The flight attendants were irascible, the devious guy in the row behind us was bean-and-cauliflower gassable and passed wind without sound then seemed as surprised as anyone else by the smell. The winds outside were fierce and the plane, (moving like an old jalopy), had to make a brief emergency landing before our second stopover. Kristína and I were like crisped cinnamon popovers. The only redeeming factor of the trip was the way people stopped us and asked if we were sisters. "You two look identical, are you twins?" they'd gush. It was a rush.

Nina LaRue arrived eight hours before us. She insisted on renting a three-bedroom apartment on oma's birthday gift money. If Maria knew what her money was used for she would plotz. The last email Nina sent said the place was Amueblado y con ubicacion super en la ciudad de Cali. In my cobbled Spanish, I translated it to, "Furnished and with a super location in the city of Cali."

The price was so good I expected a dive but the dwelling, hidden ten meters off the street behind a gigantic Jacaranda tree, promised a peaceful stay, at least regarding our living quarters. The tree was a plume of purple paradise with smooth, spindly grey-brown branches. On the reddish-brown finger like twigs unfolded flowering swans like a cheesy magician opening his hands after reaching into a top hat. Inside high ceilings rose in welcome, "Bueno, hello," natural lighting, granite counters, vibrant tiles of Verde and Azul beckoned us on. In the backyard, parse palm trees and a puny pool would help keep cool in the soggy heat of the South American summer.

"This must have cost a fortune, Nina!"

"Kiss, kiss, which one is you?" She smiled widely as, ever the dramatic Dame, she clawed Kristína and me close in a mamma bear hug.

"I'm Camille," Kristína said, "don't you recognize me?" Nina laughed at the twin joke, but since what Kristína said was actually factual, it gave me a splitting headache.

"Luc-eeee, is that youuuuu?" a male voice sang out from the other room. I looked to Nina with quizzical curiosity. She shrugged her shoulders, lifted her eyebrows like blinds pulled open on a sunny day, "We hooked up after you left, he's muy dolce y Jalapeno hot."

Out from the recesses of the house, (wrapped around the bottom in a blue batik sarong and shirtless on top), appeared Ramon, the vibrant vocalist from Jabori's band, *Paolo Paradis and the Psithurism Paupers*. "Luc-eeeee," he wrapped me tight in his arms, even tighter than the skimpy sarong he knotted tightly at his slim, brown waist. He turned to a now flustered, jetlagged Kristína who was confused by this cast of characters. "Yo soy Rrrrraaathththththth-ah-mon," he introduced himself accompanied by the full lift, swivel, and pinched bunny puppet of his artistic hand. Nina and I bit our lips.

"¿Cuál es tu nombre, Hermosa?"

Kristína already having a great time was quick on the uptake, "Mitt nafn er Kristína, gaman að hitta þig, myndarlegur," she said coyly. I was proud of my sister, no finicky wallflower.

"What does that mean?" Nina played the straight woman.

"It means, 'My name is Kristína, handsome.' Now where is the bathroom, I have to use it? I had a beer on the plane."

Nina let Kristína to the loo while Ramon poured me a chilled glass of tart lemonade. This crew was doing their utmost to make this crazy trip memorable, but I was supposed to be miserable and repentant.

Nina rejoined us momentarily, "You couldn't have had business in Peru or Brazil? What is in Santiago?"

I looked out the back door and saw Pierre, pant legs pulled up to his knees, dangling his bare feet into the pool. I set down the lemonade, which suddenly tasted too bitter to swallow. "I have to atone," I said. I wanted to be left alone.

"I'm so tired, the room is spinning," Kristína put the back of her hand on her forehead and swooned like Blanche talking to Stanley Kowalski.

"Why yes, Miss DuBois, right away," I said with my best Southern inflection; this reference fell flat with Nina, Kristína, and Ramon — perhaps it was the heat, for surely everyone was familiar with this famous play?

"They told me to take a street-car named Desire, and transfer to one called Cemeteries, and ride six blocks and get off at—Elysian Fields!" a euphonious voice sounded at the front door. There he was, leaning against the doorjamb, the most beautiful sight in South America — including Canamera Park, The Meeting of Waters, Lake Titicaca, and The Chilean Patagonia — with a wink that could topple me from across the world.

"MATT! How did you get here so quickly?" God, an intelligent man is so sexy; I teared up in joy. My stomach turned over as if I was going down the vertigo inducing Gelmerbahn funicular above Lake Gelmer in Bern, Switzerland where Pascal and I celebrated our first anniversary, just before his cancer diagnosis.

"Got our flight switched," he drawled. I threw finesse out the window and smothered him with hugs and kisses.

"Just forgo introductions and get yourselves a rthhhooooooom," Ramon said.

"Hi, Luc-eeee," piped a piquant voice.

"Matsako!" She threw herself on me like a bear cub reuniting with her mother. Seeing her elated me though I was unsure how my most private, painful moment had become a party.

Ramon noticed that I was overwhelmed and stepped forward to sort everyone out. He handled the introductions like a well-paid cruise ship director; served lemonade, and red beans, rice, and avocado wrapped in lettuce leaves all round, and gave us a tour of the place as if it were a palatial palace.

Goofy, gargantuan gargoyles that looked demented to me besmirched the largest of the three bedrooms, but Nina and Ramon thought they were gorgeous. Fine. They got that room. Matt and I got the small eggshell blue bedroom that had a bathroom (decorated by green, gold, royal, white and black Talavera tiles), for my late night pregnancy pees. Matsako and Kristína would bunk in the rose room with garish burgundy trim, and we would situate the latecomers, Brigitte and Noni, on rollways in the living room.

Matsako and a very pregnant Nina hit it off immediately and changed into bathing suits to make use of the pool. Nina's suit left little for the imagination. Somehow hot stuff Matsako looked matronly next to her! Ramon joined them. This left me, Matt, and Kristína with a chance to bond. It was like Spring break except it was summer, and my heart was breaking.

"I am so pleased to make your acquaintance. Not that looks are everything," Matt gestured towards his face in an unusual display of self-consciousness, "but you look just like the prettiest woman I've ever met." He took both her hands in his and made a genuine connection. Kristína caught my eye, taken by Matty's southern charm. "I can see you're all tuckered out though. We should chat later."

"No, no. I want to talk now! I'll just lie down and you both can sit there in the room with me." And that is exactly what we did. Matt and I sat by Kristína's bedside and chitchatted until she dozed off mid-sentence, happy with her new family, and saturated by sadness from missing Jón with every pore of her procumbent body.

Matt and I disappeared into our tiny blue room together. We reunited as only new lovers can when separated by continents, and then slept because of exhaustion, finally safe in each other's arms. We emerged fifteen hours later when the spicy smell of huevos and tortillas reminded our bellies it was time to eat again.

I cried about Luis Fernando, my only reason for being in Santiago de Cali. "I killed him, Matt. I did a terrible thing."

"Circumstance has nothing to do with character, Lucy. Don't get those things confused."

"There's no excuse. I looked down for a split second, and that was it. It was so sudden, like slipping down a water slide."

"It could have been anyone, Lucy."

"Please, don't make this less than it is."

Matt heaved a serious sigh, rolled closer to me, and brushed my long bangs back from my forehead. "It's a terrible, tragic thing, I agree, for a boy to lose his life, for a family to lose their child, for you, a good person, to feel torment due to one false move."

The truth comforted me. "I can't ever make it right, but I have an idea of something I can do to honor Pierre's life and hopefully spare others."

"What is it, Lucy?"

"I will give speeches and tell Luis Fernando's story. People think they are immune and just one text will be okay, but it's not."

Matt sat up. "I like this idea. This is good."

"I would only do this if it's all right with his family."

"Yes."

We walked into the kitchen where four shiny faces clinked Ramon's lemonade and uttered a well-rehearsed greeting, "Buenos Dias, lovebirds! They told me to take a street-car named Desire."

Santiago de Cali is located in a valley. The Farallones de Cali Mountains are to the West, the Cauca River to the East, and extended plains to the North and South. Matt, Kristína, and I wasted no time in heading seventeen miles East to Palmira: our destination was the Centro Internacional de Agricultura Tropical, where Juan Alberto Jiménez, Luis Fernando's grandfather worked as a scientist to reduce poverty and hunger while protecting natural resources. He was the only one in the Jiménez family I traced to a solid, verifiable address.

Kristína, fluent in Spanish from spending her childhood holidays visiting Seville, served as our guide on the Colombia public transit system. The trip in the tropical Savannah was seamless, but for the ghastly midday heat. I, the dimwit, had forgotten to wear a sun hat OR bring water, and so by the time we arrived, I was both peaked and parched.

"I vote we sit in the shade until Camille catches her breath," Kristína hadn't made the name change in her mind yet to Lucy. She guided me over to a bench as though I were blind.

"I second that. I'll be right back with tres aguas," Matt disappeared as if he were a mirage in my mutable mind.

Kristína and I sat in wait for half an hour and, as voyeuristic vamps, we watched an old man crack open sunflower seeds and pop one in his mouth for every two he tossed to his furry friend, a scampy red squirrel with silver dollar eyes and a tail that helmeted it's head like a Mohawk. We didn't make a peep so as not to disturb this saffronic scene. He seemed unaware of us, lost in his heavenly communion with the rascally rodent whose cries sounded like a hyena when the man stopped his friendly feeding.

I glued my gaze to the sedate South American slice-of-life scene. Soft footsteps approached me from behind; hot hands the size of a large doll covered my eyes, startling me. "Devine qui," a French voice as honeyed and familiar as the fragrance of the lavender tree in my childhood backyard prompted me to 'Guess who?'

"Brigitte!" I proclaimed and pirouetted so pointedly I caused a devise diversion — the squirrel scampered away speedily with a seed hanging from his lips. Its benefactor threw the remaining lot grimly on the ground and stalked off with a snarl.

"Camille, c'est tellement bon de te voir, mon ami," she gushed how good it was to see me.

A mechanical concern had caused Brigitte's plane to arrive late. "Go ahead without me, I'm a big girl, I'll catch up," she had emailed me earlier. Ultimately, I went ahead because I had to before I chickened out entirely; if inertia took over, I might never recover the bravado I needed for this weighty life task.

Kristína inched forward with shyness, as was her habit. "Bonjour Brigitte, pleased to meet, je suis Kristina, la sœur de Camille."

"Ah, Kristína," Brigitte faced my twin and sandwiched her as though she was a mother warming icy fingers of her babe in an arctic blast. They stood like statues, eyes locked, unable to turn away.

"Okay, ladies, tres aguas," Matt returned with a flounce, "Whoa! We now have another beauty in our midst. Brigitte?"

"Oui. Allo, Matt, I have heard so many wonderful things about you," Brigitte kept hold of Kristína as she leaned over to give Matt two feather quick kisses on each of his cheeks.

Everyone fell for Brigitte just as I did when we first met. She has a gazelle-like grace that intoxicates all who meet her. Brigitte dressed head to toe in black, her face pale, hair pulled severely back. In Paris she often dressed in a crisp white shirt that played in contrast to her now washed out Mediterranean toned skin. She stood there in the shade like a delicate negative of herself; her rose lipstick appeared garish on her otherwise natural face. My bet was that she wore it begrudgingly, just for a bit of color to perk up her weak, wan look.

Matt passed around water bottles. Brigitte, Kristína, and I held them high, "Salud!"

"To the memory of Luis Fernando and the prayer that I will somehow - in any way - honor his life." I sipped and then passed the bottle back to Matt who guzzled the rest. Sweat dripped into his half-shut eye.

"Ready?" he asked us.

"Oui."

"Yes."

"Já."

"Okay, let's go." And like the Pied Piper of Hamlin, we filed inside Juan Alberto's building behind Matt. The only one who noticed was the squeamish squirrel that came snooping back around for more treats. The skeptical look on her face transmitted uncertainty.

Matt led the way and we women shuffled close behind him, shoulder to shoulder like a three headed bobble headed sheep. Brigitte, in the middle, kept a light hold of our palms — so light it tickled. In tune with being horticulture headquarters, the light was neat and natural, but in my hellacious state of mind everything was too bright; our footsteps seemed to echo down the vast hallway like the pounding of an anvil, and I had to pee again.

We peeked in every office, each was small yet vacuous, variety was lacking: a slanted desk, a potted plant, an overhead fan, and a window with a view of the hills. There weren't any shades to block the screaming white-yellow histrionic sun streaming in like a bath tap on full blast. After what seemed as long as a Rumpelstiltskin rest, Matt stopped, turned, and announced, "We're here!" Brigitte squeezed my hand so tightly that I thought my bladder would burst.

The door to Suite 1117 was three-quarters ajar; at first glance, it looked the same as the rest. Inside stood a tall man tidying his papers — part scientist, artist, Zen monk, and pinup poster, full of greying dignity and brimming in anticipation of our sloppy spur-of-the-moment meet-up. He looked up with a measured movement when he sensed our presence.

To Brigitte he said, "Just on time. I received your email alerting me you were coming. It's nice to see you again, although naturally I wish under different circumstances."

"I wrote the email," I asserted, confused.

"I did too," Brigitte blushed. "I didn't think we should show up unannounced."

"Nor did I."

"It was good thinking on both your parts to alert me," he sighed. I'm Juan Alberto," he held out a brown weathered hand with long fingers and strong knuckles for me to shake. I didn't expect such civility. I was in fact shocked by the normalcy of the conversation to that point.

"I'm Camille." I wanted to add, "I killed your grandson," and fall at his feet and explain the car skidded and I did not understand how. I wished to explain I could barely live with myself and saw Pierre at every turn. "I would trade my life for Luis Fernando's," I wanted to assure him. But I didn't. I held my tongue and maintained the forced amicability.

It was then I noticed a picture of Juan Alberto holding a laughing little Luis set in a polished silver frame on his desk. Dried flowers flocked the base.

He held his hand out to Brigitte. "Juan Alberto."

"I'm Brigitte."

"I remember your name."

"Wait — you've met before?"

"At the police station," Brigitte explained, "I thought I told you."

"No. I would have remembered that." Juan Fernando put on his hat. *The police station?*

"Juan Alberto."

"Matt."

"Juan Alberto."

"Kristína."

Juan Alberto did a double take between Kristína and I.

"Twins?"

"Yes."

"Yes."

"Ah, my children are twins. Have you eaten?" We all shook our heads. No. "Come, let's go to lunch."

"Do NOT burden Juan Alberto with your own angst; it is NOT his place to comfort you," I'd coached and admonished myself on this for months since I first planned on making the trip to Colombia, but apparently all the DO NOT'S made me DO; what you resist persists perhaps, and I spilled my till against my will the first chance I got.

"I would have killed myself if wasn't pregnant. I thought about it many nights — I have no right being alive when your grandson died because of me. I ran because of shock, adrenaline, and fear, and then wove myself a web I couldn't get out of. I haven't thought straight since that day. I've decided whatever happens to me, I will be a voice against irresponsible driving. I wrote a speech about it." My heart was pounding.

Everyone put down his or her forks. Kristína swallowed as if food had lodged in her throat. She gulped her water and signaled for more. Brigitte palmed her eyes, bent over, and rocked in remorse. Matt set his hand on my knee for support, but I gently removed it. I needed to face this on my own.

Juan Alberto sat silent as stone while the waiter refilled everyone's glasses; the server backed away quickly when he parsed the mood around our table.

Finally, the senior Jiménez spoke. "Losing our precious angel devastated and divided mi Familia." He was a kind man, but humanity did not eclipse his grief. "I support this plan of yours." He moaned, remembering Luis Fernando's smile. "I wish you well, but your punishment, I presume, will come this evening when you meet with my son and his wife. Thank you for contacting me." He stood and laid his white linen napkin over his plate of uneaten beans and salad as though he were laying a burial shroud over his nieto.

"Here is the address. See you there. Buena suerte," he touched my face and walked away.

It was a holy zoo when we returned to the bungalow. Ramon was on the couch with his left leg propped up on three pillows. He'd wrapped ice in a towel and set it on the ankle he sprained when he jumped on a beach chair after he saw a rat run by the pool. Ew — a rat! The place was a mess of wet clothes, breakfast and lunch dishes caked with eggs and beans, and ten lemonade glasses strewn everywhere.

Nina emerged from the big bedroom like a voluptuous fertility goddess, tanned, big-bellied, wide hips swaying, glistening moist in the heat - the vicious, vindictive heat. "You're back early! How did it go?"

"Fine," Kristína and I like synchronized swimmers doing a perfectly timed breaststroke said. Yes, we twins did that; it's true. "Fine," we said only because this wasn't the time or place to go into detail about the deed, or Juan Alberto, or the uneaten Bandeja Paisa.

Ramon yelled for Nina to come help him hobble to the bathroom. "I'll be right there, babe," Nina whispered to Ramon as she disappeared down the dark hall as a rodent, swallowed whole by a vulture, might vanish. When Nina returned, Matsako and Noni were with her.

Noni and I, blissed out from being reunited so recently, were fast friends again. "Ooooooooooo!" She closed her eyes, clenched her fists, and stampeded in place, so happy to see me. We high-fived Idaho style and shared a rag-doll hug. Matt waited his turn and got the same: squeal, stampede, high five, hug. I introduced Noni around to everyone, " Noni, this is Ramon, Nina, Matsako, you've met Brigitte..."

"Yes, Brigitte, how sweet to see you again. I wish it was under better circumstances."

"Bon soir, Winona," Brigitte teared up, and Noni wrapped her in a soulful hold.

Then I presented my sister like a debutante at her ball, "Noni, THIS is Kristína."

"Well, knock me over with a feather. Kristína. Umm-um. I never thought I'd see another sight as lovely as Camille. Now I see double and haven't even had a drink. Let me see the two of you together." We posed like a two-headed poodle, heads angled in, foreheads touching. Noni was speechless.

A light flashed. We all looked up from our lock.

There in the hallway's mouth, atop the tonsils of the beast like Poor Pinocchio before the whale stood a slightly pregnant Tanu with a phone in her hand, snapping photos.

"Tanu, is that you?"

"Allo, Lucy." She kiss-kissed me and greeted Matt and Brigitte, whom she hadn't met yet.

Kristína walked to Tanu, wiped a tear from her eye and pressed her in a soft embrace, "Thank you for coming. Thank you for being so supportive of me." She turned to me, "I hope you won't be angry with me. I thought if I told you, you might object. We all need to find closure in this mess — Tanu too."

She WAS my twin, so bold and brazen.

"Yes. Tanu has helped me a lot. I'm glad she's here. I'm glad you're here, Tanu." My conflicted feelings fought inside like siblings squabbling for mamma's attention.

Ramon, who had gotten up for the hugs, lay back down with a groan. Nina ran to his side to attend to him. Matt and Matsako tackled the dishes together as I imagined they had done in Berkeley without me. The rest of us cleaned up clothes, shoes, towels, and blankets, and organized final sleeping arrangements. The two couples stayed in their respective rooms. Kristína and Brigitte who had taken to each other like pups to a pond in summer stayed put in theirs, and the three new Musketeers, Matsako, Noni, and Tanu set up cots and a futon in the living room where Ramon lay.

When the hustle and bub quieted down, I retreated to my room, reached for a pad of ivory paper, and drew charcoal renderings of the day. Three water bottles, four hands, Juan Alberto at his office, a gorgeous group huddle, and my twin and Tanu, fingers tenderly entwined in a tattered Twilight Zone.

The weather was overcast, uncharacteristic for this time of year. The police station was unusually quiet. The woman in the red coat and her yapping Yorkie were nowhere in sight.

"The final report just came in," Moreau strode into the lunchroom, shaking a paper printout.

Girard, eyebrows raised to a pointed arch, a few breadcrumbs in his beard, looked up grimly, "And?"

Moreau leaned in to Girard, "Just as we suspected."

"Why did it take so bloody long?" Joubert came over to read for himself.

"Bureaucratic red tape," Moreau mused with mellow disdain.

Jolbert's eyes skimmed the document. At the end of each line his eyes shifted and returned like a 1920s typewriter. "Hmm. Tsh. We need to get in touch with her as soon as possible."

Rousseau came in to pour herself a black cappuccino. "What's this? What's all the fuss?" She gulped the drink down like a shot of tequila. Girard shook his head, wondering how his young superior didn't just burn her tonsils. She was tough stuff.

"The final report just came in," Moreau nearly snatched it from Joubert and slipped it into her hands.

"We must tell her as soon as we can." Girard said decidedly.

Moreau's phone rang, "Allo?"

"Bonjour, c'est Leonard."

"Ah, Leonard. Do you know where she is?"

"Oui. She is in Colombia, according to my source."

"Colombia?" Girard's eyebrows rose again, "This girl gets around."

Moreau's moustache moved up and down on the phone, " Good work. We will clear you of all charges of harboring a suspect. Good day."

Leonard pulled up to Helga's house in Brussels. He sobbed with remorse for four solid minutes. He blew his nose and gathered up take away food bags and fourteen fuchsia roses. He walked defiantly up to the front door.

"Bonjour, Helga."

"Bonjour, Leonard," she took the flowers from him, "Merci!"

The door shut as Rousseau slapped the pages down, "Let her rot, she ran."

It was a mistake to go to the Jiménez house. My feet moved forward, but my hips like a Harlequin tried to pull them backwards as if a harpoon tied to a two-ton truck dragged me in reverse.

A poem sprang into my head:

"I yearn for the smell of my youth.
Mellow grass in autumn, yellowed in November
By February dead and gone.
New life is planted, the old tossed away too soon.
The bright moon will never light the shadow of gloom from the one who took the bloom."

"Lucy! Whoa, be careful!" Matt caught me as my toe snagged on a cobblestone and I stumbled, nearly falling face down on the dappled, creviced bricks.

My body and being were in two separate places. My mind was half a world away on a street in Paris as my body arrived at the top of this quiet cobbled hill, the pungent aroma of cooked chicken, onions, sweet yams, and fried plantains mingled with the moonlight. In the distance, an Afro-Caribbean drum beat, padda-peat, padda-peat, displaying Cali's cheerful nature, a perfect scene for someone else, not I. Half here - half there, I saw Brigitte as through a View Master boldly knock on a dull turquoise door, overarched in white, with two black overhead lamps like donkey ears sticking out of the brick on either side. The front window, left ajar to ventilate stale air from a stagnant day, allowed insight into the mood inside. Footsteps echoed on tiles like walking the lonely green mile on death row.

A woman clothed head to toe in shades of brown opened the door, Her browns were not the sassy sienna of Pierre at play, but the dirgeful dress of sadness, unable to face brighter pigments, and straining to break free of the grey and black she had known since last winter through the yellowing, white, balding, and dead days. She was young in years, perhaps only thirty, not much older than me, but her countenance belied her age. She looked more ancient than her father-in-law, crow's feet where smooth skin ought to be.

A man who looked like Luis Fernando all grown up stood with a supportive hand on her shoulder. He trembled, restraining himself from shaking our hands.

"I'm Luis Fernando. This is my wife, Marta, my sister María Rose, and you have met my papa, Juan Alberto."

We four filed in: Brigitte, Kristína, Matt, and me. Matt knew better than to hold my hand. They led us to a modest living room adorned with photos of Luis Fernando as a baby, a toddler, and a young boy. A life frozen in time in photographs taken in joyous moments by parents pleased as punch, unaware that their time together would end too soon.

I cleared my throat from the fuzz that settled on my tongue; my mouth was like a desert oasis, and my skin crawled like a lizard under an unsullied sun. I needed water, but didn't want to trouble them. "No, gracias," I said as I slipped a water bottle from my purse and took a tiny sip, not feeling like I deserved more. Brigitte eyed me, and I passed the bottle to her; she gulped half of it down. The swallow sounds from her tight throat ate us up.

"I'm sorry... about your son," she sighed.

Everyone shifted positions. They sat in agitated silence. The lively padda-peat, padda-peat, padda-peat mocked us.

"No, I'm the one that needs to apologize, but words and actions will never be enough," I croaked.

They met our pitiful offers of penance with silence. María Rose moved her mouth as though she was chewing gum. I expected big bubbles to grow from behind her lips, but then I realized she too was dry. She stood up and headed to the hall. We sat watching until she pivoted and waved her hand, "Follow me." We did: Brigitte, Kristína, then Matt, then me. She led us to a brown room. "Brown was his favorite color," she said. "Funny boy," her lips quivered into a sorrowful smile. The walls were brown and covered with pictures of 1930s airplanes. Model airplanes sat proud and lonely on stands without their maker to buzz them above his head; one set was half done, a glue bottle sat still open next to plywood wings, a promise of a plane that never got off the ground.

In silence they showed us a movie of their family christening Luis Fernando III. They also took out a large, stuffed photo album: pictures of him in day care, with his first lovely lass, flying a 1930s airplane kite, corralling a bunch of helium balloons, ("That was on my birthday," Marta broke the silence with a horse, cracked whisper), and petting their cat Sansibar. We learned a bit about Luis, the lost light of their lives, from Marta Luis II as Juan Alberto watched over her and María Rose bubbled like a rolling pot of boiling water.

Marta took us on a silent tour of her home. In each spot she narrated a story about Luis Fernando like the time when he was three years old and put his favorite blue bowl on the floor, got down on all fours, and ate his dinner next to Sansibar for a week so his gato didn't have to eat alone. In the backyard she showed us the stable for his planes he had meticulously built out of twigs from a grand Colombian mahogany tree. A Spiderman stepstool that Luis used to stand on to brush his teeth sat in the bathroom; his parents cherished Luis' scuff marks that soiled the Superhero's face.

The house was hollow because of the ghosts that lived there. The air was uncharacteristically cold, though it was sweltering outside. Luis Fernando followed us around with doleful pride. "Do you see him?" I whispered rashly to Matt. He shook his head, "No," and looked at me with a sad look in his eyes, aware of how harrowing and heartbreaking this was for me. "Do you see him?" I wheezed quietly to Brigitte who fluttered like a wounded dove, "No, but I wish I did." Kristína overheard me and breathed back, "Everyone sees that YOU see him, Camille. He's real to us through you."

When the tour was over, they ushered us out. There was no talk about anger or forgiveness. No screams of, "Oh, god, why?" No curses, no blessings, no chants for my incarceration, just the satisfaction of having shared their boy's lost life with me — with us. Their calmness was rattling; the stony faces, anguishing; the photos of Pierre, piercing. Juan Alberto ushered us out: Brigitte, Kristína, Matt, and then me. When we got halfway down the hill, I threw up in the bushes. It was then that a woman's wail came cascading through the dappled night air. A slow moan of a mother left alone. The padda-peat, padda-peat of the droning drum slowed like a dying heartbeat. The last swat of the drum skin hit me like a slap, then stopped. We continued down the grade: Matt, Kristína, Brigitte, me, and Pierre.

Upon our return, we noticed the light in the bungalow, which meant Ramon had stayed home to nurse his ankle while unstoppable Nina La Rue took Matsako, Tanu, and Noni to salsa dance among the sugarcane in the city nicknamed, *Branch of Heaven*. The peaks of Cristo Rey harkened them from this heavy hole like coyotes on an end of summer nighttime prowl. I didn't blame them at all and had no intent to hinder their happiness. I too yearned to poach my inner restraints and dance barefoot with my girls in the luminous hills of San Antonio that jut from the playful plains of Valle del Cauca.

Matt grabbed my hand and Brigitte held Kristína's. My heart reeled from the worst night one might ever imagine; not only had I come face to face with the disconsolate Jiménez family and their well deserved grief, but there in the dark recesses of their back bathroom hung a calendar from one of "Fabian's Fantastic Photo Shoots," in France. Fiddle fuddle. Scantily clad images of Tanu and I taken fresh after the incident in Paris would peek from the pages of next year's edition. How awkward this would be for Luis II.

Life never failed to surprise me. Existence is laborious, frothy, and unforeseen — a character with hulking arms and a dancing heart.

Matty opened the door and we four minstrels witnessed Ramon push Tanu against the living room wall, her right arm pinned behind her back. Matsako, Nina, and Noni stood by like a crowd at a football game staying a safe distance from the violence below.

"OW!! Stop it, you're hurting me!"

I rushed forward, "What are you doing, Ramon? Stop!"

"She's recording us!"

"You and Nina? Having sex?"

"No. We think she's trying to record you to frame you."

"I'm not!" Tanu bleated with her cheek pushed up causing one eye to scrunch shut.

"Then what's this?" Nina pulled a nano microphone from Tanu's collar.

"I'm NOT framing you, Lucy. You worry Jon sick being pregnant and roaming around."

"Jon, not Theo?"

"No, Theo's cool, Jon is a wreck. Tell this guy to let me go."

"And he asked for you to RECORD me?"

"Yes," she answered meekly, turning scarlet.

"Ramon," I shook my head at him. He reluctantly released her.

Tanu massaged her shoulder. "Nikos.... he will be a father. He's also worried to pieces about you turning yourself in for killing that boy."

My hand instinctively touched my belly, "You know?"

"Yes. Parlene is pregnant," Tanu looked tuckered out from the tussle.

"Parlene AND my twins make three."

"Yes, but she's pregnant with Nikos baby."

"So am I."

She looked like a little deer lost in the forest. Her legs wobbled as she asked, "Nikos is the father of your baby?"

"Babies - twins. Yes."

Tanu took two more breaths. "I suspected this in Lille. Congratulations. Welcome to the family." She left juicy kisses all over my forehead.

"Digame, You killed a CHILD?" Ramon was just catching up.

"It was an accident! The car slipped like someone had thrown bacon grease on the road."

"Camille... Lucy was texting me on my birthday, it's MY fault, I kept her on the phone," Brigitte burbled out.

"Wait? You KILLED someone —"

"With my bare hands," Matt said. No one understood his comment but me.

"... A boy... WHILE TEXTING?" Ramon was incredulous.

I looked desperately out the back door. There, I saw Luis Fernando dive into the deep end of the pool, dip down, and disappear. Frantic, I ran out, kicked off my shoes and dove in after him. Once I was underwater, I shimmied around until I saw him - it was Bertrand as a boy! I had not gotten the chance to grieve Bertrand properly. I submerged again and chased him down near the deep drain.

Two big splashes rocked the water like a tidal wave. Ramon and Matt dove in, and pulled me out. My clothes were waterlogged and clung to my crevices. I was confused, realized I was screaming and crying, "Bertrand! Pierre! Life is not fair!" Then I passed out.

If you are ever in my shoes, (and I hope you never are), you'll find out what it's like to hash out the horror in recurring night terrors of a pole toppling over and over again repeatedly. Nothing I could do seemed right enough for this wrong. They lay me on my back as though in a dream: Ramon gently palpated my stomach, "Be careful of the babies!" Nina micro-managed in her marvelous way, and so he stopped.

"Who knows CPR?" I thought I heard Matt ask, "I do!" Tanu answered. She and Ramon worked in tandem to bring me back from the brink of Boise where I was visiting my parents in a sea of sunflowers. Matsako brought me my favorite clothes. Together, she and Kristína dressed me. Matt sat still like the Buddha, holding my hand, willing me back to life. Brigitte, in a corner, rocked back and forth, singing a French love song of her youth.

"Do you ever get hit with overwhelming pregnancy cravings?" She asked me as I lay shivering like a beached whale, still in the other world as much as this one.

"Yes. I need Speculoos, (which I didn't expect to find in Santiago). I miss Bertrand."

"So do I. I'll find you some." With that, she turned to leave.

"Kristína," I called my twin over.

"Yes?"

"Would you keep an eye on Brigitte, I'm worried about her."

"I will." With a kiss on my lips, my twin ran after Brigitte.

I took a head count: one, two, three, four, five, six, seven, eight, nine of us left: Matt, Noni, Matsako, me, Nina, Ramon, a de-microphoned Tanu, young Bertrand, and Luis III.

Someone tuned down the lights. Someone else made the cots up with sheets, pillows, and blankets. Everyone hunkered in as close as they could. Our eyes closed and drifted into group slumber, while Bertrand sang us to sleep. Luis lay down next to me, content.

"Próximo cliente!"

"Próximo cliente!"

"Próximo cliente!"

"You need to settle down and get a home," Kristína reprimanded me like a mother hen as if it wasn't on my mind that dos pequeñas personas depended on my health and future.

"Próximo cliente!" The woman who bleats out commands gave a titanic yawn.

"Próximo cliente!"

Matt, Kristína, and Brigitte had accompanied me to the airport. I was there for a plane ticket to Paris - pronto. My other amigos had said their goodbyes to me back at the bungalow, wished me oodles of luck in prison, promised to keep in touch, and then swam and sunned on the banks of the Pance River.

We waited impatiently in a snaking line of sweaty people for an hour and a half. When it was my turn, I stepped up to the ticket counter and announced, "Ya quiero irma a mi casa ahora." (I want to go home now.) The heavily rouged woman looked at my ticket, shook her head and intoned, "Lo siento; necesita una semana para compare su boleto. Próximo cliente!" (I'm sorry; you need a week to buy a ticket. Next client!)

Hmm. Well, she didn't understand about my pregnancy and The Predicament. After seeing Luis Fernando's model airplane stable, I was eager to be locked up already and have it done with. I stole skittish glances back to my friends who stood shiftlessly at the head of the line. My eyes rested on the wide-brimmed hat on a kindly, browned-skinned woman in her sixties. She turned to her husband with concern. The gentleness in their expressions released something within me, and a tear dripped onto my ticket.

I turned back to the desk and with steely vulnerability repeated. "Ya quiero irma a mi casa." The agent told me to come back in a week, looked past my shoulder, and yelled, "Próximo!" I quietly and profoundly repeated my mantra: "Quiero ir a mi casa ahora."

Again, no. "Próximo cliente!"

I stood my ground. As if out of nowhere, carefully crafted Spanish (*with* correct verbal conjugation), flowed from me as I clarified I didn't care if she had to re-route me on a flight by way of China. I explained that I would stand in the bathroom the whole way if need be, but I needed to go home today. Now. Por favor.

"Hold the horns!" Matt held up his hand like a stop sign to Miss Próximo Cliente and patted my clammy forehead with the bottom of his tee shirt. "You're sweating like a whore in church, sweetie," he twanged tenderly to me, "You okay?"

I shook my head no. The kind couple stood by my side. The man spoke to the agent who called over a supervisor and, Voilà, produced a ticket for a flight back to France later that evening. We had just enough time to take Bernadette and César out to a late lunch and learn about their charitable lives as art and literature teachers for children in need.

"I wish I could do this instead of you," Kristína held me at the gate in a hug my DNA danced to; her presence completed me in ways I never knew were lacking, like when a cinnamon sunset emblazons the sky over a lackadaisical lavender field.

"Here's the key to my flat. You must jiggle the lock. My sister is out of town till Thursday, but she welcomes you. I kept Leonard informed. Ring him for support."

Leonard — oh! The thought of him made me chatter like the electric skeleton Noni and I set up at the Halloween hullabaloos at the house on the hill. Lord knows Leonard tried to help. I'd put him in such an awkward position, but I wish like wildfire he hadn't egged me on to run and instead had accompanied me to the police. If Bertrand had been there, things would have been different. Bertrand, my partner, my heart and spirit mate, was dead.

I was reminded of the last few times I saw Leonard:

1. At the service for Bertrand in Brussels.
2. Passing by him in his Uber on the street in Paris with Tanu. The face of the man in the cab, Juan Alberto, whose calm, sad eyes pierced my soul.
3. In the flat where he and Bertrand were to get married and I ran to, a wild animal with blood on my heels.

No. I would not call Leonard.

"It's not your fate, Kristína. No one can do this but me. I deserve whatever they give me."

Matt and Kristína fought over who would get the last hold of me. Matt won. He gave me a kiss as if I was off to the electric chair, the sort of kiss that would zing through my body for the whole eleven hour and fourteen minute North Atlantic flight.

Brigitte looked meek. I squeezed her hand, "Je t'aime, Brigitte," which is all she wanted to hear that day in February when she kept me on the phone a moment too long.

"Je t'aime, Belle."

PARLENE

I slept most of the way back to Europe draped in a loose purple top and flowy magenta skirt looking more like a fertile flower than a fugitive. The only flight was direct-to-London. I changed planes in Heathrow where officials detained and searched me at length. I swapped my sandals for running shoes and sprinted to my gate as fast as I could. I made my connection by a hairsbreadth. They held the plane. Drink orders were already taken.

My seatmate had a Rudolph red nose from the dreaded flu. When I woke up at Brigitte's the following day, my throat was scratchy. During the time I was too ill to leave the bed, there was a frequent late night helicopter buzz overhead. I was so convinced police planned to nab me in the dark of night I slept in my clothes.

Four days in, the fever finally broke. I celebrated by buying a fresh tub of the finest, stinkiest sardines Paris offered, (fiercely flavored by sea kelp and seasoned salt), and cycled on Brigitte's bicycle, which was a bit too big for me, to sit caddy corner to Nikos' place and wait for my feline friend to appear, as she always did.

Miss Mouskers didn't show, but a fat, fluffy cat did. He hoisted himself up to nibble the shiny, silver-skinned snacks that laid still like soldiers in a row. His paws were rapid and swat roughly at my skirt, so I packed away my wares, pet the persistent puss between his ears, and picked up a slender fish by its tail, which I tossed in the bushes for him.

As I turned to go, I saw THEM together. There they stood in front of the house, kissing and cuddling in a rash display of public affection. *"Get a frickin' room!"* I wanted to cry, but they carried on with no shame, rubbing noses and doing the two-step together.

Parlene and Miss Mouskers made a lovely team. My heart was shattered. The pieces scattered all over the planet from Berkeley to Barcelona, Iceland to Idaho, and San Francisco to Chicago, but the largest part remained in Santiago, where a boy built a stable for his planes. There was nowhere in the world I could fly that would ever numb that pain.

"Good," I thought. "Natalie Mouskers has the love she deserves. I deserve worse even than this. I'm nothing now but for the babies I have to grow." Parlene was pretty, and playful, and visibly pregnant. "Good. This woman will take care of Nikos and my cat. She doesn't seem as bad as I feared."

She spotted me — squinted her eyes like a Major League pitcher before winding up and throwing a wallop.

"Camille? What the hell are you doing here? Are you stalking Nikos? Leave my family alone. Shoo. Go. Disparaître. À présent." She flipped her hand at me like she was flicking a fly off of her salad. Before I could skulk away, Natalie Mouskers leapt into my arms. She mewed like Madame Butterfly, kissed my face, and then found the sardines. I opened the tub of treats for her. Parlene was livid. She came over and sat solidly on the bike, her arms crossed like an angry Artemis, her legs straddling for balance in four-inch heels.

"Mew," was the only word uttered for several minutes.

We sat there like that, (me on the stoop petting my cat, and she, mesmerizing me, pointed toes on pavement), hashing out a chat for two hours. When Natalie Mouskers ran into the street, Pregnant Parlene jumped off the bicycle and scooped her up to safe ground. This marvelous act shifted my opinion of her. Perhaps she was a woman of substance, and who was I to judge? What must she think of ME?

"Shall we go inside? I'd like to get out of these heels and put my mukluks on."

"Is Nikos home?"

"No."
"Are you expecting him soon?"
"No."
"Where is he?"
"School."
"School? What does he study?"
"Cooking."
"Cooking? Mr. Peanut butter and banana sandwich?"
"It's why he moved to Paris."
"Oh." I didn't know that." How could I not have known that? "Sure."

Her standing height surprised me. She is six foot tall in stockings, two inches taller than Nikos, and scads taller than me; her kids will tower over their half siblings, Click and Clack. I followed her lead with 'our' cat tailing behind.

The place looked good. It cleaned up nicely with a woman's touch. She had accessorized with red, but not too much.

"I met Nikos at an office I manage."
"What kind of office?"
"I'm a headhunter."

Shit. I believed her! Don't mess with Parlene.

Now, I try to see the good in everyone, but some folks are jerks, plain and simple. I wasn't sure about her yet. I kept my guard up as the conversation continued.

Parlene was the eldest of four raised in a poor section of Lille, of all places. She moved to Paris on her own when she was fifteen. Her parents were both sick, (we bonded over that), and she helped support her younger siblings who now lived with their aunt.

We talked through tears, worked through our fears, and emerged like caterpillars from cocoons, brighter, wider, and free. My perception of her shifted as I listened to her tale. I liked her, she liked me, and we both expressed hope for a good relationship between us three, especially since there would soon be six, with the babies in the mix.

"Do you hear about the accident?"

"Oui." Her look of sorrow was magnanimous enough to include me along with Juan Fernando and his family, which I did not feel deserving of. "Nikos doesn't want you to turn yourself in. He lies awake and worries, which means I lie awake and worry." She reached out and touched my wrist, the one with the freckle.

"I have to do what's right. I'm going to the station tomorrow."

She gasped. "What do you think will happen? Do they put people in jail for this?"

"I don't care. It doesn't matter anymore..."

"But the babies..."

"Click..."

"...and Clack."

We laughed.

"I shouldn't have run. I wasn't thinking right, Parlene. I was in shock. After they're born, it will be a horrible time too."

"Yes, I see what you mean." She got up and came back with two glasses of water. The cups had red and copper trim. "We'll go with you."

"No. I have to go alone."

"I INSIST."

"That's kind of you but..."

"We'll discuss this in the morning." She stood again signaling our conversation had ended. "What are you going to do now?"

"I'm going to see my chalk spot on the sidewalk. I want to pay my respects to Bertrand."

"May I come with you?"

"Yes, actually. Thank you. That would be nice."

"Stay here, Natalie," Parlene told kitty as she undid the kickstand on the bicycle.

"Natalie Mouskers."

"Excusez-moi?"

"Natalie Mouskers. I always call her by her whole name."

"Ah, I see. Stay here, Natalie Mouskers."

"Mew."

REFLECTIONS

The Right Bank in front of The Louvre was rowdy. An antsy after-lunch crowd gathered in groups and cycled in circles like those round cumulus clouds in Iceland before a rainstorm. There was a new kid in town, Saleem from Lahore, Pakistan — he had my spot in front of the museum and chalked up a storm.

"Wow. You're amazing! How did you learn to catch reflections in the eyes like that?"

He shrugged and kept drawing the curls of the Albanian girl who sat cross-legged on the sidewalk posing for him, "Self taught... Practice... Okay, done!" He wiped his hands on his white shirt, which was now a work of art on its own. The young lady's parents were thrilled and handed him a fistful of bills. Ah, I loved those fistfuls of crumpled bills and missed hiding them in the bean jars. The family took ten photos of the rendering and then scattered to the wind. The daughter headed this way, and her folks headed that; the portraiture had brought them together for those few precious moments.

Saleem turned his attention back to me. "You have studied art."

"I'm an artist."

"She's a chalk artiste!" Parlene proudly proclaimed.

"You are? You've got to be good to work well with chalk."

"She's the best."

"The best? Hmm, let me see what you've got. Draw a picture of me," he offered me a medium brown thick stick.

"No, it's okay."

"I insist. I would like to see the best in action. Please." He put the chalk stick in my hand and sat cross-legged as the ringleted girl had before him.

I said no five times firmly before I gave in. I'm not sure why I did it. My thoughts were a muddle. I was afraid of Saleem making a scene. Also, I missed chalking, my life and soul for so long.

As I drew, images of Bertrand, whose sweet music was strikingly silent, flowed. In my head I heard him play *Sunny Afternoon*, by the Kinks as clear as a Bow Bells. The flashbacks of my friend and our life together erased my fear of flubbing up. *I Wish I Never Saw the Sunshine*, by Beth Orton played in my memory as I swirled Salaam's curls. By the time I completed the refection in his eyes, mine overflowed with tears.

"Why are you crying, Lucy? This is much better than mine. You are a Master."

Parlene stroked her hand through my hair to soothe my sadness.

"Let me repay you. I'll do a portrait of you ladies together. I may never again have such an opportunity to sketch such a sensational doublet."

"Yes. We would love that," Parlene decided, and so we stood arm in arm with Brigitte's bicycle as Saleem worked his magic. The portrait captured our new connection, my sorrowful but radiant, flushed face, and the curved shapes of our bellies, breasts, and hips.

"Ah-ooh, it's fantastic, Saleem! What... what... what are these?" I pointed to two blurry blurbs in the background.

"Sometimes I see auras and spirits, ghosts in the distance."

I looked closely. "Bertrand and Luis Fernando.... Ah... hoo.... YOU are The Best, Saleem." We kissed him on the cheeks, took ten pictures of our portrait, and wheeled away. As we head off into the oncoming evening, Bertrand's jazzy *Waterloo Sunset* played us out.

In the morning, I awoke before dawn, dressed, ate, and head to the station alone.

"Sweet potatoes, seared salmon, and orange sherbet," my answers were monochromatic. "Vanilla ice cream with chocolate sauce and rainbow sprinkles!" Noni's were specific and colorful.

"Sautéed spinach..."

"EWWW!"

"... Green M & M's..."

"Ummm!"

"... and.... and..."

"What Cam, say it already!"

"And moldy Swiss cheese!"

"EWWW!" Noni delicately set down the miniature flowered teacup, which she held with her pinky bent just so as she was a guest of the Queen. "Tell me truly, Camille Lisette — if you could have just one last meal before they executed you, what would it be?"

Executed was a big word for us. We were seven.

"I don't think I'd want to eat. I might want music. I'd want to dance like Isadora Duncan one last time." I got up and blew like a storm around the room. "I might be upSET and wouldn't want to eat OR dance."

Noni refilled her tiny teacup with Guava punch and sipped, finger crooked just so. "Yes, Camille, but if you HAD to choose a last meal, what would it be?"

"Hmm. If I HAD to?"

"Yes," she again set down her cup.

"Avocado, Swiss cheese, grilled spinach sandwich on nine grain toast loaded with browned garlic and seared salmon, washed down with orange sherbet with a sliver of the rind curled round the top."

"EWWW!"

"What do you mean, EWWW? That's what I want, Noni. Don't make fun of me. I'm on death row for god sakes."

"Well, I want vanilla ice cream."

"GIRLS! Come downstairs, dinner's ready!" My mother's voice spiraled up the stairs as if carried on the gorgeous fumes of garlic in her special, famous seared salmon.

On the morning I headed to the station, I had scrambled eggs, Icelandic Hafragrautur garnished with blueberry Greek yogurt, gogi berries, and roasted pumpkin seeds, moistened by a splash of goat's milk, and a piece of the Speculoos Brigitte bought me in Santiago de Cali. The babies and I needed all the energy we could get on this day.

"Rrrr.... uuffff, rrrr… uuffff, rrrr… uuffff, rrrr… uuffff," a yappy Yorkie in a red velvet hair bow nipped at my heels as I turned into the blah beige building. Her human, a woman in flimsy pale pink housedress, barely seemed to notice.

"Madame, your dog is having my ankles for a snack," I wanted to snap, but I focused on my task at hand. There was no need for me to be nasty; we might not be aware of the battles someone else is fighting. My legs would survive, but Luis Fernando had not.

I looked around for him. There he was peeking out of a nearby bush. I beckoned him forward with a wave of my hand, "Come on, Pierre, I think you should come inside with me, don't you? It's a day of reckoning."

The woman looked at me like I was Cracker Jack crazy. She pulled tight on the Yorkie's lease as if she were reining in a herd of wild horses. "Viens, Bodette, la dame va bien maintenant."

"Rrrr..... uuffff, rrrr… uuffff, rrrr… uuffff, rrrr… uuffff," Bodette seemed in agreement I was not well.

"Rachelle, look who's here," a squared faced officier called out as I stepped inside. I stole a sideways glance at Luis; he looked like he wanted to punch the guy on his right-angled jaw. I was glad Luis was there; at that moment he was the best friend I had.

Mornings at the station revolved around coffee. Girard, two meters tall, stooped over his steaming café and dumped lumpy buttermilk from a stripped cup into his Café au Lait. He slurped it like a hungry babe at the breast. Jobard's jowly cheeks contracted into a fish face and he sucked daintily on a hazel Café Noisette in a small demitasse-style cup. Moreau favored Café Viennois with cream whipped into a curly cue, decorated with a puff of chocolate powder with a tanned raisin scone on the side. Sometimes, when he thought no one was looking, Moreau ate the raisins out and left the crumbles on the plate. Rachelle Rousseau, head honcho, with nary a moment of hesitation, downed a mug of piping hot espresso and then sped around in circles barking orders to keep the peace in Paris. Even Girard, who loomed over her, quivered when Rachelle got worked up over something.

At 9:00 a.m. on a quiet Wednesday, these four all stopped sipping, slurping, and gulping their caffeine to watch a pink-cheeked chestnut brown beauty fumble through the security check.

"What's in your pants pockets, Mademoiselle?"

"My... pockets?"

"Empty 'em out," Raphaël tapped a metal detecting stick on the tattered black bin on top of the conveyer machine.

"Ah—hoo." The woman perspired. She reached into one pocket and pulled out a box of colored pastel chalk sticks and reluctantly set it in the bin.

"What's that?"

"Chalk."

"Chalk?"

"Oui, for drawing."

"Rachelle, look who's here," Jobert's cheeks expanded back out like a puffer fish on steroids. Rousseau tipped her head back and guzzled half of her drink, "AHHH."

"What do you draw?" Raphaël inquired, but the lady with swan-like grace wasn't in a mood to talk.

"Mostly portraitures," she mumbled with one hand protectively over her belly, which swelled with pregnancy. Rachelle surmised this nonchatty, chalk artiste carried twins. The female officer headed over to the conveyer.

"Empty that one too," the stick pointed at a distended pocket on the left. The lass reluctantly pulled out a green granny apple, the kind that goes well with cinnamon in cider or sliced thinly in holiday pies. Raphaël tapped the stick on the bin, "Here." The woman hesitated. Rachelle

Rousseau whipped out a clean tissue and set it on the tray, "The tray is dirty, she doesn't want to put her apple there, she wants to eat it later, isn't that right?"

"Yes, ma'am." The mother-to-be gathered up an apple, chalk, a comb, small wallet, tangerine lip balm, and a tin of mini-mints congregated like freshmen at a kegger and clattered through the scanner. "Arms up," Raphaël motioned to her. She lifted arms like a falcon ready for flight, but with no delight.

The officer and the police station patron walked side by side like old school chums up to the imposing counter — one woman positioned herself behind and the other stood in front.

"I'm Camille Portraro. I killed Luis Fernando Jiménez. On February 23rd when I was driving, I looked down for a split second and hit a pole that toppled over and knocked him on the head," her voice didn't waiver or hesitate. There was no undertone of pleading for leniency. Her tone was even, clear, and glistened like the polished apple. She held out upturned wrists. A sweet freckle on the left caught the eye of Moreau, whose own wife had one similarly placed. "I ran. I was... in shock... I'm sorry."

"We've been expecting you," the officer whose shiny badge glittered "Rousseau" said.

"How was Colombia? I've always wanted to go to South America," said the fat faced one.

"Joubert, shh!" Girard scolded him.

The woman moved her wrists forward, imploring, "Arrest me. Do whatever you have to do. I'm not worthy of any kind treatment, I'm only concerned for my babies." Babies! Ah-ha, Rachelle sipped her cooling coffee, which nearly made her spit. Coffee, according to the bible of Rachelle Rosetta Rousseau, ought to burn the top layer of one's tongue off.

"WAIT! STOP!" came a yodel vehemently hurled forth.

Nine sets of eyes, eighteen eyeballs in all: Girard, Moreau, Joubert, Rousseau, security guard Raphaël, the pint-sized pregnant lady, and three patrons sitting on side benches all swiveled to look in the direction the yell came from.

"Halt. What's in your pockets?" Raphaël pointed and tap-tap-tapped with his stick.

Seven keys circled a lanyard chain hand-thread with love by a child, the uneven errors in the weave were endearing, a beat up brown leather wallet bulged with papers that played peek-a-boo out of the folds like edges of a shirt un-tucked after a sucky hard day in a stiff suit, a package of unopened, impure peanuts from a plane, celluloid crinkled, "May contain nuts, sugar, salt, and preservatives," you think they are healthy but they'll kill you — these three items spilled from his pants pocket. From his blazer came a curved comb and metal water bottle. He and his partner did not use plastic bottles, containers, forks, or straws.

The woman with him smelled like she was over-sprayed at a Freakin' Fragrances demonstration, this fruity, alcoholic scent could set off a Geiger counter for an asthmatic. "AH, AH, AH." The environment could use smell protection laws too, not only straws can strangle birds. She compliantly set a beefy leather-bound book into the black bowl.

She sported a polished silhouette accented by a look of importance, humor, and grace. The pregnant woman liked her face at first sight. Rousseau stood up straighter with regard for this figure that surely spent many hours studying till closing time in a Bibliotheque.

Her black briefcase clunked into the bowl next. Something beeped, "EH, EH, EH." She took out her pocketbook and Raphaël waved the wand until she pulled a set of keys from it, more than double the bloom of her companion: fourteen keys, she must hold high rank.

"Jon, what are you doing here?" gurgled the Granny Smith apple gal.

"Lucy! STOP! Don't say ANOTHER word. I brought a lawyer for you."

"Lucy? I thought you said you were Camille," Rousseau was losing her soft feeling for the confessed child killer.

"I go by Lucy too. It was the name of the coach's cat. You can call me Camille, that's what my last license says." She took out an old ID and plopped it on the cherry laminate reception counter.

"STOP!" Jon cried again, scooping Camille in his arms. He hugged her until the minute hand ticked twice, then stepped back and regarded her at arm's length, "You've gotten so big! You're glowing. Are you eating enough?"

"Acch-hem," Joubert cleared his throat. He meant nothing by it; he just had a frog in it.

"Yes, Jon, I am. It's so good to see you. How did you find me?"

"Tanu."

"Ah, yes, Tanu."

"Mademoiselle Portraro, I am Helene Valentine," she pumped Camille's hand in greeting, putting an end to the chitchat. "Here is my card. Theo and Jon have retained me to represent you. Please sign here." A set of papers appeared from her black valise.

"It's too late. I've just declared the facts. I must face the consequences."

"WAIT! STOP!"

"Halt. What's in your pockets?" Raphaël pointed and tap-tap-tapped with his stick.

"Oh, for the love of..." Girard paced impatiently. He couldn't get through this circus without his mug of coffee. He took a few swallows. It was cold, just the way he preferred.

"Acch-hem," Joubert cleared his throat again.

"Pour l'amore de Dieu, go get a glass of water, Joubert," Rachelle snapped at him like the Yorkie had at Camille's ankles. He excused himself to do just that.

Ten sets of eyes, twenty eyeballs in all: Girard, Moreau, Rousseau, security guard Raphaël, Camille /Lucy, Jon, Avocat Helene Valentine, and the three entertained patrons sitting on side benches, all swiveled to look in the commotion's direction.

"THERE SHE IS! LUCY, WAIT, WE'RE HERE!"

Raphaël lifted his hat and wiped perspiration from his forehead. The synthetic threads from the sleeve of his uniform left scratches on his nice pink skin. "Halt," he said with a tired sigh to the two tinsel town type beauties, "Do you have anything in your pockets?" He pointed and tap-tap-tapped the bowl with his stick. "Empty them here."

Eleven sets of eyes, twenty-two eyeballs in all: Girard, Moreau, Joubert, Rousseau, security guard Raphaël, Camille /Lucy, Jon, Avocat Helene Valentine, and the three patrons on side benches, (one man was chewing on his nails because oh-the-drama-of-it-all; a lady sat tap-tap tapping her foot every time Raphaël tapped his wand), all swiveled to look toward the new participants.

Helene humphed. Her papers were unsigned. She clicked her pen on and off twice, "Please, I need your initials, here, here, here, and here." She flipped arrogantly through pages, unused to being ignored.

"Nikos?"

"Oh, my sweet...!" The man with the lead actor's face-and-physique rushed up to the confessee and buried his face on her shoulder. He dropped to his knees and cradled her belly in his palms like it was a magical orb containing valuable hidden secrets of the universe, "... and my sweet babies!" He kissed the bump like a woodpecker, not leaving an inch un-pecked.

Rousseau rolled her eyes, (though if one looked close enough, one could see tears in them), "All right, folks, let's get some order here."

Ignoring the swagger of this alpha officier de police, a tall woman, also burgeoning with new life, appeared just behind the dashing man. "Lucy, forgive me. I told Nikos. I could not let you do this alone. We are family now."

"Parlene!" The two pregnant women kiss-kissed and hugged, twisting to the side to make room for their bellies.

Overwhelmed with emotion, Lucy absentmindedly took out her apple and bit into it. The tart juice exploded on her tense tongue and oozed down her constricted throat. She closed her eyes and allowed herself to get swept away in the fresh apple aroma and tangy taste; for a few moments, she blocked out the pandemonium and could well have been in an Idaho apple orchard on an August day.

Someone kept clearing his throat, "Acch-hem, Acch-hem." Madame Valentine cried, "Papers, papers," as she click-click-clicked that ballpoint pen. Hands were lovingly and protectively placed on her shoulders. In the regal reprieve of the ripe fruit meadow, mourning doves cooed and bubble bees buzzed as Pierre picked apples with the childhood abandon she had robbed from him.

The BIZZZZZ of the bees turned into a ringing "Belle" in her ear and she opened her eyes to see a new man standing there.

"Leonard? What are you doing here?"

"Acch-hem," Joubert stood, "I called him. I thought he would want to be here. His involvement with this case is deep."

"Joubert! You didn't clear this with me!" Rachelle's wily look contorted her handsome face in a most unbecoming way.

"He ran it by ME," Girard stepped forward, all 6'4" of him. This was finally his moment to assert some usurped authority from the last year. This was HIS commissariat, and he was displeased with the untoward direction things had taken like a car on an AutoRoute speeding the wrong way with faulty brakes. "We'd better take this conversation into a back room. NOW!" Then he began pointing and asking questions, "Who are you?"

"I'm Camille. I killed Luis Fernando."

"I'm confused," Moreau piped up, "I thought you were Lucy."

"She IS Lucy," Parlene, Nikos, Leonard, and Jon responded with a harmony that brought to mind a barbershop quartet.

"Okay, you come with me."

"I'm her avocat," Helene offered, "As soon as she signs HERE, HERE, HERE, HERE, and HERE."

"Is this your lawyer," Girard hefted his pants two incher higher by inserting his thumbs in the belt loops.

"No. I've never seen her before. I don't need a lawyer, I have the truth."

"The law doesn't care about the truth, Lucy," Jon moaned, "Please, Helene Valentine is the best there is."

"I could use a good avocat," the nail-biting man from the bench jumped up, raising his hand.

"So could my son," the foot-tapping woman enjoined.

"Who are you? Who are you? Who are you?" Girard and Joubert tried to sort out the Greek chorus and determine if anyone else was part of the action.

"WAIT! AM I TOO LATE?"

Fourteen sets of eyes, twenty-eight eyeballs in all: Girard, Moreau, Joubert, Rousseau, security guard Raphaël, Camille /Lucy, Jon, Avocat Helene Valentine, and the three patrons on side benches, Nikos, Parlene, and Leonard all swiveled to look toward the new person, (undoubtedly with pockets), who appeared in the doorway.

Lucy could barely bring herself to look. She closed her eyes and took another big bite of the best apple she had ever tasted in her life. The sound of the CRUNCH and the texture of the flesh as her incisors pulverized it so completely into pulp eclipsed everything. "UMMMMM," she moaned, living fully in that moment.

"Set your bag and book on the tray, empty your pockets, please take off your hat."

"By the tray, do your mean the black bowl?"

"Yes, the black bowl."

The woman moved so swiftly, no one got a good look at her until she approached the reception desk. She seemed to sail like a schooner on smooth seas, yet her speed reminded Leonard of a cougar he'd seen on a nature show the night before. It coiled then sprang from the bushes like a rocket to Uranus.

"Hello, Lucy. I got here as quickly as I could from Colombia. A flight opened up last night." She kiss-kissed Lucy, who froze, unable to utter a word. Of the trio of responses of shock: "fight, flight, and freeze," freeze gripped a hold of Lucy. Her joint were stiff and immobile as though webbed with icicles.

Leonard knuckle-rubbed his eyes as if he was a two-year-old waking up after a three-hour Graham cracker and grape juice sugar-induced nap.

"Belle?"

"I'm Camille, but you can call me Kristína if you like. Either way, if you're looking for Camille, I'm your girl." She shook hands with the four attending officers and then held her wrists out for cuffs.

Moreau scratched the bald spot on his head until the skin began peeling "YOU'RE Camille from Colombia?"

"Oui," her French was perfect.

"Who is this then?" Moreau pointed to Lucy.

"That's Lucy."

"What are you doing, Kristína? I'm Camille."

"You're pregnant, Lucy. I am Camille, and you are Kristína, correct?"

"Yes, but..."

"I'm Camille, see, no freckle," she turned her wrists around to show Rousseau that she had no freckle, "Camille." She turned to Nikos, "Do I have a freckle on my wrist?"

"No."

The woman called Kristína handed the blue book to Parlene, who was standing closest to her. "Open to the bookmarked page. Read the passage halfway down the left side."

Parlene complied, who wouldn't? "Kristína Alicia notices everything; not a detail goes unnoticed by her. She loves flowers. Her eyes trace each outline: petals, stems, and leaves. I think she will be an artist. Camille Lisette moves her bitty body to the music like a miniature hula dancer. I think she will be our Isadora. Both of my babies have excellent taste in tunes from Ella to Big Bill and Bonnie; these girls get it. They have soul."

"Below that," the woman with the hat said.

""So, who do I choose? It's been three months now and I am clear that financially and logistically I can't give them both what they need. I blame myself for not being enough. I'm not functioning well in this situation and my wish is for what is best for my loves. When Charles offered to raise one of them, I concurred this is a gift to all…"

"Below that," Kristína leaned over and tap-tap-tapped as if she were auditioning for Rafaël's job. "Right here."

Parlene continued, "After many late night calls, we agreed to stay in close touch, share photos and stories, and introduce the girls when they are twelve, no earlier, no later. Since I can't choose, I handed the burden to fate; I flipped a coin tonight. Heads for my blessed one who has a sienna-colored freckle on the inside of her left wrist, tails for my Picayune princess with the pliant grin. Heads is the one I shall keep, my Camille. Tails goes to Charles who arrives tomorrow at half-past three."

Kristína showed her wrists again, "Arrest me, I'm Camille."

"But Lucy has the freckle," Parlene objected.

"They mixed us up." Lucy whispered.

"What exactly is going on here?" Rachelle didn't like to be played for a fool.

"What's your name?" Girard wanted so badly to be in control, but he did not understand what he was witnessing.

"My name is Lucy. People also call me Camille, Cam, Cammy, and Belle."

A quiet voice in the background commanded, "Empty your pockets," but no one was paying any attention.

"Are you twins? You look like carbon copies."

"They appear to be. I've only had coffee to drink, but I'm seeing double."

"Who are you?" Girard turned to the second auburn-tressed lass.

"I told you, I'm Camille, but you can call me Kristína."

"So, you're Camille?"

"Yes."

"And you're Camille?"

"Yes."

"Camille, I just need your signature, here, here, here, here, and here," Helene Valentine was game to tame any Camille she found herself in vicinity of. She ruffled the papers and clicked her pen.

From the back came a male voice with a bit of a twang, doing shtick, "Who is on first? Yes. I mean the fellow's name. Who. The guy on first. Who. The first baseman. Who! The guy playing first base. Who is on first. I'm asking you who's on first! That's the man's name. That's whose name? Yeah. Well, go ahead and tell me. That's it. That's who? Yeah."

Fifteen sets of eyes, thirty eyeballs in all: Girard, Moreau, Joubert, Rousseau, security guard Raphaël, Camille /Lucy, Jon, Avocat Helene Valentine, and the three patrons on side benches, Nikos, Parlene, Leonard and Kristína/Camille all swiveled to look behind them.

There stood a tanned twosome. The man had a burn on his face that affected his right eye and ear and pulled his handsome grin higher on that side. The woman, a waif who looked like she might blow away at the next big gust, was not a stranger to this station.

"It was me! I did it, I kept her on the phone telling her I loved her, asking if she loved me!"

"Matty! Brigitte! What are you DOING here?"

"We got seats on the plane right after Kristína's. We used the old, "Quiero ir a mi casa ahora," routine.

"Próximo cliente!" Lucy raised her fist and shouted out. Matt, Brigitte, she and Kristína all laughed. The four of them hugged all round and Matt held Lucy's hand, "Hi, Belle," while Brigitte cuddled up to Kristína; they gave each other a quick but passionate kiss.

"Camille?" Leonard asked Kristína.

"Já," Kristína said. "No!" Lucy said.

THE PARIS PREDICAMENT

"ENOUGH! Enough is enough is ENOUGH! You're turning the station into a circus," Rachelle's face was incarnadine with splotches of eggplant hues. She smoothed her shirt, re-cuffed her sleeves, and began organizing papers on the desk. Order. She craved order.

"Girard..."

"Yes?"

"DO something!"

Meanwhile, Brigitte took it upon herself to introduce the cast of characters to each other, since she knew everyone, included the officiers at this station.

"Look, we have some big news about this case, and we need to talk to those who think they were suspects in the back room." That narrowed it done to two. Lucy and Brigitte. "I'm her fiancé, practically her family, and I'm not letting her out of my sight," Matt got a bro pat on the back from Nikos for that. "I'm not letting Kristína out of MY sight," Brigitte interjected.

"Are you two engaged?" one grifter asked.

"Will you marry me, Kristína?" Brigitte took out an Irish friendship ring to propose with. "Yes, yes, I will! I love you, Kristína."

"And I you love, Brigitte!"

There was not a dry eye in the house, even Raphaël had to borrow a pack of pink tissues from Raquel.

"I have to pee." Parlene could NOT wait anymore. "So do I," Lucy was in the same pickle with her baby challenged bladder. "Okay," Joubert asserted, all pregnant ladies to the loo, follow me, right this way..." he led a train of three: Parlene and Lucy, with Rachelle in the rear, " Mazel Tov," Matt whispered to Rachelle as she tromped off behind the others.

"Look here," Girard twisted his moustache and said to Matt, "Are you expecting any MORE of your friends to be popping round this morning?"

"No. We're good. Nina La Rue, Ramon, Tanu, and Noni are still partying in Colombia. I think this is all for now.

"How is Tanu?" Jon inquired.

"She's good. She sends her regards to you and Theo."

"Who's Theo?"

"Theo is my husband and the father of Tanu's children. They used to be in love."

"Oh," said Moreau and Joubert, clearly lost.

"Nina la Rue, the great niece of Mrs. Van der Heffelin?" Rachelle was curious to know. Lucy back from the bathroom as well answered that, "The same. She's one of my besties."

A collective officer gasp sucked the air out of the station. "She's very influential in Paris," Moreau said. "Her grandmother contributes yearly to our..."

"Acch-hem!" This time Joubert cleared his throat on purpose to shut Moreau up.

"Yes, and Lucy means a great deal to her," Matt leaned his elbow on the counter and gave a southern wink. Matt knew how to work a room, that's for sure.

"Are we all here?"

"Not yet," Nikos explained, "My lady takes a while. She's always worth the wait though."

Girard, Joubert, Moreau, Rousseau, and Helen Valentine all looked at their watches. They seemed skeptical.

"Who's on first?" Leonard asked.

"He's on third base, "Jon replied.

"Camille, come with me," Girard said.

Both of the twins stepped forward. They turned towards each other and squared off.

"Lucy, you're pregnant."

"Yes, I am, Kristína."

"I'm Camille."

"Only on paper, according to our móðir."

"What — you don't believe Jónína?"

"I didn't say I didn't believe Jónína."

"Then what are you saying?"

"I'm saying I'm Camille. I lived as Camille. Camille hit the pole that landed on Pierre that ended up being the cause for his death."

"Who's Pierre?" Rousseau looked up from the furious notes she was taking.

"Camille, sign here, here, here, here, and here," Helena slapped her papers on the table.

"SHUT UP!" both twins shouted at the avocat.

"Pierre is Luis Fernando," Lucy added in a hush. "I appreciate your love and concern and selflessness, Kristína, but I'm Camille. I did this, and I take responsibility for it."

"It was I. I did it," Brigitte said, "I kept you on the phone. It was my fault."

Girard sighed, "Okay, the three of you, come with me," he waved his hand and turned to walk down the hall.

"I'm Lucy's fiancé, I'd like to come too."

"Suit yourself."

"I'm her lawyer..."

"Helene, stop," Jon pulled Mademoiselle Valentine back and pulled out a roll of bills, "How much do I owe you?"

"Oh, my tab will make your head spin, Jon, you'll receive it in the mail," Helene Valentine brushed past Nikos and Parlene, (who flipped her the bird). She knocked into the lady and then her delinquent son who fell into the bench and bounced to the floor with a bonk to his head that knocked him out momentarily.

"AHHHH," a collective gasp blew through the crowd like the W~A~V~E at a winning baseball game.

"Johnny!" The mother cradled her son's head in her arms, "Are you all right, son?"

"Ow. I don't know. I think so," he rubbed scalp, dazed. "What are YOU looking at?"

"Who, Johnny?"

"That pipsqueak over there," he pointed toward Lucy.

"Moi?" She held her hand to her chest.

"No, the little kid next to you."

"There's no one there, Johnny. I will get you to the hospital. I'd like your card, Helene Valentine so I can SUE your fancy pants."

"I can't give you medical advice, Mademoiselle, but he may be okay — that's Pierre, he accompanies me everywhere."

Moreau dropped his head in his hands and moaned, still confused.

"Do you want to press charges?" Joubert asked Johnny's mother.

"I'd like to reserve the right to."

"Mademoiselle Valentine, your card, s'il vous plaît."

Helene took out five cards and handed them round to the four officiers and Johnny's mum, "Here, here, here, here, and here. Everyone saw the little urchin tripped me."

"I didn't see that alleged trip, but the cameras caught the whole incident," Rachelle pointed up to the corner.

"About that bill, Helene..." Jon's inflection lifted up at the end in a questioning tone.

"Never mind. It's forgiven. Forgiveness is the way of the Lord. À tout à l'heure. Bonne chance, Camille... and Camille. Accidents happen," she shrugged, her valise bouncing against her immaculately dressed figure as she fled.

"I need to go back to bed," Rousseau silently pled as she straightened the stapler, hole punch, and ruler and gathered stray paper clips into a cup.

"You four, come with me," Girard led the way down a stark fluorescent hallway. First Kristína, then Brigitte; they touched fingers, as new lovers do. Then Matt bravely led the way for Lucy who turned behind her and muttered to Pierre, "Five. We all five will come."

Girard led the three foreign iconoclasts, one French beauty, and a ghost-mirage to a small dank room with a large Alder wood table and industrial Walnut chairs arranged around it in perfect formation; no doubt the handy work of Rachelle Rousseau, who'd set them four inches apart, JUST so.

"Have a sit. Café anyone?"

"No, thank you."

"No."

"No' thanks, have you got a wee bit of water?" Brigitte inquired.

"Yes, Sir," Matt needed the caffeine kick, what with the jetlag and stress and his fiancé being in a mess and all.

"How do you take it?"

"Black is fine, Sir."

"JOUBERT!"

"Girard, you called?"

"One black Café and three bottles of water, si vous plait." Girard sat directly across from Lucy and Kristína, flanked by their partners on either side. "Now then, Camille," he nodded to Lucy.

"Oui, officier?"

"And Camille," he nodded to Kristína.

"Já, officer?"

"Here are the drinks, who gets the Café?" Joubert seemed unnerved. The tray was shaking.

Matt raised his hand, "Coffee here, much obliged, Sir."

"Now then, as I was saying, Camille..."

"Oui?"

"And Camille..."

"Já?"

"There were four véhicule accidents within a ten kilometer range on February 25."

"HUHHHH." Everyone turned to look at Matt. "Sorry, coffee's too hot. Continue, please."

"Now then, ACCCCTTT," he cleared his throat. "JOUBERT!"

"Yes?"

"Would you mind bringing another water for me?"

"Not at all. Coming right up."

"Merci. Now then, where was I?"

"Four véhicule accidents within a ten kilometer range," Brigitte helped him along.

"Right. There were four véhicule accidents within a ten-kilometer range on February 25. All of them happened with one-half hour of each other."

"That's a LOT of accidents in a short amount of time," Matt swirled the drink, breathing in the pungent aroma.

"I didn't do it. I just slid, like a slippy-slide - I don't know how that happened - and hit that pole," the Lucy-Camille was defensive.

"You slid. This is exactly what I'm saying. There were four accidents, UMMM, well, the um, the Jiménez boy was the only death, in fact the only injury, part of that had to do with a faulty pole. The store-owners received citations to fix their unstable awning the week before, so several unfortunate factors came together to create tragedy for the Jiménez's."

"What were you saying about the four accidents?" Brigitte perked up after she heard about the wobbly pole; the more the pole was at fault, the less she was.

"Well, ahh, what was your name again?"

"Brigitte."

"Well, Brigitte, there was a véhicule leaking oil like a racehorse losing water before a race."

"Losing water, you mean faire pipi?" Kristína-Camille was trying to keep up.

"Faire pipi. Leaking all over the streets of Paris in our district. The roads were slick from the storm, anyway. You wouldn't have been able to prevent that accident. We had to cordon off the area, preserve the scene, clean up the mess, and have forensics test the oil."

"Tell her," Kristína-Camille pointed to Lucy-Camille.

"I heard," there is such a thing as positive shock, and Lucy was in the throes of it. "So... it wasn't my fault?"

"No, Camille. It wasn't your fault."

Lucy sat with this for some time, and her sister, friends, and Officer Girard gave her sacred silent time. Rousseau snuck in the back and sat by the door. She watched Lucy-Camille and Brigitte excuse themselves from the burden they had carried for so long now. This emotional anvil had dragged them and all the pieces of their lives down to depths previously unfathomable to the carefree spirits they were on February 24.

"I still feel responsible. I came here to do the right thing. I came here to turn over my life to let due process have its way with me."

"Well," Girard slapped his knees. He stood, "Now you're just going to have to make new plans for the day." He held out his hand and offered it to Lucy to shake, "It's a real pleasure to meet you. You drew a portrait of my daughter several years ago. She still has the photo on her wall. I'll be glad to tell her what a kind, honest person you are."

"But I stink as a human. I killed Pierre, and I ran!"

"Pierre... do you mean the Jiménez boy?" Rachelle stood too — in judgment.

"Oui, Pierre is my name for Luis Fernando."

"You shouldn't have run. That was bad."

"I *know*." I was in shock. "The car slid, it just... I lost control of it."

"We ought to press charges for leaving the scene of an accident."

"Rachelle, the girl is not at fault. There is no crime. She was in shock, the car slid from the oil, the pole was unstable, and it was a bad set of circumstances. She's here, she's remorseful, and she'll have a long life to think about it. The family does not want to press charges, and I see no reason to do so. There is no need, Rachelle, to make any of these lovely young people feel ashamed or shackled to guilt and grief for the rest of their lives."

He put his hand on Lucy's shoulder as a father might, "You're free to go. I hope you allow your spirit to be as free as your body when you walk out this door."

Lucy looked around in a panic for Pierre. There he was over near the door, just behind Rachelle. She didn't want him to leave — he was part of her now. He trained his eyes closely on her. By the looks of things, it didn't seem like he would leave her side just yet. They both needed, perhaps, to spend more time together.

"Why did it take so long to tell her this?" Kristína exerted significant effort to control the anger in her voice. "She's been through hell, you know."

"We did a thorough investigation. We had to match all four accidents to the same spill. It took some time to do it right. The police don't always bat a thousand. This time we did."

Matt gave Lucy an Adam-in-the-wilderness type hug, like a passionate big black bear. They disappeared in each other for a few minutes. Kristína and Brigitte did the same.

"All right," Moreau popped in to say, "I need the conference room cleared in ten minutes. Say your goodbyes now."

"Thank you, Officier Girard, you just gave me back my life."

"Le plaisir est pour moi, Camille."

"Call me Lucy."

"The pleasure is mine, Lucy."

I hadn't felt a soul-satisfying slice of sunshine since the sky fell upon me that frosty February day just before the twins hijacked my womb.

Hadn't had a sense of calm and UN-calamity since my waist was tiny, the width of which Pascal could fit his gangling hands around, practically touching his fingertips together.

Hadn't contemplated even the possibility of a free, fecundus future that involved my growing fetuses, in OR out of France.

I was ready to sift through the shards of this nettlesome Paris predicament that pulverized my predilection for pep, but first, before scuttling with my posse out of the dim dredges of the commiserate's clutches, I had a question for Madame la Commissar.

"Excusez-moi, Madame Rousseau. Have you found the driver of the véhicule responsible for the rash of road grease?"

"Oui."

"Is he or she charged with anything?"

"No. We believe a rock from a pothole punctured his car. We couldn't track down the exact cause because he drives for a living into many towns. It was an accident."

"What did he say when he found out?"

Rachelle looked up curtly from her busywork, filing and re-filing papers to avoid full contact with me. "It's not for me to say. He turned himself in a few weeks after the accident. He knew of the death, had discovered the leak, and put two and two together. Ironically, Camille..."

"Lucy."

"Ironically, *Camille*, this man picked up the grandfather of the boy on the way to see him in hospital before he died. This prompted his guilt, I suppose. I'm sorry," but she didn't seem so, " I shan't say more. Bonne journée. Au revoir." She dismissed me.

"Was anyone charged in this crime?"

"No. The city gave the store a week to fix the pole. Everyone and no one was at fault," she was angry. It was frustrating to be a police officer when you couldn't procure justice for a grieving family. "I have a boy his age," she seemed to hiss, "Good day." She stormed away.

I ran to catch up with my friends.

"What did you talk about?" Brigitte was all twitter.

"What did she say?" Kristína chimed in.

"The driver did not face accountability, nor did the store-owners. No one did. The Jimenez's don't have closure."

"It looked like she was pitching a fit," Matt observed in his droll way.

"She was. She has a boy the same age as Luis Fernando. It's personal for her. I can see why," all four of us put our hands on my belly as a collective sigh washed over us.

"Yer friends are waitin'. Come on," Matt pulled me along. We exited the imposing doors of the station and ambled down the steps. When our feet hit pavement, us three women gave a squeal. Brigitte even spun a few circles as if she were on her skates dancing on the ice.

"There they are! LUCY!" Parlene waved.

The four of them flanked us. Nikos, Parlene, Leonard, and Jon.

"Hey, what's happened?" Nikos seemed nervous.

"Are you free?" Jon joined in.

Only Leonard was silent.

The eight of us piled into a booth made of mushroom leather at a local cafe that served gorgeous vegan cuisine. Being a vegetarian in Paris, one now had options that didn't exist when I arrived as a student. Everyone but Leonard was upbeat — he was unusually sullen. I assumed I knew the reason for his morose mood so I pushed away my dish, (though the fluffy quinoa garnished with shredded radishes, dried cranberries, parsley and cilantro pepper, topped with lightly charred sweet onions and garlic called to my rumbling stomach), and took him by the arm. "Let's go outside for a minute."

We stood around like bumbling third-cousins-once-removed meeting for the first time at a family reunion. We were at a loss for what to say. I finally penetrated the tense standoff, "I'm sorry for your loss of Bertrand."

"Thank you. It's clear how much Bertrand and you meant to each other."

"I miss him so much, it's like they amputated a leg and I hobble now, unable to dance."

"He would want you to dance."

"And you too."

Tears formed in our eyes, but an emotional chasm remained.

"You did an amazing job reading my poem, 'Our Bertrand' at his life celebration ceremony in Brussels. There wasn't a dry eye in the crowd."

"You WERE there."

"Yes."

"I thought I saw you hiding in the back."

"That was me."

"Margaret said you hugged her, acted weird, and dashed away."

"I did. How is she?"

"She's fine," he whispered as though her well-being was a secret.

"I shouldn't have asked you to harbor me. That put you in an uncomfortable spot."

"No, Belle, it was I who is unfair to you."

"How so, Leonard?"

"It was my car that leaked oil that day."

"What? You! YOU are the driver?" This shook me like a six point earthquake.

"Oui."

"Wait. YOU are the driver whose car left puddles of slippery grease?" Now I was whispered.

"Yes. Oui. It was me."

Brigitte came out to check on us. "Everything all right? Your food is getting cold. You must be starving." Her words slowed as she sensed the tension between us. "I'll just see you both inside. Belle, Leonard was supportive of me at the station. He made sure I was okay."

"I'm sure... he did."

"I'll just... umm... I'll be inside. Come in soon — you're missed. We want to talk about what happened with you there."

"Okay, we just need a few more minutes, don't we Leonard?"

"A few more minutes ought to do it."

Brigitte retreated to Vegan Haven.

"I picked him up and drove him to the hospital."

"Who? What are you talking about now?"

"Señor Alberto?"

"Ah, yes, Juan Alberto. An extraordinary being. He met with me in Columbia."

"He liked me. Trusted me. I drove him and his family around during their ordeal in Paris."

"That must have been... awful."

"It was."

"I saw you drive a Latino family. I made contact with the elder's eyes. I wonder if..."

"That was him, yes, I saw you on the sidewalk."

"Oh," I sat down, "Nothing is as it seems. Reality lifts the rug on us time and again."

"I have some writings of Bertrand's and one of his guitars and a harmonica he left for you - if you want them."

"Yes, thank you. I do."

"Lucy! Come in, you must eat. We're gettin' tuckered out in there and want to celebrate with both of youse. I'm fixing to dig into your meal if you're not coming back to lunch."

"I'm coming, Matty!" I turned to Leonard, "Join us?"

"No. I couldn't. I have nothing to celebrate."

"I understand, but we want you there. I want you there. We're in this together, Leonard. It was everyone's fault, and no one's fault. Look at you, you need nourishment."

He hesitated.

"Do it for Bertrand."

LUCY IN THE SKY

"Bonjour, Lucy!" Felicite, the former front desk agent at Hôtel Plaza Athénée clasped my hands with her meticulously manicured fingers and stepped back, her full charming smile flashed teeth whiter than a full moon in June, "Look at YOU, Mademoiselle Petrokov! Ahh, félicitations! When are you due?"

"Soon, Felicite, soon! Congratulations on your promotion!"

"Merci, I'm the morning manager now," she pointed proudly to her employee pin and blushed in the sweetest way. Crimson circles appeared and then disappeared on the apple of her cheeks as though painted on with an invisible brush and then blown away by fairies. "Well," she put a hand to her chest, "We better get you to your room quickly so you can begin the portraitures before you pop!"

"This is my fiancé, Matt. Would it be all right if he stays with me? He's just visiting Paris for the first time."

"It's your room in your private hours. Do as you wish. Ralph! She's here! Mademoiselle Lucy is back. Show her to her suite, s'il vous plaît."

"Lucy! Welcome back. You've been a stranger for too long!"

"Ralph! It's so nice to see you. This is my fiancé, Matt. Matt, Ralph."

"Bonjour, Monsieur," Ralph greeted Matt with all the graciousness he could muster, though he was jealous.

"Pleased to make your acquaintance, Ralph," Matt sounded endearingly out of place in Paris. It was precious to see him gawk at the skylights and look bemused by the blissful bustle, as I had done earlier in the year.

"Congratulations to the both of you, when are you due?"

"Soon!" Matt and I echo-chimed like bing-bong bells, "Soon!"

Ralph gulped and grabbed our bags, "I can see! Right this way. We've put you in the same suite as before, Lucy, compliments of..."

"Compliments of Maria Van der Heffelen!"

"Maria! I didn't think you were arriving until tomorrow! It's so wonderful to see you! Matt, this is Maria Van der Heffelen."

"Pleased to make your acquaintance, Mademoiselle Van der Heffelen."

"Madame," I whispered to Matt.

"It's perfectly all right to call me that, young man, it sends me back to my youth, but bitte, call me Maria."

"Pleased to meet you, Maria. I appreciate how kind and generous you are to Lucy."

"Oh, pssh, that's easy to do. She's an ABsolute delight. And look at you, carrying TWINS, Nina tells me! You're getting humongous, but you're still too petite. Do you eat enough? We must fatten you up with delicious French food while you're here. When are you due?"

"Soon, soon!" Ralph and Felicite harmonized like zebra doves at sunrise.

"Well, take care of yourself as you need, but chin up, we've got ten days booked for you; one session each morning, and two at night. You ought to make a steep pile of Euros to sock away for the babies. Are you having boys or girls?"

"I don't know."

"You don't know?"

The piano player, Cristoff, whooshed on by, "Félicitations! Congratulations! So nice to see you back." Then he kiss-kissed me and within seconds sat on his bench and played Frank Sinatra's rollicking rag, *Bim, Bam, Baby.* Matt's eyes danced with fiery delight, "Hot dog," he snapped his fingers along to the jazzy tune.

"How are you going to pick out names?" Mademoiselle Maria lipped to me. I immediately thought of Jónína. "I'm not worried about conventional names. My Icelandic mother used to say, 'Many people don't take the time to know themselves, instead they are self-justifying, manipulative puppets. It's those that explore the inner realms I'm interested in.'"

"Ja, that's all lovely, dear," Maria waved her hand, "but you still need to give your kinder somewhat NORmal names. Don't set them up for a fight they need not have in life."

I smiled and lost a bit of blood as I bit my tongue to keep myself from bashing my benefactor and her old world ways. "My children will have lovely names. I'm certain you'll approve."

"Yes, well…" she sniffed, "Your Icelandic mother? Whatever do you mean?"

"You'll meet my sister soon. We'll take you to lunch and tell you the whole story. Our mother, Jón, didn't identify with gender."

Maria scowled. "Be that as it may, Lucy, that you had a progressive, free-thinking parent, don't give your kids weird names or I will CLOBBER you. Bis später! Pass gut auf sie auf, Matt, oder du wirst von Maria hören," she ta-ta-ed off to her day.

"What did she say?" Matt asked me.

"Take good care of me or she'll clobber *you*."

"Right this way," Ralph led us through the lounge.

"Any song requests, Lucy?"

"Play my song, Cristoff," I winked. His fingers flew over the eighty-eight keys.

Lucy In The Sky With Diamonds rang in my head all day.

I floated through ten days at the Hôtel Plaza Athénée like a helium balloon that was whooshed skyward. It was the first time since February that my psyche had latitude to roam. My dewy liberty produced more profound portraitures than I knew were possible.

"Oh mein," Herr Bandemer gushed, "This likeness you have drawn of me reflects my innermost thoughts and prayers."

"Lucy, you have a gift," Mimi Sorenson, the Danish jazz singer scatted, "A gift, a GIFT, a gggggifTa. I learned something about myself by the light you marbled through my eyes."

I bought a set of Mason jars, filled them with white, red kidney, and navy beans, and tucked rolls of cash inside. My mind ticked through the many financial needs I had: to fund a modest wedding, use as a down payment for a home, pay Madam Trouli for the time, hassle, and upset of finding the lipstick scrawl and dealing with my ransacked flat; pay off my school loan, sock away for a college fund for the kids, and begin a business with Matt.

"Lucy, you're a hit again! How would you like to do this once a month?"

"Are you serious? I would LOVE to, Maria, but when the twins come, I don't think I can stay overnight for a week."

"Nor can I afford you to. You'll be living close by, I understand?"

"Yes."

"And your fiancé is moving to France?"

"Yes, he is."

"But dear, what about citizenship, weren't you just here on a student visa?"

"Matt's father's parents are French. Lamoureux."

"It has a nice ring. Matt and Lucy Lamoureux"

"Actually, Matt Lamoureux and Lucy Petrokov. I've changed my name enough to last a lifetime."

Gina Messina, the Sicilian Soap Opera star entered regally through the lobby, "Farfallina, I'm on my way now to get a facial for our sitting this evening."

Felicite interjected, "Fräulein Messina, you look as fresh and lovely as a flitting butterfly."

"Grazi, Felicite, but just, I'd like to get the savory oatmeal, sea salt, and peppermint scrub treatment first.

"See you at 8:00!" I wove her away and got back to the grilling by Madame Van der Heffelin.

"What will you call the children then? You will not give them strange Hippie names, will you, dear?"

"Hippie! That's it! Hotdog, I dig it, Danke, Maria!"

"What did I do?"

"I'll tell you soon, I have to go now."

"WAIT!" she commanded.

I turned, flushed, "Yes?"

"What will you call them?"

"Petrokov-Lamoureux."

"Hmm, it has a ring. What about their *first* names, dear?"

Nikos, Parlene, and Matt strolled over. The four of us had a double date planned before my evening sessions. We would play a round of mini-golf.

"Whose first names?" Matt asked, jumping in the conversation midway.

"The babies," Parlene surmised correctly.

"She let me choose one name," Nikos puffed with pride, "If she's a girl, Camille."

"Camille, wasn't that your name?" Maria turned to me.

"Yes, in a manner of speaking."

"What if you have two boys, or one of each, or..." Maria was unsettled by the prospect of these unsettled details.

"Mine will be a girl," Nikos blubbered like an excited and scared-to-death father-to-be of three.

"I'm a spur-of-the-moment person, Maria. No worries. The baby's names will come. Bis später!" And off we went.

Matt stayed a week until work commitments pulled him back to Berkeley. It was wrenching and wrong to be apart again and we wasted no time in planning our nuptials, which made all the sense in this haphazard world.

"Sometimes I wish my life was normal."

"That will never happen, you're exquisite."

"And YOU are incorrigible."

"Ummm."

"Get a room," an American passing by joked.

"We have one! A Suite!"

"UMMM!"

"Paris Lovebirds," the American sped off.

BE YOURSELF

We held the wedding in the garden at Hristina's home in Seville when the twins were four and a half months old. They arrived early, eager to take part in this precious, peculiar world and we wasted no time in picking a date, drawing up our invitation list, and reaching into the bean jars to help those who needed a financial boost. We wanted our dearest surrounding us on our special day. We crammed as many as possible into Grandma H's house to sleep. Theo, Jon and their rapidly growing sprouts, (Harquint, Gilberto, and Bub), rented a room in a nearby hotel, and the rest slept at a hip hostel down the road.

The weather in Seville was a glorious 26.11°c. The affair was quirky yet classy, down-to-earth yet extraordinary, cozy and brimming with love. I wore a tie-dye rainbow splashed sundress. Matt wore jeans and a white tee, as per my request. He wanted to dress it up, so he slipped on a cornflower blue sports jacket, a teal bowtie, and his trademark jaunty grin.

Our guest list included: Kristína and Brigitte, my bridesmaids, who wore their dance and skating outfits respectively as our theme was *Be Yourself!* Nina LaRue and Ramon arrived together. They now say they are just friends, but I don't believe that. Ramon woos Nina's from Brooklyn to France as Nina bought a petite flat in Paris on Maria's money. Madame Maria Van der Heffelin honored us with her presence. She and Hristina hit it off like seaweed in miso soup or two women who had both lived through the Second World War and survived with their lives, integrity, and sense of humor intact.

Matsako made a brief stop in between her courses in Kyoto where she studies architecture. She and Kasey, who red-eyed over from Berkeley, were busy catching up; Kasey was so overjoyed to see her Matty with a loving life partner she was verklempt.

Tanu glowed in a golden gown, hand tailored to fit her growing belly. She wore three-inch hoop earrings and an armful of tinkling bangles. She was the only one to dress elegantly, but the theme WAS *Be Yourself*. Noni arrived with Adam the amphibian guy as her plus one. He was more prince than frog and we expect their wedding invitation soon. Nikos and Parlene beamed through the three-day foray.

Four of Matt's friends, five of my favorite portraitures clients, two sweet, squirmy twins, and one cat, Miss Natalie Mouskers, who dined on sardines as the rest of us celebrated with homemade vegetarian fare, were there. Captain Fun brought balloons, which he tied into animals for each guest. Jon and the kids had a great time. Little Bub even put down Babar to latch onto Miss Mouskers, whom she nuzzled like a mini me.

Tom Haines and Adeline flew from Beirut on a boost from the navy bean jar fund. Ralph made the trip to represent the crew at the Hôtel Plaza Athénée, while the others stayed in Paris, unable to take time off; even Aunt Molly came as herself in ski goggles and boots, which she swapped for shorts and sandals in the soaring Spanish sun.

Bub was the flower girl. Her dad Theo walked me down the aisle. When Matt winked at me, my heart stopped. Luis Fernando appeared to me as the ring bearer in a pale blue shirt and tiny black tux with tails reaching past his rear, his black ringlets bouncing as he walked. With one last big step forward, he handed the Lady of the Lake to Matt who took it and put it on my finger as a biplane roared overhead with a banner that read, "I love you, Lucy!" on one side and "Yes, a thousand times, yes, Matt!" on the other.

My lost loved ones were all there at the reception, dancing with flair. "I'm happy for you, Belle," Bertrand said. "I love you, honey," came from my mom. "You'll always be my girl, but you're in good hands with Matt, Mrs. Petrokov-Lamoureux." The creative mind is a beautiful thing when geared towards love.

Our vows were simple: "Life is unfair. Life is beautiful. I love you and will be by your side through it all."

EPILOGUE

She appeared in the doorway of *Hungry Hippies*, our burgeoning vegetarian café, a modern day muse in blue jeans, a raspberry beret, and boots of the most convincing faux Spanish leather. I hopped up from my special typing spot in the booth across from the bronzed colored paper mâché statue of Luis Fernando. Matt and I spent two months perfecting Pierre's likeness. We used home movies, photos of the boy, and his clothes for measurements, all provided by the Jimenez's. Above his head and artistically placed throughout the establishment hung some of his prized antique planes, flying into eternity.

"Kristína!"

"Lucy!"

We kissed-kissed-kissed as two halves of a whole do. We'd were complete before meeting and then found out we were part of something greater than we ever could imagine when we learned of each other, (Kristína - Camille at twelve, and Camille - Lucy, at twenty-seven).

"How was your flight?"

"Uneventful, just the way I like 'em." She took a bite from the parsley-garnished pecan loaf in my plate. "Umm, you got this recipe down pat."

"We added sundried tomatoes and cilantro."

"Well, that sure kicks it up. How's business?"

"Fantastic! The place is busy beyond our wildest dreams, as you can see." I gestured to tables filled with patrons in between bites of gorgeous green sesame oil spritzed salads or freshly cooked pea soup simmered just right, with delight, by Ralph, our Chef-in-Chief.

"This place is definitely the bomb." She soaked in the artistic atmosphere. On the back wall I painted a gigantic garden with laughing fruit and vegetables splashed sensuously floor to ceiling. Icelandic fairies flew figure eights between pumpkins and pomegranates. Matt had carved each booth to unique splendor. We attended every detail in our place with love.

"Is this the new menu?"

I grinned, "Yes. What do you think of it?"

"Let me have a look." Her eyes widened as she scanned the pages I had illustrated moments at a time in between breast-feeding and changing nappies.

Roasted cauliflower with roasted garlic tahini sauce and pomegranate, spaghetti squash or shredded zucchini pasta, broccoli crust pizza with roasted pine nut pesto, amaranth-lentil pancakes, millet burgers, Brigitte's Babaganosh, ten of our top-tested salads, and a soup special for each day of the week.... and we were just getting going.

"Where's Matt?"

"Out buying produce. The kids have him wrapped around their pinkies."

"What are you doing here?"

"While the twins are sleeping, I write my story."

"Oh, wonderful, you started. Did you figure out a title yet?"

"Yep."

"Well, don't wait until next Tuesday to tell me — spit it out!"

"*The Paris Predicament.*"

"Perfect! How's it going?"

"Good. It's a ride. It's hard to live through some situations again, but it's also cathartic and uplifting. I hope the story will help people."

"I should write a book too."

"You should. Your story is amazing. What would the title be?"

She looked at Luis Fernando and then back at me and without batting an eye deadpanned, "*The Parallel Predicament.*"

"Do it!" I laughed, not knowing if she was serious or not. "How's Brigitte?"

"Hot."

"How else? What is she up to?"

"She's busy with school, she loves it, and every free minute she has she runs around the house, climbs the stairs and goes down the slide."

"Wheeeeeeeee!" We both lifted our arms with glee, causing the customers to stare with wonder.

"I'd love to put a slide into our suburban Parisian condo — spice it up."

"As if a view of the Eiffel Tower isn't enough..."

"All right," I looked at the rooster clock on the wall just about to crow, "I better run. Thanks so much for watching the twins."

"My pleasure," she stood, eyes shining, "I can't wait to see how they've grown."

I walked her through the kitchen, past cries of, "ORDER UP. Bonjour Kristína. Bonjour Ralph," and back to the nursery we built just behind it.

"Sammy is a little fussy today..."

"Did he sleep last night?"

"Yes, the whole night."

"Excellent!" she high-fived me, a habit she picked up from Noni and me in Santiago.

"Our little girl looks more like you every day."

"Well, she's my namesake, after all. Where are you speaking today?" We spoke in hushed tones to not disturb the wee ones.

"A high school on the East side."

"How's it going?"

"Great. Once a month is a sane schedule to keep for these speeches. I want to do this for the rest of my life. The kids ask a ton of thoughtful questions. It's important for them to hear how one second can change the course of their lives and end someone else's."

"Hi, Sammy. Hi, Cammy," Kristína cooed to the two who just opened their afternoon eyes. "Allo, Mademoiselle Camille," she picked her up like a pro Auntie.

"Up, up!" Sammy lifted his arms for some attention.

"Well, hello to you too, Monsieur," she handed Cam off to me. The four of us stood together, twins holding twins, free as birds. Life is wild.

ABOUT THE AUTHOR

Sasha Lauren, poet, artist, professional organizer, and screenplay consultant, was a globetrotting licensed massage therapist for cast and crew on feature film-sets. She won first place in the Channillo Publishing short story contest for *The Country Fair,* and first place in Writers Assembled contest for, *The Paris Predicament,* which is her first dramatic novel. She loves to review films, study world culture through art, and juggle.

https://www.facebook.com/SashaLaurenAuthor/
https://www.facebook.com/PoetryIsMyPrayer/
https://twitter.com/SashaLauren5
https://www.instagram.com/sasha_lauren_portraits/
https://www.instagram.com/sasha_lauren_artist/
https://www.linkedin.com/in/sasha-lauren-6858684/

NOTE FROM THE AUTHOR

Word-of-mouth is crucial for any author to succeed. If you enjoyed *The Paris Predicament*, please leave a review online—anywhere you are able. Even if it's just a sentence or two. It would make all the difference and would be very much appreciated.

Thanks!
Sasha

Thank you so much for reading one of our **Women's Fiction** novels. If you enjoyed the experience, please check out our recommendation for your next great read!

City in a Forest by Ginger Pinholster

Finalist for a *Santa Fe Writers Project Literary Award*

"Ginger Pinholster, a master of significant detail, weaves her struggling characters' pasts, present, and futures into a breathtaking, beautiful novel in *City in a Forest*.
–*IndieReader Approved*

View other Black Rose Writing titles at www.blackrosewriting.com/books and use promo code **PRINT** to receive a **20% discount** when purchasing.

Lightning Source UK Ltd.
Milton Keynes UK
UKHW040748101020
371356UK00001B/3